# The Inheritance of Peter Tye

### by Andrew Worrall

SOFTWOOD BOOKS

SUFFOLK, UK

Published and Manufactured by Softwood Books

EU Responsible person: Maddy Glenn
Office 2, Wharfside House, Prentice Road, Stowmarket, Suffolk, IP14 1RD
www.softwoodbooks.com, hello@softwoodbooks.com

EU Rep:
Authorised Rep Compliance Ltd., Ground Floor, 71 Lower Baggot Street,
Dublin, D02 P593, Ireland
www.arccompliance.com, info@arccompliance.com

A CIP catalogue record for this book is available from the British Library

Paperback ISBN: 978-1-9192349-0-8

Hardback ISBN: 978-1-9192349-1-5

*For the inheritors: Jennifer, Darcey, and Cian*

'...for the growing good of the world is partly dependent on un-historic acts; and that things are not so ill with you and me as they might have been, is half owing to the number who lived faithfully a hidden life, and rest in unvisited tombs.'

George Eliot, *Middlemarch*, 1874 (from the final sentence).

'Should the child have parents "with secrets" he will receive from them a gap in the unconscious ... This unknown phenomenon comes back from the unconscious to haunt and leads to phobias, madness, and obsessions. Its effects can persist through several generations and determine the fate of an entire family line.'

from Nicholas Abraham: *Poetics of Psychoanalysis* (1978), quoted in 'Tools for a New Psychoanalytic Literary Criticism: the work of Abraham and Torok', Rashkin, Esther, *Diacritics*, Vol.18, No. 4 (Winter, 1988, pp31-52).

'History is a playground. The facts are Lego. Make of them what you will.'
Alan Bennett: *Diary, 28th of January, 2015* (quoted in *The Guardian*, 14th of October, 2016).

# Contents

# Part 1
# Keziah

# 1: Peter, An Indian Silver Bowl

## January 2021

I live next to a country churchyard. Funeral by funeral, the graves march closer to my cottage. On this icy day, when I am locked indoors by winter and a worldwide pandemic, it seems that death seeks to leap the hedge and encroach upon me.

When I moved from Ipswich twenty years ago, after the death of my dear mother (and sole companion), I felt lucky to have found this cottage. The ghosts from next door may have put other potential buyers off, but such things didn't bother me. I am a genealogist, and that churchyard became a convenient metaphor for a lifetime spent with the dead, piecing together their lives and relationships.

My commissions are provided by people who feel themselves in need of heritage. 'Who am I?' they ask. 'Why am I drawn to this profession or to that place?' I do my best to provide an answer, or to let them down gently, for few of us are really the lost cousins of royalty or inheritors of precocious talents.

Sometimes an executor asks me to find the missing heirs to an estate, or an adopted son or daughter searches for their birth family. I keep meticulous notes and indexes - each discovery corroborated, every development in the story referenced.

I lead a solitary and systematic life, committed to facts and evidence. It has all been quite satisfactory. I have no family of my own; never felt the need, and other people's children seem just to be distractions, for them as well as for me.

When I first came here I walked around the churchyard and examined its stages of neglect. I tripped on a half-buried stone kerb and brushed away the yellow and silver lichen to see names and dates from centuries before our own. Those are the ones that excite me: the graves where no one leaves flowers or tidies up, the gravestones which are toppling, uprooted by the untended yew, cracked by centuries of frost and damp river air, because there will be the unexpected finds and untold stories. Every person leaves an inheritance, whether they are remembered or not.

Furthest from the church porch is what they used to call the paupers' grave, where nothing marks the grassy mound. *This should be my rightful place*, I think. There will be no one left to mourn me. No note of my passing, except the required entries in the official registers of death and probate. No wife, no children. A few acquaintances, perhaps, who will say, 'Did you know, Tye's dead?' and pass on quickly to more hopeful topics.

As that prospect comes closer and my contact with the rest of the world has reduced to almost nothing in the face of the pandemic, I confess to feeling, for the first time in decades, a slight sense of deprivation. Years ago, I would have spent my days stirring the dust of record offices, in redundant schools and libraries confected with the smell of goat skin, old paper, and the droppings of flies and mice. Now, I'm mainly retired and conducting investigations only when it pleases me, so I sift remote digital databases for virtual fragments but without any great enthusiasm.

Tonight, at the beginning of the year, I have made a resolution. On this night I will start a new search, and it will be no commission; this I will do for myself. This will be my inheritance. I must find my roots, and then I must discover the descendants who will inherit all, though I feel apprehensive about what I might find.

There is almost nothing left which belonged to my ancestors. I have a few black and white photographs of my parents, a clock, a couple of watches, an anonymous, indifferent oil painting of a river scene, and, here on my desk - and most mysterious of all, an old, Indian silver three-footed bowl. It is a family heirloom, which my mother said was given to her by Aunt Eliza Evans who once lived in India. That is the only story known to me. Why was it bought or given? Why has it been kept? Who was Aunt Eliza? I have no photograph, I don't know what she looked like. What did she sound like? And what was she was thinking when she gave the silver bowl to my mother?

The bowl is less than four inches tall. It has six facets, each with an engraved image of the Hindu goddess, Lakshmi. She is the goddess of good fortune and wealth, here portrayed in various poses. I peer closely at her. She has four arms, a narrow waist, and bountiful breasts. I caress her with the ball of my thumb. Below three of the facets are stylised lotus flowers; the other three sides are supported by the feet of the bowl, which are each in the form of a lion's paw. The whole has an elegant proportion and decoration. Though small, it draws my eye, and when handled it sits comfortable and cool in my palm.

Who was Aunt Eliza? I have not yet been able to place her in the family tree. She died long before I was born, and the Indian connection seems so unlikely amongst my Suffolk ancestry that I am inclined to dismiss it as one of those little legends which haunt a family and cause the rigorous genealogist much misdirection. And so there is a puzzle to be solved, a conundrum whose answer is lost to time, and I am suddenly aroused. It's not the silver goddess's full figure which excites, but the promise of a quest. Once I get started I can puzzle on, regardless of the clock, until I find a solution, or the trail runs cold.

I make a cup of tea and take it to my office. My mother, when she was alive, would bring tea and toast to my desk and leave, knowing to say not a word to disturb my concentration. Alone now, I can sit and tap away for hours, sketch charts on stacks of gash paper, fill my databases, and open half a dozen search windows until my back protests or I am called away by the pressure on my aging bladder.

You must know where to start. It's no good just putting 'Eliza Evans' into one of the search engines; there will be a thousand indiscriminate results. I start with my mother's date of birth. She said she was a young woman when Aunt Eliza gave her the bowl, and that Eliza died soon after in Southsea, Portsmouth. So I must search Hampshire in the 1930s, and not just the death registrations. If Eliza were giving away silver to her niece then there was probably a will and a registration for probate. There might even have been a death notice in the local paper. All are at my fingertips. I find that there are a couple of Eliza Evanses who died in Southsea in the right period. They left wills but I don't recognise the names of any executors. But I can deduce dates of birth for these ladies and, from there, find their marriages. One of them was called Eliza Ellis at the time of her marriage to J G Evans, an engineer. The name Ellis rings a bell.

I put Bach on the computer - one of the unaccompanied cello suites - as stimulus, and reward for a good start, and check Ellis in the family database.

There is an Anglo-Irish family called Ellis who lived in Ipswich. Isaac Ellis left his Ipswich dockside slum in 1875 or thereabouts.[1] With his wife, Sarah Jane, and their three children, Eliza, Charles, and Kate, Isaac moved to Station Road, Plumstead, in Kent. Internet archives tell me that the son, Charles, became a gunner in the Royal Horse Artillery.

I smile whenever there is the prospect of a military record, since army recruiting officers and clerks set down revealing details - including family relationships - when fulfilling their own bureaucratic purposes. They share my delight in factual records, and these I can fashion into a narrative, like a palaeontologist who can construct a whole dinosaur from a box of bones. So it is with Charles Frederick Ellis (number 64691) of the Royal Horse Artillery - later the Royal Artillery. His records survive. He was stationed in India from early 1889 to December 1895.[2] He lists Eliza Evans, née Ellis, his sister, as his next of kin, and gives her address not as Plumstead or Ipswich but Bally Gunge, Calcutta.

Oh, such joy, such an adrenalin rush! I am perhaps the first person to read this record in the one hundred and thirty years since an army clerk filed it away, and certainly the first to attach any significance to it. It is corroborative evidence for my mother's story that she had a great aunt Eliza (related somehow) who went to India, where she acquired a silver bowl.

I make a careful note, attach it to the computerised family tree, and take my teacup to the kitchen. There is a bottle of single malt I bought myself for Christmas, and this is the right moment to open it.

Back in my office I look through the pale gold tumbler at the silver bowl and picture how it once sat in a Calcutta bungalow, in the 1890s, to be admired by a young wife and her husband (an engineer on the Indian railway, I discover) and by her soldier brother who dropped in for tiffin when off duty.

Was it Gunner Charles Ellis who had recommended the very silversmith who had fettled the piece?

'Lakshmi, memsahib. Goddess of wealth and prosperity,' says the craftsman. 'Good fortune to you and your home. May India prosper the memsahib! This is a very good price.'

Eliza, my distant cousin, runs a white finger across the raised decoration of the silver bowl, tracing the repoussé work in tacit admiration. I touch the inner chasing and, through a millimetre of silver and more than a century of time, a momentary tremor links us, a shimmer in the space-time continuum. Lakshmi, bringer of good fortune connects Eliza, Charles, my mother, and me, in a way the Calcutta silversmith could never have foreseen, though, in his craft, would know was always possible.

I raise the whisky tumbler to my lips and drink to these ancestors, to their continuance, for we are suddenly all here, convened by the archives and the bowl: our gaze, our touch, our atoms and DNA, and their ripples within my blood.

Here is no cold artefact but a symbol of a quest which will make all time present. Here is my inheritance. Here is what I offer to those who come after. Light is refracted between screen, bowl, and tumbler. It is a long time since I have been so bewitched, so intoxicated.

When I was a child, I was attracted to shiny, unattainable things. Almost the only object of value in my parents' terraced, red brick Ipswich home was the Indian silver bowl, prominent on the utility sideboard in our cramped dining room. This beautiful artefact seemed unconnected with anything else in the house. As I grew capable of independent thought, I found myself in sympathy with the bowl: I, too, had little connection with anything else within those four walls. I was even unsure of my connections with my parents, who seemed alien inhabitants and in a different dimension to me.

By the time I was nine years old I was a solitary only child, but my imaginary life was rich and full of friends. I convinced myself I had been abandoned at birth, or snatched and exchanged, like a child in some old tale that I might have read at that age.

In the years after the Second World War, my father worked long hours for little money in a tannery. It was a dirty Victorian brick building full of animal hides, stinking vats, and brooding machinery which frightened me. Sometimes, when I was still in primary school, he took me to the factory on a Saturday morning. He was duty-bound to check that the building was safe at the weekend. I remember being left alone on empty floors while he did his rounds. Outside, a goods train rattled past, its metal wheels grinding and squealing as it sauntered round a tight bend. Inside, the wooden floors creaked, and the high windows were thick with dust and spiders' webs. There was the sweet odour of tanning hides, somewhere between nausea and seduction. At every moment I expected some sinister figure to emerge from the shadowed corners. Once, an alarm sounded whilst my father was not there, and I did not know whether to run or stand still. It seemed a lifetime before he came to collect me, and he didn't appear to notice that anything might have been wrong. Even now, more than sixty years later, I can see myself pretending to be calm, not showing the frantic dread and relief which engulfed me as I hurried to keep up with his purposeful stride out of the building.

Ours was an ordered, bounded life, and not unhappy, but there was an unspoken understanding that the world outside was hostile - my parents had lasted through a world war, sometimes together, but more often apart because of his military service - and survival depended on order, good discipline, and not expecting too much. I learned only much later that my mother had been bombed out of her Ipswich home and my father had ended the war as a British military policeman amongst the dire privations of Berlin. All this was invisible to me then; unknown, because no-one would talk of such things to a small child. Our house was a place of secrets, and I became convinced that things were not as they seemed.

The parents I believed I deserved were very different from the ones I had. My fantasy parents were rich. They would give me a bicycle for my birthday, not the wretched toy scooter I actually received.[3] They would not make me eat cabbage for Sunday lunch, and I would not have to sit at the table until my plate was clean. They were not those parents talking quietly downstairs behind a closed door.

Perhaps the people who called themselves my parents were simply hired to look after me by my real parents, whose ancient lineage and closeness in blood to the royal family prevented them from caring for me themselves.

I was convinced that one day a letter would come, probably from one of the big, detached houses above Christchurch Park, and I would be claimed by my rightful parents. They would arrive in a very large car, probably a silver Jaguar Mark IX,[4] and anything I wanted I could have, if I asked nicely. I had an ancient pedigree which commanded all this.

The old Indian silver bowl on the sideboard was the one sign that this must be true.

That was my first interest in family history.

There must be a story to unearth, I thought, and the silver bowl was its single piece of physical evidence. At that age I did not know how to take my exploration any further.

Meanwhile I discovered that there were other lives which I could enjoy, and some of them were much more outlandish than the urban riches that I dreamed of. In my imagination, fed by frequent trips to the local library, I could inhabit distant planets and lost islands. I could journey in the remote future and, especially terrifying, the dinosaur-inhabited past. My childhood reading, I see now, fed my longing to escape. That was what the library offered and, ever since, I have been unable to resist the sight of old books or the feel of time-worn archives and ancient artefacts.

By the time I went up to Grammar school I was a constant reader - spending long nights with a torch beneath the bedclothes - and a writer. There were imaginative narratives of heroic derring-do, usually in rocket ships or submarines. They owed much to Jules Verne and *The Eagle*.[5] Sometimes I wrote the stories down, but more often they were part of my rich, imaginative life; my secret world.

I was enchanted, too, by real-life adventures. In the world I would inherit I was sure I would be the hero, the adventurer. People would write stories about me, like the ones written about Sir Edmund Hilary or Captain Cook. Perhaps I would write stories about myself, and these would be true, with black and white photographs of exotic places like those in the *Children's Encyclopaedia* in our bookcase.

In my first week at the new school, a well-meaning master set a piece of homework to describe an evening at home. Here was an opportunity to present my creative credentials, and I thought myself well able to bring such a scene to life, even if there would be nothing at all heroic about it. (It never occurred to me to imagine a fictional scene: he asked for facts and that's what he'd get.)

I had a small desk in the box room where I slept, and I laboured with a messy pen: Platignum, as we all seemed to have in those days, filled from a bottle of Quink.[6] I found it difficult to keep a blot-free page and my fingers were perennially dyed blue-black, so I wrote in pencil on scraps of paper and copied out.

It was laborious, but I was pleased with the result. I listed and detailed and described, and I thought my parents would be as proud as I was of this first piece of homework for my new school. I went into the small back room where they sat on either side of the empty fireplace; it was not yet far enough into autumn to be burning coals. My father was reading *The Daily Telegraph* and my mother was darning his socks. They looked up and smiled.

'All finished, Peter?' asked Mother. 'Can we see?'

'I'll read it to you if you like,' I said.

I could sense the excitement, the encouragement.

'That would be lovely, Dear.'

They turned expectant faces towards me. My father folded his paper across his knees and my mother paused her sewing, laying aside the wooden mushroom and the wool.

'*An Evening at Home,*' I announced. '*When my father comes in from the tannery we sit down for tea. My mother cooks egg and chips and sometimes we have beans as well. I like a slice of bread with margarine but sometimes I spread dripping from the Sunday joint on it …*'

I read on. It was full of facts: every small detail of my family's behaviour, such as my parents' secret conversations in the kitchen with the door closed, or the sound of the trains to Felixstowe which rattled past the end of our small garden. I was, I think, merciless in precision. Finally, I came to an end and looked up at them expectantly.

'You can't give that in,' said my father.

I looked at him in confusion.

'Give me the book.'

His smile had gone. I held out my writing to him.

My father took the book - a lined and stapled affair with a blue card cover (blue was for English) - and carefully bent it back along the thin spine. Silently, he made a neat excision of the page I had written on and then removed the other half from the back of the book so that the only way to tell that the page had gone was because the book was now slightly thinner. He held up the sheets he had removed. The blank sheet from the back of the book he put on one side for my mother to use for her shopping lists, the written-on sheet he folded and then tore precisely, three times, and dropped it in the wastepaper bin beside his chair.

I can still feel the horror of the moment. It was the sudden jerk, as when a roller coaster plunges over its summit and part of you is left behind.

'Write it again, Peter,' he said.

'Again?' I was shocked and tearful.

'Do you think anyone needs to read about how we live? These are private things.'

'But ...'

'Do it again.'

And he thrust the book back at me.

I slipped out of the room, fearing to look either of them in the face.

I retreated to the little desk in my bedroom. I thought I had never written anything so well. But no, I had exposed the details of family life. A teacher would read about us, and this would be like turning the bricks and mortar of our house to glass and letting in the public gaze. I had destroyed the carefully constructed curtain walls of home as effectively as any German bomb.

I would have to write a new piece which would present those few details which could be for a public audience in as favourable colours as possible; something that I knew to be untrue, but which would pass my parents' domestic censorship.

There cannot have been anything which I gave away in the original which would have been to the family's detriment, unless it was an un-gilded description of an aspiring post-war, working-class English family.

I was wounded to an extent that I can still remember the texture of the scene to this day. It changed my life and the way I work. Now, for my clients, I write what the evidence dictates, but only what I judge that people want. If a story might embarrass, I keep silent until I know the client is prepared for such a thing.

As for my own family history, I have had a foggy terror, twisting about my shoulders, which has stifled me for more than sixty years. I have not been able to write what I think and feel, so I have kept silent.[7]

Yet now that I am alone in my cottage and threatened by the cold of winter and this apparently unassailable Covid, the imperative to penetrate my family history has become overwhelming. In front of shimmering screens, with the cold night beyond, staring at an Indian bowl, I imagine the stories which the silver might signify, the stories which govern me and tell me who I am.

I will, at last, collect the odds and ends of my heritage, finding where the fragments fit together and where they do not, trusting that I have the imagination to fill in the details. There is no-one to censor me now. The few friends I have are scattered and as unable to meet me as I am to meet them. My parents, and all those adults who knew me as a child, are long dead. There is a thread of liberation woven into grief.

There is no jeopardy, except to my own sense of who I am. Facts might be emotionally troubling, but they no longer threaten punishment. Facts can be collected and relationships established beyond reasonable doubt.

To return to my most recent discoveries, Eliza Ellis married an engineer called Evans. *Fact*. They went to India. *Fact*. Her brother was a soldier there. *Fact*. Eliza acquired a silver bowl in Calcutta. Not necessarily a fact, but, given what my mother thinks Eliza told her, and the appearance of the bowl, then it's more likely than not.

When I see the lives of these ancestors, diagrammatised, I might be looking at a map of my subconscious. Here are my foundations, the secret spaces hidden below, with their struts and buttresses. Or, since I am organic, they are the mycelium of my toadstool existence, hidden beneath the surface while I have my brief appearance in the sun.

Looking up from the screen I can see though the study window, in the moonlight, the church's grey elegance peering back at me over the hedge, and I glimpse the rows of gravestones. They stand jagged against the uneven frozen grass. For many years I filed and indexed our own family gravestones whenever I came across them, sought out records of births, marriages, and deaths, and entries in censuses, but I could not imagine what each signified. I would not imagine their lives, their horrors, but now

I make tentative steps towards assembling my inheritance. I will tell the story as I think it really was because I am all these people. I might even find some comfort in filling my silent study with their presence.

My father would, I now think, have appreciated all my careful record keeping in files, databases, and relationship diagrams: he had neat copperplate handwriting and setting pen to paper was, for him, always a painstaking skill. But he would probably have asked, 'What on earth is the purpose? Who needs to know, Peter?'

I gaze at the silver bowl, seeking inspiration. Lakshmi seems to speak to me from one of her six faces: 'Once the self exists it can never cease. It is good to seek to understand this.'[8]

The memory of Eliza was treasured by my mother. Whatever memories Eliza carried within her surely informed my mother's own life, just as she has passed the same gifts, in silver and in memory and in some shared DNA, down to me.

I finish the Scotch and shut down the computer. I polish my finger marks off the silver bowl and place it by the keyboard. Tomorrow I will begin to discover who else may have haunted us.

In the days that followed my discovery of Eliza Ellis and her brother I struggled to make sense of the Ellis family and their connection to my mother. Her mother, my grandmother, had been a Miss Root before her marriage, and she was descended from a George Root, my great-great-grandfather. I couldn't find any connection to an Ellis, and it seemed that George Root didn't exist in the archives before the 1870s.

Then I discovered a record of a woman called Harriet Keziah Root, living in Ipswich in the 1840s, who had a son called George.

Living in Ipswich in the same decades was another woman called Harriet or Keziah Sparham who also had a son called George.

Both mothers and sons would have been the same age as each other.

I tracked them in the archive. In the census and birth, marriage, and death records, George Sparham and George Root were never present at the same time: if there was a Keziah and George Root in the 1841 census there was no Keziah and George Sparham. If Keziah and George Sparham existed in 1851 then there was no Keziah and George Root. I dug further and they each seemed to have brothers, sisters and wives with the same first names and of similar ages. I realised that Sparham and Root were the same person.

Then I found some pages of newsprint from 1836 where Keziah Root and Keziah Sparham were reported as the same person - 'Sparham, properly Root,' wrote the reporter. She was surely my ancestor.

And Lakshmi said, 'Give the woman her voice.'

I put the search for Eliza Ellis to one side to listen to Keziah Root.

## 2: Keziah Root or Sparham

### Ipswich: December 1836

I was sure my George would die of cold that night. We was in St Clement's Churchyard all evening. There was shelter where the path came close to one of them great stone walls as sticks out by the door. I been there before 'cos it was a place people passed and I reckon those folks found themselves uncomfortable close to God when they had to take a turn about the old church. If you was sitting with a hand out, there was a chance the passers-by might place a farthing in it and look up as if to say, 'Look I paid. Now let me walk on.'

We'd been there for six hours or more, me and George, huddled together while the snow drifted against the stone. There were few enough walking the town that night. I had next to nothing to show for our vigil. Dear Lord, it were cold! The first snow had fallen early in October.[9] Winter had started then and never finished - not till long after Christmas and the great storm.

That was still to come, and anyways, Christmas never meant much to me. Just another day, like this one, like any other. Same pains, same nab nannies[10], same goin' wet-shud and never warm. George was six years old, jest a little squit, and limp as a rag. He was always a silent, clingy child. 'A seemed to live deep inside hisself, and he wouldn't be parted from me. Sometimes that were to our advantage. The verger's wife passes and looks at me like she'd look at any whore, but then she sees George, and me cradling him, and she won't look me in the face, but she finds a coin to throw in my lap.

People judge you out the corner of their eye. If I'm alone then I'm a whore and it's a tanner and I have to give out, if you understand me. Or I gets nothing. These days usually nothing.[11] If I'm with George then it might be a ha'pence and all I got to do for that is hold me hand out. Ha'pennies, even farthings, do add up. Sometimes I have to make the choice, to bring George with me and risk him freeze to death or leave him at home and we all starve.

We hung around St Clement's[12] for hours. There was half a moon, and the snow lit us up enough to keep us in the doorway. I heard the clocks strike ten. George was whimpering, asleep, and I was pulling him in close to me when I saw the man's boots - saw them rather than heard them in the snow.

Thick soled, shiny, black, high boots. They'll keep the cold out well enough, I thought. Then I looked upwards and saw the fine black cloak, the cane, and the tall hat.

'Please, sir,' I said, 'the boy ain't eaten today.'

He stopped. He spoke softly and kept his distance. His questions riled me, though.

'Where do you live?'

I looked at George and then I stared the gentleman down, wondering what this was about. Wasn't it clear why I was there? If I had a warm home to go to, I wouldn't have been out in the snow.

'I mean no harm, woman,' he said. 'Are you of Ipswich? Who is responsible for you?'

Then I knew straight off, he was from the Poor Law or the magistrates. He wanted to know if I was his responsibility or could they move me on.

'I live in Ipswich, sir,' I replied. This were true. We had lodgings close by in Back Hamlet at the time.

'Where was the boy born?' he said.

I looked at George. He were turning blue with the cold. He were shivering and I knew he were frightened of this strange man.

'Walpole, sir,' I said.[13] 'And he's a good boy, but he needs to eat, sir. Nothing all day, sir.'

'And you shall have money for him,' he said. 'Now, tell me your name and your story so that I can help.'

I've heard this sort of thing before. Some men seem to need to know all about you, others would rather treat you like a piece of furniture. I reckon as the trick is to give 'em as little as you think you can get away with. Either way you got to make 'em pay for the use they make of you.

'I am Mrs Sparham, sir,' I said, which was true up to a point because I'd been with Sparham for twenty years. It were important to seem as though you cared to be respectable.

'And you're originally from Walpole?

'Yes, sir.'

'And you have more children?

'Oh yes, sir. Four, sir.' Which was as true as it needed to be, 'cos my other girl was all grown and married and widowed.[14]

'Your husband, Mr Sparham, lives with you and supports you?'

'Oh yes, sir, when he can,' I said softly, looking as pitiful as a sailor's wife who's just heard her husband's ship's overdue. I looked down at George, just to remind the man that I had a child dying in my arms. George snuffled and coughed.

'Is he at home now, your husband? Is he in work?' said the swell.

'No, sir. He's gone away to find work.'

'To Walpole?'

'Me'be, sir. Back to his wife, I should think.'

'I thought *you* were his wife,' said the man, stooping to get closer to me as if he were afraid that he hadn't heard aright.

'I thought so too, sir.'

'Whatever do you mean, Mrs Sparham?'

'Fifteen years we been married, sir. All proper and writ' down at St Matthew's Church, sir, and we had four children. He's a saw-yer, sir, so sometimes he has to travel for work, and after George here was born he went back up county, and then I discovered that he had a wife up there what I never knowed about ...' Now I started to cry, rubbing my shawl across my face.

It wasn't all pretence, neither. Of course, I knewed he had a wife. I'd been their maid. She was a fearsome old baggage and neither him nor I could keep her content. So Sparham and me kept each other happy when there was a chance. He'd had enough of the old missus a-maggin[15] at him, and he said he'd take care of me. So off we come to Ipswich. But I wasn't going to tell my gentleman any of this.

'Now, Mrs Sparham,' said this fine man. 'If what you have told me be true then you have been badly treated, and I am minded to enquire what can be done to help you. My name is Cobbold. Here is a shilling, but I will tell your story in the appropriate quarter, and we shall see what may alleviate your suffering.'

Then he is off out of my face and down the path with a purposeful tread through the snow, and I thought to myself, *What have you done, girl?*

You see, this town is full of Cobbolds. They own the brewery and the beer shops and the inns. We're all tied to that family; many men work for them and then give them back their money on rent for the houses they live in. They drink Cobbold beer in Cobbold public houses. Cobbolds are mayors, magistrates, bankers, and landlords. They own Ipswich. Now I'd told this 'un enough for 'im to own me twice over.

George was some place between sleep and awake now. His breath was coming in short bursts and the tiny wisps of steam on the cold air were getting fainter. *Best go now or he'll be dead before I reach our bed*, I thought.

I gathered him up and trudged back home, finding his brothers, Alfred and James, were out, but our Jemima, his sister, were in front of the small fire.[16]

'Come to bed,' I said to her. 'Huddle together and we'll soon be warm. We got money for breakfast, now.'

The children were soon asleep.

Jemima was only ten year old herself, and she and George bunched together like those children in the forest in the old tale. But I couldn't rest until James and Alfred were in (they're twelve and fourteen, and weren't about to tell me where they'd been. It's not a month since James was arrested for carrying a quantity of lead which wasn't rightly his.[17]). Even when the boys had fallen into bed beside me, smelling of ale and the dung heap, I couldn't rest my mind from Cobbold. I had his shilling, but he'd had much more from me, even if they was only words. What would he do with them?

It's like I was always telling the children, 'Protect yourselves, 'cos no one else will look out for you. It don't matter what these folk say about wanting to help. They'll just do whatever is to their own advantage. So be like those dodmans[18] in the yard. Pull yourself into your shell and don't give nothing away or you're like to get your head chewed. Especially, never tell nothin' about your family.' And now there was I giving it all away to a bleddy Cobbold for a bit of silver. That's what cold and a belly full of air do to you.

George's breathing was steadier now, and we all warmed each other in the bed, so I suppose I slept, but whenever I did wake I were troubled by what I had said to Cobbold and lay there cursing meself.

Saturday was rent day, but we'd already spent Cobbold's money. There had been broth and bread and George ate well. Sparham still hadn't come home so we were short, though James had a couple of bob for me (I didn't ask where from), and one way and another I could scrape enough together. I was just going up the court[19] to buy more bread when the rent man came down the alley. He were a thin, grey man, all buttoned up against the cold, and clutching his little leather satchel to his chest.

'Mrs Sparham,' he says. 'Stay a moment.' He stands in my way and makes his usual performance of having me wait while he searches the bag for his book and pencil and licks his finger to find the page.

'Now then …' He's slow, for a man built like a whippet, and

now he looks me in the eye for the first time and smirks. 'You had a pay day,' he says. 'Don't tell me you don't have no money. You're already a week behind.'

'But Mr Bentham, I wasn't about to ...'

"'Cos you been consorting with Cobbolds.[20] If you can't pay up you can go and see your new friend and get him to give you one of his cribs ...'

'I don't know what you're talking of. Here. Here's my money.' I hold the coins out in my hand but he doesn't take them, not yet.

'No, of course you don't know what the whole town knows!' he jeers.

There are others in the court now, idling and watching. ''Cos we all live cheek by jowl, it's easy enough to gather a crowd. There's Mrs Sparrow and Mrs Worledge with their noses in everything, and children who stop their larkin' 'cos they can see something more exciting is brewing. He has his audience.

'What you on about?' I say. 'The only Cobbold I know is the beer what you've been drinking.'

He waves a copy of the *Chronicle* at me.

'Here you are,' he says. 'The report of the meeting about the Poor Law in the town on Wednesday.[21] Your Mr Cobbold, who is soundly against the new law and thinks that us poor rate payers should be burdened by every pauper that shows their face at the overseer's door, met you and told the meeting - the public meeting, mind - all about you.'

'He never!'

'He did.' And the old heathen, Bentham, reads it for all to hear in his most pompous voice:

*Last night, between 10 and 11 o'clock, as I was going home, and whilst passing up St Clement's Hamlet, a poor creature called after me. I stopped and she related her story. She had with her a child, about six years of age; she said her name was Sparham, and that she belonged to Walpole in this county,*[22] *that some years ago she married a man who, she subsequently found, had a wife elsewhere. She, however, did not discover this fact until she had borne him 4 children, and these she is now compelled to maintain as well as she can. She applied to her parish, at Walpole, and was told they had no business with her, and that the children did not belong to Walpole. Mr Gooding, at her entreaty, had since written to the parish officers, and the answer received was, 'We can allow Mrs Sparham, with her four children, 9d a week' (shame). If this were the case it was scandalous (hear, hear).*[23] '

'Well, it is scandalous,' I says. 'You can't keep a roof over the heads of four children, or food in their mouths for nine pence.[24] Even if it's a stinking sty like the one we live in. You should be ashamed of the place. We all pay good money.' I look at Ma Worledge and that busybody Sparrow - I need them on my side, not laughing at me.

'When are you going to clear the midden, Mr Bentham? When you going to mend the pump?'

'Ar, when?' says Sarah Worledge. 'We ain't had clean water for months, and the stinking thing's frozen solid now.' She pulls a couple of her children to her and looks ready to go into battle.

If he wants to make a show of me, him and his silly voices, I've got the gawpers on my side now. Folk is coming in all round us. The court is small and crowded and Bentham is edging towards the covered passage leading out on to Back Hamlet.

'Now, no more of that, Mrs Sparham,' he says, standing on his dignity, which he doesn't have much of, being foxy and generally disliked. 'There's plenty more who'd take your room, so you just pay up and go your way quietly.'

I paid most of what I owed, and we parted, scowling, but you can imagine what it was like for me after that. I wasn't in my shell no more. I were a public spectacle. Every time I stepped out someone would ask if I'd seen my friend Cobbold, and snigger behind me back.

'We saw you was in the paper.'

'How much did Cobbold give you?'

'Does Sparham know?'

'You want to hope no-one shows him what you said, his business being all over the town.'

'He'll be off out of here if he doesn't want to be in court for bigamy,' said Ma Worledge, who was probably only trying to make mischief between us, though maybe she was right. But I didn't know where he was so he'd already made himself scarce.

On it went like that: all my life was dragged out in the papers and everyone had an opinion. I could see my neighbours looking at me over their shoulders and yammering on, as if they didn't all have their own little secrets. I knew where some of them got their wages. I knew who had been out on a quiet, moonlit night and come back with red meat. I could guess who was here because they'd trouble elsewhere.

So I held my head high and said, 'I'm Mrs Sparham,' even if I could truly only call myself Keziah Root.

*You got to brazen it out,* Sparham would have said.

It were worse with the gentry, of course. We weren't anything to them 'cept the subject of their chat and a reason for their arguments - mainly about money. These men in top hats don't like to be made foolish, so each must have his say. The very next week, there I am again in the paper, and there is Bentham, the rent man, to wave it at me and read it out.

> *'Mrs Sparrow or Sparham, properly Keziah Root's case. - This woman is the mother of five bastard children, three belonging to St Clement's parish, two of whom are boys, aged 14 and 12, had been in constant earnings during the summer of between 6s and 7s each, and has received orders for the Poorhouse. The Board of Guardians conceiveding it improper that they should remain with the mother, in consequence of her character; but they refused to go into the house.*[25] *The woman now receives weekly from this Union one stone of flour for the third child, a girl aged 9; she herself and one child, for whom 9d a week is allowed by the Blything union*[26], *belong to Walpole. She ran away with a man named Sparham, while living in the service of his wife, and knew perfectly well at the time she married him, that his first wife was alive. She had one child by another man.* [27]

It was Christmas Eve by then, eleven days since I'd met Mr Cobbold in St Clement's, and wasn't that a nice present from these men of the workhouse board - advertised as a whore to all the town, my children told they had a lying slut for a mother, and me expecting Sparham home from wherever he was that very night.

My 'character,' they talk about!

What about their characters? Don't suppose they thought about that as they tucked into the Christmas goose and smiled on their wives and children. Do they suppose I don't love my children? Don't I do the best I can?

The night before Christmas, and George, Jemima, James, and Alfred all snuggled with me in the one bed.

'I want to stay like this forever, Ma,' said George, suddenly.

'I wish we could,' I said. 'Now go to sleep. I bought a meat pudding for tomorrow,' I whispered. 'And there's tatties.'

'Will Father be here?' asked George.

'He'll do his best, I'm sure,' I said. 'Now sleep, or you'll never find out.'

He wriggled and kicked as he dozed, but it wasn't that that kept me awake. Me mind turned over and over. God knows I loved my little George, but we should never of 'ad him. I told Sparham, 'I'm too old.' More than forty years old, I was, when I fell with child for the sixth time[28].

'I can't keep away,' James Sparham had said, leering and grabbing at me. We were as bad as each other. I couldn't resist him from the moment I first met him in the missus' pantry twenty years before. We both knew right off that we was in trouble. Thank God he travelled all over for work: if we'd lived in each other's pockets it wasn't just five babies we'd have had together.

And now look at me.

He's away and I've got Alf and James and Jemima and George, and though the older two do as they please, Jemima is still a year or two from being put out to work. As for George, he may be sickly, but he ain't dead yet, and he'll be keeping me company until he's strong enough to go brickmaking with his brothers. They do worry me, see. I dunno where it will end. At least when Sparham do come home I'm too old to get any more bastards off of him.

I love James Sparham, but people don't see that. It makes me angry. I won't be judged.

I tightened my grasp around the sleeping George. He felt my tension and whimpered. I tried to relax but all I could see in the pitch-black room was a vision of meself when I was just a young woman, kneeling in the pantry of Sparham's home at Walpole, hard brush in hand as I scrubs at the flags and Sparham creeping in behind.

'You got sawdust in your beard,' I'd say to him.

'Brush it out, then,' he'd say. I'd get close, threaten him with the sudsy brush, then run my fingers through his beard.

'I got shavings inside my shirt, too,' he'd say.

'You'd better take it off and I can shake it out for you.' He'd make a show of unbuttoning. He were slightly built, but he had a powerful, hairy chest.

'Oh, let me help,' I'd say and go to pick the shavings off his skin. He'd laugh and pull me in to him, then press me back hard against the pantry door.

I loved him in those days when I was young and it was our secret, and he said he loved me.

Eventually, we left the mistress. Being a sawyer, he had to move round the county from one job to another. Sometimes I went with him and sometimes I stayed put in Ipswich with the children. Every time he came back home there were shavings to be picked from his skin and sawdust in his beard. I got these children, and I hold them to me now in the blackness of our rough bed. I have the pictures in my head of his naked arms and his beard, but now they jingle-jangle along with the faces of Bentham and Ma Worledge and a man in a tall black hat. Sure, it's a tangled mess, but you got to live each day and there ain't no use moping or longing for things you ain't got. You take what's available.

'Come home, James Sparham,' I muttered as I fell asleep.

When he got back that Christmas morning and heard about the newspaper and the gossip in the court from Ma Worledge's lad, the poor boy wore the black eye he earned for his cheeky words for a se'nnight after. George and the others got their meat pudding and James and me drank the whole of Christmas and I was picking sawdust out of his beard whether there was any there or not.

# 3: Peter, Locked Down

## March 2021

I am surrounded by images from the newspaper archives, the confusing handwriting of census clerks, and neat computerised family trees, but my thoughts reach out to Keziah. She has more to reveal, I know it, if I let her speak in her own voice.

Lakshmi speaks to me too, from one of her six faces. She repeats, 'Once the self exists, it can never cease.' These phantoms are my inheritance. They swirl around my study, populating my world.

I feel some urgency to hear them speak. Sixty-five years have passed since I first tried to write about my family life and since, like Keziah, I was told to keep the stories private.

I have diaries full of pointless reflections on an ordinary life: my progression from school to university (Liverpool; History), to a certificate in archival studies, to my first post in a county records office. As I flick through them, I see that I complained a lot about ignorant bosses and patronising clients. I notice how rarely I recorded my relationships with family or friends, and now I find I cannot even remember many of their names.

A journey with no interest, not even to myself.

My father died while I was at university, suddenly, before he and I could discover an adult relationship. We remained mysteries to each other, I think. We had little in common beyond a name and his wife, my mother. I had to demonstrate the expected reaction to his death but could only think that he and I had missed an opportunity, had passed beside each other like two souls who walk down a widening street on opposite pavements, not speaking and hardly noticing the other's presence.

At the end of my time in Liverpool, I went home to Ipswich to be with my mother, in the same cramped terraced house where I had spent my childhood, and I remained there while I worked in record offices, doing what I thought of as my apprenticeship.

My father had, in his thorough fashion, procured an adequate pension and good insurance. We had a little inheritance, and, with mother's support, I set up my probate and ancestry research business. Mother threw herself into being my administrative assistant. It was the most adventurous step I would take. It wasn't a lucrative business, but we both found it satisfying work, and we could live quite comfortably and work in the house, which had long since been paid for. Upon her death, I sold up and moved to my cottage by the country church.

It has been, by the standards of the heroes of my childhood, a small life, though I think it has had its uses. This tale of ancestors stands fair to be my most original bequest to the future.

I am, however, time sick. A pandemic is stealing what little space I have left to complete the work. Every moment is past before it has really been present, and all I can think is *When, and how, will this story end?*

In the dead of night voices in my head whisper, *What's the point? This virus has arrived and you, old man, are an easy target.* I'm frightened, I admit it.

I hide away and avoid other people because everyone is a threat. This solitary quest is one of the few purposeful things left to me. The present is uncertain, and there is safety, as well as richness, in the past. I want to believe that out of these archival fragments I shall find the foundations for my own life. Perhaps I will find inheritors for these stories.

Keziah's life was far less secure than my own. Perhaps she, too, sought an explanation of her present self by searching what she knew of the past.

# 4: Keziah, Elizabeth, and Charles Mallows

## February 1837

In the New Year, James was away, and I could meet my girl, my first child, Elizabeth. She wasn't Sparham's daughter, and he didn't like being reminded of it, so she kept away when he was home.[29] (There was a lad at the first place I worked and I fell pregnant, lost my place, had to go home to my ma. It were mainly her that brought the girl up while I worked where I could. That was how I came to skivvy for Ma Sparham).

Before she was twenty, Elizabeth had lost both her husband and her child. That's a tale worth the telling, if only to warn the other children, and because it keeps coming back to haunt me. We live with our mistakes, and year by year they pile up like broken crocks on the dunghill, sharp edges and bits of pattern showing through shit.

At the age of seventeen, Elizabeth married a rogue called Charles Mallows.

She wouldn't listen to me and there was no father around to see him off. She wouldn't listen to Sparham, her stepfather, either.

She'd been a young girl when Sparham and me found each other. Sparham took me, her mother, away and then started to give her those brothers and sisters. When Jemima came along,

Elizabeth was fifteen year old, and that was the last straw. Why would she hang around to look after our brood? Charles Mallows appeared, showed an interest, and that was that.

I couldn't blame her. It were just a pity Mallows were such a divil. I knew his history and I could see that he'd do her no good, but she wouldn't be told.

'He's had a difficult life, Ma,' she'd say, though there ain't no reason why his was worse than anyone else's.

'He can't help himself. He's good at heart.'

All the truck that you hear a thousand times from girls who get themselves charmed. I should know 'cos it was my story too. Things repeat themselves in families - well, they do in ours, and I don't know as you can ever escape the wheel as it keeps going round. My Elizabeth, poor child, didn't really stand a chance.

Mallows was ten years older than Elizabeth.[30] He was jack-sauce, hulking about and never earning an honest penny if there were a dishonest one to be had.

He worked with horses when he had to. He was good with Suffolk heavies, I give him that. I seen him with them a time or two, pulling the drays for the brewery. But the horses were steadier than he was. He had work one week and then none for a month 'cos he couldn't keep sober, and when he was drunk he fought or let his tongue run away with him. Whatever money he had slipped through his fingers and back to Cobbold or one of them other puffy brewers.

Elizabeth saw him in the town. He was out of work and got hisself sent to the old St Clements' parish workhouse. A strappin' youth like he was, they'd have him work to pay his way, but he refused so they took him to the justices who sentenced him to hard labour in the house of correction. 'Idle and disorderly,' they said he was.[31] Ten hours a day on the treadmill.[32]

It was supposed to teach you a lesson, all that pointless labour, though I think it's really just to remind us all that we're on that wheel we can't escape. Either way, it didn't work for Charles Mallows. Out of prison, back in the workhouse, he were refusing to toe the line again.

It were a few days before Christmas (Christmas again, must be seven or eight year back) when he and his mates, Welham and Gladding, got silly-bold with drink. They were soon back in court and into the gaol for another twenty-one days of hard labour.[33]

Then, within three months of coming out of prison, he married Elizabeth at St Margaret's,[34] and a few months later she was pregnant. They had a little boy, Frederick, my first grandson (and I still had Jemima toddling around - and George, God bless him, were two years in the future).

Now, when I met up with Elizabeth, a few weeks after I'd encountered Cobbold at St Clement's, I found her on the street. She was alone and lost, leaning against a wall, dawzled[35] with hunger and hardly able to stand. The bodice of her dress was all torn and a cuff hanging loose. She been beaten, fair swinged, by some fellow - a soldier, she said - who'd gone off without paying 'cos he said she was poxed.

'Which I ain't, Ma,' she said, sniffing.

She were in a dreadful state, and I reckoned the pox was the least of her ills.

I took her in and fed her as best as I could, and she slept a bit into the evening. There was no little Frederick with her of course. No, there wasn't no Fred, because he died at a year old, and though she'd had others, there were none she'd been brought to bed of. Her pretty face, and she had been a pretty child, was lined and pitted, and I thought she might have passed for my cousin or my aunt, so old she now looked.

And Charles Mallows? Oh, he was long gone out of all our lives, and I can't say I was sorry. It happened like this.

When Fred was born, Charles Mallows seemed to see sense for a while. He got work and kept it. There's nothing like having a child to make a man grow up, and I began to think he wasn't so bad as he'd seemed. But now he had to keep Elizabeth and the babe, and the ten shilling a week he could earn with the horses hardly paid for food and rent. It was midsummer, but he knew that once the winter came on he would need new boots and a thick jacket. Elizabeth needed shoes, too, and the child was sick.

Thomas Rainbow's shoe shop in Harmony Square[36] was too much temptation for the couple. Rainbow had only recently opened his business. He was not yet twenty years old, and had never done his time, but he knew enough of cobbling to provide for the poorer folk who had begun to patronise him.

His was an untidy little cottage. To the right of the door from the street, a counter divided the room and Rainbow sat behind it on a low stool, bending over his last. There was the tang of glue and tanned hides. Fragments of leather and spools of thread littered the floor. A few odd shoes, awaiting repair, lay limply on the counter with a couple of newly made pairs. Behind the front door on the left were shelves bearing more new boots and shoes and some well-worn pairs which were also for sale.

Rainbow were a tall young man, thin, with a blemished face. When Charles and Elizabeth went inside she looked at the man and the state of his shop and thought, *No woman lives here.* She turned her brightest smile on him and asked to look at the boots on the counter.

'Oh, Mr Rainbow, such lovely leather,' Elizabeth said.

Rainbow blushed.

Charles Mallows stood by the door, watching on.

'May I try these, please?' she said.

'Surely, missus,' he stammered.

She walked back and forth in the new black boots, held her foot up and twisted it and raised the hem of her dress to admire the effect.

'And what do you think, Mr Rainbow?'

'Why, they suit you fine.'

'Don't you think they're a little snug? I think they pinch my toes. Feel them for me,' she commanded the cobbler, who came round the counter and knelt at her feet to check the fit.

'They'll soon stretch a little,' said Rainbow, feeling Elizabeth's delicate toes for perhaps a second or two longer than required.

'But I'm sure the left shoe is tighter,' she said.

He examined the other foot with even greater care.

'I think you'll find them perfect,' he said, reluctantly rising to his full height. Elizabeth walked about once more, then said,

'Oh, I'd love them, but I'll have to save my pennies. Thank you so much.'

She unlaced the boots quickly and placed them back on the

counter. With a final smile at Rainbow and a look of longing at the boots she turned and took Frederick out of the shop. Charles Mallows, who had been examining the boots on the shelves behind the door, had already left, unnoticed by Rainbow.

It was only at the end of the day, as Thomas Rainbow counted his poor takings and made some attempt to put the shop in order, that he realised that a pair of fine horseman's boots and a pair of lady's button boots were missing from his shelves. He pondered the events of the day. It didn't take him long to guess that it was while he was preoccupied with the pretty woman with the delicate feet that his shoes must have walked. Hard as he tried, he couldn't for the life of him remember what the shadowy man who was with her had looked like.

Elizabeth and Charles might have got away with it if they hadn't been daft. You see, Rainbow would stand outside his shop whenever there wasn't a customer or shoes to mend. He didn't look at folks' faces, he looked at their feet. When some passer-by had good shoes which needed repair, he'd engage them in conversation.

'Street's so muddy ... sir like to go dry-shud?' or 'Madam, seen this latest style ...? New from London ...'

So when he looked down and saw a pair of dainty feet with nearly new boots which he'd had in his own hands but a few days before, he cried out, and as luck would have it there was a constable at the end of the lane.

Elizabeth, babe in arms, couldn't run, so she tried anger.

'These are my boots. My husband got them for me ... No, I don't know where!'

'But they're hardly worn in, nearly brand new,' said Rainbow.

'I look after them. I've had them months.'

'I saw you in my shop last week!'

'You never!'

'We'd better check with your husband,' said the policeman.

'There's a pair of fine gent's boots that went at the same time. He'll be wearing those, I warrant,' said Rainbow.

The cobbler closed his shop and he and the policeman escorted Elizabeth back to her lodgings. They walked down the Woodbridge Road, along St Helen's, and into Upper Orwell Street. The constable kept Elizabeth's elbow tightly gripped, and Rainbow, puffed up like a pigeon, hopped along on her other side. She led the men off the street into a tight courtyard and towards a flight of wooden stairs on the outside of an old building, part stone, part timber.

When they reached the heavy wooden door at the top, they seemed to be going into what might once have been a room above a stable, or the subdivided loft of a warehouse. The floor was bare, and its twisted planks were worn to a shine by generations of feet. It was dominated by a large, high, iron bedstead covered with an assortment of quilts and blankets. There was a curtain across one end of the room and a washstand in the corner. A cradle, a stool and a bent wood chair completed the furnishings. The ceiling was low, and, on this late summer's day, the room was stuffy and smelt of baby, mother's milk, and unwashed clouts in a bucket, though there was order and care in the attic's arrangement.

'Where's your husband?' asked the constable.

'Working, of course,' said Elizabeth, who, now that she was

off the street and in her home, found herself protective and cross. 'You seen enough, then?'

'We're going to have to search for those boots,' said the constable. 'Stand by the door,' he said to Rainbow, 'and don't let her leave.'

Elizabeth put the baby in the cradle and fussed with it, trying to ignore the violation of her room. The constable got on his knees and lifted the blankets from the edge of the bed. He reached beneath and emerged with a cleaned chamber pot and then a trunk.

'Don't you go messin' in there,' said Elizabeth. 'Them's my things.'

The constable lifted the lid and pulled out linen and clothes. In the base of the trunk were the girl's marriage lines and a sprig of heather. He shut the lid.

'Very well,' said the constable, standing and toeing the trunk back beneath the bed frame. 'Now what's behind that curtain?'

'Just old clothes,' said Elizabeth, quietly.

The constable paced to the end of the room and snatched the curtain to one side. It concealed a deep alcove with a brass rail from which hung a mass of men's and women's garments. Partially concealed behind them were a couple of shelves. One was stacked high with more clothes and handkerchiefs, whilst the upper one supported a shiny top hat.

'So this is where the quality of Ipswich lives,' said the constable, snatching a handful of garments from the rail and throwing them on to the bed. There were woollen shifts and smocks, a fine fur-lined cape, and a delicately embroidered silk dress.

'Played that trick before, thieving from honest shop keepers,' said the policeman, knowing full well that a woman like Elizabeth doesn't have such a wardrobe.

'I don't know where they come from. My husband gets them,' said Elizabeth, having the sense to claim her innocence. And to herself she said, *Why shouldn't I have lovely things? Don't I deserve to be well dressed? These men will take it all away. I know it.*

While the policeman set to and threw every garment he could find on to the bed Elizabeth slumped in the chair, rocked the baby in its cradle, and quietly wept for the dream of colour and elegance, silver and gold, which the space behind the curtain had represented to her, and which was being demolished before her eyes.

'But there's my boots!' exclaimed Thomas Rainbow. On the boards below the shelves were a pair of high-topped boots. 'I'd know them anywhere,' and he picked them up and held them to him as if afraid they might resist arrest.

The constable waited until Mallows came home and took him straight to the town gaol, him having been arrested before. And that was the end for my Elizabeth and Charles Mallows. Within a month, at the next Sessions, he was sentenced to seven years transportation.[37]

Transportation to Australia. It's us who's left behind that suffer all the agony. It's like a death, 'cos the transported never came back to tell you what it were like. He were gone in a flash, and my Elizabeth, nineteen years old, left with an empty heart, a sickly child, and little more than the clothes she was standing in.

And here she is, six years later, on the town - called 'Long Lizzy,' now, heading for the poorhouse and worse. I look down at her feet, her old boots unlaced and unstitched and her ankles filthy under the too-short hem of a patched dress.

I can't leave my own daughter weeping on a street corner. She's chilled through and I wrap her in my shawl and half drag her through the lanes until, as I said, we make our court and my ground-floor room.

I don't have a chair, so we climb onto the bed where we sit, making the best of a smoky fire and a jug of beer, while the wind whistles in the chimney, the snow settles on the windowpane, and George scratches at his itching head.

'Sit here, boy,' I say, and work through his hair for the leece[38]. He's patient enough with my rummaging, and I can see he's taking everything in.

'What's happened to us, Ma?' sniffles Elizabeth.

'You got to fight, girl,' I say. 'There ain't no use bawling. You've had it no worse than a 'undred others. We got to get you washed and repair this fine dress.'

'"ull just get torn again.'

'Then grow your fingernails and hold a knife in your sleeve. For God's sake, child.'

She don't look convinced, but George, he look at me with eyes wide.

'What you thinking, boy?' I say, but he says nothing.

I'm thinking, *Whatever happened to Charles Mallows, the fool? What has he done to us?* I know we'll never see him again: no one returns from Australia, and his little baby is dead, so you could say as there's no evidence he ever existed, but we ain't the same as we were before he showed up.

We're going to have to live with the ghost of Charles Mallows.

Charles Mallows sits on a rock at Dawes Point and looks towards the sea. It is the year 1838, and Charles is approaching forty years of age, though he looks much older. He rarely thinks of Ipswich at all since he is no more given to introspection than to future planning, but this moment, he thinks, may be some kind of turning point. He looks at the grey, choppy waters in front of him and stares without truly focussing on the rough headland across the bay and screeching gulls searching the swift-flowing tide. He has in his hand a piece of paper headed 'Certificate of Freedom.'[39]

'I am,' he says to no-one but himself, 'free to go'.

It is the first time in his life that anyone has told him he is free. Most of the time people have told him to stay and to obey and accompanied their commands with oaths and beatings, shackles, and prison doors locked against him. For a moment he visualises damp stone and unforgiving iron. He shudders and looks at the uncomfortable space around him.

Cool waters lap at his feet. It has been raining but the clouds are whipping across the winter sky. He pulls his shirt around him.

He is a small man, slightly built, five feet, one and a half inches, with brown hair, grey eyes, and a sallow complexion, mottled from the sun and wind. He has a broken nose which is twisted and scarred. Scars fracture his left eyebrow and neck, as though he had once been slashed with a knife or whip, and the middle fingers of his right hand bear the kind of marks which come from fending off a blade.

He has the twitch - the result of a lifetime of flinching. He has, however, given as much punishment as he has taken; his right hand is deeply scarred across the knuckles where it has connected, much to his satisfaction, and more than once, with some other man.

He clambers to his feet and, finding it easier to think when he is doing something physical, climbs higher up the smooth, ancient rocks. His mind flickers through the memories of his tribulations. They are scattered like the light through a blown windowpane. Perhaps a life of beatings has left lesions in his mind as much as his skin.

He still remembers his boy, Fred. Lizzy was young when he married her, and Fred had been born the following year. There was excitement, even hope and joy. Elizabeth was a fine lass, and for a moment he wonders what she is doing now. She is sure to have married again, and Fred should be seven or eight years old.

In his mind's eye he can see the boy playing in the streets round Fore Hamlet. Is he a good boy? Has Elizabeth brought him up good? 'I had hopes for him,' he says out loud. Then he catches himself. *I had hope for me too*, he thinks.

But hope is a starvation diet. There was just never enough. He had tried to work, and he liked horses, so he had become a groom. He pictures the fine Suffolk heavy horses that had stood like red statues over him yet had yielded to his firm hands. For a moment he can see flashes and manes, feathered hooves, and sorrel coats.[40]

'It ain't fair,' says Charles, to the squabbling gulls and the rain-filled sky. In his mind's eye he sees the ghostly figure of the shoemaker, Rainbow. 'Eight shillings, he said those boots were worth, which was a lie.' His voice is lost in the hungry wind.

Since the moment of his capture he has had no freedom, as though made to walk at the tail of one of his own horses. Hands cuffed. Banged into the police cell, then before the magistrate and on to the Borough Gaol. Fettered and taken to the sessions. Sent down. More irons and carted to Portsmouth. Flogged below decks on the hulk, *Leviathan*. The warder, a nasty piece of work, writes in his ledger, 'Charles Mallow: Bad'.[41] But by then Charles has stopped struggling, stopped pretending that there was freedom to be had anywhere but in his own, belaboured head.

For six months Charles rots with the grand old ship to which he is chained. Through October, November, and December of 1830 he lives with rats and lice - human and the other kind, and the rain drips through the decks from above and seeps up the rotting timbers from below. The warders laugh at him and his fellows: 'Housed at His Majesty's expense in one of His Majesty's finest ships. Why, didn't you know she fought at Trafalgar? Home to great captains and Admirals she was. And you complain!'[42]

On 12th of December, 1830, back in Ipswich, Frederick, Charles's son, is buried. He is one year old. Charles is not told. When sentence was passed in Ipswich he had been transported out of place and time, forgotten, except by clerks who recorded the passing of his carcass as they would also record the passage of a barrel of pork or a cask of rum.

In January and February 1831, it snows in Portsmouth. Water and blood turn to ice. Charles shrinks further inside himself. Towards the end of March the prisoners, in manacles, trudge or are dragged on board the *Georgiana* to transport them to Australia.

The ship's surgeon, John Tarn, keeps a journal and records that the prisoners are generally young men and lads and appear in a tolerable state of health although not in full vigour in consequence of confinement, scanty diet, and other causes.

Charles finds himself bunking with seven other men. They sleep, cook, and eat together, and keep their deck space clean under fear of punishment.

In the Channel they shiver and cough.

In the tropics, Tarn writes, 'Many of the prisoners complain of lassitude, want of appetite, and general debility.'

In the Southern Ocean, they are beset by storms. The ship leaks and the prison deck is foetid and perpetually wet. They are heading into winter again. At least they are made to exercise on deck every day if it is not blowing a gale, and the rolling seas sluice their accommodation. Whenever possible, stoves are lit, and the men can dry clothes and blankets.

Of the one hundred and eighty-two convicts on board, only two die during the seventeen weeks at sea. This is reckoned a great success by the authorities, but Charles does not know the dead men or very much care about them.[43]

Charles Mallows arrives at Sydney Cove on 27th of July 1831. He is gaoled at Parramatta. He endures. It's all there on paper, in his hand. Date of trial: 20th of September, 1830. Transportation on *Georgiana*: 1831. Freedom: 9th of June, 1838. And Dawes Point, where he stands now, is not on the River Orwell, but in Sydney Harbour.[44] The birds do not sound like Suffolk birds. The sun, when it shines, is harder than the Suffolk sun. Even after seven years, the trees and the flowers trouble him with their unfamiliarity. He sits and contemplates the meaning of freedom in this unfathomable place. He can find no meaning.

Now that he is free, he is free to starve. He stumbles as he climbs higher up the rocks then turns away from the sea and towards the inner harbour. Someone there will give him work. He has that week's *Sydney Herald* and on the second page an advert: 'GROOM WANTED. A man of good character, who is competent to take charge of a pair of horses and to make himself generally useful in a store - liberal wages will be given. Apply to the undersigned, Isaac Simmons.'[45]

And for a man of poor character, Charles wonders, perhaps the wages will be a little less liberal. He embraces his freedom, such as he can, and walks into a future in which he leaves not a trace in the archive.

# 5: Peter Considers Charles Mallows

## April 2021

Keziah is in my head on these chilly afternoons, chattering away through the medium of Lakshmi. I run the ball of my thumb over one of her six images on the silver bowl.

'Is this all true?' I ask Lakshmi.

'That is not the necessary question,' she replies. 'The structure of the story is true enough. You have the evidence, which you persist in showing in your notes. Somehow this seems to satisfy you. I don't know why.'

'But I want to tell a true story,' I object. 'This is my bequest to the future.'

'Impossible. The past is never true. All those irrelevant notes about old battleships and lost places - who are they meant to convince? What you need to write is something that is real, something living. Your ancestors deserve that much.'

'Show them to me,' I command (I am talking to an engraving

on a piece of silver. Am I now as dawzled as Elizabeth?).

'Once you unravel these stories you will not be able to forget them. Once you are alive to them you will be changed, even by those who are not related to you but who troubled the lives of those that are.'

'Like Charles Mallows?'

'Charles Mallows. He disappears from your precious archives but he won't be forgotten by Elizabeth or Keziah. You can't escape him either, because I have shown you more of him than they were ever to know. And whether you know them or not, these phantoms are inescapable.'

In my garden, the frost has given way to snowdrops and then daffodils. There are buds on the trees and moorhens have returned to the pond to nest. It is only humans who are locked down. I don't often crave company, but at this moment I wonder whether I am missing out, with only spectral beings from the past to converse with.

I am relieved that Keziah Root, otherwise Sparham, has found her voice. She had existed in the records, but, previously, others such as Cobbold and the overseers of Walpole and Ipswich have spoken for her. And Charles Mallows may be no relation, but even his absence creates ripples in the family unconscious like those brief circles on the pond where an unseen fish has come and gone.

There are voices in my head and an unnerving feeling that perhaps I am not what I thought I was and that my exploration will reveal places I never wished to visit. These are not the imagined palaces of my childhood. These are not the sort of things I thought the silver bowl might have contained. I examine it closely once more. Lakshmi is gesturing in each panel. In one she prays and in another seems to wave me forward, in one she is in repose, her hands drooping across her knees, while in a fourth she dances. The gestures seem to say, 'Everything changes. Anything is possible. More stories will be disclosed to you if you will only listen.'

I walk out into the sunshine and sit by the pond in a silent search for inspiration. A kingfisher dashes before my sight, sees me, and darts fearfully away. I wish it had stayed but am blessed by the brevity of its appearance. I breathe more deeply, watch the breeze trouble the ferns, and try to sum up, for, surely, I am doing something different from my original intention. I have become a novelist. How has it come to this? Father would, I think, have ripped the pages out, yet there is no other way to give this heritage life.

Keziah, my three-times great-grandmother, and George, her son, were unknown to me. Now their story has gradually unfolded. There are hard facts: birth, marriage, and death records, and the newspaper reports, in so far as they can be believed. There are suppositions - such-and-such an event must have given rise to some reaction or another. Then there is imagination, of feeling and conversation and changing relationships. I base my narration on a sort of empathetic understanding, which equates to experience (limited) multiplied by emotion, and always subtracting the gaps in my knowledge. I say this as a form of justification: do not assume that this account is true except in so far as it is real to me. Anyone else in the family who examines the same facts will come up with a different story. They will ascribe a different set of meanings to whatever they see before them. I shall leave all the evidence in the endnotes. Perhaps I should leave some wide margins for the next imaginer to make their own contribution. The kingfisher, calling from somewhere down the river, like the squeak of a rusty bicycle, says, 'Don't lose your nerve now. Your father is no longer looking over your shoulder. Trust the story to flow, bright and unhindered. It has to be told. It has to be told.' I wonder if my father is listening. Out of the dappled sunlit calm of the garden the bird flies to an overhanging branch of the oak tree. It plunges into the pond, returning to its perch with a small, silver fish, then swallows and shakes itself. Flying droplets of water catch the declining sun and the bird resumes its silent pose, punctuated by gulps of the fish in its gullet. The kingfisher is always purposeful. There is no sign of doubt that comes between desire and action. It knows what it wants and is always scheming to get it.

*Get on with the story*, I say to myself. *No delay.*

I retreat to the computer. The Charles Mallows story is finished, even though I can't forget him. I still don't understand the relationship to Eliza Ellis, and why she gave my mother an Indian silver bowl. Perhaps what I must do first is go further back: who was Keziah and where did she come from? Whoever her parents were, they will be part of the weave and weft of my story. The more I reach towards the beginning, the more I enrich the pattern of the present. Time is pliable and multi-layered, and I need to follow the threads.

# 6: Keziah, the Origin Story

## 1760-1830

As she huddles with George, her youngest, and Elizabeth her first born, in a cold, miasmic room, Keziah begins to spill out what she knows of the family story, trying to answer Elizabeth's lament.

'What's happening to us, Ma?'

'It's a tangle,' replies Keziah. 'That's nothing new. Us Roots, we get caught up in things we never bargained on. Your grandfather was a good man but that didn't save him. Too trusting. Lucky to survive.'

Suddenly Keziah wonders whether the answers are to be found in the family's history and thinks that perhaps there is no harm in telling her children all she knows.

What happened to Grandpa, then, Ma?' Elizabeth says, wanting to be distracted from her own pain, her lost child, and lost husband. Little George raises his head and looks at me. I might as well tell. There is nothing else for us to do as we lay on the bed in the cold, darkening room.

'I'll tell you a story,' I say. 'You know Walpole, where you was born, Georgie?'

'No,' says the boy, but there is a flicker of interest. He likes stories.

'You was born there and we lived there a time when you were all young. It's more than two days walking from here, beyond Framlingham where I was born.[46] My dad, Samuel, was apprenticed to a shoemaker in Framlingham - Old Hayward. I think Pa reckoned he was on the up then. He had a craft and Hayward liked him; liked him enough to let him marry his daughter, Ann - my mother. I think everything was good enough for a year or two, but there wasn't enough work for two men in a small place like Framlingham. Samuel had to take to the road when his apprenticeship ended, working day by day wherever he could. I don't know exactly how it happened, but he fell in with Henry Cone, a young butcher from Halesworth.

'This is all fifty years ago, so I can't swear to it, but this Cone had an older brother, John, I think. They'd worked together in the butchery trade, but John had been hanged for stealing a horse. That were up at Rushmere, on the heath, I do believe, where they always hanged condemned men.' [47]

George looks up.

'Who was hanged, Ma? Was it my granddad?'

'No! Listen. This man, John Cone. His brother, Henry, met granddad, and caused a right fuss for us, too. Our lives would all have been different if Pa had never met Henry Cone.'

Keziah pauses for a moment. She'd never really thought about it like that before. Her father had had a good trade. He'd married a girl whose father was prosperous. Life must have looked set fair when they married, but then father met Henry Cone.

'So, what happened, Ma?' says George.

'Henry Cone was sure that evil was in his family blood. He boasted about his brother to anyone as would listen. One of his bar-room friends was your grandpa. The ale flowed, I shouldn't wonder.

'Tell the story properly, Ma,' says George, impatiently. He snuggles into the crook of my arm, and Elizabeth, too, gets closer.

'So, this is how it was,' I say. 'Your grandfather and this Henry Cone were sitting in an inn - I don't know which one, before you ask - and it's at the end of the day and they are sitting in a corner at the back of the snug.'

Henry Cone said, 'You should have seen my brother at the end. He was a good man. All he wanted was to feed his family. He buys an animal and there's little profit in it. The farmer does right enough, but the butcher not so well ... And when the master can't make ends meet ...'

'Ends meat, you might say' said Samuel Root, laughing more than is necessary at his cleverness.

'It's the journeyman what gets laid off, as you well know. Take the high road, son.'[48] They drank, contemplating the precarious nature of their lives.

'I hear you married Ann Hayward, young Root,' said Cone.

'I was her father's apprentice. It suited us all well enough.'

'Her father's a wealthy man,' said Cone, with the thoughtful air of a man who has a vision of gold sovereigns and fine clothes as well as hearty meals.

Samuel sensed that he may suddenly be stepping into dangerous territory. Best to play down expectations.

'Not at all. All's for the shop', said Samuel. 'Leather, and such like.' There is another long pause while Cone sees that he's been headed off and considers his next tack. They drink deep and watch the motes from the inn's guttering fire dance in a shaft of evening sunlight. The smoke-blackened beams suggest a degree of solid permanence which cradles them.

'You've got to have property,' mused Henry Cone.

'Just so. There's nothing in it for us poor men,' said Root.

'This journeying from place to place …' Cone let the words hang and wondered if Samuel would choose a new direction for the conversation.

'You do get to see where the folks as have the money live,' said Samuel, who was confident that he had diverted Cone from looking at his own family.

'You, Samuel, understand me exactly,' said Cone, sitting back and drinking deep once more. 'My poor brother did his best to live within the law, but when a fine mare ambled in his way what was he to do but halter it. He was unlucky, is all.'

The men sat in further silent contemplation of the injustice that led to one poor butcher's execution. They called for more of Cobbold's ale. Cone moved closer to Samuel and whispered.

'It don't have to be like that. Look.' He produced from his greatcoat a pair of crumpled newspaper cuttings. The first was dated Halesworth, 14th of February, 1785.

Samuel read it aloud, slowly and quietly, his finger underlining every word.

*Whereas on Saturday night or early on Sunday morning last, the dwelling-house of William Revans, baker of this town[49], was burglariously broken open and entered by some person or persons unknown, who broke open a bureau in the said dwelling-house, and stole therefrom a canvas purse containing Twenty-eight Guineas and an Half; also broke open and carried away the drawer or Till of the shop containing a large quantity of Halfpence and some*

*Silver. Notice therefore is hereby given, That if any person will give*
*information to the said William Revans of the person or persons*
*who committed the said robbery, so as he or they may be brought to*
*justice, the persons giving such information shall be entitled to and*
*receive a reward of Twenty Pounds, to be paid by the inhabitants of*
*the said parish of Halesworth, on application to the parish officers,*
*upon the conviction of the offender or offenders.'* [50]

'Was that you?' asked Samuel.

Cone stared back at him, impassive, and said nothing.

'So it was, and you didn't get caught,' he muttered. 'I won't tell.'

'What's to tell, son? Two years ago, that was, and no evidence.
I didn't do it. I wasn't there. No one saw nothing,' and he smirked.

Before Samuel could think of any innocent comment to make
Cone unfolded the other fragment of the *Ipswich Journal*. The
corner where they were sitting was in deep shadow now and the
paper was smudged and creased. As Samuel held it up to catch the
light from the candle in its sconce Cone said, archly, 'Someone's
getting notorious.' Samuel read:

*Whitehall September 23, 1785*

*Whereas, it has been humbly represented to the King, that the*
*several Burglaries and Robberies herein after mentioned, have been*
*committed within these few months past, within the town and neigh-*
*bourhood of Halesworth, in the county of Suffolk, viz.*

*A Burglary and Robbery in the dwelling house of William Revans.*
*A Burglary and Robbery in the dwelling house of Henry Nursey.*

*A Burglary and Robbery in the dwelling house of John Wilkinson.*
*A Burglary and Robbery in the dwelling house of Robert Reeve.*
*A Burglary and Robbery in the dwelling house of John Cooderham.*
*A Burglary and Robbery in the dwelling house of Mary Burgess.*

*His Majesty, for better discovering and bringing to justice the persons concerned in the burglaries and robberies above mentioned is hereby pleased to promise his most gracious pardon to any one of them, who will surrender himself to one of his Majesties justices of the peace for the said county of Suffolk, and discover his accomplices therein, so that one or more of them may be apprehended and convicted thereof.'* [51]

More money! In addition to the twenty pound reward offered by the parish, forty pounds was allowed by act of parliament, and twenty pounds and the promise of a pardon to any accomplice who turned the burglar in. Yet no-one had put a finger on the butcher Henry Cone. So much money!

I pause in the telling. It is quiet in the room as Elizabeth, George, and I take in the story: the King, all those crimes, and all that money.

George pipes up. 'That is a lot of money, Ma, isn't it?

'More than you can imagine, boy,' I say, ''cos it is, like the promises in old fairy stories.

Elizabeth says, 'None of it come our way, did it?' and she snorts.

'Back fifty years, in the snug of the inn,' I say, 'my dad must have wondered how he could turn this tale to his advantage.

What would happen if he went to his father-in-law and told him about Henry Cone? But, before he could think through what might happen, another thought come to his mind: *Why is the man showing me this?*

Samuel pondered. He reckoned he and his wife could live for years on those rewards and with a bit of jobbing work he'd be a made man. So why had no-one claimed the reward?

He thought quickly. Henry Cone's accomplice must have been his brother, who was executed for another crime, so Henry was now working alone. But these crimes were more than eighteen months old. Was Henry unable to work on his own? Was he looking for a new accomplice? He pushed the papers back to Henry.

'That man's in great risk,' he said at last.

'Maybe,' said Cone, tucking the cuttings back inside his coat. Nothing more was said. They drank companionably until it was time to part. Both men wondered whether anything had really happened between them, and, if it had, what the consequences would be.

I pause again and look at the children - Elizabeth and little George.

'So, what do you think happened next?' I ask.

'I do think Grandpa went to the king and claimed the reward, but then he probably lost it all again, which is why we ain't living in a palace,' says George.

Elizabeth laughs. 'He wouldn't do that. He'd know no-one would believe him. Who'd believe a Root? Anyway, he'd not want to see another man swing. When you live on the road you got a know who your friends is,' she says wistfully, and I see her touch the bruise above her eye.

'You're right,' I say to Elizabeth. 'He was a gentle man, your grandpa.' In my mind I can see his quiet, sad face, long and thin, like all the men in our family. I look at George and for a moment I can see a likeness, and I hug the boy closer to me.

'Was that all, then?' says Elizabeth. 'I never heard of this Henry Cone. What's he got to do with us?'

'If only my pa had never met him,' I say. 'People like Cone, they're like lice, the way they live off you,' and I crush another nab-nanny from George's head between finger and thumb.

'My ma told me all about what happened, because this was just the start - the beginning of why we're living as we do now.'

On St Valentine's Day, 1787, the sky fell on Samuel Root's head, or so my ma put it. He was in Ipswich, having got work in the town, when the constables from Halesworth came calling. He was sharing a room in *The King's Head*, and he was in the public bar when his supper was interrupted.

'You Samuel Root?'

'Why …?'

'We have the warrant for your arrest.'

'Who's warrant?'

'Mr John Wade, Mr William Revans, and Mr Charles Hayward,' said the constable.

'Charles Hayward - the wife's father?' spluttered Samuel, astonished by this turn of events.

'So, you do know them. It's the right man, lads,' said the constable with a triumphant air. 'Bind him!' The constables lifted him roughly from his chair and bound his stiff arms behind his back.

'We won't get him back to Halesworth tonight,' said their spokesman. 'Landlord, have you got a room where we can keep him under lock and key till the morning?'

'I ain't done a thing,' said Samuel.

'You know Henry Cone,' said the constable.

'I've … met him.' Samuel felt his guts turn inside out.

'He says you were his accomplice.'

'I never!'

'We have him in Bury Gaol. He has money and goods belonging to these three gentlemen including your father-in-law and he says you helped him get them.'

'I never. I'm just a shoemaker …'

'So, you best look to your soul…' said the constable, playing to the spectators in the bar.

Samuel, shouting and struggling, was bundled down to the inn's cellar and the door locked and barred. It was dark, damp, and cold, on that February night. Samuel had a sudden, horrible vision of his future. He had done nothing wrong, but he knew Cone. If he had decided to play him false, then Samuel Root was sure he was doomed. If found guilty of the offences he had seen listed in the newspaper, he would be hanged.

Samuel was frantic. From the rooms above, he could be heard trying to break out of the cellar. Then it went quiet, but the constables weren't to be deceived. They posted a look out, and, soon enough, found Samuel trying to squeeze through the cellar grating into the street. They pushed him back and tied him tightly.

When he was brought before the magistrate on the following day he was remanded to Ipswich Gaol. He was charged with breaking into the house of William Revans 'in the night of 12th of February 1785, and stealing thereout twenty-eight guineas, half a guinea, some silver, and halfpence.'[52] But the big surprise for my father was that the warrant showed that he had been charged on the oath not only of Revans but of Henry Cone, now also a prisoner in Ipswich Gaol.

Samuel had a month in gaol to contemplate what had happened to him:

> *If I had near twenty-nine guineas to my name, then you show me where it is now. I've not seen that much in one place in all my life ...*
> *You ask my wife, Ann. She's Hayward's daughter. We'd never steal from him ...*
> *I was his apprentice - he'll speak for me ...*
> *Henry Cone is lying. He's trying to save his own neck. He's trying to claim the reward for his own crime!*
> *How much longer in this place? Freezing, it is. I'm dying in here. They'll be carrying me out.*
> *Twenty-nine guineas!*

And so it went on, from day to day, with Root terrified of what was to come. There seemed to be no way out. No words of comfort reached him.

'Tell us where the money is,' ranted the constable, a grizzled fellow by the name of Goodale, who only enjoyed being parish constable in Halesworth in as much as it allowed him to extort bribes from suspects and inducements from property holders.[53]

'I've seen no money.'

'But you talked to Cone. You told him about your father-in-law. Cone had Hayward's candlesticks and three pair of boots from his workshop. Now how did he know just where to find them?'

'I don't know,' says Samuel Root, his voice sunk to a whisper, caused by prison sweats and anguish. 'I don't know. I told him nothing. I was Hayward's apprentice. I married his daughter. I wouldn't hurt them.'

'You're a penniless cobbler with a wife and child. You'd do anything to make money,' said the constable. 'I've seen it before. Men would cut their granny's throats if they thought it would keep a roof over them and they could get away with it.'

'But I didn't ...'

'Speak the truth, lad.'

'Let me talk to my wife. Let me see my father-in-law. They'll tell you I'm honest.'

There was a long pause, as if Goodale was sympathetic and trying to find a way out for Samuel. When he spoke again, he was suddenly kindlier.

'I hear your wife's a lovely girl,' said Goodale. 'A merry dancer, I'm told. This will be doing her fair looks no good at all. Worrit sick, she'll be.'

Silence.

'If you hang, there'll be no shortage of takers, even with her child.'

'What can I do?' groaned Samuel. 'It's my word against Cone.'

'That's right, lad,' said Goodale. 'What can you do? Cone's a rare villain. He'll hang for sure. But you … it would be a sad end.'

'So, what must I do?'

Goodale allowed the silence to deepen once more, as though trying to conjure a solution.

'The only way I can see,' he said at last, 'is for you to tell the judge everything you know about Henry Cone. Where you met him, what he asked you, what you told him. You got to give evidence for the king. And you got to get that sweet wife of yours to give evidence about where you were when the burglaries were done.'

'But I can't see Ann when I'm locked up in Ipswich.'

'That's a problem, surely,' said Goodale.

'Would you go and see her for me,' pleaded Samuel.

'To Walpole? That's fair out of my way, from Halesworth,' says Goodale.

'It's less than three miles!'

Slowly the penny dropped for Samuel. Wearily, without looking Goodale in the eyes, he said,

'Look, I don't have much, but we can pay you for your time. I'll write to Ann and to her father. They'll come to court and swear for me. You tell them what they need to say. And I'll tell the judge everything I know about Cone.'

'Now that seems like a worthy plan, young man.' Suddenly business-like, Goodale was out of the cell to fetch paper, pen and ink and Samuel Root felt as though a flickering flame of hope might be dancing before him as he dictated his letter.

In Walpole, Ann Root, nursing their baby son, was in turmoil. Had her husband really burgled her own father and been accomplice in so many serious crimes? When Goodale turned up with a frantic letter from her husband she was both relieved and troubled.

'Yes,' she said to the constable, she knew exactly where her husband was on the nights that the burglaries were committed. 'Yes,' she would swear in court. 'Yes,' she would talk to her father and persuade him that Samuel should be treated as witness not defendant. And 'Yes,' there was a half sovereign which she had kept by and sewn into her skirt which, if he would spare her a moment, she would release for him, and she was confident that her father would be as generous again, were he to visit the old man. No-one, she assured Goodale, wished harm on Samuel, who was honest as the day was long (*Just so long as someone was watching*, she thought to herself).

At the beginning of April 1787, Mr Justice Ashhurst[54] sat in the assize court in Bury St Edmunds when Samuel Root was brought up from the cells.

In Keziah's Ipswich room, on a cold February evening in 1837, the children, George and Elizabeth, hang on their mother's words, living every turn of their grandfather's story. Now Elizabeth interrupts, angrily.

'Dear God. You don't never want to end up in the assizes, George. I saw what happened to my Charles. They call you up, read your name, someone says, "This is what he done, your honour." You ain't allowed to explain yourself, and the judge says to the jury "Make your decision," and they all huddle together and say, "Guilty, Your Honour," he reads the sentence, and they take you down, and it's all over in the time it takes to drink a pint of ale.

'She's right, George,' says Keziah. 'Pray you don't never find yourself in the assize.

'I won't, Ma,' says George, though he doesn't understand what it all means except that it must be terrible if his mother and his sister are so frightened by it.

'Anywise,' says Keziah, 'this Ashhurst sat down at eleven in the morning and before he took his luncheon he'd had six men in front of him, and each one of them he sentenced to be turned off - hanged, George - 'cos they was burglars and thieves, and one man who was sentenced for stealing a bell from Dunwich Church.[55]

And after lunch the jury found another five men guilty.'

'Did they all have to hang, Ma?' says George, looking frightened, as though his own life depended on it.

'They did, George.'

'But what about that Henry Cone?' asks Elizabeth.

'He was one of them, charged with burglary of Mr Revan's house.'

'And what about Grandpa? Wasn't he one of them?'

'He didn't do anything wrong,' mutters George, and looks about to cry.

'Now here is the strange thing, children,' Keziah says. 'That Ashhurst must have heard twenty cases between his breakfast and his dinner, and the court was full of people crying or cheering according as how things went; chiefly death or acquittal, and it were bedlam. And just as it looked like things were coming to an end - so my father said - this old judge with his grey face and lantern jaw[56] turns his deathly gaze upon all the people and lawyers and prisoners there and says, "The following are reprieved ..." and he reads out eight names, and the last is Henry Cone, "...who will be transported to Sydney Cove for the term of his natural life."

'And then he says - and my father was fair fainting by this time -

"Have the record show that I find no bill against Joseph Hempstead and ... Samuel Root."' [57]

'But what does that mean?' says George.

'It means that he were free, innocent,' says Elizabeth.

'It means that no-one came forward to give evidence against him,' says Keziah.

'Well, I hope Henry Cone suffered for what he done,' says Elizabeth.[58]

'But Grandpa was safe,' says George, and gets off the bed and searches beneath for the piss pot.

'My pa was never the same after he came out of prison,' Keziah says. 'He got this sort of twitch, as though he expected someone to come up and hit him. Folk didn't like looking at that. And he couldn't keep a job for long. Once you been in gaol, even if you was not guilty, no one wants you around,' Keziah says, hugging George and grasping Elizabeth's hand. 'See, this is why we're poor. Pa and Ma travelling all over to get work and never being able to stay long. Couldn't put down roots, you might say.' She didn't laugh, while Elizabeth looked puzzled until she realised the unexpected joke.

'We're Roots without roots,' says Elizabeth, laughing mirthlessly too, and George chuckles, though he can't make out why this is funny. *People don't have roots*, he thinks. *That's just silly.*

'So, what happened to Grandpa?' asks Elizabeth, who knew that, for a short time, she had lived with him, but that he had died when she was still a small girl. She has no clear picture of him in her mind. (For a moment, she is terrified: how can someone so important suddenly become invisible to you, an absence in your memory, a ghostly, foggy hole in your brain?).

'What happened, Ma?' says Elizabeth, urgently.

'We were poor. He couldn't always get work as a shoemaker. He made beautiful things from leather, but he couldn't make a living. There was me and your Uncle Samuel, my older brother, and then they had another baby, Titus, but he died. Soon as I could I was away and living in, with one job or another, so I didn't see much of Ma or Pa for a bit. Next I knew, he was in prison again.'

'What had he done?' says George, frightened, curious, and excited, all at the same time, about this man he had never known but must, somehow, be important, because Elizabeth and his mother seemed so serious.

'Perhaps he hadn't done anything, again,' says Elizabeth.

'They said he'd burgled his master's shop. He and ma were in Mutford then. It's not much of a place. A few shops and work-shops at a crossroads on the way to Lowestoft. Got a church tower that looks like a factory chimney, as I recall. He was working for a miserable old man called Margerom, and I suppose he went back one night and broke in and stole some shoes. This time I think there was no doubt, though of course Pa said it was money he was owed for work he'd done and never been paid for. But that didn't wash, and though he must have been an old man by then - more than fifty, I should think, they come down on him and sentenced him to seven year transported. That were a crying shame. He were back in the Bury Sessions and got seven years!' [59]

*Just like my Charles,* thinks Elizabeth. *And all about boots and shoes! Nothing changes.*

'I went to the court with my ma,' continues Keziah, 'and we sat there and wept and waved to him, thinking it would be the last time we saw him, because how was a man of his age going to survive months at sea and the horrors of Australia with hard labour and everything?

'Lord, we were in a state. He may not have had regular work, but now the only money ma had was what she could earn or me and my brother could spare, and how could we see her go into the workhouse?'

'But Grandpa didn't go to Australia, did he, Ma?' asks George, who was thinking of the ships which mysteriously appeared and vanished again from Ipswich Harbour, and the strange men with even stranger language who shouted and heaved on ropes, and who laughed and cursed at a young boy who got in their way. It might be rather exciting to go on a boat to the other side of the world. But George dare not say anything, since his mother and sister look so sad.

'No, George, he didn't go, thank the Lord. They sent him to the hulks at Portsmouth. He did all his years, less a month off for good behaviour, staring at the filthy water of Portsmouth harbour. He said he never got dry in seven years. They found he could work with leather, so they had him mending and making. When he came home, he was like the husk of a man, with a thin, hard skin and nothing much left inside. Almost the last I remember of him was when he came to our wedding, mine and Sparham, and he died soon after.[60]

Elizabeth is aroused and angry once more:

'So, Grandpa escapes the transport and comes home to his wife and children, while my Charles gets sent to Australia never to return and I lose him and our baby. It ain't fair, Ma!' she cries.

'Course it ain't,' says Keziah. 'You was never promised a fair life. Blood and tears is what we're born into. Now, get off your arse, fill the kettle, and poke some life back into that fire.'

# 7: Peter Finds a Witness

## May 2021

There are new lambs in the meadow across the river. I can always find a reason to leave the screens and keyboard, and the darkness of Ipswich past, to walk the solitary Suffolk lanes and savour the light of a new season.

Something fresh has happened in my history. Keziah and her children have found their voices and will not be denied. That which connects me to these previously unknown folk - my four-times great-grandfather, Samuel Root, his daughter, and grandson, something in the blood, the soul, has burst out in its own spring. Their voices come to me, distorted by time and overlaid by the words of more recent generations and fragments of learning, but are not to be ignored because they are what has made me.[81]

What's more, the penny is beginning to drop about the number of events already in this tale that might have stopped the family's history dead: poverty and starvation, a freezing church-yard, the gallows. The reason I'm here at all is that these things didn't happen.

If genealogy is the search for a sure foundation, then these Roots demonstrate survivability, which is a greater inheritance than wealth or status. They have nothing to insure them against the winter, the day without food, the landlord's demands, or the illusory promise of riches. For Keziah, sitting in the snow or huddling in bed telling tales to her children, the fragments of family history were no comfort. I wanted a story of hope and happiness; something that would have pleased my parents, not repetitive cycles of crime, punishment, and poverty. Yet I know there is an arc leading from Keziah to me, and somewhere things began to change for the better. How was she not dragged down? How did she and George survive?

Twelve years after Keziah's encounter with Cobbold in 1836, George and his older brothers, James and Alfred, had not only survived but were well known in the Ipswich slums. Their names appear in court records and the newspapers, and other witnesses come forward to fill in the details. One, PC Samuel Bragg, was destined, so I imagine, to play a key role in the lives of the Root or Sparham family. He was an upholder of law and order, a no-nonsense type, with a strong moral code, and the more I get to know him in the archive the more I trust him. I should have liked him, I think, and my father would have pointed him out as someone to look up to - a man of character and purpose.

I can see him in his old age: now ex-Superintendent of Police Samuel Bragg, sitting in his inglenook in Bedford (his final posting and place of retirement) and drawing on a churchwarden pipe. He would seem to be posing for one of those oil paintings of the late nineteenth century which were bought for tin lid illustrations by the purveyors of tobacco or chocolate. Ask Bragg about the Roots, however, and he is not in the least comforting: he swears like the trooper he once was, spits into the fireplace and shivers as if a whole lifetime of uncomfortable memory were crawling just beneath his skin. He has plenty to say, so I shall let him speak for himself.

# 8: Samuel Bragg Recalls Keziah Root's Family in the 1840s

The moment I got to Ipswich as a young constable, 1848, my inspector warned me to look out for the Roots.

'Bragg,' he said, 'this town is a cess pit, and your duty is to keep more of these young scoundrels from falling deeper into it.' He recited their names: Pryke and Friston, Southgate, and Root, alias Sparham. 'Look out for them. Whatever they're doing, it will bear investigation, whatever they say, it will be a lie.'

I'm sorry if they're your family, but it's the truth. Filth is what we trudged through, then, in Ipswich, moral and actual. Anywhere down by the Rope Walk, Long Lane, and the Potteries was foetid and the rats, human and otherwise, ran in and out. They'd tell me I shouldn't blame them, that they knew no better, that they hadn't had a chance. It was nonsense. Let me tell you why.

I've got to go back a few years to when your story started, in 1836. I was a driver in the Royal Artillery that year. Not yet twenty, and I was in Canada with my horses, and we were ready for a battle. Those French settlers thought they wanted a revolution, but we soon convinced them otherwise.[62] November of the following year, just as we were preparing, I fell from a hayloft and dislocated my shoulder. 'Why didn't you seek medical assistance?' they said afterwards. Well, it was the eve of battle, and I didn't want to be left out or called a shirker. Tough enough with a name like Bragg. When you're not perfect, 'nothing to brag about now, son, eh?'

It wears a bit thin. Later, when the excitement was over (it didn't last long), I saw the medical officer. By that time, it was too late, he said. I couldn't lift my arm above my shoulder, though the rest of me was 'tolerably perfect,' according to his report. 'Bragg will be able to contribute something towards his livelihood,' said the medical board which discharged me. In other words, the damage was all my fault and they could pension me off without a proper pension.[63] By the age of twenty-two, I was back in Essex and looking for work - which I found soon enough, joining the local constabulary. All you need to do is stand up straight and show a bit of moral fibre.

I was in Essex, police constable for Tendring and all the villages around, with pretty Susanah who I married almost as soon as I got home. Before we knew it, we had three babies. At that time, Essex had one police force, and the chief constable was about moving you on from one place to another every few months, so it seemed. Five years, four houses, and Susanah with her arms full and no mother to turn to.

So, when Ipswich, just across the Stour, was looking to recruit a constable, I thought, well, I might as well make a move as I want, and it's a growing town, so a bit more excitement and less running round the countryside (how wrong I was), and it had its own force - so no being sent hither and yon by some bigwig who knows nothing about the place he's policing. What's more, the constables they had in Ipswich were a bad lot, forever being relieved of their duties for drunkenness and worse,[64] so it seemed to me that I could make a reputation and show what duty meant. But you've got to know the folks, you see. I got to know those

Roots, alias Sparhams, which is what made all the difference.

Let me be precise about this family. First there was the father, James Sparham, sawyer and adulterer. This is only rumour, mind. He'd left before I came to Ipswich. Some say he was dead, in Bury or somewhere. Dead and buried. Anyway, he needn't concern us.

Then there was Keziah Root, or Mrs Sparham, as she liked to be known. Unmarried mother and bigamist. One of the least deserving paupers in the stinking warren which was St Clement's. I don't need to explain to you what she was up to, though by the time I knew her she was old and surviving as a char or beggar or on the parish. It was the smell that I remember most of all. Whether it was the midden in the court or her linen or the drink, you came away from her with your skin crawling. I shouldn't judge, I suppose; she had rheumatics and her fingers were all curled under, so she might have found it difficult to keep herself clean.

There were three boys: Alfred, James, and George. They were all ferrety-looking youths. Alfred I hardly knew. He was a brickmaker when he wasn't in prison, and often went to Norfolk for work, leaving his family behind in Ipswich.[65] But James and George I knew all too well.

'See here,' said my old inspector, reaching in his desk for his ledger. 'It's this young James Root or Sparham you want to sort out. He keeps slipping though my fingers. Has been for years. They wanted him in the workhouse 'cos his mother was wanton, and she couldn't cope with the lads, but he'd rather stay outside, forego the shelter, and gain whatever he could however he could. Look here, *"2nd January, 1837: Ipswich Borough Sessions, charged with stealing lead affixed,"* - affixed St Clements' roof - and what happens? He got off! Mind you, we kept a firmer eye out after that and got the little rat eventually.' He turned up another page. 'There you are, see: *"October 1838. James Root. Guilty of larceny and sentenced to six months and a whipping."'* A few old scores being settled there, I shouldn't wonder. It didn't do any good, of course: he was back inside for stealing - eighteen months this time - in the spring of 1840.[66]

Anyway, that was all before my time. When I knew James Root, he was brickmaker, burglar, procurer, and poacher. He had fists like iron, and I couldn't lay a hand, legal or otherwise, on him. Best I could do was have him for damaging a farmer's gate![67]

I nearly got him for burglary.[68] A colleague of mine, PC Hentzer, was on the beat shortly before one o'clock on some February morning. As he stood in the shadows, down in Tavern Street, who should appear but James Root, George Gooch, and Elias Woods, hugger-mugger and up to no good, though silently. Hentzer watched and followed them as they turned past the Great White Horse Hotel, up Northgate Street, and into St. Margaret's Ditches. They may have been slippery, but they weren't quick enough to see they were watched.

They reached a greengrocer's shop and set to work on the shutters, quietly shaking a bolt free, and soon the window was wide open.

Gooch leans his back against the wall, giving Root a leg up. Woods walks a few yards away as if keeping watch, and PC Hentzer, expecting to be seen at any moment, breaks cover and asks the rogues whether this is their lodging house. James Root is, by this time, with one knee on the windowsill, while Woods is retreating up the lane. A conversation ensues, with Gooch saying that it's his house and Root claiming he's just offered to help his friend 'cos they'd been working and drinking late. You can believe the second but not the first. The conversation gets louder, and a woman looks out from next door. She says she's never seen Gooch before and he doesn't live in the house.

Hentzer notices that Woods has scarpered and, while he's listening to the woman and searching for Woods, Root and Gooch run off. Hentzer runs back to the station house and all the available men sets off in pursuit, including me.

I find James Root curled up by the cinder oven at Mr Cobbold's brewery. It hurt me to wake him!

We watch Gooch's house - the one he actually lived in - and, sure enough, the fool crept home at breakfast time and was soon in handcuffs.

Woods wandered the town until he was picked up, and all three were before the magistrate at eleven o'clock that morning. They were remanded to appear before the Recorder a couple of weeks later, and that's when it all fell apart. Nobody had seen Woods trying to enter the shop, so he wasn't charged, and he turned evidence for the defence. He claimed that they were look-ing for a house belonging to a woman they did business with (if you see what I mean) and had simply mistaken the address.

Then up pops the solicitor, Rouse, to say that there was no evidence of a burglary, and they didn't have tools for housebreaking, and they had answered all the police questions, so must be let go. And the jury believed him!

You could tell the Recorder was a bit stunned, but he knew the score well enough when he spoke to them. He said to Root and Gooch:

'The jury are quite correct in their conclusion. Take care of yourselves. It is not long since you were convicted; you are well known.'

And he smiled at me from the bench, as if to say, 'bring 'em back, but make sure the charge sticks next time, Bragg.'

Well, I did my best. I went to see old Keziah.

'You see them sons of yours stay out of trouble, missus,' I said. 'That James will be transported or worse if he don't watch out, and what's he doing to your George? Leading the young lad to bad ways, too.'

It were like water off a duck's back for folk like those, but you've got to try, haven't you?

I had James Sparham, alias Root, before the magistrate in the summer of 1848 for theft, and again he got off. By that time, they were calling him 'Witty' Sparham down in Fore Hamlet. 'Witty slipped through your fingers again, Bragg,' I had shouted at me in the street. I knew I had to take him down. Then just before Christmas the constable in Woodbridge got Root for fighting. He was sentenced to two months in prison for beating a fellow's lights out.

As I recall, Root had a tattoo on his arm which read, 'James Root May 7, 1840,'[69] and the man had made some comment about needing to have himself inked to remember his own name. Not a clever thing to say to Root, who then took it upon himself to tattoo his name on the poor chap's memory.

Root spent Christmas 1848 in the clink, and came out in February, but I suppose it's the events of March 1849 you really need to hear about. There was a full report in the papers at the time.[70] I was a nine days' wonder because of it, which is very appropriate because of the cautionary poem which I tell my children.[71]

If you're going after a specimen like 'Witty,' it's all in the planning, and planning means intelligence. If you're looking for stolen jewellery or silver you go to the pawnbrokers, and if you make friendly, and offer to look the other way at times, they'll give you a sniff in return, especially if they don't trust the rogue they're dealing with. It's the same with poaching. Your small-time poacher just does it for himself and his family, but once they get into a gang and start going after sheep and cattle, they've got to earn a few bob from the carcasses. That means behind the bar in a none-too-particular public house or with the connivance of a friendly butcher. So, it pays the scrupulous policeman to let land-lords and butchers know he has an eye out, and that I did.

There was a butcher called Pryke, and you already know that the inspector had warned me about him, and he was in cahoots with Root, alias Sparham, but if he thought it might be in his interests he would give me a tip. I met him in the market.

'What's your news, Pryke?' I said.

'There's a full moon on Friday.'

'And where might it be shining brightest, lad?'

'Best on the river,' he said. 'Freston or Woolverstone, I shouldn't wonder.'

And that was all I needed to know.

There's lush pasture all along the south bank of the Orwell, and rich farms at Wherstead, Freston, and Woolverstone. It's just a short sail across the river from Ipswich, or you can go round by the Stoke Bridge and along the Wherstead Road.

Friday, 9th of March, was indeed the night of the full moon, and my guess was that they'd be going on the water. It's where your local knowledge comes in. You see, when Henry Pryke was at market in Ipswich, he lived with his brother in some nauseous tenement in Long Lane, and in the same house was James Wardley. Wardley was a boatman, well into his sixties, but he had a neat little yawl - sort of a large rowing boat with a sail, and if there was a crime on the river or around the docks you were as likely as not to see Wardley's yawl beating a brisk furrow away from the scene.

Folk on the river called it the 'Pirate Boat.' They'd steer clear of it. But talk to Wardley and it was always a case of, 'I wasn't there, Mr Bragg. They must 'a taken the boat without permission, Mr Bragg. I know nothing, sir. I'm just an old man, and I can't no longer climb in an' out of the thing ...' There was always another old fellow in the bar of *The Myrtle*[72] to claim that Jimmy Wardley was with him at the time.

Friday comes and I said to the inspector, 'I'll make my patrol down Wherstead way tonight, if I may, Sir.'

'You got a sniff, Bragg?'

'It's a bright night for poaching, Sir, and I did hear that someone might be crossing the river.'

'Carry on, lad,' he said, and it made me feel proud to be trusted and I was determined to fulfil that trust.

I went south across the Stoke bridge and turned down the Wherstead road. It was a bright, still night with a chill in the air, I recall, but one of those nights where you feel alive and your whole body loves the ground beneath your feet as you march along.

Now, there's a point a couple of miles south where the

Wherstead road cuts close to the river and a nice, gentle beach. Redgate Hard, they call it, since it's where the lane to Redgate Farm comes down, and it's good for grounding a boat. Open country, so good viewing, but with deep ditches and convenient hedges to hide in.

Soon after eleven at night, I was ready to spring my trap. I'd just passed the junction heading towards where the Freston brook comes down to the river when, up ahead, I could see four men crossing the field. The ground rises and they was caught in the moonlight clear as day.

I couldn't rightly tell who they were, but one of 'em looked like James Root, alias Sparham, and anyway, what would four men be doing crossing a field out there at night.

*I've got 'em*, I thought, but four against one wasn't good odds. I had my service cutlass and revolver, you'll understand, but four of them could give me the run around. I needed to get them red-handed, and I could see they were travelling light, so I needed help. I ducked under cover of the hedge and slipped up the lane towards Redgate Farm. Five minutes and I was banging on the door of James Beart. It took forever to rouse him. When he did open, he was barring the door with his long-handled axe and his huge bulk, but he recognised me soon enough.

'Come, Jimmy, and bring your weapon,' says I. 'You have poachers, but we can trap them. There'll be a reward, I don't doubt.'

'Who?' he muttered, sounding like a man who had just woken from a particularly deep sleep.

'The crew of the Pirate Boat. Witty Sparham and his mates from Fore Hamlet.'

He grunted, grounded his axe, and pulled on his boots. 'Where are they?' he said, like a man who would rather beat their brains in than ask questions.

'Come,' I said. 'We'll find the boat first. They must return to it, and we can ambush them.'

He smiled and followed me out into the lane. I'm not a small man, but he towered over me, and that made me feel more secure.

We walked back down to the Hard and there, sure enough, pulled up on the strand, was the yawl. The sail and mast were down, and the oars stowed. They'd put a kedge out against the ebbing tide, but she was hardly afloat. There was no-one about. There was no name on the boat, nothing to distinguish it in a court of law from a dozen others up and down the Orwell, so I needed to secure my evidence.

'Right,' I said. 'First thing, we'll mark it, and you must witness so that we can be sure.'

I took my cutlass and climbed aboard. There was a seat athwart and I cut it twice, taking deep chips from the underside.

'Take this chip,' I said to Beart, 'and mark what I've done.'

'I'd know this boat anywhere,' he said.

'Yes, but we've got to prove it to a judge, Jimmy.'

'Nicely,' said Jimmy, smiling, and took his chip, seeing how it fitted into the seat.

'Now we'll let the tide help us. Get the anchor,' I said.

We put the anchor and cable aboard and pushed the boat through the thickening mud. We were in above our knees, but one last shove and she was adrift downstream.

'She'll fetch up at Woolverstone, I shouldn't wonder,' said Beart. We watched the boat bobbing away under the silver moon.

There was no-one else about to see it.

'They'll be back to use it for their escape,' I said. 'We'll have to guard the road and keep a keen watch on the Hard. More men are what we need.'

'I'll get John Southgate from Freston,' said Beart, and set off back up the lane. I went back to Wherstead to knock up John Gosling, another farm labourer. He was a well-set-up young man who'd been known to give a poacher a hard time. I thought I could rely on him[73]

When we gathered again at the Hard I sent Gosling and Southgate along to guard the road at Freston Brook. If the poachers were to come back to their boat they had to cross the stream at that point. Beart and I hid ourselves in the ditch behind a hedge at the bottom of Redgate Lane from where we could see the place where the boat had been.

It must have been well after midnight, and the moon was sinking. It was still and cold and the tide continued its fall. Acres of mud, shining dully like wrinkled tin, lay in front of us and the damp rose to rust our limbs. My damaged shoulder screamed at me. Nothing moved, though I knew Root and his gang were out there somewhere. An hour passed, and then another.

Beart said at last, 'They've gone back another way. Perhaps they saw us.' Then, 'I'll walk back up the lane towards the farm. If I don't see any sign of them, I'm going back to me bed.'

I could hardly complain, so I wished the fellow well and thanked him and settled to my solitary watch.

I didn't know if Southgate and Gosling were still on guard at Freston Brook and I didn't want to discover myself to the felons by going to find out. I stayed in my hideout.

In those hours before the dawn, when the moon is down, the temperature falls and the body cries out for a place of comfort, then even I can feel the tentacles of despair. What absurd catalogue of chance had led to me crouching in a damp ditch on a Suffolk shore? Why was I in pursuit of these poor men? I've spent my life defending the law, in this country and abroad. I've got to believe I'm better than the rogues and rebels I fight. In the light of day I do, but alone in the damp dark I wonder whether the life of a lamb and the wealth of some gentleman farmer is worth it. What would it take for me to turn poacher and join the likes of Root? Only the fear of capture and the desire for the respect of worthies.

I don't remember, of course, if those were the thoughts I had then. I expect the excitement of the chase kept me on my toes, as well as the fear of failure, but there have been times since when I've wondered what it was all about and why I didn't let well alone.

If I had been indulging in such maudlin sentiment, I was fortunately interrupted by the sound of footsteps on the road. One man. I could hear his heavy boots on the gravel and then slithering in the mud. He paused, then walked on a little. He sniffed and spat, then became silent.

I tentatively raised myself to a crouch and pulled myself high enough to peer through the hedge. There, about eight paces away, was a thin man in dark clothes with a large canvas bag, like a sailor's bundle, over his shoulder.

It wasn't Root but one of his cronies, Isaac Prentice; a seaman who occasionally lodged in Ipswich between voyages. A seaman who seemed to be missing his boat!

I struggled over the hedge, and the slow-witted man didn't

move or even turn around. Perhaps he thought I was one of his mates come up behind him. Once I was on my feet and had my cutlass in my right hand and my left on the pistol in my pocket, I shouted at him to stand or I would shoot. He took one look and decided to take the risk and run.

He dropped the bag and made away across the Hard and towards the receding water. Perhaps he thought he'd stumble across the yawl - as I say, the moon had set by this time and it was very dark - and he sloshed onwards into the mud, flinging his body about in his desperation to see the boat, but of course it was long gone.

He set off seawards and I followed him, we both getting deeper into the water. When it was halfway up my thighs and I could feel the mud sucking me down I shouted at him again, telling him I'd shoot if he didn't come back (though I well knew that the chances of a percussion cap firing in all the damp were slim, and, at twenty yards distance, I'd probably miss.) He said he'd stop, but he pressed on. He must have been up to his chest by then. I determined that there was nothing to be gained by chasing the fool through the Orwell, so, keeping him in my sight, I made for the bank and the road. Prentice now seemed to be swimming.

I stood on the bank and shouted at him and he shouted back, but I suppose neither of us could hear what the other was saying.

Just at this moment a Brig, the *Etherley* of Ipswich, as I discovered later, came into view, sailing down the river on the ebb tide. Slow, and fully laden, she was keeping a good watch.

It was George Chambers, a porter on the ship, who heard our shouting and alerted the mate. He and a sailor called Harrison were told to take the ship's tender and investigate, since there were two other boats - one going upstream and one down - from which someone might have fallen overboard.

I saw the ship's rowing boat pull into view. I shouted all the more, telling them that it was a wanted man in the water and that they must bring him ashore to me. Days later, Chambers swore he didn't hear a word I said, never even saw me, but he recognised Prentice immediately - another sailor, you see. He and Harrison lugged Prentice on board their skiff and all Prentice would say, apparently, was that the water was dreadful cold.

The men of the *Etherley* thought he'd fallen overboard from some ship and was suffering fit to die of exposure. At least that's what they said afterwards, though I suspect it was just shipmates sticking together and putting out the law. Anyway, I could see the *Etherley* heaving to and the skiff making for her, so I thought, *Well, I know where to find you now, but what did you have in that great, canvass bag?*

I was cold and wet as I hurried back to the road. The bundle lay where Prentice had dropped it. I dragged it into shelter and, with my tinderbox, steel and candle made enough light to see.

Inside the grisly bag were roughly butchered chunks of mutton: two legs, a shoulder, and several other smaller pieces. That was enough. Now for the hue and cry! Southgate and Gosling were still watching the road at Freston Brook. They'd heard all the shouting and came along to me, so I left the poachers' spoils in their custody.

I ran up to Redgate Farm, shouted up Beart once again, and requisitioned a horse. I rode back towards Ipswich, but the creature was tired and reluctant and I never roused it much above a walking pace. As I rode into St Peter's parish, at Stoke, I came upon two other constables. I left the poor old nag with one of them, and the other, Mason, and I, tramped across Stoke Bridge and down towards the docks.

'If the brig landed Prentice on the Ipswich shore then he'll be making for his lodgings in Fore Hamlet,' I said. 'We'll cut him off.'

Well, Mason wasn't convinced, but he was up for some excitement on a cold March night, and we hurried though the silent lanes before breaking into open country at Greenwich Farm.

It just wasn't Prentice's lucky night. There he was, slinking along by the hedge and shivering. He was dressed in black, with a sou'wester covering his head, but I knew my man. We forced him back against the hedge.

'Constable Mason,' I said, 'be my witness. This is the man I have been pursuing.'

And to Prentice I said,

'The charge against you is that of having a quantity of mutton in your possession, supposed to be stolen.'

'Oh!' he said.

'Your clothes are wet,' Constable Mason said to Prentice. 'Why?'

'I fell overboard,' he said, without further clarification.

The time by the church bell was just after three a.m.

We took the pathetic fellow back to the police station and I noted everything down. Prentice's clothes were stained with mutton fat.

'As good as red-handed,' I said, but Prentice didn't reply. He just steamed by the station fire until we locked him away.

There was no time to waste. Where were the rest of the gang, and what evidence could I gather to put before the magistrate? I hurried off to Prentice's lodgings but there was no-one there, and no evidence of poaching, so I marched back through the town and out once again on the Wherstead road.

I must have walked close on fifteen miles that night, all-in-all. Word had spread, the sun was coming up over Felixstowe way, and by the time I got to Woolverstone Park, the home of Mr Berners (the retired archdeacon of Suffolk who was an ancient gentleman of considerable means), his men were already out searching the estate and counting their sheep.

It took some hours, but by midday his steward, Dale, was able to confirm that two sheep were missing. During the afternoon his men brought in two skins with the marks of rough butchering upon them and several parcels of mutton tied up in handkerchiefs, shawls and two old aprons. But of the other three gang members there was no sign.

I was sure Root, Prentice, Henry Pryke (my spy), and a man called Charles Lucas, were in that boat and had butchered them sheep, but proving it all to a judge and jury was another matter, and a jury could ignore the evidence because they wanted to spare the man the worst of punishments. Of course, by this time you were no longer hanged for sheep stealing,[74] but transportation for seven years was common, and if you had a bad record that could be for life. Either way, it was a death sentence so far as the man and his family were concerned. It's only in novels that transported criminals ever find their ways home.[75]

When the case came to trial it wasn't quite the triumph I'd hoped for. Prentice was doomed from the beginning. Caught red-handed with dripping meat, dripping clothes, and his face marked by half a dozen men, there was no way he was anything but guilty. We even had a butcher show that the meat came from the same beast as the skins in the field.

But the other three were different. No one was prepared to swear they saw them and there was not a bit of evidence found on them.

Then up pops Susan Caley, elderly widow of Fore Hamlet, all coy and respectable, who said that Root came into her house and told her there were two policemen after him, 'Or one, he could not tell which, and he was told young Pryke cut the sheep's throats, but he had nothing to do with killing the sheep.' As much nonsense as you can imagine, and, of course, no-one thought to tell the jury that Caley was a friend of Keziah Root and was living next door to her and James Root, alias Sparham's brother, George. Caley's son, like James, worked as a brickmaker too, so they were all thick together. It's what happens, you see. They close their ranks in Fore Hamlet, especially in the face of the landowner.[76] The stolen mutton could feed their small society while his reverence across the water wouldn't miss a couple of beasts. Typical of 'Witty,' too, that he attempts to lay any possible blame on to Pryke - and plausible, since Henry Pryke was a butcher by trade.[77]

So, it was no surprise to me that at the Ipswich assizes, on 6th of July, Root, alias Sparham, was again acquitted, together with Lucas and Pryke, though Prentice was sentenced to transportation for seven years, which was some kind of reward for a long, cold, wet night.[78]

I'm nearly at the end of this story. I'm sorry it's not an uplifting one, though there was perhaps a glimmer of hope at the end: a few months later,[79] Root was strolling down the lane from Fore Hamlet and into Holywells Park, the land of Mr John Cobbold, brewer, whose coke oven had once given him a warm crib. He was in the company of Robert Friston, James Lucas, and his younger brother, George.

I don't believe he was a bad lad, young George, but just in bad company, and I might have helped him a little by seeing him caught that day. You see, they were intercepted by Arthur Lee, the gamekeeper, and charged in the magistrates' court with trespass in pursuit of game. James Sparham, alias Root, was fined ten shillings, or one-month imprisonment in the event of default, and the other three were given five shillings fines with twenty-one days for default.[80]

After that, I think that James Root had Cobbold in his sights. He seemed to think he had a score to settle. How many times that winter he tried to poach on the brewer's land I don't know, but in March 1850 he was there again, lurking by the ponds. Armed with a stone, he knocked down a duck and prepared to walk off with it. However, he was seen and recognised, I think again by Lee. Though he dropped the duck and ran away, the word was out, and he was caught at Stowmarket, fifteen miles away.

The prosecutor, Mr Dasent, made a fine speech, and he told the Ipswich Sessions, 'The prisoner has long been a notorious character.'[81]

At last, the jury found him guilty. Then, of course, his whole history was rolled out, and the judge sentenced him to be transported for seven years.

I must say, I had a quiet ale at Mr Cobbold's expense that night. No-one was sorry to see James 'Witty' Root, alias Sparham, sailing away from the Orwell for good.

Young George - he can't have been twenty - was nowhere near the duck hunt, and I'm pleased to say that I had a few words with him about the company he kept. It may have made a difference. I remember he turned Queen's evidence soon after. I'm not a vindictive man; I just expect a fellow to take some responsibility, to live in peace with his neighbours and with himself. It's not so much to ask, is it?

# 9: Peter

## July 2021

A torpid day. I am hiding from the heat, sat at my desk, and staring vacantly at dust on the computer screen. Covid restrictions are now lifted but I am reluctant to go out. It may not be given to a genealogist, whatever his childhood reading in *The Eagle*, to be an action hero, but I have been vicariously excited by Constable Bragg. He knew Keziah and George. His dealings with them may have changed George's life, and therefore mine. I should rouse myself.

Witnesses to these Roots are crowding in, like ghosts shimmering amongst the trees. Having had little to go on only a few months ago, I find that every time I address the archives there is a hand on my shoulder and a delicate voice in my head. It is the Indian silver bowl sitting beneath the computer screen which conjures such spirits. Today, the panel facing me shows Lakshmi in a twisted pose with arms raised. She seems to be opening the bowl still wider and revelling in the summer heat, which reminds her of Calcutta and a house in Bally Gunge.

'So, what happened to James?' I ask her. 'What was the impact on Keziah? How did George take it? And what does it mean to me? And what about Eliza Ellis: what is our connection to her?'

'Be patient,' says Lakshmi. 'Soon you will hear George in his own voice, but first he must be free of his admired older brother, James.'

'Are there archives?'

'Enough to save you from too much imagining,' she says, grinning.

'The archives spark the imagination,' I retort.

'Listen.'

In March 1850, Henry Betts, the governor of Ipswich Gaol, wrote that James Root had 'Twice been convicted before for larceny, and has been summarily convicted five times. The whole course of his life has been bad from his infancy.' His conduct is described as 'Very bad, has shown much bad feeling'. Within days, James, prisoner 5021, is shipped off to Millbank Prison,[82] where he is held in silent and solitary confinement. According to normal procedure, he would have remained there for three months prior to transportation, but James was kept at Millbank for ten months and eighteen days. However, the governor described his behaviour there as 'good.' Every day he waited for transportation down the River Thames and transfer to a ship bound for Australia, but nothing happened.

Then, in the winter of 1851, James was sent to the prison hulk, *Warrior*, laying at Woolwich. As each day passed in the freezing damp of his wooden dungeon James wondered what would carry him off first: disease or an Australian transport ship. But, while he remained in sight of the Kentish shore, he felt some hope. The *Warrior's* records show that his behaviour, though initially poor, improved as time went on.

Perhaps he got wind of political events beyond the confines of the prison deck. By the early 1850s the conditions which had given rise to transportation as a punishment were changing. There was a move against the practice, both in Britain and Australia. The longer James Root stayed in the hulks the less likely he was ever to see passage down under. Even so, it was something of a surprise to me, and would have annoyed Constable Bragg, to find in *Warrior's* records that, on 24th of March, 1854, he was released on licence. He had served just over four years of a seven-year sentence[83].

Immediately on his release, he took up with a woman twelve years his junior called Sophia Thorndike. As man and wife, they lived itinerantly throughout the East of England while James followed his trade as a brick maker.

Their first child, George William, was born nine months after his release from prison. Three more children followed, and on 8th of February 1863, Sophia and James were married in Ipswich. Though he stayed out of prison, James ended his days in the Ipswich Union Workhouse, where he died on 17th of January, 1877, at the age of fifty-five. My 'witty' three-times great-uncle was buried at St Clement's, Ipswich, three days later.

The widow, Sophia, moved to the Fens with their younger children. She took in a lodger - a bricklayer called William Cutting - whom she married, and he took James's youngest son, William, as his labourer. Sophia and James's oldest boy stayed in Ipswich (and caused trouble).

And Keziah?

Keziah's life was precarious from the start. She had an unreliable, naïve father, and a bigamous chancer of a husband.

'I still got my George. He's a good boy,' she says to me in my imagination. 'He were a soldier, you know. Nothing can destroy him. He's got ideas. And you, you who dig all this dust, what is the point? Live life as it is, not as it was or might have been. Each day was a new start for me. We did our best and, if it mainly didn't end as we had hoped, at least I clung on. There ain't much margin between living and dying.'

I feel thoroughly chastised. Too comfortable, complacent, and told off by the imagined ghost of a very distant ancestor.

What margins do I live between? None so treacherous as those hemming Keziah, though I become less sure with every day that passes. The virus has begun to mutate and the threats multiply. Despite the summer weather, I am consumed by thoughts of mortality and family mutability, of the bequests I might make and the lack of any descendants to leave them to.

The days have passed their zenith; the apples are already ripening.

When I die, I should prefer my ashes to be scattered in the river, allowed to flow onwards, rather than for my corpse to be planted next door in the churchyard, supposing there is anyone to carry out that obsequy. Or perhaps interred in the garden. A convenient spot would be below the sumac trees. There is a message in those trees which suits a genealogist. When I first came here twenty years ago, I thought of the sumac as a single specimen. It was exotic. Its blood-red flower spikes appeared before the pinnate leaves, and I enjoyed its barren, twisted branches and deeply etched trunk. But it had a secret. It was spreading beneath the soil and, as it matured, new trees, its clones, rose all about. Where I left the grass uncut, new, whippy stems appeared overnight. Those I pulled at revealed their long roots and runners and they gave way to my weeding only with reluctance. Those I left alone soon brandished their own spikes like a mediaeval army. They were one connected specimen of multiple generations surviving through their hidden persistence.

So, I have stopped my destruction. A sumac family grows here now. Some roots I live with and will die with, some I pot up and leave by the gate for passers-by to take. That is all I can do with that inheritance, except fertilize them with my ashes.

I had once thought Keziah of little account. She didn't satisfy my childish ambitions for my ancestors. She had no riches or position to pass on, yet without her I am nothing, for there would have been no George, nor anything that followed, including the Indian silver bowl. I need to follow the secret runners and find where Root, alias Sparham emerges once again. What bits of his inheritance did he keep and pass on in his turn? How did he mutate? Will he lead me to Eliza Ellis, owner of the bowl? George is nearer to me in blood than Keziah or her father and her other children, and I need to dig about in his archive.

'He will speak to you,' says Lakshmi.

As the sun fades in a sullen sky, I must listen and write.

# Part 2
# George

# 10: George Sparham, Alias Root

## May 1852

George Sparham, alias Root, wakes suddenly. A shaft of early morning sunlight has rudely discovered him through the filthy, cracked panes of the room in Fore Hamlet which he shares with three other people.[84] Their tenement is in a court off the street and only a minute's walk down Coprolite Street to the docks where George works, and to Packard's manure factory.[85] The stench from the factory is appalling. George coughs and turns on his straw mattress. Across the small upper room, he can see Keziah, his mother, asleep in the only bed. Beside her is their lodger, Charlotte. Next to George, on another mattress on the floor, Charles Lucas is also still sleeping. Charles, the confederate of his brother James (who is now under sentence of transportation), is another lodger. George would like to see Lucas in chains too. Any moment all three will be awake, but for now this is the time to think and plan and decide whether to go through with 'it'.

George would like to stay hidden, but what he intends to do will draw attention, since his plan is to escape. Though he calls himself Sparham he knows that he is, essentially, a Root, like his mother, and Roots keep out of the sun if they want to survive. George knows, however, that he can no longer endure this room in the hideous squalor of Fore Hamlet. He is twenty-one years old - a man. Time to make a move.

James's sentence of transportation had turned all their lives upside down. You could never have accused James Sparham, alias Root, of being a stable influence, but he had been a provider. When there was brickmaking there had been an income, and, at any time, James seemed to produce small windfalls of meat or money. 'Ask no questions, you'll be told no lies,' he told their mother when she asked where the bounty came from. He gave George a wink and a playful punch. Outside their room he was fierce, wary, and dark: inside he was their man. There was no need back then for lodgers to help them to pay the rent.

James was eight years older than George. The little boy had tagged along as soon as he could, making himself useful, running errands, taking messages, and handing on packages of this and that.

'Here's a ha'penny. Get us a beer and bring it to the brick works.'

'Tell Mrs. Hudson I have a soldier for her. St Clement's Churchyard. Now.' [86]

'Take this to my mate Charley. Make sure them coppers don't see you. There's a penny when you get back.'

James had been kind to him and stood up for him. Other lads didn't mess with George because there was always James to contend with. Life had been fun, and he'd felt important. George knew all the courts and alleys. He could slip from one yard to the next, through the crowds of men, between their legs and below their eye lines. Sometimes there were apples to be taken from distracted stall holders or a bucket of coal to be filched from the Wet Dock wharf. Rats could be caught and sold on to Mr

Goodwin, the innkeeper at *The Royal Albert*. At twopence a rat, it was worth the bites and scratches. Ratting sweepstakes were popular, then. There was money to be had, and it was another day when George could eat.

He reflects on the kaleidoscope of his history. But there is a shadow. He can't remember exactly when it stopped being a game, but, little by little, he had grown up enough to know that this wasn't what he wanted.

Perhaps it was when he went to the Sunday school at the Tacket Street chapel; they read him the Bible and he soaked up stories where God was always looking over your shoulder and threatening punishment. If God sees everything, what escape is there? Or perhaps it was the day when, at the age of eleven, he started at the brickworks alongside his brothers. That was hard and heavy. He learnt to hate clay and brick dust. He froze in the yard through the winter and his hands cracked and opened as he lifted pugged clay to the moulds, pressed it down and dusted it with sand. His shoulders bent under the weight of the moulds as he carried them to the drying ground.

Each year he thought, 'I cannot do this for another day,' and each year he did.

Or perhaps what changed him was the first time he was caught for poaching. He was seventeen and it was just before Christmas.

He had been out to Nacton with James and the boys, but the keeper had got them before they could take a thing. It was Sir Philip Brooke's land, one of the biggest nobs about, so you didn't have to be caught red-handed to be sent down.[87]

Two weeks of the treadmill. It wasn't going to break him, but it was close.

When he came out it was like he'd made a name for himself, and for weeks George snuck out whenever the moon was up to try his luck. When they got him again, in September, he got another twenty-one days. He was all bravado when he went in, but this time it was truly crippling. His body was broken, his mind torn apart. For the first time in his life, when he began to think about his future what he saw was a blank.

There were men in the gaol who were walking skeletons, who were old men at the age of thirty, who seemed to know no other kind of life but prison, the streets, and the workhouse, and who had no family who cared for them or for whom they cared. One of them, seeing him as he propped his exhausted body against the dripping wall of the exercise yard, said to him, 'You're one of us now, lad.' He shuffled off across the yard with the stooped, dragging gait of a man who has spent too many years in irons.

*No, I'm not*, said George to himself, *but as he looked after the man he thought, but the next time I come here, I will be.*

A few days after he came out of gaol (leaving James inside to serve out another week of his sentence), Bragg, the policeman, came up to him in Fore Hamlet. He was the copper who had Prentice transported and was smarting that he didn't get James at the same time.

'I'm watching you, George Root', he said.

'I ain't Root, I'm Sparham.'

'I know who you are and what you are,' he said.

'You got it in for us,' said George.

'No, son. You're doing this all by yourself.' Bragg drew himself up, as if standing to attention and sniffed the autumn air. He looked steadily at George and took a pace towards the boy.

'Of course, it doesn't need to be like this,' said Bragg, quietly.

There was a long pause. George was longing to walk away, but Bragg held him with his eye.

'You're not a bad lad,' he said, and left his words hanging.

'You remember Pryke?' Bragg said. George nodded. He was the butcher who occasionally went out at night with James and the Lucas boys.

'He doesn't seem to get in much trouble these days. In fact, he's been quite a help to me.' Another pause, to let it sink in, then he turned with a, 'Have a care, young George,' and walked firmly away.

It didn't take George long to work out what all that was about. Henry Pryke sometimes went out with James and more than once he'd been picked up by the keepers, but Pryke was always acquitted or 'no bill.' [88]

'You'd think that Bragg would have him in his sights, but he seems to be pleased with him,' said George to himself. 'So perhaps he was Bragg's informer, running with the hare and the hounds. And if Pryke can do that, is Bragg offering me something too? And if he is, does he expect me to inform against my own brother? That I'd never do. Who does he think I am?' He could feel himself getting angrier. Next time he saw Bragg he'd tell him something he wouldn't like! But he also remembered the story Keziah had told him about his grandfather, Samuel: you needed to know which the winning side was.

When James came home a few days later, he was wrecked

worse than George had ever seen him, and wild, too. George tried to tell him about Bragg, but as soon as he mentioned the man's name his brother went off like gunpowder, fizzing and spluttering with anger.

James now seemed to be out several nights a week and getting more and more reckless. He didn't mind who saw him. They'd call out in the lane, 'There's Witty. Where's the moon shining tonight, Witty? Bring us home a leg.' So it was that he went after one of Cobbold's ducks, got seen, bolted, found at Stowmarket, tried, and gaoled.

It was now a couple of years since James had been sentenced to be transported, though he was still in the hulks. *All for a bleeding duck!* thought George.

*I'm not going the same way as James,* he thought. *I'll just keep my head down.* He resolved to be quiet and hidden away, like Roots should be.

With James in prison Keziah said they had to take in lodgers to make ends meet, even though they were living in only one room and sharing their stove and the privy with other families in the court. A succession of men and women came and went - usually one at a time but now there were two, including one of those Lucas boys who'd egged James on. *All of us in the one room 'cos we no longer have James's earnings, and I can't do nothin' about it,* thought George, bitterly.

Some weeks after James was sent down, Bragg had been on George's tail again.

'Sorry to hear about your brother, George.'

'You ain't sorry. You're laughing.'

'That I am not,' said the constable. 'It always hurts to see a young man sent to the other side of the world when there ain't no need for it. I was in the army; one thing I learnt is that you have to save yourself. Though of course, if you choose the right side, then there's plenty of others who'll watch your back. Remember Pryke.'

'You want me to spy for you!' said George, angrily.

'I want you to stand up for what's right. I want you to do yourself a favour at the same time.'

'I won't betray anyone.'

'Being on the right side isn't betrayal, it's survival,' he said. 'Those lads didn't help you, did they? The only one who did was your brother, James, and they just stood by while he got sent down time and again. Who have you got to stick up for you now? Your father's dead, your sister and Alfred are married and away, your mother don't know what day of the week it is most of the time ...'

'You leave her out of it!'

'I've nothing against her, George, but she can't do anything to help you.' He let that sink in. 'But there are those who can and will if you let them.' And, again, he stalked off.

George thought, 'I'll say two things about Bragg. He's persistent and he lets you mull over something on your own. It was as though he knew what you would end up thinking before you'd worked it out yourself.' And for a moment he remembered a starving winter afternoon, lying in bed with his sister, while his mother told them the story of his grandfather, Samuel, and the rogue, Henry Cone.

*That won't happen to me*, said George to himself. *Got to save meself.*

Finally, a few days later, when George came across Constable

Bragg on his beat, he'd made his mind up.

'So, what do you want me to do?' he said.

There was a public house on Holywells Road called *The Happy Return*. It was a short walk from Cliff Quay, tucked behind a dilapidated archway. It had a discouraging aspect, belying its welcoming sign: *Return if you must*, it seemed to say to any except those who were known in this corner between the docks and the factories of St Clement's. But it was a favourite with sailors and those who made their living from the river and the port, so it was no surprise to find the fisherman James Breckles and the sailor Ernest Gooch (both teenagers) in conversation with James Lucas (brother of Charles).

It was ten o'clock on the evening of Friday, 12th of April, 1850, and the young men were preoccupied with the events of two nights before. They had taken a small wherry belonging to Gooch's stepfather and sailed down the Orwell to its confluence with the River Stour and from there upstream to the Essex shore and into Ray Creek.

It had been a difficult voyage. The rivers they navigated seemed to be slow flowing, but the tidal range was twelve feet or more, and the currents confused. The unskilled could find themselves aground on the wide and gently-shelving mud flats, but Breckles and Gooch knew their way around. They knew where to expect sandbanks, and if there was danger of being seen they could find secret inlets and wooded coves in which to hide.

They had to avoid the river traffic, too. Ipswich was a busy port with many wherries and brigs making use of the new dock. A collier of two hundred tons or more from the Tyne or the Wear lumbering up with the tide or returning empty at a sprint on the ebb would never avoid you in the dark and would run you down.[89] Crossing the main channel into Essex, waters could be a hazardous business, especially on a moonless night such as this was, but Gooch, Breckles, and Lucas were capable and cautious. They worked silently in the small boat, alert to the shifting winds and the tell-tale ripples of the water over mud banks. They looked to each quarter for other traffic and listened for voices and slapping sails which would carry easily on the light airs. They communicated with each other in whispers.

At last, they successfully anchored alongside a chalk embankment at a remote farm known as Ray Island.[90] They never doubted their indestructibility as they climbed out of the boat and into water so cold it took their breath away. The soft mud hidden underfoot pulled at them as they waded through the shallow water of the creek and climbed the bank. At the top was a turnip field and, by the starlight on this clear night, they could see the silhouettes of a large herd of sheep.

What they did not see was Superintendent Mason from Ipswich, on the hunt for a felon called Branch, who, the policeman thought, might be on Ray Island. Mason was on the lane beyond the field and largely concealed by a ragged hedge. He had detected a movement to his left and stood motionless, wondering who might be abroad at such an hour - it was already midnight - and in so unpopulated a spot.

He wondered if it were Branch, but he did not expect the man to be in company with others. As they approached him, concealed as he was at the top of the field, he recognised the Ipswich men. He smiled to himself, guessing what they were up to and sensing the opportunity for another arrest that night. But he was a man alone and, being in pursuit of Branch (whom he soon captured), he simply stored the information away for future action when he returned to the police station.

The three poachers knew nothing of Mason's presence. They were intent on mastering the sheep without the flock scattering.

In the darkness they spread out and crouched like sheep dogs. The sheep saw them, and their heads popped up quizzically. The men lay still and waited. The sheep returned to grazing and the men closed in on the flock. Like a game of grand-mother's footsteps, each time a sheep looked up or turned its sharp ears towards one of the poachers the man became a statue. When the sheep relaxed its guard, the men crept forwards once more.

At the last, as Breckles approached the flock from the wind-ward side, the animals moved away from him and two walked directly into the waiting arms of Lucas and Gooch. These beasts were quickly seized, turned upon their backs and had their throats cut. As they bled out on the cold earth the poachers inexpertly butchered them where they lay.

Now the men felt the urgency to get away. The whole flock was frightened and restless and the poachers were suddenly fearful of discovery.

They dragged the dismembered carcasses down the field and stumbled through the mud flat back to the boat. The wet skins were cumbersome, and the men felt horribly exposed as they wrestled flesh and fleece over the gunwale. All three men were cold and bloody as they climbed on board and sailed for home. Lucas set about further butchering, throwing the bloody skins and guts, weighted with bricks, overboard.

'What will we do with all this meat,' said Gooch, his nervous gaze constantly flitting from watching the river to viewing the grisly scene in the bottom of the boat. 'There's too much to carry through the streets when we get back, and we can't leave it on the boat. My stepfather might find it.'

'Hide it on Hog Highland,'[91] said Breckels. 'No one goes there. It's Cobbold land.'

'We can each take some for the pot,' said Lucas.

When they got close to home, they pulled into Hog Highland and loaded half the booty into a canvas bag and put it in a ditch. By then it was nearly four in the morning. The clouds were hiding the stars but very soon the first hint of dawn would begin to seep up the Orwell, people would emerge for work, and the danger of discovery would increase.

They did their best to clean their blood-stained clothes, hid some of the meat in the little cuddy on the boat, despite Gooch's protestations, returned the mile or so to Cliff Bight to moor up, and made off home with the rest of their gains.

Two days later, the three poachers still had a major part of their haul to dispose of, some on the boat and much more in the ditch on Hog Highland. The consequences of the crime, and the difficulty of disguising it, were beginning to come home to the young men. Gooch, responsible for the boat, was in a particular sweat as he sat in *The Happy Return* with Breckles and Lucas.

It was at this moment that George Root, alias Sparham, came through the inn door with another mutual friend, Robert Friston.

'Tell George,' whispered Lucas. 'He'll help. You can trust him, what with what happened to Witty. My brother's living with him and his old ma.'

'George,' shouted James Breckles across the bar, 'what would you do with a couple of dead sheep?'

'I'd not shout about them in a pub, even *The Happy Return*,' said George quietly. 'Whatever you've been up to, I don't want to know.'

'But you'd like a juicy shoulder of mutton,' said Lucas, smirking.

'I don't know nothing about that,' said George and turned away to buy his ale.

The conversation drifted, and George and Friston asked no questions, but before the hour was out Gooch said, 'Come to the boat,' and leaving the pub the five young men wandered down to Cliff Quay.

Once on board, Breckles threw back a large sail cloth to reveal a heap of sweating mutton. Then the whole story of Wednesday night came out. Root listened but the three poachers became heated as they debated what to do.

'Take what we can between us now and throw the rest overboard,' said Gooch.

'What do we do with the bag on Hog Highland?' asked Breckles.

'Leave it where it is. Forget about it.'

'Never,' said Lucas. 'Let's divide all this between us and tomorrow we can go to Hog Highland and do the same with the rest.'

'But if the coppers see us?'

'They won't. You worry too much.'

The argument went back and forth, fuelled by beer, until, one by one, the poachers dropped off to sleep in the warm spring afternoon. In the end they bought more beer and settled down for the night. Next morning, Saturday, they went their various ways, and most of the meat was left on board.

Later that day, George met Breckles again, in the centre of Ipswich.

'Come to the boat,' said the young fisherman.

George, cautious and silent, ambled along beside him. On their way they passed Constable Bragg and another policeman coming away from the docks.

'They've been to search the boat, I'll be bound,' said the nervous Breckles.

'Keep calm, James. I'll find out where they've been,' said George.

'You can't!'

'I know Bragg. He'll talk to me.'

George approached the policeman while Breckles watched, horrified, from a distance. What was said between Bragg and Root no-one knows, but after a brief and apparently friendly conversation, George rejoined his friend and they continued to the boat.

'Bragg ain't been to the boat,' said George, once they were well out of earshot of the policemen. But he didn't say what else they had talked about.

When they got to the waterside Gooch was already there. They boarded the wherry and sailed to Hog Highland. They were there within twenty minutes and, to their relief, the bags of mutton were untouched.

As they gathered the meat, they saw John Marshall, Mr Cobbold's bailiff, approaching. He was some distance away, so, keeping low in the ditch, they scrambled towards the cover of a copse. Gooch led George and Breckles to a large hollow tree. Gooch climbed it and, while the bailiff relieved himself a hundred yards away and gazed meditatively at the wide and gently flowing Orwell, the other two men threw all the meat up to Gooch. Then they lay low for half an hour until, confident that the bailiff would not return, they recovered the meat.

'What do we do now?' asked Gooch.

'Take it into Ipswich and see who will buy,' said George. ' Perhaps Pryke the butcher is around, or you could hawk it round the pubs. It's Saturday. There'll be buyers for sure.'

As they walked back to town, lugging the bag, the two policemen were lying in wait. Gooch and Breckles dropped everything and ran. George stood, apparently transfixed.

'Why lad, what have we here?' said Constable Bragg.

At the end of May 1850, the case came to the Quarter Sessions in Chelmsford. In the dock were Breckles, Gooch, and Lucas. George Sparham, alias Root, was the star witness for the prosecution.[92]

Mr Chamberlain, the farmer from Ray Island, attested to the fact that he had lost two sheep on the night in question.

'How do you know the carcasses recovered by the police were from your sheep?'

'They'd been grazing on turnips, your honour. They were lean and not fit to be slaughtered or eaten.'

Robert Kemp, an Ipswich butcher, confirmed the state of the meat. Then George took the oath. He told his story of the Friday night and Saturday up to the point when he was detained by the police. Robert Friston was called and confirmed everything. Both he and George were cross-examined at some length, with the defence lawyer drawing attention to their criminal records, but no fewer than three policemen filled in the circumstantial details.

There was little doubt in the minds of the public in the crowded courtroom about the way the case was running. These were Suffolk men in an Essex Court. It was an offence against the livelihood of a local farmer. In his conclusion, the defence lawyer, Mr T Chambers, contended that the whole case relied on the evidence of George Sparham - 'Who was entirely unworthy of belief' - and that the defendants should be acquitted. The local newspaper reported that 'after some hesitation the jury found the defendants guilty, but strongly recommended mercy on account of them being young men and, as far as they knew it, it was their first offence.'

Things became heated in the courtroom. The prisoners had friends and family in the gallery who were immediately fearful of the outcome. Police Superintendent Mason was recalled and strongly objected to the jury's recommendation.

'These men are all suspicious parties,' he said. 'They are continually under the eye of the police, your honour.' The gallery groaned.

Mr Chambers did his best to delay things and allow a period of reflection away from the public eye.

'Nothing in the indictment shows the value of the sheep, your honour. It should have. By the farmer's own admission, these sheep were not fit to be eaten. In fact, they were half-starved and so worthless. The farmer has lost little or nothing, since he would have had to keep feeding them. The injury occasioned by this crime is unquantified. Your judgment should be reserved,' he said.

The prisoners' friends in the gallery muttered in agreement and the judge rapped his gavel. The policemen in court shuffled, but the judge was having nothing to do with the defence argument. It was a crime to deprive a man of his property, regardless of its value. As he sentenced each of the three young men to transportation for ten years the gallery erupted in grief.

'A death sentence would have been more merciful.'

'Think of the families.'

'Justice!'

And some quietly muttered the names of George Sparham and Robert Friston.

With the case over, the two witnesses slunk off to a distant ale house, hoping to avoid the prisoners' friends and families. Early in the evening, they made their way to the railway station and took the train back to Ipswich. As they walked home from Ipswich station, in the company of Robert Kemp the butcher who had also given evidence for the prosecution, they were accosted by a small gang of women.

'Here they are. Get the bastards!'

Robert Friston was jostled, his hair violently pulled.

'Get that Kemp, filthy traitor. We'll burn your shop down. You should roast with your meat. If you want to keep your customers don't keep company with the coppers.'

Another woman, Maria Bloomfield, shouting 'rogue' and 'traitor,' according to witnesses, struck George in the eye.

Police arrived and three of the women were taken away. In the magistrates' court, the following morning, Maria was fined one shilling plus costs and the other women were reprimanded and discharged. [93]

'Witnesses must be protected,' said the magistrate, though the assurance did little to hearten George. As he walked through the streets, he felt like a marked man. It was as though everyone knew who he was and thought of him as a traitor. He no longer had brothers to protect him. He was frightened.

In the weeks following the verdict, the ranks of the Ipswich poor closed against George. Was he running with the hare or the hounds? Bragg wanted him with both but he wasn't sure he was running with either.

'Roots best stay buried,' he said to himself.

He got up each morning, made bricks, and avoided company as much as he could in the overcrowded courts of Fore Street and Back Hamlet. His mother found it more difficult to get work, too. They let out space in their room to first one and then a second lodger - Charles Lucas, a distant cousin of the James Lucas who had run with his older brother and was now himself to be transported. Charles was a form of protection for minimal rent, but he did nothing to improve the atmosphere.

Back in the close room George shares with his mother and their lodgers he struggles between sleep and wakefulness. Two years have passed since he was in court in Chelmsford. Now that he is a man, he can make his own decisions. He doesn't need to listen to his mother, or Bragg, Lucas, or any of the fickle friends who surround him.

He looks at the crude tattoo he had made on his left arm:

'*James*,' it reads, in honour both of his father and his brother. His father is dead. His brothers have all gone.

On his right arm he has inked a pattern of stars: we are under the heavens and they are our only constant. Bragg had talked to George of getting out into the world, of sailing abroad with the army and living somewhere fresh. Beyond the harbour and the grey Orwell there is a greater world where he can find opportunities. Or hide.

He gets up, sluices himself in the yard below, and walks away from St Clement's, up the hill towards the Norwich Road and the Ipswich barracks. For the last week he has seen the recruiting sergeant for the Ninety-sixth Regiment of Foot barking his invitation.

'Join the colours, lads!'

'Money in your pocket just for putting your mark here.'

'See Her Majesty's Empire and be paid for the privilege.'

'Why, this very year we're in India, and last year we were in Australia.'

'Australia,' thinks George. 'My brother is going to Australia. Why not?'

It is Tuesday, 11th of May, 1852, and George is leaving home.

# 11: Peter

## Autumn 2021

When I was twelve years old, I had the mental image of time as an undulating road stretching ahead of me. In January I could see the year heading towards a distant horizon, peaking somewhere around the end of summer, gradually dropping into remote November darkness, before exploding in brief joy around Christmas. The pandemic has changed things. Even though lockdown is officially ended the horizon is lost in a grey fog no more than a day or two ahead. We wear masks and move like phantoms. All is uniformly flat and dismal, and danger is concealed behind each hedgerow. It seems sufficient that I survive from day to day, living with my ancestors and no one else.

It doesn't matter that my painstakingly constructed family trees lead from one generation to the next. I only see these people piled up as in the paupers' grave. My life encapsulates them all, and I will soon be among them, covid or not. I have learnt that all time is now.

When I contemplate my death, I think of my inheritance. I don't know what I shall leave, apart from a crumbling cottage, an overgrown garden, and a silver bowl, unless it is these stories. I don't know who I will leave them to, unless I can find the inheritors in the family tree.

The more I feel the urgency to get things straight the more difficult it seems to achieve anything. Archives are still largely closed. 'If we had anything for you to look at you would have seen it online already,' seems to be the response to all queries. All the world looks inwards, and I can only retreat further into my family tree, with its voices and their echoes.

Keziah had so much to say but now I want a hero to drag me from autumnal despair. Perhaps George will fit the role despite his unpromising beginnings.[94] He started as a frozen child, a victim in the snow, and has shown a capacity to learn. But he had surely betrayed his friends, involving himself in their crimes and then turning against them in court. Maybe I am putting the least objectionable interpretation on the evidence: was he a stool pigeon or simply doing what he must to survive?

How does George feel in May 1852? Surviving from day to day is perhaps all he has ever done, but now, as he approaches the Ipswich barracks, I feel envious of him. He is setting out on a journey. As a child I had thought it would have been me going off on adventures, and that I would have been the first in the family to live such an enlarged life, but chiefly I have spent my time in darkened rooms with old records, and, each day, I become more fearful of walking through an open door into unknown territory.

Now I face up to the smallness of my own world, unless liberated by George's adventures and his willingness to speak to me.

# 12: George

## 11th of May 1852

'Sir,' said George, removing his flat cap and bouncing slightly on the balls of his feet, as though about to make a run for it.

'Sir, is this the way in?'

Sergeant William Whittingham of the Ninety-sixth Regiment of Foot[95] turned and looked down at the young man who had appeared silently behind him.

'What do you want, lad?' asked Whittingham, slightly irritated to find himself addressed by someone he hadn't seen coming. He jerked his head back as though about to utter a parade ground command.

'Joining, sir,' said George, almost at a whisper. He looked at the sergeant's bright red jacket, his sash, his thick moustache, and tall black shako. He saw how the soldier must see him: a shabby, dirty young man, with two front teeth missing.

'Speak up, lad!' said Whittingham. Although he had heard perfectly, it was important to start as you meant to go on.

'Want to join up, sir,' said George, a little louder.

'Want to join up, Sergeant!' said Whittingham.

'Yes please, sir. I think so, sir.'

'Saints preserve us,' said Whittingham, in the stage whisper he used in public to register his lowest level of irritation. 'Follow me, lad.' He turned smartly and marched inside the barracks and along two sides of the parade ground.

'Keep off the square, lad!'

*Why keep off what square?* thought George but dared not ask. He marched behind the sergeant, trying to keep up and in step with the taller, bulkier man. They reached an office in the far corner. Inside the dark panelled room was a table and a chair. Whittingham sat behind the table; George stood and mangled his grubby cap. With great deliberation the sergeant placed a printed form squarely on the blotter on the table where there was a pen tray and inkwell. Whittingham took a steel nib and fitted it with care to a pen from the tray. He dipped the pen in the ink and looked at the blob on the nib; dissatisfied he ran the nib over the inkwell to reduce the load then held the pen like a poisoned dart above the blotter.

Only then did he look at George. He looked him up and down, from his matted hair to his scuffed boots and then back again. He looked into George's eyes, and for a moment Root felt as though he were undergoing one of Bragg's inquisitions. Finally, the sergeant spoke.

'Name?'

'George … Sparham … Sergeant.'

'Well done, lad.'

If George had hesitated about using his father's surname it wasn't because he knew his parents weren't really married in the eyes of church and state. Rather, he had wondered whether this wasn't the moment to take an entirely new identity. He would not be known as George Root. As Root he was proclaimed a bastard. Better stick to Sparham, for now.

'Place of birth?' asked Whittingham.

'Bungay, Sergeant.'

'Suffolk?'

'Yes, Sergeant.'

'Age?'

'Twenty-one.' [96]

'Trade or calling?' George looked bemused. 'What do you do, lad?'

'Brickmaker.'

The questions continued and it was all written down in Whittingham's careful script.[97] Then he was marched to another room and George was measured (five feet, six and a half inches[98]) and identifying features were recorded: hazel eyes, dark brown hair, dark complexion, and tattoos on both arms. Two teeth missing and a cut on the ball of his thumb.

'Why do they want to write all this down?' George asked a soldier, Private Cope, who was walking him from one room to the next.

'So they can identify your body when you dies of cholera. Now take your shirt off and the doctor will give you an injection.'

'What's this for?' asked George.

'India,' said Cope.

'That's not what I meant,' said George, but the man wasn't listening, and before George knew it he was back with Whittingham who picked up his paper again and read back all the answers he'd given.

'Do you understand?'

'Yes, Sergeant.'

'And you are signing on for ten years and will receive a four pound bounty when you are attested by the magistrate tomorrow. Are you prepared to sign?'

'Yes, Sergeant.'

'It is now thirty minutes after noon on 11th of May 1852 - see, I'm writing it down - and you are now enlisted. Cope, find this man a bed and take him to the mess. He stays in barracks until we've seen the magistrate and I give him his number and pay book. Welcome to the Ninety-sixth, Sparham.'

'Thank you, Sergeant,' said George, trying to sound like a soldier, but Whittingham had already turned away and Cope smirked at him and said,

'Come with me.'

As the two men sat over a bowl of stew and some bread, Cope said,

'Well, my friend, you done it now.'

'What have I done?'

'I didn't think you'd 'a' knowed. You've signed away your life, that's what you done,' said Cope. 'And you won't get nothing much for it.'

'Four pounds and a pension,' said George. Cope laughed. He said,

'You look at your pay book when you get it. Four pounds in and three pounds, seventeen shillings, and six pence straight out again to pay for your uniform.[99] As for your pension, every time you get a black mark against your name, go absent or suchlike, they dock your pension until you'll probably be paying the army when you get out - if you live longer than ten years, that is, which, by the look of you, ain't likely.'

That night, as he tried to get to sleep in the half-empty barracks room amongst a handful of unfamiliar men, he thought, *I'm dry and I'm fed. This is better than prison or the floor in Fore Hamlet. I don't have to go to the brickworks tomorrow and break my back and burn my hands. Instead, they'll send me away from bloody Ipswich - maybe India, but perhaps Australia, and I'll see our James and we'll have some fun ...*

He was woken by a bugle, turned out for breakfast and a medical inspection, and twenty-four hours after he agreed to be enlisted, he was brought in front of the magistrate, Charles Burton.[100] Burton looked hard at George.

'I know you, lad.'

George thought it best to say nothing.

'A Sparham. You got brothers?'

George hesitated to answer, and Burton perhaps thought better of digging up family history. If this Sparham could be signed up and sent away then it was one less potential nuisance for the electors and rate payers of Ipswich. The magistrate turned a baleful smile on George.

'Well done, lad. Keep your nose clean and you'll make a fine soldier. Now, I have to ensure that the Sergeant here has done everything right, according to the book, so I ask you questions and you say "no" each time. Understand?'

'No ... I mean, yes, sir.'

'Do you object to the manner of your enlistment?'

'No, sir,' said George.

'Do you belong to the militia?'

'No, sir.'

'Do you belong to any other regiment or service - navy, marines, East India Company?'

'No, sir.'

'Have you ever …?'

'No, sir.'

'Have any of 'em ever found you unfit to enlist?'

'No, sir.'

'Now, see here, Sparham, I am writing in your name on this paper to show that you swear on oath that everything has been done correctly and you are willing to serve in Her Majesty's Ninety-sixth Regiment of Foot. I don't suppose you can write?'

'Not much, sir.'

'No matter. You will make your cross in the middle of your name and Sergeant Whittingham and I will both sign at the bottom. Well done, Sparham.'

'Thank you, sir,' said George, and he made a neat cross on the paper.[101]

As Cope marched George out of the office, he could hear a murmured conversation between the magistrate and the sergeant and a sudden burst of muted laughter. Nearby, a church bell struck the third hour.[102]

*Out of the frying pan*, thought George.

'Straight ahead! Shoulders back! March!' shouted Cope.

George found himself outside an open storeroom. Cope pointed.

'Bucket. Mop. Tap on the wall. Now clean your muddy footprints off the tiles back as far as the guard room. I'll tell you when you've finished!'

And as the soldier walked away, he looked over his shoulder and said,

'Welcome to the Ninety-sixth, lad. You're off to India.'

# 13: Peter Dreams of India

## January 2022

I write 'India' and it as if the silver bowl in front of me trembles into life. We are about to go away, George and I, and Lakshmi dreams of home.

'You are going nowhere,' says Lakshmi to me.

'But it's winter, here. The garden is bare, the days too short, and I need sun.'

'But you know you cannot travel, not that you ever enjoyed it much when you had the opportunity. You will have to listen to George and use your imagination.'

She is right. I live as if an invisible tether confines me to the cottage and garden. I must be content. Perhaps I am even hopeful. It is a new year, I've been vaccinated, although a new strain of virus threatens. No one knows what the risk is.

'You and George are one and the same,' says Lakshmi, 'for George does not know what he faces, yet he will never cease. But that doesn't mean he remains what he always was. Think of the dragonfish: in the lake it swims and fights; when the lake dries the fish is transformed. It breathes and walks.' [103] She looks at me with open arms from her most sedentary pose, cross-legged on a lotus.

I find that I am prepared to be led by the two of them, Lakshmi and George. I had thought that I was in control, but, like Keziah before them, they have taken charge of the story.

# 14: George and the Ninety-Sixth

## 1852-1854

'Like a furnace in here,' says George Sparham to no one in particular, flopping on to his mattress.

'You should have been in the old Lahore lines,' says the man on the next bed - Private Charles Edwards. 'This is luxury.'

They are side by side in the new barracks at Mian Mir, Lahore.[104] George has only recently arrived, and found himself assigned to the same section as Charles Edwards. The two men seem to enjoy each other's company even though Charles is a Norfolk man, and some years older than George.

George has come through his month of basic training at Chatham, has been shipped out with a batch of new recruits on the long voyage to Calcutta, and has faced the burning march across Northern India to reach the current home of the regiment guarding the north-west borders of the East India Company's domain. The Cantonment at Lahore is commodious, and George feels that he is expected to appreciate the care which the army is taking of him, but he has his doubts. The bounty he was paid when he signed up is mostly taken back to buy his kit. His shilling-a-day mostly goes to pay for his food: a pound of flour (often adulterated or infested with mites), a pound of meat (of dubious origin and quality), vegetables, and tea (without milk).

The army, he has discovered, is a hard master, and can be

tolerated only as long as you keep your neck in, but he is obedient and has adopted the tactic of silence in his relations with most of his comrades. In Ipswich, it was getting involved that caused him trouble. It was caring about his brothers and their friends that made him exile himself, so here he will do what is required of him, not make close friends, not give himself away, but just wait and see how the land lies.

Charles Edwards is the one exception to his rule. Charles has seemed a quiet, steady sort of chap, and quick to show George the ropes when he first arrived at Lahore. He told George which men of the company were to be avoided and who was to be trusted. He took him to the market stalls where he could buy fresh food or palatable coffee. They talked together about their families.

'You miss Ipswich, George?'

'Not a bit, Charles. You miss Norfolk, then?'

'Not often. I miss the sea, and the long sunsets.'

They lie in silence in the almost deserted barrack room. There is the distant sound of men at leisure, shouting, kicking a ball through the dust.

'Curlews,' says George suddenly. 'I miss the sound of curlews across the river.'

'A sad sound,' says Charles Edwards. Another long pause.

'The birds here are disgusting blighters,' says George.

'It's true,' says Charles. 'They're just waiting for us to be corpses.'

Their conversations were often like that. Charles Edwards didn't make any demands. He didn't probe George's past, with the result that Charles was the only man in the regiment that George has shared confidences with.

They are both in a section under the command of a fussy lance corporal called Isaac Tyrrell.[105] He is not an unpleasant man, not a parade ground bawler, but he likes things done by the book. He is keen to please his superiors and so his section must be keen to please him, if they want a quiet life. George and Charles want quiet: they do as they are told, turn out smartly, are uncomplaining, never volunteer but never shirk, and the immense boredom of life in camp is thus made bearable.

It is insufferably hot in the barrack room, and now, early evening, they rouse themselves to sit on the veranda. They smoke their pipes. George's pipe sits comfortably in the gap where he is missing his two front teeth. The sun rapidly sets and, as the temperature drops to something more comfortable, dust hazes the air and they look towards the distant hills where a silent lightning storm flashes but no rain falls.

'Not Suffolk, is it?' says Charles, simply trying to be companionable.

'The folks at home wouldn't believe what it's like here,' says George to Charles.

'Just like prison, mate, but with flies and snakes and the shits.'

'Prison with servants, two meals a day, and ginger ale!'

Isaac Tyrrell walks along the veranda towards them, pulls a chair over, and flops down. They nod to each other. Tyrrell is keen to join the conversation.

'Whenever could you have lived so cheap and have a hot joint of meat for breakfast, George? And for just a few pice.'[106] says Tyrrell.

'You could be dead of diarrhoea by evening, though,' says Charles Edwards.

'True enough,' says Tyrrell. 'Did I ever tell you about what happened when I first arrived here?'

Charles and George know what is coming so say nothing and wait for Tyrrell to get into his stride.

'Just after I arrived in India,' says Tyrrell, 'four men of my company reported sick and were taken to the hospital by the sick-bay orderly, Corporal Blanchfield, an Irishman - a bit of a joker, he was. At the breakfast table, one man asked, "Corporal, how is my chum Vardon?"

' "Dead. Buried," said Blanchfield, all matter of fact.

'Turns out, the four men who had gone to hospital the day before were not only dead but actually buried without our knowing a word about it.'

'That's terrible,' says George.

There is another long pause. Dysentery takes more men than any Pashtun jezail, as the men well know.

'Bael fruit,' says Charles. 'That's the answer. On toast. Three times a day. And whatever you do, don't go to the hospital.'[107]

'He's right,' says Tyrell. 'Bael fruit jam from Khan, the apothecary.'

That, and prayer. At church parade on Sundays, they pray more fervently than they were used to back in England. For George, disease and death is another reason for not making close friends.[108]

The desultory conversation between the three men goes nowhere. The regiment goes nowhere. There is no fighting to be done, just drills and exercise and, in their free time, seeking out the pleasures of Lahore, whether in gardens and temples or in the Heera Mandi, where dark houses provide music and dance and all manner of sensual pleasure in upper rooms.[109]

# 15: Peter Meets George in Heera Mandi

## 1976/1853

I feel a sudden shiver down my spine. I had forgotten all about Heera Mandi until this moment. It is as though George has placed an arm across my shoulder and we are walking to the Heera Mandi together.

On a late summer evening in 1976, I was staying at Faletti's hotel in Lahore. I had a wealthy client in Pakistan who was intent on proving his Anglo-Indian status and he had flown me out - one of my very rare trips abroad - to look at the limited documentation he had inherited. (I recall that, though I followed up every tentative lead back in England, I could prove nothing about his British ancestry, and he was left disappointed.[110])

Faletti's is now, I believe, a luxury establishment, but then it was somewhat out of time and grandly fading.[111] Beyond the imposing gates, a wide, poorly maintained drive led to a pedimented entrance and long colonnades.

There were uniformed bearers with high starched turbans. They escorted me silently through dusty halls. Slow ceiling fans hardly disturbed the oppressive air. The bedroom was spacious and its bathroom provided tepid water through much-painted Victorian pipework. A vast dining room was almost empty of guests. I felt I had been transported to a waiting room to the past.

After dinner, I approached the frock-coated concierge and said I wanted entertainment for the evening. I couldn't countenance the thought of being isolated in this dismal palace for the rest of the evening. He was guarded.

'What is it you want?'

'Just some music - local culture.'

My request was obviously a matter of some concern. The concierge was reluctant until I pressed the matter. Then he turned away into his little office. There were conversations with an unseen person within, and a discreet phone call. When he returned, another fellow materialised at my side. The concierge said, 'Go with this man,' and I was led rapidly (it seemed surreptitiously) to a car. There was no explanation. My silent guide sat beside the driver.

We left the hotel grounds and, soon after, the main road. Unlit, narrow streets wound between black tenements which all seemed to have their backs turned to us. After many turns and my complete disorientation, the car stopped at a junction. There was no one else on the street. I had become used to the overcrowded ways of Lahore, so this was unsettling. Surely, I should not be here.

'We get out,' said the guide, and the driver opened my door, gesturing to a dark opening between high walls.

'Where are we?' I asked the guide.

'Heera Mandi, Sir.'

I got out.

'I wait,' said the driver, and got back in the car.

My guide and I walked down the alley. Just as my eyes were becoming accustomed to the darkness, the guide stopped before a windowless wall and a door opened a crack.

'Quickly,' said the guide, pushing past a door keeper, who immediately slid the bolt behind us. We entered a small, spice-scented courtyard where barely visible shuttered windows rose into the gloom. A smear of moonlight caught the top of stonework four or more storeys high. It was as if we were standing at the bottom of a rectangular well, like being inside a particularly gloomy Doré print.[112]

And George was there beside me.

I only know this now, fifty years later. I sense him. We breathe the same, heavy air, feel the same nervous excitement, and wonder what we are about to experience.

The guide has disappeared. George and I follow a house servant up steep stone steps and through another door. We are invited to remove our shoes before being shown into a carpeted room - clearly a performance space, because, at the far end, are musical instruments and stools. George and I are seated on the floor against deep cushions. We are offered water, which we both refuse, fearing disease, and we wait.

After some minutes there is movement. Two men and two women appear through a door close by the instruments. It seems that they have prepared themselves hurriedly, like a family that had not expected visitors. There is hushed conversation, but since neither George nor I speak Pashto, and they do not speak English, there is no spoken communication across the room. It seems these performers are gauging their audience and deciding what will make up a suitable programme. We wait in silence.

Sweet incense perfumes the air and a sarinda[113] player strikes up, and then a tabla. The music is restrained, almost religious, the mood expectant. There is much repetition but with subtle variation on a theme. After some minutes, the music becomes faster and more brittle. A woman in a brightly coloured dress, emblazoned with tiny mirrors, dances. Another sings.

The performers hardly look at each other, and not at all at us. They keep their distance, each in his or her bubble, and all is decorous, though I do not feel comfortable. The room is filled with invisible walls, as though none of us know how to react or respond in our isolation. There are occasional shouts from the musicians. Encouragement, warning, passion? I have no idea. The quarter tones, the detailed and practiced movements, the sliding, keening intonation, keep me on edge; the language of this music is as foreign as the idiom of the street. There are meanings to this performance which are hidden from me and from George but could be a prelude as much to a massacre as any other passion. Nothing is explicable and I am troubled by its strangeness. George also seems nonplussed; this is not like any music we have heard before, in Ipswich or elsewhere. He and I sit in silence.

We watch and listen for nearly an hour, bound by uncertainty but caught in the moment, the movement, the humid, scented air, and the aching sound. The performers seem to have an inexhaustible repertoire, but it is never clear where this is all going or what is expected of us. We have no guide or book of etiquette; we can only sit where we are until anxiety or weariness overtakes us.

Eventually, there is a pause in the performance, and I rise, fumble for my wallet, and extract some rupees which I bestow on the guardian of the door. I have no idea whether this is too little or too much. I am led back to the stairs, to my guide, the courtyard, and the driver. Nothing is spoken. The bouncing, black, Ambassador car hurries me back to Faletti's. Uniformed watchmen salute me as I walk through the silent, dimly lit arcades to my room where I recline, but cannot sleep, under the slow fan.

George has not come with me. He remained in Heera Mandi, and what happened to him on that summer night, and at what hour he returned to his barracks, I have no idea. But I know that George was there with me and is with me again whenever I hear a sarinda and tabla.

We are bound together by that room and that music. Time has not stood still but melded so that we exist simultaneously, then and now. George does not know what is going to happen to him, or to Lahore. My archives tell me of generations which bind us, and of events in his family which he could never foresee. Libraries will show that revolt, war, partition, and millions of deaths separate us, and, though the music will be unchanged, the players and the listeners will have different faces and will hear differently. But George and I will share that time in Heera Mandi.

Fifty years on, I sit in the armchair in my cramped office and listen to Munir Sarhadi[114] play the sarinda through my ancient record deck. Before I left Lahore, all those years ago, I bought the LP in the gift shop at the hotel gates. I rarely play it, but when I do I am taken back to a carpeted upper room enclosed by dark streets and blank walls. The instrument and its music have an uncanny humanity, like an impassioned monologue from a restless phantom. One moment it is whispering in my ear and the next retreating into distant mountain desolation beyond the Khyber Pass. It has always sounded like a soul reliving a tumultuous life of joy and pain. The ghost of George inhabits the music and fills the little room. I say to him,

'You survived! We are here, and we were there. I exist because of you.'

I look at the silver bowl on my desk. It has turned once more and Lakshmi is in the pose of a dancer. She has a knowing gaze. She knows that George also paid his rupees to the doorkeeper at Heera Mandi but took a different turn on the way out - that he was joined in an upper room for a sinuous dance in which he was an intimate partner.

'Don't you regret walking away?' Lakshmi says to me.

I have no answer. When I got home to Suffolk, I talked to my mother only of the lack of evidence for our client and the failure of the work. I never mentioned Heera Mandi.

George, however, in his twenties, was eager for a soft caress. His brief interaction had little consequence for him, but who knows what result for a dancer of Heera Mandi. Lakshmi knows. She knows that I share a morsel of DNA with a family which now resides in Bangalore, Dubai, and Birmingham, and whose members are as ignorant of me as I am of them.

'You're imagining,' I say to Lakshmi, horrified at her leap into a whole new story.

'Am I?' says Lakshmi.

'But what about the archives, the history?' I am indignant. The scaffolding I have so carefully erected is being pulled from beneath me as I write. 'There is no evidence for any of this!'

'Cling to facts if you want to,' she says, 'but you must learn to do without. Archives do not define your life. Look within yourself. Look outside.'

Her eyes close, she becomes still, and I will get nothing more from her this night.

I wanted to unravel a personal detective story, such as I have spent my working life doing for others. I wanted a straight line of cause and effect which would lead, without too many detours, directly to me, now, and would help to explain me to myself. I wanted a journey of exploration where the end was assured, there was little personal jeopardy but a tidy piece of research to leave for another generation. It is not to be. I need time to understand where all this is going.

Help me, George. Tell me your story.

# 16: We Come Home

## 1855/1976

When folk hear as how I were in India, they alus want to know what it were like.

'Were you in the Mutiny, George?'

'Did you fight the Afghans, George?'

'Did you see tigers, George?'

I give 'em a bit of a smile and turn away. I tell them nothing. Best to keep your secrets, I find. Answer one question and you just get asked another.

There are stories that play in my mind over and over. I never saw real fighting, but there was always something to fear. Cholera was the worst killer, but there were snakes, scorpions, and other insects such as you've never seen (and I couldn't name). On guard duty, you were on the alert: some Pashto with a knife could do for you and be away before you'd time to call out. Always there was the heat so that your uniform was soaked with sweat and rubbed the creases of your body into open sores. No-one in Ipswich wants to hear any of this, so I've got one story that I tell the youngsters, just to keep them off my back.

There're these huge birds - greater adjutant cranes, standing anything up to five feet tall. They were scavengers of the dung heaps and refuse pits. They had massive bills. Each evening, when the bugle sounded to call the regiment to dinner on the verandas round the barrack square in Lahore, the cranes flew in. The men fed them scraps and they would eat anything, being especially partial to animal carcass.

'Tie a bone to a long piece of twine with a brick on the other end. Watch the buggers swallow the bone and then try to fly,' said someone.

It were really comical, seeing them birds hop and dance across the parade ground, pulling a brick and trying to get away. Flying upside down and sicking the thing up. Then another idiot bird would pick the bone up and try the same trick.

One day, some ass in the company filled a bone with gunpowder, stuck a fuse in the end, and lit it. The bloody bird snaffled the lot and, before it left the ground, its head and neck exploded and we was all showered with bits of gizzard. They stopped us teasing the birds after that. There's always some duzzy fule as goes too far.[115] I'll see that bird flying all over the parade ground and feel the bits of blood and flesh in my hair for ever now.

Some things - and they ain't often the most important things - your senses capture and they won't ever let you forget. You got this picture gallery inside your head and you can't turn it off, and it might reappear at any time (like I can see my mother and the snow and a man in a black hat, and I can see them women shouting at us outside the railway station in Ipswich, and James in fetters, and PC Bragg standing just a bit too close to me. It all comes back, and if I don't want to remember then it's best not repeated).

Within a year of its arrival in Lahore, the regiment was ordered back east. We marched to Allahabad[116] and then on to

Dinapore,[117] on the south bank of the Ganges, arriving sore-footed and with cankered necks. There we were largely confined to barracks. The enemy at the gates was cholera. It did for the locals, and we could see bodies floating down the Ganges, consigned to the water when there was no wood for the cremation ghats. The regiment prided itself that the epidemic was kept at bay (only one soldier died, and he was in another company), and some men said that it was a good thing the Indians had disease to fight and so many of them died, otherwise they might have been giving us trouble.

In the autumn of 1854, word went round that the regiment was to return to England, but at the same time a request was made for officers and men to remain in India. We'd have to transfer to the Forty-third or Seventy-fourth regiments, which were under strength. I couldn't make me mind up. India sort of gets inside you, and after two years there were times when I thought I might never go home, but more often I thought about my mother and my brothers and wondered what had become of them, and how it would be better if I didn't cut all ties. And what was I going to do about a wife? There weren't no prospect of meeting the right kind of woman out in India. (The wrong kind of women could be had for a rupee or less, but the right kind were out of reach for a private in the Ninety-sixth.)

We talked about what we would each do. Charles Edwards was all for going back. He'd been with the Ninety-sixth in Australia for five years before India, and the regiment had been in India nigh on six years.

'Time to go home,' said Charles. 'Eleven years away is enough for any man. Besides, if I go to another regiment, I'll lose my seniority and good conduct pay. Should make corporal any day.'[118]

'No future for me in England,' said Isaac Tyrrell.

We were sat by the Ganges as the day cooled. Ten times as wide as the Orwell back home, the river was. Slow and heavy, grey as lead, and secret as a grave. It flowed between low banks, and you couldn't tell where the land ended and the waters began.

We'd peeled off our jackets and trousers and sat on the sand, watching the birds seeking their roosts, and masses of flotsam pass by on the current. There were rafts of vegetation and logs, or perhaps they was crocodiles, or even bloated bodies what were dead from the cholera. It wasn't a pretty picture.

'I shall stay with the army in India,' said Tyrrell.

'What do you see in this place?' I said, 'Look at all the death and misery.'

'I can live like a duke here,' said Tyrrell.

'You can die before breakfast and feed the vultures by sunset,' I said.

'You'd have to join another regiment and start at the bottom,' said Charles Edwards. 'The Forty-third is all Welshman and the Seventy-fourth all Jocks.[119] I'm ready to see my service out, wherever the Ninety-sixth take me. What about you, George?'

'I don't know,' I said. There was a long pause. While I tried to make my mind up, another body floated past. A carrion crow had settled on its face and was pecking at an eye socket. The bird paused and gazed at me before returning to its feast.

'I reckon I'm not much in favour of this India. Too close to death. Too hot, too dry - except for the monsoon, when it's too wet,' I said.

'And the smells,' said Charles.

'The dung of India smells much the same as the dung of Ipswich. But the disease and the snakes and the insects - I could do without them. You've always to be on your guard,' I said, and thought, *I don't understand these Indian people neither; can't read what they're thinking. Don't know what they're saying when me back's turned. I could never relax here.*

'I don't want to go back to England,' said Tyrrell, again.

'The regiment could be sent anywhere,' Charles said. 'We could be back here in a year. Just so long as it ain't Crimea. They're bound to keep us in England or Ireland for some months, and the Russkies will be done with by then.' [120]

We went to and fro like that for days, but finally Tyrrell volunteered for the Forty-third while Charles and me stayed with the Ninety-six and looked forward to the boat back to England.

After some weeks, we embarked on flat-bottomed barges, pulled by steamers, to drift down the Ganges to Chinsurah. Life were easy for a few days, watching the wide plain pass by on either side, though it were sweltering and the canvass shades we rigged didn't do much good.

'What was it all for, Charlie, coming to India?' I asked Charles Edwards, as we lay in our undergarments on our sweaty, vermin-infested mattresses, crushing the ticks between finger and thumb.

'We done no fighting,' I said.

'"cept these lice,' said Charles.

'We marched up and down and dug camps and emplacements. We didn't conquer nothing.'

'We flew the flag, George. We never let them forget who was in charge. And thank the Lord we're getting shipped out before the locals decide to do something about it,' he said.

When we got to Chinsurah we were in barracks again. More guard duty and marching up and down in the sweating heat. More loafing around. We were twenty miles north of the port of Calcutta, and the word was every day that we were expected to board the transport home.

Some of the lads found that you could escape at night through the women's jakes and make free with all the pleasures of the town.[121] I didn't go. I lay on my charpoy and remembered the scent of the spice markets and the dark alleys of a summer night in Lahore; of the blind doorway of Heera Mandi, where jasmine-fragrant skin was so delicate it seemed to melt. It was one good memory out of three years or more, and I didn't think I wanted to spoil it.

I enjoyed the town during the day when I had a pass out. I knew we were going home, so each visit somehow seemed to take on more meaning, as though I was trying to capture memories. The bazaars were exciting, the ways different trades clustered together, jostling for space and custom. There were stalls with mountains of bright spices, there were fruits and vegetables which I knew I'd never see again, and, round another corner, there were trestle tables piled high with brass and copperware.

Most enticing of all were the silversmiths on the road to Ballygunge. I could hardly believe that such riches existed among the chaotic squalor. You could just walk up and handle precious items which might have been manufactured yesterday or shone for a hundred years. My fingers could wander over their intricate carving, feeling the different textures. The large pieces were not for me: too grand. I preferred the smaller pieces which made me look closely to uncover their secrets.

I remember one workshop and its jumble of wares. Among them there was a small, three-legged bowl which fitted neatly in the palm of my hand. It had six panels, each with a goddess figure - the same goddess - in different poses. A dancer, I thought, like in Heera Mandi. She looked at me with sharp, silver eyes, challenging.

'Lakshmi,' said the silversmith. 'She will bring you good luck. Much fortune, sahib.'

I laughed. I was drawn to it, but what would I do with it? What a fool I would look with a delicate silver bowl in my knapsack, even if I could afford to buy it.

'I give you very good price,' said the silversmith. That was what they always said.

I smiled at the man, but I wouldn't start haggling. For a few seconds longer, I allowed my fingers to explore the pretty thing before putting it down amongst the piles of precious goods. Someone else would buy it eventually.

I turned, held up my hands to show that I hadn't filched anything, muttered, 'Thanks, matey,' and walked away, though looking back as if to suggest that I might return. The silversmith had already turned to busy himself with something inconsequential, as if no sale was only to be expected and of no consequence, though I am left with another picture which doesn't fade from my memory.

That were probably the last free moment I had in India. When I got back to barracks, I had to clean my kit and prepare for inspection before the regiment marched down to the harbour. I wasn't loaded down with mementoes as some of the other men were. I had a couple of brass coins of little value, but mystically engraved, which I kept in my pocket for years - don't know what happened to them - and a thin silk scarf which eased the pressure under my uniform collar and was easily concealed from inspection. I don't need things to remind me of India, because everything is locked in my head and it comes to mind when I don't want it to. India is not somewhere I belong, just a phantom thing.

Then again, where did I belong? The Ninety-sixth would have to do.

In December 1854, George, and that portion of the regiment not remaining in India, boarded *The Bride of the Sea* and sailed into the West. The journey to the Thames took more than three months.[122]

One hundred and twenty-one years later, I was in Pakistan, following in George's footsteps without realising it. When I set off for home, I boarded a PIA Boeing 747, and was in England within a day, arriving in a tumultuous thunderstorm on the day that the great drought of that year finally broke. I returned to my archives and lay aside adventure, except in my imagination.

George and I were both much changed by our time in India/ Pakistan. He did not seek excitement but, when it crossed his path, I detect a new confidence in his response. George had grown up. I remember the music of Lahore and the scent of spices on the stifling evening air. I stored it away and it was sufficient. There is world enough in the archives. I have rarely travelled abroad since (turbulence doesn't suit me).

Until now. Lakshmi and Heera Mandi do something to the fabric of time. I had thought that time was a thing of dates, clocks, and spreadsheets, progression from past to present: one the building blocks of the other, and both laying foundations for the future. Samuel begat Keziah begat George, and so on, until it reaches me. If our stories overlap, they do so in an ordered way, charted by records of birth and death.

Now I find that George has not died. His Indian army experience changed him, his destiny, and his family. He is born again, if only to me, and I cannot live without him. I have a stake in his story, which I feel compelled to tell because it is my story, too. Each time I pick up the silver bowl, some fragment of its history unbalances me.

'Find the rest of the history and write it down. That's the only way to settle,' says Lakshmi.

From England, the Ninety-sixth Regiment travelled quickly onwards to Ireland where it formed part of the Dublin garrison.[123] George was still with Charles Edwards.

# 17: George in Ireland

## 1855-1862

When I took the Queen's shilling, I'd had enough of things never being quite certain. I reckon that trouble had looked me out and I wasn't about to go looking for it myself. It's an odd thing to say, but I reckon I thought the army was safer than Ipswich: that I'd be better protected. I should think, looking back, as how Charles was part of that protection, being more like an older brother to me than James or Alf had ever been. We listened to each other and helped each other when it came to solving them pesky problems with people which I suppose we all have.

I knew Charles had a plan, too - something I'd never had. By April 1855 (when we were in billets in Dublin), he'd been in the regiment for thirteen years and knew that he'd no more than eight left.[124] He was worrying away at his future. He was nearly thirty-four, had three good conduct badges and the pay to go with them. He was a corporal now, and knew he'd likely get to sergeant. He might not be the handsomest man in the regiment, but he stood tall and strong. I said to him, 'Get married, lad, while you've still got your legs and we're close to home.' (I'd seen too many wives, sometimes whole families, buried in an Indian cemetery.)

Still, he was in some doubt as to how to go about it until I said, 'You could do worse than one of these Irish girls. You seen that lass as serves in *The City Arms*? She's sure seen you.'

Very quickly we had become regulars there, and, by the early summer of 1855, Charles took up with Maria, who was behind the bar and was the daughter of a local policeman. She was twenty and dark, but with the greenest eyes, and she was smart and nicely spoken. Her father and Charles got on well from the start: two men who understood a bit of discipline and order.

I said to Charles, 'If Maria won't have you her father will, for sure.'

For two or three months, things went well, and there was soon an understanding between Charles and Maria. However, there's nothing certain with the army, and at the beginning of September we had orders to up sticks and march the thirty miles to The Curragh. The army had built a new camp with wooden barrack blocks out in the desolate heath, and the rumour was that we were there for training for the Crimea.[125] So, no sooner was Charles engaged to Maria than they were parted.

I was sorry for him, but I soon became even sorrier for myself, 'cos I went down with the most fearful fever. I'd suffered it a bit in India; hot sweats, pains in the stomach, and dreadful squits that made you double up, and once the crisis passed you lay on your mattress, weak as a baby, and shivered. So it was for me, at the start of 1856, at The Curragh.

'Too much porter last night,' said Charles, laughing at me, but he knew what the matter really was. 'You're all over yellow. Let me help you to the sick bay.'

I was sore bad for a week, with Charles looking in on me twice a day, and when the worst was past, I was as weak as a kitten and my head was full of wool. I couldn't think straight at all and sleep was no good. I'd strange nightmares full of horrible beasts. I could see bodies floating on a great river, crocodiles opening their jaws at me, and giant birds exploding. There were black courtyards between high buildings and no way out. I cried out in the night and gave everyone a start. They kept me in the base hospital for days and gave me laudanum. By the end of January, I thought I was going mad. I knew I had to get out of there.

Early one morning, I pulled on my trousers and boots, slipped back to the barracks for my greatcoat, and walked out of the camp. I had no idea where I was going except that I had to get away from them beasts. Whenever I closed my eyes they came at me, so I slipped away across the heath before the sun was properly up.

Don't ask me where I went. I walked until I found a country lane. I turned the way that seemed the easiest until I tripped and fell. I climbed the bank at the side of the road and sat with my head drooping on my chest. A carter going towards Dublin picked me up and I climbed amongst his baskets of vegetables and bales of straw, where I lay and shivered. We must have joined the main road, but, well before the city, he turned aside.

'That way to the packet steamer,' he shouted, and left me as the dark of night closed around me. Perhaps he thought I had a pass to go home to England. I could hardly stand or walk. The best I could do was huddle in a hedge, curled up and shivering. I hoped to sleep but feared to close my eyes because of the night terrors and the killing cold. I truly wondered if I'd see the dawn.

I know that I rose and walked onwards before the sun was up. I walked all day, and by nightfall I was in Dublin. I found a poor inn where I could buy stew, bread, and stout, and they had a bed I could share. I slept in my greatcoat with my purse hidden inside my shirt. The following day (I think), I set off again, further into the city, but I needed to avoid the barracks and the police 'cos I knew I'd have been missed at roll call and they would have sent messages on to Dublin, expecting me to try to get back to England. I'd have been stopped at the docks.

I had no wish to go to Ipswich in the state I was in, and I couldn't go back to The Curragh where I'd be flogged and imprisoned. I hid in back streets, away from the city centre. Days passed. Sometimes I felt strong, and the fever left me, but sometimes I know time went by without me reckoning it. I couldn't have told you whether I'd been absent for three days or a week. I turned my coat and trousers inside out so that I looked like a tramp (and there were plenty of us about) and not like a soldier. I found the warm places to rest at night, like the back of bakeries where you might even find a stale loaf to eat, and I made the few shillings I had last as best I could.

After some days, I felt the fever had passed, and though I wouldn't say the nightmares were gone, I could get a few hours' sleep without waking in horror. I suppose the laudanum was all out of my system as well as the illness. Then I came across a brick yard which was another warm place to be at night and because I knew the trade I got some day work and enough money to spend the night in a lodging.

It came to a Sunday night, and I'd been absent for three weeks. I found a bar to drink in and began to think about what to do. Try to escape to England? I was likely to get caught going on or off a ship. Try to lose myself in Ireland? But it felt a mean, low place.

There was little work and even the Irish were leaving to go abroad.

So, go back to the Ninety-sixth and face the punishment? The country was at war with Russia and if I were away for more than a month then the charge of 'absent without leave' would become desertion. What might stop them from branding me, or transportation, or worse?[126]

I needed a friend to help me, but the only friend I had, Charles Edwards, was back in the camp. The bar I was in had become noisier as I sat and contemplated my fate. The glass of stout in front of me wasn't helping any. Then a couple of local policemen marched in. I hid in my corner and hoped they wouldn't see me while I watched them out of the corner of my eye. They stood at the bar and surveyed the scene but it didn't seem they were looking for anyone in particular. They talked quietly with the landlord and enjoyed a drink. Their presence made me think.

I did have a friend in Dublin, or at least someone who I thought would treat me fair and give me good advice: PC James Malone, Maria's father. He'd tell me what to do, I was sure of it. Maria would speak up for me, if only for her Charles's sake. Suddenly this seemed to be my only hope; I couldn't think of anywhere else to turn. I wondered how to tackle it. Not tonight, I thought; it's too late on a Sunday evening. But tomorrow I would smarten myself up and go to his house before dinner time and hope to find both James and Maria at home.

When I knocked at their door Malone himself answered. For a moment he couldn't work out who it was:

'By the Lord, George!' he exclaimed. 'What ails you? Come in my boy. Maria! Get this young man coddle and boxty.[127] He looks half dead!'

It was only then that I realised that the mark of illness and rough sleeping must still be on me.

'My God, George,' she said. 'You're green and white like a leek. What have they done to you?'

Malone pushed me into a chair at their table and Maria brought food and drink. Piece by piece I explained what had happened and, when I was done, James Malone said,

'It's a mess, right enough, George. Every day you stay away the punishment will get worse, and the more difficult it will be to go back at all.'

Then we talked about the alternatives, like trying to hide away in Ireland and taking on a new identity, but everything seemed worse than going back and facing the music.

'I'll help you, lad. Tomorrow morning we'll go straight to the Royal Barracks in the city, and I'll explain that you are giving yourself up and that you have been grievous ill and not in full command of your faculties, but that you want to go back to the regiment. And you'll stand up straight and look smart.'

'Anyone looking at your scrawny, yellow features will see you've been very ill,' said Maria.

Malone was good as his word. At the barracks we presented ourselves smart and early and I was taken into custody. It was 28th of February and I'd been away for twenty-nine days, they said. I was put in handcuffs and carted back to The Curragh.

'District Court Martial,' said the adjutant. 'You've been away too long for me to deal with you. And you took your uniform and boots.'

So, a few days later, I was in court, and, though there was folk as spoke for my previous good behaviour and for my sickness, they sentenced me to fifty-six days in prison and took away all my pension.[128]

'You're very lucky, lad!' said the sergeant. It didn't seem like it, but I did feel somehow as if I'd come home. I wasn't flogged or branded, as could have happened, and though the work was hard the food was better than we'd been getting in the barracks, and, gradually, I came to feel more myself again.

By the end of April, I was back in Dublin because the regiment had finished training at The Curragh and been sent back to the city. So I was with Charles and he was with his Maria again. We sort of picked up where we'd left off four months before, though every day we expected to be told we'd be off to Crimea.

The order to move finally came in the middle of July, and it was not for Crimea: we were to be the Gibraltar garrison! No fighting, though some of the men complained they weren't getting a chance to have a go at the Russkies, and others that we'd be away from home for years again. Of course, that put Charles in a frenzy over Maria. Within the week, he'd been to the adjutant, and, being a corporal with good service, he was given permission to marry her. What's more, she could be 'put on the strength,' as we say, which meant the army would pay for her to travel with the regiment and for the two of them to live in married quarters. So, there was a wedding to be organised, and three days later Charles and Maria were in church, and for three days more we had one great party!

The Malones knew how to party. PC Malone put money behind the bar, and most of the lads from the station house dropped in at some time that afternoon, and that evening, and the next day. Malone lived only a few doors up Prussia Street from *The City Arms Hotel,* which itself was next to the old Jameson's distillery. This was a party that seemed to fill the whole street for days and days.

The Ninety-six was not to be found wanting either. They must have taken it in shifts. They were there to see Maria and Charles to the bridal suite and they were there to cheer the blushing Mrs Edwards the following morning, and the morning after that. I missed my roll call on the 24th, and the following two days, and was duly arrested again, but then so were several of our mates and the punishment was not severe.[129] In any case everything was at sixes and sevens as we prepared for embarkation. On 30th of July we marched down to Kingstown Harbour and boarded the steamship *Cleopatra.*[130]

I saw less of Charles once we got to Gib, him being allowed to billet out of the camp, but come the autumn, things took a nasty turn for me again. By the middle of October, I was all a shiver, and for a few days I was the hottest thing in Gibraltar. 'Malarial fever,' said the surgeon. 'Souvenir of India. Touch and go, but he's a strong young man.' I was in hospital for six weeks, and as shaky as a leaf when I first returned to the living. Charles and Maria were good to me. Maria brought me her special stew, saying she had to fatten me. I was on light duties but, soon after Christmas, I picked up a chill. I was in hospital from January to March and began to think I'd never see England again. When I finally came out, I looked like a ghost, so Maria said. Malaria's a bastard thing and keeps turning up when you least expect it. You may never quite shake it off, regardless of the quinine or Warburg's tincture.

Charles used to say that that's what did for my army career. I might have been a twenty-one-year man like him, and made the sergeant's mess, which is nonsense of course - I were never cut out for giving orders. From then on, I was always afraid of the unexpected weakness striking me down.

After Gibraltar - we was there for nearly a year [131] - Crimea was over and it was home service for the Ninety-sixth: the Isle of Wight (Charles and Maria's first child, James, was born there), Aldershot, Plymouth, Manchester, and back to Ireland, which Maria was delighted to see once again.

In 1858, Charles had finally got his sergeant's stripes, and a couple of years later, when, as ever, we were short of men, he was sent recruiting. Detached from the regiment, it was an easy life as long as he convinced the starving poor, late prisoners, and masterless men to put their mark on paper. The other benefit was that he could return to his native Norfolk and finally think of a permanent home. He took this little place in Thetford.

Best of all, he could select a man to go recruiting with him, and he chose me. I'd had a change of fortune all right. My illness had not come back for a couple of years and all those nightmares and sweats seemed to have gone. I knew the ropes of soldiering and we'd had so many new recruits, including some very young fellas, that I was often nursemaiding. I got the first of my good conduct badges, which was a bit of a turnaround after my time in prison in Ipswich and The Curragh. I'd even learnt to read and write after a fashion. So, there I was, living with Charles and Maria and set loose to parade around Norfolk with Charles, both of us in our finest uniforms, sounding off about our adventures and the fine life to be had in the Ninety-sixth.[132]

We were recruiting in Norfolk for near enough eighteen months. I never travelled south, never saw Ipswich during that time. Something kept me away. The voice in my head said, *You're happier than you've ever been, George. Don't do anything to disturb it. Go back and the tentacles of the place will grip you again.*

Now, you could say that George Sparham had had the easiest life the army had to offer. You'd be wrong, of course, because no life lived in Her Majesty's service is easy. If you're lucky you've got good mates, like Charles and me was - fellows that you can rely on, but the rest of the time it's hard beds and harder discipline, short rations, and long hours in all weathers in all parts of the world, and always at someone else's beck and call. But it is true that I'd not yet faced the cannon's mouth. The nearest I'd come to death was a brush with all the creatures and fevers that India, that vile cess pit, had to offer.

So, we was congratulating ourselves on missing the Russians and the Hindoos,[133] when the Americans started to fight each other.[134] To put it simply, our Canadian colony[135] was at risk from all these fighting Yankees. The masters in Whitehall were of the opinion that, having lost the major part of America eighty years before, they weren't about to lose the rest, so the army must be sent once again to defend it. This time it meant the Ninety-sixth mobilised for war. 'Come back to The Curragh and prepare,' they said to us, living our quiet Norfolk life. We packed our kit and, with a small band of our newest recruits, returned across the Irish Sea, leaving Maria and the child behind. That was a hard leave-taking, and so much harder for Charles.

September 1861. According to the newspapers we was to go across the sea immediate, but of course there was hanging around waiting for equipment and for ships to be procured, so, rather than being snug with Maria and her cooking, Charles and I was living in barracks and taking the occasional pint with the in-laws in *The City Arms* and hoping to God that if we didn't drown on the voyage or freeze in the wilderness we'd do our duty and live to see home once more.

Christmas Eve, 1861, in Dublin, not a one of us but was thinking holiday and family, yet we were formed up for a six-day march in the rain. Twenty miles or more a day. A final night at Fermoy, and then quick sharp to the port of Queenstown, which the locals call Cove.[136] It was impossible to get warm and dry. A gale had been blowing in from the Atlantic for days and the harbour was full of shipping. All the talk among the seamen was of the impossibility of braving the ocean at that time of year. I had a gaze at the local newspaper which listed the ships that had been fighting the storm. It also had a useful letter from a traveller telling us how impossible it was to travel anywhere in the great freeze of a Canadian winter.[137] Otherwise, it was just news of how the great in our countries couldn't determine the American future and how we soldiers must pay the price.

It was a few days after Christmas that the regiment embarked, having first become soaked to the skin as we piled into our little cutter to take us across the bay to the shipping lines, lugging our over-full kitbags up the side and down below as the rain whistled in horizontal. Charles and I sat in our exhausted state with our backs to a bulkhead, braced against the iron hulk, which was pitching to and fro, even at anchor.

Charles said to me, 'George, lad, if I don't get back, and you do, look after my Maria.'

'We're as like to go together, Charlie.'

'Swear.'

'Aye.'

We need say nothing more.

We were set to sail late on 30th of December. We were on the *Victoria*, a screw steamer, newly refitted, they said, and with two tall masts. I said to one of the tars, 'We're all right then, mate, with both steam and sail.'

He laughed. 'You think so, soldier? Here we are full of coal and iron, guns and baggage, not to mention the human cargo. If the wind's against us, and the sails down, the engine ain't big enough to give us steerage way, and if the engine breaks down - as it will, the sails ain't big enough to blow us across this 'ere 'arbour.'

Now, I suppose you might have been on one of those pleasure cruises off Felixstowe pier. Well, this couldn't have been more different. First off, we didn't sail nowhere. We sat at anchor in that god-forsaken harbour for six days while the wind crazed through the barren rigging and a quarter of the regiment puked and groaned. That ship stank despite the fresh air blowing into every dismal corner. Finally, on the sixth day of the new year, the captain decreed that the wind had dropped sufficient for us to venture out to sea. Once past the headland, it was straight into the teeth of a westerly gale. The ship wallowed, the sails were furled, and we blundered on under straining steam, so slow that the same piece of land was in our view for hours.

'Told you,' said our friendly tar, with a grin which would freeze your waters.

For a couple of days, the weather improved, and Ireland fell away behind us, but, on the third day, the wind picked up again. Spray and rain drove us from the decks.

'It'll pass by nightfall,' said Charles. It didn't. Each squall was replaced by a greater one. By the 13th of January we were in the midst of a hurricane. Remember, we'd been on this damned ship for a fortnight now. Tar said he thought we was no more than 600 miles from home, and at this rate we'd be aboard for three months. He seemed to be enjoying hisself, ribbing all us landlubbers as we retched and shivered.

The sea got up to such a state that no amount of steam could keep the ship straight. We clung to bunks and stanchions as the whole creaking mass of steel twisted and jumped like an un-broke horse. Baggage came loose and we could hear ordnance crashing in the hold, like to break through. Then we shipped water. We could hear huge waves breaking on to the decks. Next all the boats were ripped from their davits. Everything above our heads was being turned to wreckage and the din was horrible. I thought the thin bulkhead was about to be peeled back like bark from a rotten tree. Charles was huddled on the floor, hugging his knees, his face grey as the metal coffin we were entombed in.

'This is it!' he shouted, and other words I could not hear, as, with a shudder, the whole ocean descended the companion way and washed us across the deck. Charles and I ended in each other's arms, forced into a corner while the filthy, freezing water threatened to extinguish us at last.

Now, you're saying that I wouldn't be telling you all this now, and, indeed, you wouldn't be here neither, if we had gone that moment into the deep. Of course, we survived, but it wasn't through our own efforts: Providence, my friend, took us to the very edge of hell, and then preserved us, though He needed our help, too.

With the ship filling with water, one of the boilers was put out and the engine room flooded. With little power, the captain could barely keep the ship head on to the sea, let alone make progress. We fell into a trough and lay there. The hands pumped for all they were worth, and we did what we could to seal every place where the waters washed in. Then we waited.

Back in Norfolk, Maria had a great bible with an engraving of God blowing on the face of the waters depicted there. But this wasn't God's work. This was surely the Devil, and I thought of Noah and Jonah and the disciples on the Sea of Galilee, and I prayed like I never did before, and I gave myself up to His care, and we waited some more.

I said to Charles, 'You know, I lived my young life in the parish of St Clement, patron of seafarers. He ain't done much for me in the past, but I reckon it's time for him to come up to the mark now.' Charles sat in his own silent world, and whether he was praying or thinking of Maria and James or just blanking out everything, I wouldn't know.

After many hours, Charles said, 'The wind has dropped.' This time he was right. The tumbling was less and the mighty noise had subsided, but I had been too terrified, too taken within myself (if you can make sense of that), to have noticed.

Then we began to think whether everything was not lost after all. We had lasted a day and a night in that mighty hurricane and when we climbed from the depths and stood on the devastated open deck, surveying the boats and davits turned to matchwood and the great hatches torn from their fastenings, we saw the sun rising behind us in the east.

With frightening slowness, the captain turned the ship across the flattening waves, and we headed back the way we had come. Some sails were set and the boiler eventually relit. After nearly a week without a proper meal, the galleys were set to rights and the stoves lit so we got hot food again. Charles and I sat back-to-back against our bulkhead and, though the stew tasted of salt water and the bilges, we spooned it down in a rush and belched and laughed. Sometimes you just rejoice in being alive.

Three more days it took us to reach Queenstown once again. We had been sixteen days at sea in the face of constant storms and, when we got to harbour, did we get ashore, and did they throw garlands round our necks and parties in our honour? No. We sat at anchor for three days more, confined to our sodden berths on the sodden ship, while messages went back and forth between Queenstown and Dublin and Horse Guards requesting permission for this and chitties for that before officers and men could be released on to *terra firma*.[138]

If I had thought that that must have been the end of our Canadian adventure I still didn't know the Army and our London masters. 'Ours not to reason why,' as his Lordship wrote about another, recent military debacle. The Ninety-sixth was slated to go to Canada and go to Canada it must, regardless of the state of the weather or the ships, or even the need. With us back in Cork, there was general confusion, with other regiments giving up their billets for us and moving back to Dublin and our officers charging round the countryside looking for forage for men and horses.

Four weeks we sat around and froze or marched around on empty stomachs just to stay warm. All the time, the fear of having to go back to sea hung over us. One day, Charles came across an old copy of the *Illustrated London News*,[139] a journal noted for its sympathy to the working man and knowledge of his condition (I jest), which wrote this about the Trent business (as they were calling this panic). He read it out to me:

> *'More than 10,000 men have been dispatched with extraordinary celerity, and it is gratifying to know that they have left our shores under circumstances which leave no doubt as regards their comfort and efficiency. The extra warm clothing, which has not been procured without difficulty, is of the best quality, and perfectly suited to the sharp winter the men will have to encounter. This extra clothing has in every case been so placed in the ships as to be accessible at any moment, and will be distributed to the men on the voyage should the weather be such as to require the use of sealskin caps and similar articles. The number of transports wholly chartered by the government is thirteen, all powerful steamers.'*

Perhaps it would have comforted Maria, had she read this piffle. Word came through that we were off again, back to the same 'powerful steamer' that had served us so well before.

'Couldn't you stay away?' said Tar. 'Don't you start thinking we'll get any further this time. If this ship gets to Canada, I'll be a Red Indian.'

'So where are the sealskin caps and the rest of the cold-weather gear?'

'You puddled?' he said, and sloped off to belay this or sling that, as sailors do. Charles and I made for our comfortable bulkhead and claimed the dry spot once again.

We set sail on 13th of February, and the weather was as stormy as ever and the hateful iron coffin slapped and slopped its way as bad as before. We were no faster than slow marching pace, the engine belching black smoke and straining like a broken cab horse while the westerly gale did its best to blow us back to Ireland.

We were about three or four days out, with a day to run to the Azores and fresh fuel and water, when the engine finally gave up the ghost. The throbbing in the guts of the beast ceased and the wind cursed through the rigging. Soon after, it seemed to me that the ship sat lower in the water, and now we were in a cart with the horse dead between the shafts and sinking in the mud.

'What now?' I asked Tar.

'There's water in the boiler room, coming up through the bilges, and the boilers are out, again,' he said.

'So, what now?'

'We got no steerage way, so we'll topple over in the next sea that hits us broadside, or we sit here till we die of thirst, or some other poor fool comes along and takes us in tow.'

'So, what ...?'

But he'd stomped off, and all of us of the Ninety-sixth were left to contemplate our fate. It's all very well for a soldier on land where you know that, at the last, you can take the course of things in your own hands. You don't sit around waiting to die unless your officer commands it. But this sea is one unnatural element. I was helpless as a new-born, and Charles and I sat contemplating the great hereafter and deciding that, if there was a choice, we'd rather drown than die of thirst. And if that sounds like bravado, we may have said such things to keep our spirits up, but I was frightened sick. My stomach turned over and Charles said to me, 'Don't forget to breathe, George.' I think I must have been holding my breath, waiting for the waves to break over us.

One of our officers appeared with an instruction to stand to and a command to follow the orders of this young engineer officer, Lieutenant Ardagh. Now you normally slip away fast when an engineer officer appears 'cos it usually means digging or building or some other unsoldierly activity where you break your back and skin your knuckles only to discover that all your effort was for nothing at all. But this man said that it was either follow him or drown, so off we went to the bowels of the ship.

It was dreadful night down there. The water had risen into the bunkers, so the coals had turned to liquid blackness, and every man and machine was one black, too. The whole dismal scene was illuminated by a few lamps and candles throwing hellish shadows. You could taste the air, and I can feel it in my throat and nostrils still; you could have drowned in it sooner than breathe. Because the boilers were out, the pumps were being driven by the hands, but one by one the pumps were failing, choked by the coal slurry. What was most terrifying was that we could feel the deck tilting under us. The more water came in the more it flowed towards the back of the ship. We were going down by the stern.

'Right, lads,' said the cheery engineer lieutenant, who seemed to be enjoying this seventh circle of the hereafter like he'd paid handsomely for the privilege and intended to get his money's worth, 'If we're to get to the Azores we must empty the shit out of this bathtub by hand. There are buckets and to spare. You make a chain right up the companion ways and you keep filling and lifting and pouring over the side until this deck's as dry as Delhi, and then we relight the boilers and we chug along fine. Now get to it!'

Well, there didn't seem to be any other option, and we could already feel the freezing mud arising further up our thighs, so we started. And I must tell you that that was perhaps the finest action I have ever seen the Ninety-sixth engaged in.

Every man worked together and knew his place. The *Victoria* may have been the deadest of machines, but we moved better than a well-greased pump, and soon we could feel that the water was no longer rising. It was still coming in, though. For every bucket we sent up, half a bucket came in from somewhere beneath our feet.

'We must have sprung a leak.'

'Someone's pulled the plug out.' And, daft as it seemed, that was pretty much what had happened.

That was when Sergeant Charles Edwards became a hero, and I was proud to be at his side. There were some of the men who seemed to lose all heart, but he and I bent our backs and set up a rhythm like a steam hammer.

Waist-deep in the nastiest slime, Charles took a bucket, filled it, and lifted it up to me. And he didn't do it once, or for ten minutes or just an hour. He was relentless, so that the men above us in the chain were shouting 'hold on George and let me catch a breath,' but 'No time for that unless you want it to be your last,' was all Charles had to say. And do you know how long this went on? Four and a half days.

Every once in a while we changed the teams over, but if we got an hour's rest in four we were doing well. Stale water and rum, stale bread and bully[140] were our only refreshment, and always Charles was first back on the chain gang, with me just behind him. We was black from head to toe, like fairy-tale imps, with eyes glistening in the darkness, our black beards set like stone and our wiry bodies dipping and twisting, lifting and swooping, in and out of the shitty, liquid coal. Charles was an inspiration to us all, and I think I did not let him down. It seemed to be the action Charles had been born to.

Little by little the level of the water fell. After three days, the great hearths of the boilers were emerging from the flood. The stokers lit kindling to dry the fire boxes and men were sent to find any dry wood in the ship, smashing tables, chairs, and the officers' bunks.

Fire breeds fire in even the dampest place: the more heat dried the coals, the more coal burned. First one boiler then another smoked and spat into life. Six hours after the first flame had been coaxed from the tinder, there was enough heat in the boiler to raise a little steam. The fire cheered us all - a sign of hope, but Charles and I just went on filling buckets.

'We ain't going anywhere yet, lads,' said Charles, and he was right, of course. If the bailing stopped for a moment the waters rose once more, and it took hours more for the steam pressure to move a piston and turn the great propeller shaft. Only then did we feel the beast shake itself and grumble. It was a great body brought once more to life, and we were in the heart of it. The chains which moved the rudder crashed and we knew that the captain was finding steerage way.

Painfully slowly the ship came round to head into the wind. Now we were not a leaf bouncing in a stream but a leviathan under the control of a mighty tail. And as fire made fire and steam built in the pipes, we knew the brute was moving.[141]

It was another day before we made landfall at Horta in the Azores. On the evening of 28th of February, 1862, four hundred men emerged onto the quay and, like the black angels of the Bible, we fell to solid earth.[142] Some kissed the ground and others just sat in exhausted silence. We knew we had won our freedom from certain death, and Charles and I laughed and cursed and lay on our backs. We ran down to the scrap of sandy beach and sluiced each other down in the sea which had suddenly become our friend and comforter.

Charles should have got a medal for helping save us all, but the Army don't award nothing for staying alive, believing, I suppose, that life is reward enough.

This is just about the end of the story. We spent six days in the Azores while they made the ship seaworthy again and then we all sailed back to Plymouth, the War Office having discovered that there was no threat to Canada after all and we could go home and sleep safe in our beds. I think I hardly slept the whole voyage, feeling that if I didn't stay on watch we might hit disaster once more. Charles, however, slept like a baby, and said afterwards that he dreamt the whole time that he was in the arms of Maria.

The regiment moved on to Shorncliffe, near Dover, and I

did then have a surprise. There was a letter from the War Office, written while we'd been waiting in Ireland for our second Atlantic cruise, to instruct whoever needed to know that all my stoppages and loss of pension were to be restored to me and that I was to get a second good conduct badge and pay.

The Army is a mysterious animal. I never discovered how that came about, but perhaps Sergeant Charles Edwards had put a word in someone's ear.[143]

For the next few months, we filled our time round the south of England, then in the summer I completed my ten years. I could have stayed in the Ninety-sixth, but Charles' time would be up within another couple of years, and I had begun to think that perhaps it was the moment to go back to Ipswich and see if I couldn't find myself a wife like Maria and settle in one place.

I talked to Charles.

'Should I go back to Ipswich, Charles? I don't know what I'll find.'

'Does it matter?' he said. 'You're a different man to that shabby youth I first met in Lahore. You carry yourself well, for all you're built like a bantam cock, and you take no nonsense. You've been schooled; you can write and read tolerable well. You've got your good conduct badges, and you'll get a good discharge. When you're back in Ipswich, and settled and have a wife, you can come to see Maria and me in Thetford - it ain't no distance.'

He painted a picture of the comfortable life he would have when he drew his pension, and I thought, *Well, it won't be so cushy for me*, but a woman like Maria to come home to would be a change for the better. And he was right that I would be a different man if

I went back to Ipswich.

In August 1862, that is just what I did.

I made another decision when I left the army. I'd been George Sparham of the Ninety-sixth, but in Ipswich I was Keziah Root's youngest boy, so from then on I decided I'd be George Root once more (most of the time, anyway). It was an easier name to sign than Sparham, too.

# 18: Peter's Inheritance

## Spring, 2022

It is April. I have been vaccinated again and feel more secure against the invisible invader. I have given Keziah and George such life as the witnesses, Lakshmi, and the documents offer up to my imagination. The Indian silver bowl still sits beside the computer, and I notice the scrap of paper placed inside it long ago by my mother: 'Belonged to Eliza Evans, née Ellis, whose husband had been in colonial service - lived Calcutta. b.1867 Southsea, sister of Gt.-Gt.-Grandmother.' I recall the satisfaction of finding Eliza and her soldier brother, Charles, living in Ballygunge in the 1890s.

Lakshmi is looking at me: she is in a forward-facing pose with her hands resting on her wide-spread knees. She seems to say, *Have you only just cottoned on? This is the moment I have been waiting for. Understand the connections. I am the link between Root and Ellis.*

'George saw you in a silversmith's and could not bring you back to England.'

'Poked, caressed, and rejected me. I had to wait another thirty years.'

'Please explain?' I say to Lakshmi. 'I don't know anything about this Eliza Evans, née Ellis.'

'So find out!'

She is right, and the story is at my fingertips. I'd already found the Eliza Evans who died in 1934. Now I discover a brief notice in the *Hampshire Evening* News which says that her executor was a man from Plumstead, and I know that that is the place where I last saw her siblings. More surprising is that the paper calls her 'a lady' and says that her estate is worth more than six thousand pounds, which would approximate to half a million today. No wonder she could afford to give a young girl, my mother, a silver bowl! She is rich beyond anyone else I have come across in this tale. Is this the inheritance I dreamed of as a child? Where did it all come from?[144]

To be doubly sure that I have the right person, I go to the government probate office website and pay one pound fifty to call up a copy of Eliza's will online. There can be no doubt. Since she had no children (the 1911 census tells me that), she makes bequests to distant relatives, including two hundred pounds to George's son - and my great-grandfather, George Lionel Root of Ipswich. Five hundred pounds was left to a nephew of his, Lionel Ford (whose name I remember, but don't recall ever meeting). Most of her wealth goes to friends I have never heard of, including, tantalisingly, 'Miss Elsie and Miss Pamela Johnson of Gun Carriage Factory, Jubbulpore, Central Provinces, India.' I have no idea who these maiden ladies are, but I am startled to be in India again. The balance of her estate – close to two thousand pounds, I estimate - she gives for the charitable works of the Woolwich Polytechnic Masonic Lodge.[145]

Not much money for us, then, but the will is, itself, an inheritance, and the information it contains will remain as part of my bequest to the future.

Here are the foundations for a hundred other tales. Like Eliza, I must find people who will benefit.

If I am to do that, I must establish the link between George Root and Eliza Evans, née Ellis. How do the families become connected?

# 19: George and Hannah

## Ipswich, 1862-68

'The foundry's fearful hot,' says George Root.

He is in *The Neptune Inn* on Fore Street, and into his second pint of Cobbold's.[146] Beside him is a regular companion, John 'Irish' Ellis, a sawyer with as big a thirst as George's. George has spent several years in Ireland, so it is natural that the two men have drifted into each other's company.

'Another pint, Irish?' asks the landlord.

'I oin't Irish!' mutters John.

'Ah to be sure,' says the landlord. 'And where was it you were born?'

'Athlone, alright, but that don't make me Irish. My pa was a proud Englishman!'

There was much merriment to be had from John Ellis, which he generally took in good part. Father an Englishman, maybe, but his mother (Catherine, née Dunn) was an Irish lass from Athlone: a princess descended from a chieftain whose family went back to the dawn of time, he said (though what she was doing living in Rope Lane and working as a charwoman he never could quite explain), and she'd gone back to the ancestral home to give birth to him.

'But I'm English. I am English,' he mutters, in his cups. 'English as any of yous Suffolk eejits …' as his head flopped back on the settle until he woke to his own snoring.

'English as any of yous, and I'll beat anyone who says otherwise.[147] Now where's me shillelagh?'

Yes, he could laugh at himself and make the room laugh with
him. He had a prodigious capacity for ale, and you only had to
worry when he 'went on a drunk,' as he put it. Then he was handy
with his fists and got into many a fight. He reminded George of
some of his Dublin friends.

The first time George saw him, Ellis had just come down
from a two-week bender and a visit to the magistrates' court. He
hadn't been up for being drunk and disorderly but because he'd
spent all his wages and left his wife and children to be supported
by the parish for two weeks.[148]

George and John became friends - the sort that fall into
each other's company whenever a thirst needs quenching, for
if a foundryman needs a drink then a sawyer, with his gullet full
of sawdust, needs two (so he says). They were of an age, though
John Ellis had crammed a wife and three or four children into his
thirty years.

'Got to look after your family, George,' says John Ellis.

'By putting them on the parish?' says George.

'I'm paying, ain't I? Annie don't go without, nor my mother.
Family's important. I've got responsibilities. But a man has a thirst,
too. And if I get lively they say, 'it's the Irishman' and lock me
up. No justice. Now, help yourself and help me out. Marry my
sister. Take her off me back and lay her on her own. She won't
disappoint.'

George says nothing in reply, but he can't pretend to himself
that he hasn't been attracted by the sight of Hannah Ellis, John's

younger sister. When he had taken John home, celebrating his release from prison with another 'drunk,' he had caught sight of the girl in the street. She lived with her mother, just round the corner from John's house in Alfred Street, and she must have been on the way home from visiting her sister-in-law and nephew and nieces. She glanced at the men over her shoulder, grimaced at the sight of her reeling brother, but gave George a small wave before she was gone. She was elfin: a slight body with a pointed chin and a few freckles, and the greenest eyes - like Maria Edwards. He had felt a shock, as if a fiery splinter from the forge had momentarily settled on his skin.

'Mebbe she'll walk out with me,' says George.

'She asked me all about you,' says John. 'Get on with it, lad, before some other beggar sees her. You been a lucky bleeder: ten years in the army and never fought no-one. Get yourself a wife and you'll find what it's like to meet the enemy.'

George doesn't rise to the bait. It's no use trying to explain to civilians what army life was like. No use trying to explain the dangers and the loneliness to men who could go home to a family every night. You make your bed and you lie on it. It could have been so much worse, he knows. Ipswich is a garrison town and there could be a dismasted man hanging around on any corner, rolled up trouser where a leg ought to be. George had all his limbs, his sight, and his hearing. The scars he did have were well hidden, and if there were days when the malarial fever came back and turned him inside out then he sweated and kept silent. He never wanted to be a hero, just survive. Maybe marrying Hannah Ellis wasn't such a bad idea.

Sunday afternoon, at the end of August, is still and hot. He bangs on the door of a house in a passageway off New Street, behind St Clement's church. It is an old building, much decayed, and the Ellis family occupy two rooms and a lean-to on the ground floor. The door is opened before George can rap a second time, as though he had been watched for, and when he walks into the small room it seems that the place is full of women. It is, in fact, only three: Catherine Ellis - mother and widow, charwoman and Irish princess, sits by the empty stove and, despite the heat of the day, is wrapped in blankets; Hannah is standing, coatless but with her little hat already in place, looking as though she can't get out of the room fast enough; beside her stands her younger sister, Sarah, gawping, pale and silent. A youth stands in the doorway to the back room. He mutters a greeting to George. He is Charles, Catherine's son and the man of the house (or so he sees himself, though he is only sixteen years old).

'Good afternoon, Mrs Ellis, Charles,' says George.

'You're away, then,' says Mrs Ellis without any further greeting.

'If Hannah is agreeable, I thought we might walk up to Christchurch and the Arboretum.'[149]

'I should like that, George,' says Hannah in a soft voice.

'Get ye gone, then,' says Mrs Ellis.

It is a steady uphill walk to reach the park. Hannah clings to his arm and he moderates his military stride. He suddenly feels so responsible for the slight girl by his side. It's different from being with men, he thinks: for a start, he has no idea what she is thinking, and he doesn't seem to have a way of asking her. Best just to walk on quietly.

Inside the park they stroll beyond the lake and find a grassy bank to sit on. The place is full of families out for a Sunday afternoon walk, children belting around, and married couples, arm in arm. There are parasols and smart straw hats, Sunday suits and polished black boots. George wonders what each man does: clerk and shopman, schoolmaster and doctor, each with his own dignity. And there are workmen like himself: men who have spent six days in noisy, smoke-filled factories or breaking stone and digging dirt but now determined to be seen at their best. George looks out on the scene and thinks, with a clarity he has rarely had before, *This is where I should be. This feels like home.* He looks at Hannah, who is observing everything with the same intense gaze as himself, and thinks, *And this is who I should be with.*

'I'd like a bonnet like that,' Hannah says, gazing at a woman who is just then walking past and wearing a straw hat with a large, upturned peak, deftly decorated with feathers.

'You'd look lovely in it,' says George, who then surprises himself by adding, 'You'd be the loveliest woman in this park whatever you was wearing.'

'Fool,' she says, but smiles and tilts her head away.

*That's done it, then,* thinks George. *No going back now.*

For a moment they sit in silence and George wonders what Charles Edwards and his Maria would think. He is sure they would be as pleased with him as he is with himself. When he thinks of Maria, he sees the tidy little house in Norfolk, and he is warmed by a sense of the comfort he witnessed there. He knows Charles and Maria would approve of Hannah, but his thoughts quickly return to the present. (There is no space for images of wild seas, baking Indian plains, or the music of sultry rooms.)

Once Hannah and George start to talk, it seems there is no stopping either of them. They talk of their work: the physical drudgery of his, despite the satisfaction of seeing sheets of metal turned into useful implements, and the delicate sewing she does as a stay maker. They compare their hands: Hannah lays hers across his and they examine the different places they each have callouses and cuts and she laughs as he folds her hands between his.

They talk of families, especially fathers.

'I was only eight when dad died,' Hannah says. 'He seemed like a giant - black hair and really big hands. Bigger than yours, George,' and she squeezes his fingers.

'I were fourteen or fifteen when my pa died,' says George, 'but he was away up in Bury. We never saw much of him. Bit of a lad, I reckon, but he was a sawyer and travelled for work. Died of a cancer gnawing at his guts. What did your father die of?'

'Pneumonia - and grief,' says Hannah. 'At least that's what Ma says.'

'How's that?'

'Did my brother John never tell you about Charlotte?'

'No, never.'

She is silent for a moment. George can see she is considering how to tell the tale. When she begins her voice is soft and distant.

'There were six of us to begin with: John, Charlotte, Isaac, me, Charles, and Sarah,' says Hannah. 'Isaac's gone to Ireland now, to our mother's family, for work. John, Charles, and Sarah you know.'

'So, who's Charlotte?' says George.

'Mother won't hear her name so don't you never let on I said anything. She broke our father's heart. It's what killed him.'

'How was that? Is she dead?'

'Probably. We don't know. She was a bad girl. Got caught time and again, thieving. She were only fourteen when they sentenced her to transportation to Van Diemen's Land. That were the year before Dad died.'

'I'm sorry,' says George.

'Don't make no difference to me,' says Hannah, suddenly defiant. 'I hardly knew her. It's one less mouth to feed. If she were going to come back she could have done it by now.[150] I 'spect she's dead. I hope she was sorry for what she done.'

George feels Hannah's tension and change of mood. He will ask no more questions. He realises that if he is going to marry this girl then he will be marrying her family and their ghosts too, and it's best to live by their rules, not upset the balance more than he already intends to do by taking Hannah from them. Ten years in the army have taught him to keep his mouth shut when faced with things he doesn't understand. Now is such a time. And how much of his own family history will bear scrutiny?

One day soon he will tell Hannah that his own brother was sentenced to transportation, though he never left British shores. He will also confess to his own prison record, and she will make light of it and remind him what a fine man he has become.

They sit on the bank for a little longer and then take a rambling walk back towards New Street. Hannah walks close to him.

He thinks he will save a sovereign and offer to buy her a straw hat in the latest style, and she will laugh at him, tell him not to be silly, the summer is past, but that perhaps she will save it for their wedding, when she will need a new dress.

It takes him less than three months to propose to Hannah.

She is six months beyond her twenty-first birthday, and he need ask no-one's permission, but anyway everyone seems happy enough. George finds them a room in John's Court, off Albion Street and close to the iron works, and close enough, but not too close, to Hannah's mother.

It is 30th of November, 1862, when they marry, and there is a sprinkling of snow on the ground. Keziah, his mother, is at the church, shuffling on a pair of sticks. She hardly knows where she is, and as she stands, solitary and shivering, by the church door, George has a sudden memory of her sitting in the snow with her hand out, and he is a little boy again.[151]

He quickly turns away, gazes at Hannah, and embraces his new wife.

Perhaps them was the happiest days I ever had. For the first time I had a room of my own to come home to and a wife who seemed to be as happy as I was. We looked after each other. I had that feeling of someone else who wanted me to be content, and I did my best to make her feel that way too. I know I'm clumsy and I didn't have much to say for myself, but I think she felt protected. I hope so. Sometimes I just wanted to wrap her up against the world and sometimes I was afraid to touch her, afraid she would break like fine china in my hard hands.

I can see us now, on a Sunday, walking by the river, Hannah's hand on my arm and her in her little boots and summer hat. We were a proper pair. All went on as before, but better. She sewed, taking in piece work, and kept our room so neat. She made new curtains and I bought a china vase for the silk flowers she would sew from odds and ends of material. I found us a second-hand bed and she embroidered little flowers at the corners of the sheets; they seemed like a love token. That autumn was the warmest I ever known in England, but when winter came, we could close the curtains and keep each other warm.

Perhaps you could say that our happiness was catching, because, within a few months of us being spliced, my brother James, who was six years out of the prison hulks, turned up in Ipswich with his woman, Sophia Thorndike, and their two children, to get married. He'd been in Cambridge, brick making, but was now a coal porter down the docks and living almost next door to us in Albion Street. Hannah and me were the witnesses to their marriage, and it were a marvel to be signing their certificate as 'Mr and Mrs Root.'[152]

I couldn't see Sophia and our 'Witty' staying together. He may have put his criminal ways behind him since he escaped the transport and hard labour, but he always seemed twitchy, disappearing for days at a time, and Sophia was a handful. When he was at home, she told him what's what, and when he was away, she did whatever she wanted. Within weeks of their wedding, they were off to Cambridge again, and I wasn't sorry to see them go. But Hannah and me was happy as a pair of cooing doves, as she said, and not too mindful of other people, especially not of my brother and the hussy, Sophia.

You wouldn't say our life was easy, not by the standards of today. There were always other people around and outside our little coop. Fore Hamlet was cold and dirty with a midden in the court and water from the well that was none too clean. The landlords cared nothing for the shoddy tenements they put up.

In the winter the soot mixed with the slime on the walls and we breathed in the staleness of it.

Hannah was never strong of body, though her will was fierce. It was more than two years before she gave birth to young George Lionel. I looked at the two of them and never felt such pride, like looking at one of them old bible pictures of Mary and Jesus with Joseph looking on. But even as I watched him feed from her it seemed as though he was sucking the life out of his mother. She was determined he was going to live (when it seemed half the babies in Ipswich died before they weaned).[153] We called him George Lionel: George after me and Lionel because Hannah said it meant he would be a lion, but there were days when I called him leech. Six months after the boy was born, her eyes were sunk and her chest heaved with a dreadful cough. She couldn't feed him any longer and sometimes she could hardly stand or feed herself. I watched her fade away, her skin becoming pale and thin, cracking like parchment, her breathing shallower, a constant cough. Then blood.

She died just before the boy's third birthday. How can you tell anyone else what it's like when you go from complete happiness and knowing that life is as full as it ever can be to an emptiness that hollows out your soul? She spent herself on me and then on our boy.

I was at the forge, beating out ploughshares, when the word came.

'Just you and the lad now, George,' they said. I hammered at the iron until the fiery metal was as bruised as me and I couldn't lift my arms above my head.

'Here's Mrs Squire with your boy, in the yard. Go home, man,' the foreman said. I pulled myself up, shoulder's back, and marched towards them, but all I could see was the space in between us where my Hannah ought to be.

It was Valentine's Day, 1868, when we trudged up the hill to the new cemetery.[154] The weather was mild and the coffin as light as if it were empty. I would have carried it alone, hugging it to me as on that day I should have hugged her, but of course I did as was expected of me and walked behind the bare cart with John Ellis, her brother, Mr Squire (the smith), and a handful of others.

The right things were said, and the sharp east wind was blamed for damp eyes. Then we drank, quietly, in a back room at *The Albion* and went early to our homes. I lay in our bed and George Lionel snuffled and twisted beside me, poor motherless boy, and dribbled on her fine embroidered sheets. He was too young to understand, and that was a blessing, 'cos what could I say? That nothing was ever fair. That whatever the curate said, there was no comfort to be had anywhere. That there was no sense to be made, not by men anyway, of the way the wheel turned. That just as you think you might rise, that you have kicked off the snow and ice you were born into and survived the brutal fires of India and the sinking sea of a cold Atlantic and come at last to a warm bed, that just as you think there might be kindness in the world, the wheel reaches the top and reminds you that it is time to fall.

I thought of the Hindoos and their acceptance of everything that came along and their belief that we come back in a new and better place if we have, like Hannah, done no harm. That we never cease. So I said to myself, I will tell the boy his mother has gone away to be the princess she was born to be. And one day she will be a queen, and then we shall see her again where she is waiting for us. And that is what I did say, and I began to believe it myself.[155]

Having sorted all this out in my own mind, I got on with things. There was work to do and a three-year-old boy who missed his mother. Maria Squire, the smith's wife, who had young children of her own and who'd been with my Hannah at her death, looked after him for ten days, but a man needs looking after too, and she had her own fellow. In any case, the answer was on my own doorstep.

I was living at 1 John's Court by the beginning of 1868, just back of the Orwell Iron Works where I toiled.[156] (It was grim, and the miasma there perhaps one of the reasons my Hannah died). At number 6 was Clara Elizabeth Southgate with her little daughter, Rose.[157] I'd known her man, another old soldier, before he died. Now here we were, widow and widower, with a small child each, and living hugger mugger. You wouldn't say it was a love match, not like me and Hannah, but it was convenient for us both and we knew we could get along if we didn't expect too much from each other. To do anything else would be to throw away money we didn't have. And over the years we found affection enough - enough to have two more children together.

Hannah had been in the ground less than five months when Clara and Rose moved into number 1 with George Lionel and me. Clara and I were married that July. I prayed for Hannah's blessing and told her it was all for George Lionel's sake, which were partly true.

Clara didn't need a protector. She was no piece of porcelain. She had a mind of her own. I liked to see her get on with things and I had few complaints. Most of the time my life was quieter than I had known up till then. Not so many ups and downs, though there were to be some surprises.

# 20: Peter, Lakshmi, and Clara
## Southgate

### August 2022

It is one of those unpleasant English summer days - too hot, too heavy, not sunny enough - and I am sitting at the computer, clueless. The Indian silver bowl has turned again, and Lakshmi is in a defensive posture - arms raised, and palms turned against me.

'What have you achieved so far with all your rummaging?' she says.

'I've got lots of facts I didn't have before. I understand the relationship between Root and Ellis, the reason why I have you in my hands! Eliza, who bought you, was Hannah's niece - daughter of her older brother, Isaac. My mother was right when she wrote that note she left in the bowl: you belonged to the sister of her great-grandmother! I'm enjoying the discoveries and filling in the gaps. I am surprised to find that I even enjoy the emotional ups and downs.'

'You enjoy!' sneers Lakshmi. 'Your father was right. What is the point of exposing all this family business? You have a pick and mix of facts and emotions, and you think you're explaining yourself by amplifying a few slender bits of information. Just accept that these phantoms are there and don't go digging for truths you can never know.'

'You're very hurtful,' I say, 'and you've changed your tune. I'm finding that sometimes distance from the events brings clarity.[158] And the people and their stories are changing. They aren't becoming much more prosperous, and they continue to be hit by one crisis after another, but they seem to be less ground down by it all; just a little bit more in control of their fates.'

'I don't know where you're going with all of this. You've yet to explain how you think these Ellises are important, except that Hannah gave birth to your great-grandfather. She didn't live long enough to bring the child up,' says Lakshmi.

'Harsh. The Ellises are important because their DNA and their history were passed down through Hannah and George to George Lionel and to his daughter, my grandmother, then to my mother, and eventually to me. And Hannah changed George. He was a different man, a different father, through having met her. As for you, you were seen by George in Ballygunge, you were left in a silversmith's shop and ignored, and then a young woman, Hannah's niece, bought you and brought you back to England where, not long before her death, she gave you to my mother. And I retrieved you from the sideboard in our dining room. Is that clear enough?'

'So where to next?' asks Lakshmi, slyly.

'I think,' I say, 'I have two important tasks. One is to complete the story of George, because I think the family tradition of hiding the truth is to be found with him. The other is to explore those Ellises. I said I was going to establish my inheritance for the next generation - all those descendants of James Ellis and Keziah Root. What happened to Charlotte, Hannah's transported sister? There is more to this family saga than merely following the DNA. As George realised, you don't just share yourself with one other person; you marry a whole family and all their history, known and unknown, too. Every time a new person turns up there's another carrier bag of odds and ends to be stored away before being passed on (should anyone want it or not). It's a wonder any of us can move for the luggage we're knee-deep in.'

I contemplate Lakshmi and her silver bowl.

'You're also a piece of my luggage. Don't forget that it was you who told me that we never cease, that death means nothing.'

I fondle the bowl and twist it again. One of the panels shows Lakshmi at her most agitated with all four arms in movement, her left leg raised and her right foot on tiptoe as if she is about to sprint out of the scene.

She says, 'So listen to Clara Southgate, George's second wife, and ask yourself what impact she had on the Root-Sparham-Ellis dynasty, of which you are an heir.' [159]

# 21: Matriarch, The Story of Clara Southgate

## 1836-1904

The first time I married, you would probably say it was for love, though in truth that was only part of the reason. The second time, when I married the widower George Sparham, it was entirely for reason. Experience is something you either suffer or learn from, and, in my case, I knew I had to learn from the past or live with my own stupidity. I may not have had much education, but I wasn't stupid.

The minister at the Tackett Street Congregational church used to say, 'Your lives have meaning. You must make a difference. What will you say to the Lord when he asks you what difference your life has made?'

His words have always stayed in my mind, and each week in church I look back and tell God that, with his strength and guidance, I have made a difference in this way and that. It hasn't always been plain sailing, but George and the children have prospered, and I give thanks.

I was the oldest of nine children. My earliest memories were of playing in the mud by the River Deben. Father, George Cracknell, was a boatman, and we lived at Ramsholt, next to the inn. Mother and father would do anything to earn a few pennies: she was a lovely seamstress and took in sewing; he would trade on his own account while he sailed barges up and down the river.

Every year or two, the tiny cottage became a little bit more crowded as my parents produced yet another daughter. By the time I was ten, there were five of us girls alive, with the first boy on the way. We children looked after each other. We were tough; you would wonder how we all survived, in and out of the water, roaming the fields and woods, but in those days every adult in the hamlet took it on themselves to look out for the children.

I remember we had friends, Lydia, Robert, and William, living next door. Lydia was the oldest of us all and bossed us. Down the lane, at the water's edge, was the shack where a young mother lived, with her four children that we weren't allowed to play with. I didn't understand what was wrong with them, but our mothers wouldn't have anything to do with that family, though perhaps it was different for our fathers.

When I wasn't out playing, mother was teaching me to sew, which seemed to come naturally to me, and by the time I was ten I was helping her.

Children these days don't know they're born, expecting everything on a plate without any effort.

When I was thirteen, mother had yet another baby (the one before had died), and she worried about all of us squeezing in to our two rooms. Five girls sharing a bed, with the baby in the cot - you can't imagine it these days.

My father saw an opportunity. He had much business in Woodbridge, just two or three hours up the river, and mother was doing outwork for Mr Samuel Cullingford, the linen draper, and his wife Anna, who was a milliner. They had a growing business in the Thoroughfare, and, before I knew it, I was an apprentice milliner, sleeping amongst bundles of cloth in the attic and bent all day at the bench.

The work was hard, but the Cullingfords were not unkind and there was always food on the table. Woodbridge seemed a vast town after Ramsholt, and I saw folk of every quality. The mistress had me learn to talk to her ladies (they were always ladies even when we knew they were not) and to be respectful.

Of course, millinery is a great competition for women. They wanted to know what the latest fashion in London was, even in our country backwater. Mrs Cullingford was always having to try new patterns, and, for those customers who couldn't afford a new hat, there was the latest colour silk or some fresh lace or a feather to be sewn in. I enjoyed the work.

Some Sundays I walked across the fields to Ramsholt to see Ma and Pa and all my little brothers and sisters - there was eight of them in the end, though by the time baby James had come along, father had set up in Woodbridge, dealing in anything he could find a market for, and my mother was dressmaking, which often also meant little pieces of work sent down by Mrs Cullingford.

I'd been in Woodbridge about six years when George Southgate came along. He was fresh out of the army, a Coldstream Guard. Tall and thin with a mix of pride and wariness, and a silky beard you could run your fingers through.

I loved him from the moment I saw him, despite his wound. He had an ulcer on his neck which made it impossible to wear the uniform and the army had got rid of him. They said it was none of their fault but, I ask you, how would a man who went fit into the guards, who served at the Tower of London, and who fought the Russians at Alma, come out after six and a half years with a weeping hole in his neck if the army hadn't done it to him?[160]

Bad food, lice, and starched collars is what caused it - that and sleeping on hard ground in the snow. He wouldn't talk about it, of course - just a quiet dignity and discipline. He went to work in the Ipswich brewery where his honesty and sobriety appealed to his masters, as to me.

I married him, and we moved into a tenement in John's Court in the town. It wasn't clean, not like I was used to, and it didn't help Southgate's illness, but I sewed and he brewed and we were happy.

I was only twenty when we married, and everything seemed possible. There would be children and perhaps we would set up in business and we'd dress ourselves well and Mr and Mrs Southgate would be people of note.

I suppose I don't need to say that it wasn't quite like that. As I tell the children now, it's much more difficult to get out of the mire than to wander into it. In Woodbridge, in a pretty shop and on the arm of a fine soldier, I was at the centre of the world; in Ipswich, in that dreary slum, cold and damp sapped all our joy and Mr Southgate became more and more frail.

Nor were there children - not at first. When my little Rose did eventually come along we'd been six years married, and I wondered then how many years it would be before she would be fatherless. My happiness withered into a sort of dread. When I became pregnant again in little more than a year, I knew that hope had given up on me, for Southgate wouldn't live to see his son.

There was one lucky chance. Another soldier and his new

wife moved into our court. George Sparham, or Root, had been a soldier too, and was much of an age with my George. They had soon become fast friends. Hannah, his wife, was a sweet little thing. Young, of course and, it seemed to me, a little lost. She wasn't strong and I had to put her right about a few things. They arrived not long after I'd had my Rose, and it was clear that Hannah longed for her own child.

Looking back, I find it difficult to remember exactly what happened when. I know it seemed like one calamity after another. First off - it must have been the summer of 1864 - Hannah and I both found ourselves with child. Both of us were trepidatious, though for different reasons. I didn't think my child's father would live to see the baby, and Hannah, with her hacking cough and shortness of breath, wondered whether she'd survive a birth. We held each other up during that autumn.

Just before Christmas, my husband, Southgate, died, and I followed his coffin with one babe in arms and a great bump under my thin coat[161].

There is nothing quite so desolate as a mid-winter funeral where the wind from the sea whips your skin and the sun sets almost before it has risen.

Hannah Root held my hand.

Then, within three or four weeks of each other, in the spring, our babies were born: two little boys, both called George after their fathers. It seemed then that we were almost one family with all the men called George.

We women did work as we could, taking in sewing, and minding two babies and our Rose, who by now was toddling everywhere and keeping us amused when she wasn't maddening us. George - Root, that is - worked harder than ever, and seemed to have taken responsibility for me, the wife of his old soldier friend, as well as his lovely Hannah. Babies are fragile bodies. Within the year my little George seemed to be giving up the fight and, come September of 1866, he died. Our little guardsman gone to join his daddy. I wept for them both.

Meanwhile, Hannah's George Lionel seemed likely to live, though a quiet and docile child. Hannah herself was fading before our eyes, and there were days when she passed her baby to me with a pitiable look in her eyes as much as to say, 'you've lost two Georges, but there are two more here I give into your care.' Or perhaps that was just what I wanted her look to mean. We lived cheek by jowl all this time and, little by little, there came to be no difference between my room and theirs, children in and out as they chose, and adults too. Hannah kept more and more to her fevered bed and George relied on me for his son's thriving, and for his own.

Little George Lionel was still only two when his poor mother died, but I think by then he already saw me as his ma. He never really missed the thin, white spectre as she faded out of his life.

Don't judge us. We made things work, and when George Root and I married within six months of Hannah's passing it wasn't more than an official seal on the ways that we had found together through our mire. Surely, we said to each other, this is the end of our troubles. But we also said it was down to us to make things change.

You could see the town changing. There were new buildings everywhere. Eventually we moved out of John's Court and had a house where we didn't have to share the privy.

Plough Street, where we moved to, might have been tucked between the brick works and the iron works, the air dusty in your mouth, and the place had its share of cheap lodgings with rough men who needed to be kept in their place, but we had our own yard, a window at the back, and a front step we didn't have to share with anyone. But for me it was what the children could get.

George Lionel went to a proper school. He was the first one, I think, to have real schooling in our families, and he was a good scholar.

His father wouldn't stand any nonsense, and the boy knew that if he got caned in school then he'd get it again at home; but, generally, he didn't need such encouragement, and soon enough we had a lad at home who knew his letters and could read the most difficult things out to us all. He took pride in his learning and in teaching his sisters, and I took joy in him as if he were my own flesh.

It wasn't always plain sailing. My husband's problem - and it became mine - was that his family kept turning up on our doorstep. George was the youngest one of four or five and they'd all been up to no good when they were young. 'Clara', he'd say, 'we had to stay alive. Our parents couldn't keep us, so what can youngsters do but thieve a little?' I'd let that pass, thinking that we Cracknells never would have done such a thing. Woe betide George Lionel if he ventured from the straight and narrow. At least George Root, his father, had been a soldier and learnt to pull himself up.

Which is not what you can say about his brothers and sister. Jemima we didn't see much of. For all her little larcenies in the past, she was married with children and now appeared straight enough. Ambrose Alfred was much the same, sort of settled down with Mary Ann who was a sweet little body, and he was off all over Suffolk and beyond making a living as a brickmaker. He was older than George and he'd had his tragedies, such as twin children who'd died before they were a year old. He was a rough sort, but I suppose I didn't mind too much when he turned up to quench his thirst with George.

It was the other brother, James, that I couldn't stand. Nasty, weaselling man; thin with a sharp face and pale eyes. Furtive. There was no secret about his criminal past - poacher, thief, sentenced to seven years transportation but ended up doing less than that in the hulks. To some, it seemed he always managed to get away with things.

As soon as he was out of prison, he had taken up with a Norfolk woman, Sophia Thorndike. First there were children and then they got married when he was in Ipswich during one of his periods in work. My George and his Hannah had been witnesses and we all had a bit of a do afterwards. Then there were more children - including more twins, but one of them was dead a year or two later.

Sophia was a caution. Though she must have been at least ten years younger than James, she gave as good as she got from him. Sometimes they lived together and sometimes apart. Sometimes the children were with one and then with the other, sometimes in Ipswich and sometimes up in Wisbech - and you may know what they say about the folk from those dull, flat, wet parts: as mad as a barrel of eels.

Eventually James and Sophia parted entirely, and Sophia stayed in Norfolk with a fancy man ten years younger and a couple of her children, and James tramped to Ipswich with the older three. And then he died.

I can't say I was sorry, though of course I did say it, but whenever he was around, we were having to pick up the pieces, like looking after the children or redeeming his clothes from uncle,[162] and forever listening to his mithering on about Sophia and everyone else who'd done him wrong.

My George was eight years younger than his brother, so he sat and nodded and groaned in sympathy, but we both knew this was just another sore man with a chip on his shoulder. I don't doubt he was clever. They called him 'Witty' in his youth when he was up to all his tricks and leading his little gang, but it didn't get him anywhere, and I'd have called him 'Witless.' Anyway, he died - that must have been in the winter of 1877 - in the union workhouse. He was not yet fifty-five years. Heart disease and dropsy did for him, they said. He just swelled up and his heart gave out. *Did he have one?* I thought, but that was perhaps too unkind.[163]

James was dead, but he had the last laugh.

This is how it happened.

His eldest boy, that he'd brought to Ipswich with him, was another called George. Now he was usually George William Thorndike, or Thorndick, 'cos his mother, Sophia, hadn't been married when he was born, but he also went as Sparham or Root if it suited him, and depending on who was asking.

'George William Thorndick, alias Thorndike, alias Sparrow, alias Root,' it said in the newspaper,[164] which was wrong and confusing, there being more Sparrows than Sparhams in Suffolk in them days.

It was always the 'Sparham, alias Root' way, to dodge and duck. Like father like son. James and young Thorndike had the same casual view of other people's wives and property, though little Thorndike got frighted after his first brush or two with the law and generally went straight, or as straight as you would expect a travelling bricklayer's labourer to be.

He'd been working up Wisbech way with his mother's folk and we saw him from time to time, as I said. He came to his father's funeral, and my George treated him like his own son whenever he turned up. He'd have a drink with him and a natter, but I never knew what they were on about.

It was sometime after James' death that my George and I moved from the stinking midden of John's Court into Plough Street. We had four children by then.

There was my Rose (Southgate's daughter), a good little seam-stress, if a bit flighty and too inclined to walk out with any lad who asked.

Then there was George's son, George Lionel, who became a printer's apprentice as soon as he left school. (His father was proud - 'the first one in our family to use his brains to earn his crust.')

And then there were our two babies, Clara and Ada, who George and I doted on and determined to bring up right, and in that I think we were successful, because they both married good men.[165]

With four children, ten years between them, we needed space, and if a little terrace cottage off Fore Hamlet wasn't a palace then it seemed like a real step up for us. There was even room for George's nephew, George Thorndike (or Sparham or Root), when he seemed to be spending more and more time in Ipswich. Before long he was taking jobs down here and not going back to Wisbech at all. He was labouring on the new sewers, and I soon realised that it wasn't the work that was keeping him here but my daughter, Rose.

Now you need to understand that though George Thorndike was family, he wasn't related to me and Rosanna so I didn't see no harm in their friendship, though I could have hoped for someone with better prospects, and younger - he was nine years older than her. All the same, she seemed smitten right enough, and before we knew it they'd both asked my permission to marry (she was only seventeen, so I could have said no). I remember it now, her giggling and blushing and being as sweet as sugar, and him standing back and looking embarrassed and making promises to look after her and giving me a bunch of flowers (which he probably filched from Holy Trinity churchyard). What could I say? In September 1880, they tied the knot. My George (her stepfather and Thorndike's uncle) seemed happy, if as quiet about things as he usually was, and everything went off simply fine. The newlywed Mr and Mrs Thorndike moved into 4 Plough Street, next door to us, where Mrs Fisher, an elderly widow, had a spare room and welcomed the rent. Lovely, I thought.

It was the autumn of the following year that things got tricky. Rose had a baby: another George! (Why is every boy in this family called George?) Anyway, no sooner than it was puking itself over its mother and me - it was my first grandchild, so I was prouder than I would admit - when I had a letter. An unknown hand from somewhere in Cambridgeshire, and when I opened it an unknown

name, to me anyway: a Mrs Frances Clarke of Wisbech. It went
something like,

> *Dear Mrs Root,*
>
> *Excuse me writing to you since we have never met. But I am
> informed that your daughter thinks she has married a man called
> George Thorndike. What you do not know is that Mr Thorndike
> is already married to my daughter Louisa and I would consider it
> a great service if you would send him home to us here in Wisbech
> to his wife and darling children who miss him so much.*

Well, there was more, and I can't remember the exact words because I screwed the wretched paper up (and later I burnt it, not
wanting to keep the evidence by me) and ran next door to my Rose
who was nursing my dear grandson.

'What's this? It can't be true, can it?' I said and showed her
the crumpled letter. She read it and went white as her apron and
grabbed my hand.

'But we went to the registrar together and he swore he was a
bachelor,' she said.

'He did. I was there,' I said, trying to recall exactly how it
happened. Then I remembered.

'No, he didn't! He sent us with the shilling, but he wouldn't
go himself. He said he was at work.'

'He said there was no other but me. And he paid his shilling
and everything,' said Rose, tears streaming.

'Why would this woman send this letter? Have you ever heard
of a Mrs Clarke? Did he ever mention a Louisa?' I asked her.

'Never.'

'But he came down from Wisbech. It's where his mother is. What's their game? Has he got some woman up there with child and they're trying to get money out of him?'

'But if his mother knows about this and she knows about me and she knows he's married me - his father's brother's step-daughter - why would she make trouble for us?'

And so we went on, but the men, these George Roots - one alias Sparham, the other alias Thorndike - being at work in the forge and on the sewerage - were not yet there to share our fury.

When they came home, I am not ashamed to say there was a row that could be heard from one side of Plough Street to the other. First off was Rose.

'Ma's had a letter from Mrs Clarke,' she said to Thorndike, our sewer rat, who was first in.

'Do you know a Mrs Clarke, Georgie?'

'I'm sure I don't,' he said, and I could see a sort of red rash spread up his neck and his mouth broke into a dreadful grin. Rose was about to explode. She poked her finger into his chest.

'When were you going to tell me that you already had a wife?' she said.

Then she was sitting in a chair sobbing enough to break anyone's heart and Thorndike the rogue, with his hands in his pockets, standing in the corner like an infant that's been caught stealing cakes.

'What are we going to do, George? What will we do?' she said over again.

Just then my George came in. I showed him the letter.

'What do you know about this?' I said, because right away I

thought how could he not know that his own nephew had got married years ago, before he and I had got hitched?

'Why didn't you tell me that he was married before he came courting my Rose? Did you think he'd never get found out? Did you tell your sister-in-law, Sophia, that her son had married my Rose? Look at my poor girl, and her with a newborn, too - what's she going to do now?' One question after another, round and round.

He sat in his chair and sucked his pipe through that gap in his front teeth and said nothing, blank and pale, and I thought how it was always men that let you down in the end. Then we all sat or stood, weeping and sighing, and waiting for the floor to open up under us.

Eventually I realised that someone had to take charge, and the first thing was to get Mrs Busy-Body Clarke off our backs. She mustn't be allowed to make us into the guilty parties. I turned to the whey-faced cheat standing in the corner.

'You, my lad, had better make yourself scarce before we have the police here. You can be sure your other mother-in-law won't waste a minute in telling the authorities if she thinks it's going to improve things for her daughter. I don't care where you go but we don't need you bringing your trouble here. You've done nothing but harm to my Rose, and she's too innocent to realise the man you are, and she'll live with the consequence forever, but at least it will be without you.'

That went down well with Rose who curled up and bawled, and the baby bawled too, and George Root said nothing, and George Thorndike got red in the face and stammered a lot of nonsense like, 'It ain't my fault,' and 'it weren't half a marriage.'

'How can you have half a marriage? Did you come here to make the other half? Make two women unhappy instead of just the one?'

'It was her fault - Louisa.'

'So, you admit it!' (More bawling from Rose.) 'And you and she have children?'

'It wasn't a proper marriage.'

'If you've got marriage lines and two children then it's as proper a marriage as it's possible to have,' I said.

'I couldn't live with Louisa. I can't live without my Rose.'

'Well, you're going to have to learn how to. We can't have you here now. You ain't properly married to her. I can't have my daughter living in the wrong. And remember, she is still my daughter. She isn't of full age yet, so she still does what I say ...'

'Oh, Ma ...'

'I should never have listened to the pair of you. I gave my permission. I swore you two were fit to marry,' I said, and I was pacing up and down like a caged beast and the four of them (including the baby) just shrunk away and wouldn't meet my gaze.

'What do we do now?' said Rose.

'He leaves. Now.'

'But what shall we do, me and the baby? Where shall we go?'

'You'll come and live with me. We need to save the money on the rent of your room, since there'll be nothing coming in from this fool.'

'But where do I go?' said Thorndike.

'Back to your proper wife and children and just hope that you don't end up before the magistrate or you'll do harder labour than you'd get from any woman, more's the pity,' I said.

There was much wailing and complaining, but I was adamant. The following day Thorndike signed off from his job on the sewerage, paid up the rent, and packed his bags. I didn't wait around to see him off and I think even Rose gave him a chilly farewell. Whether he went to his wife in Wisbech or off somewhere else for work I neither knew nor much cared. His Louisa would probably be stupid enough to take him back, but I just wanted him gone.

Then there was his other mother-in-law to be dealt with.

*Dear Mrs Clarke,* I wrote, *I cannot but express surprise at your letter. I am sure that there must be some mistake, but I must tell you that I have no idea where Mr George Thorndike is. He is not here, but should he turn up, I will certainly tell him to take care of his wife and children.*

As you can see, I was trying to sound sympathetic without giving anything away. Nothing of this must come home to us.[166] Finally, there was my George Root, keeper of the family secrets.

'So why didn't you tell us your brother's boy was already married?'

'I couldn't be sure.'

'What's not to be sure about? He either was or he wasn't. Why do all you Roots think that you can be two opposites at the same time? Sparham and Root. Two sides of a bad penny.'

'But I didn't know for sure. I heard he had a woman up that way, but it wasn't my job to check if they had a licence. When he came here, I just wanted to see our Rose happy.'

'Oh, so you did it all out of the goodness of your heart!

What did you think was going to happen?' I said.

'I didn't think he'd lie.'

'What, him, the son of 'Witty' Root? You told me yourself your brother couldn't tell the truth to shame the Devil. It's in his blood.'

George was as silent as ever, thinking, I suppose, that if I thought there was bad blood in the Roots it applied as much to him as his brother. I didn't mean that - it was the anger talking - but it hung in the air like the smell of the privy, and we sat in silence. I never knew what he really knew. Anything for a quiet life, was my George, and he just sat in the corner and smoked his pipe and hoped things would blow over. Which they didn't.

At 5 Plough Street, me, George, the children, with Rose and her baby, settled down, and for three months or so all was well enough. Then just after Christmas a police officer turned up with a straight face and a bag of questions.

'Constable Garnham, Ma'am. Do you know a man called George Thorndike, alias Sparham, alias Root?'

You can imagine the rest of his questions, having heard me tell the tale. Garnham wouldn't thoroughly answer my questions but, from what he did say, it seemed that the sewer rat had gone back to his legal wife, that that had suited neither of them, and interfering old Mrs Clarke, out of maliciousness, or as a way of putting him on the road again, had reported all to the police and he'd been arrested. Garnham seemed to know everything but struggled to untangle the detail of the story.

'So, this man's father's brother ...'

'... is my husband, George,' I said.

'And he is the stepfather of Rosanna, or Rose, Southgate,' continued Garnham.

'Because her father, my first husband, was George Southgate, who sadly died. Do you want to see the death certificate?' I said, wishing to be helpful and distracting at the same time.

'So,' he began again, like a man who is lost in a marsh fog and is struggling to find the path to safety, very slowly, 'if your present husband is uncle to the alleged bigamist, Thorndike, how did he not know that he, I mean Thorndike, was already married?'

A good question, but I wasn't about to let the cracks show in front of the police.

'Sergeant,' I said ('cos it's always a good idea to promote men in authority to feed their vanity), 'how were we to know that he'd married at all? His father, my husband's brother, has been dead for several years, and the young man lived up North, and we had no contact with the family at all. And when he turned up in Ipswich, we were only too pleased to give him a home, and we took it in good faith that he was a bachelor. We are devastated.'

I let my misery hover in the air between us. There was a long pause while the young man looked about him and then, having thought he'd found a new piece of safe ground, said slowly,

'But you told his wife's mother that you didn't know where he was when he was living here all along.'

'But when I wrote that letter I didn't know where he was. We were glad to see the back of him, Sergeant.'

Well, that was stretching the truth not a little, but it seemed enough to make him try another tack.

'And where's your daughter? She needs to make her complaint.'

Now I'll say this for Rose, she could see that it would do her no good to get tangled with the law over this. I'm sure she hoped to see her man back, her having no prospects whatsoever as an eighteen-year-old girl with a little bastard at her heels. As soon as she'd seen the policeman arrive, she'd vanished through the yard, baby and all.

'Well, Sergeant I'm sure I don't know.'

'It's Constable Garnham, ma'am.'

'I'm sure you'll soon be a sergeant, and we're so glad you caught this rogue, Thorndike,' I said and smiled at him. 'And you make sure that he doesn't ruin any more young women, won't you. I wouldn't say he's beaten her, but he's left her in poverty and rags. If it weren't for me and Mr Root, she'd be in the workhouse.'

'When your girl returns send her to the station. I need to talk to her.'

'Of course, officer. Thank you.'

He trudged away, looking no happier than when he had arrived.

'I hope you're satisfied with yourself,' I said to George when he came home and I could tell him all about the visit I'd had. He sat with pipe grimly clamped in his set mouth. It's what he always does when he doesn't want to say anything. I was thinking, the apple doesn't fall far from the tree. Look at the mess his own father had left: wife deserted, bigamist, and children left to thieve on the streets and huddle in the snow. That wasn't going to happen to my Rosanna or her child, nor for that matter was it going to happen to me and our other children.

George just nodded and said, 'Hmm ...'

Before we knew it, the case came to the police court.[167] Rose had been made to put in a complaint of bigamy against her husband and I had to say everything before the magistrate. George Thorndike was committed for trial at the assizes, six weeks away. If the magistrate's court was a tribulation for me, with all these people staring at you hard and judging everything you said and the way you said it, the assize was far worse.[168] It was all robes and wigs and uniforms and people talking like no one ever talks in real life with 'm'Lord' this and that. There was George Thorndike in the dock, ragged and sorry for himself, and the men of the jury in their Sunday clothes, looking like they'd hang a fellow before they'd look at him. The judge scowled at everyone, his gaze taking in the whole scene in such a way that everyone was silenced. I did wonder how I could have saved us all this, what with all those people who had come to gawp at us with our dirty linen to be washed in public. Then up stands Thorndike and the clerk reads out:

'George William Thorndick, alias Thorndike, alias Sparrow, alias Root, you are charged that you did feloniously marry Rosanna Caroline Southgate at Ipswich on the 5th of September 1880, your wife Louisa Thorndick being then alive. How do you plead?'

Thorndike stood in the dock and twisted his cap in his powerful hands. For a moment he bowed his head as if in prayer and then, when the attention of the whole court was on him, he looked up and in a surprisingly jaunty voice said,

'Guilty, to a certain extent, m'Lord.'

People in the gallery laughed and there was applause from some young men. A woman shouted abuse which I will not repeat, and lawyers raised their eyebrows and looked at the judge, across whose stony face there was the glimmer of a deadly smile. *What can you do with such a man?* they seemed to be saying to each other, but I could have told them all that this was the son of 'Witty' Root talking.

A Mr Simms Reeve was the prosecutor. He was bowing and scraping to the judge and making out that George Thorndike was devious and a thoroughly bad lot, and he called me to give evidence.

'Mrs Root,' he said. 'It is your daughter who this man, Thorndick or Thorndike, seduced into marriage, is it not?'

'Yes, sir,' I said. Then he made me tell the story all over again, how I welcomed Thorndike into my house and that we never knew he was married. I didn't say a word about George being the villain's uncle and no-one asked me. It was over in a blur and I sat down.

Then Mr Reeve called 'Detective Sergeant Garnham' to say all the things that he had done, and I smiled at the policeman to show that I was right all along on his promotion from constable. Then a churchwarden from Wisbech swore to the first marriage. He showed the vestry book which was passed around. After only ten minutes the case seemed to be decided and Thorndike was obviously guilty, so we all thought.

Then things seemed to fall apart for Mr smug Simms Reeve.

'Where are the wives?' said his Lordship.

'I regret, m'lord, that they are not present.'

'And the mother of the lawful wife, Mrs Clarke, who made the original complaint?'

'Again, I much regret, not present, m'lord.'

His Lordship looked very displeased. He wrinkled his nose as though smelling that something was not quite right. Will that toad Thorndike get off? I wondered to myself. There was a moment's silence, then his Lordship spoke:

'Gentlemen of the jury, since the defendant has pleaded guilty we will not trouble ourselves with hearing anything more from him. All the records are clear and there is unassailable evidence of two marriages, which constitutes bigamy on the part of the defendant, and is contrary to law. You may now, therefore, gentlemen of the jury, consider your verdict.'

They huddled together, spoke in whispers for less time than it would take to cross the Cornmarket, and pronounced our George Thorndike 'Guilty' and looked very pleased with themselves for making such a sophisticated decision.

His lordship looked down his spectacles at the prisoner, roasted the whole court with his gaze, and said,

'Young man, this is a serious offence which must be punished. It is a very great injury to a woman who is led into a supposed marriage with a married man. However, in your case we have not seen these women. We know very little of the circumstances of the case,' and here he gave a particularly hard stare at Mr Simms Reeve, who seemed to shrink in his place while attempting a ghastly smile, 'and I therefore sentence you,' resumed the judge, 'to three months' hard labour. Take him down.'

Then, would you believe, the wretched Thorndike gave me a smile and a wave as the warders hustled him down the stairs at the back of the dock. I went home to report all to George and Rose, and how the whole piece was over in fifteen minutes.

I couldn't understand what had just happened. Thorndike

had been given half the usual sentence, so Sergeant Garnham told me. I'd been made to give witness in court but no-one else had stood by me, and it felt as if these wives and Mrs Clarke had come to some sort of private arrangement about what was going to happen, and I wasn't included.

Some lines had been drawn, but which side of them me and my Rose were on I didn't know. I still don't, if I'm honest. We never talk of it, of course, but it is as if I go around with a scar upon my back. No-one sees it but I know it's there. An imperfection which I cannot shed. A wound I did not choose, from a time when I wasn't as in control of things as I like to be.

I could never quite forgive my George for not admitting he knew about Thorndike's first marriage, but we carried on much as before. And after three months, Rose had her George Thorndike back! He stayed with her and forgot Louisa entirely. (I heard she eventually took up with another man who had been her young lodger.)[169]

Soon after his return, we had a family discussion, me, George and George Lionel, Thorndike and Rose.

'We are starting again,' I said.

No comment.

'I'm not going through that again,' I said. Silence.

'We will put everything behind us. We are the Root family of Ipswich. We will put behind us Thorndicks and Thorndikes, Sparhams, Sparrows, Sparkhams, or any other name. These names are history that we do not need to remember.'

'We put down Roots,' said my George, who seemed to think the whole affair had a humorous ring to it; a sentiment I could not and do not share.

It's nearly twenty years since that court case which none of us speak about. Rosa and Thorndike are still together as man and wife and have two thriving children.[170] George Lionel, my stepson (George and Hannah's child), prospered at school - his father and me saw to that, and he's a master printer for the local newspaper with a wife and children of his own.

I have pride in our family. I think back to running barefoot in the River Deben and of the distance I've come since, and I reckon I have made a difference, like that old preacher commanded. If there are family ghosts I don't think of them.

# 22: Peter

## Autumn 2022

Late afternoon. Misty. Rain and leaves are falling in my garden. Lakshmi appears to be in silent prayer - she does not want to be interrupted. Our time together in India seems to be long in the past and our story is edging towards the twentieth century, to those ancestors whom I met in person or whose stories were told to me at first hand.

Would Clara find me a disappointment? I want to apologise to her for digging up these tales, but I feel I owe it to Keziah and George and Hannah: they survived, and I'm here because of them.

I had sympathy for George as a starving pauper and even as a petty criminal when he seemed forced into crime just to survive. I have been conflicted when he turned Queen's evidence against his friends. I rejoiced at his decision to leave it all behind and become a soldier and even found reason to think him heroic. He found love and I was relieved. I hoped that he and Hannah would live long and fruitfully. It all seemed to matter because they were my people, my unconscious ancestry and personal heritage, and I revelled in it.

Now I encounter bigamy once again, and George's apparent willingness to cover it all up. I know I am becoming censorious, and this is not my role. I am Peter Tye, listing and cataloguing interesting finds, but the closer to me the events become the more difficult I am finding the task. I don't think that family heritage is merely traits repeating themselves. Bigamy and other crimes, a propensity to hide from the world: they're not how I see my inheritance, nor what I wish to bequeath. I should just grasp the page, rip it out of the exercise book, and find something more wholesome to report, because that's what families do. I can see my father's disquiet as he sits, half-concealed behind his newspaper, and my mother saying, 'Can't you tell a nice story, dear?'

Lakshmi has finished her meditation. I say to her:

'Clara is not one of us; not a Root or Ellis, except through marriage, yet she may have made all the difference to George Lionel. The Roots were particularly good at surviving. It could have all ended in the snow outside St Clement's Church, or on the plains of India, or in the cold Atlantic, but it didn't.'

'You might as well say that good luck was on George's side.'

'Or that he just became successful at keeping his head below the parapet and above the waters. It seems to me that, before Clara, George Root, alias Sparham, was bound upon the turning wheel and that it could have raised him up or left him drowning. What Clara had was a conviction that the wheel could be stopped, even turned, by the force of her will.'

'She made it possible for George Lionel, their son, to start writing his own history.'

'Appropriate, then, that he was a printer, adept at shuffling type around in the forme and chase, just as I shuffle text on my bright screen.'

As the sun sets, I can see the redness reflected in my garden pond, rippling in the slight breeze. I suppose that all these events made us the family we are, but is it any use knowing about them now? They shape us, whether we know the details or not. There are ripples in the pond which bounce around. They become weaker with each generation, but the present is modified by every variation.

Where next? When I started this pursuit of my family, one of the few pieces of evidence I had was a death certificate for George Root. He died on 2nd of April, 1907, at Myrtle Road, Ipswich. 'Paralysis and old age,' it says. He was seventy-seven years old, but he was still employed as a labourer with the Dock Commission, not a stone's throw from where he lived. Myrtle Road had been a further improvement on Plough Lane: the houses had tiny front areas and doors with ornamental lintels and a literal 'step up.' George Lionel, his printer son, was by his bedside when he died, and he registered the death. Perhaps he even typeset the memorial notice in the *Ipswich Evening Star*.

Clara had died three years before.

I have a line of succession: Keziah, George, and George Lionel Root.

'Do you feel better for that?' asks Lakshmi, staring at me from one of her more mischievous poses.

'A little more complete, I suppose. Like finding I am part of a bigger picture and quite liking what I have found.'

'There is always a bigger picture. You can never know its end.'

Which is why I shall go on. I am not the person I was when I started the investigation. All those professional quests into other people's ancestry and inheritances affected me not one bit, but now I have stories of Roots and Sparhams, Ellises and Cracknells, and they have changed me. I am surrounded by people I never knew existed. My personal heritage has a different quality: my own, thin experience is compounded now with all these other lives and they make me rich in ways neither I nor they could ever have foreseen. We have shared adventures.

I am greedy for more.

# Part 3
# Charlotte

# 23: Peter in His Garden

## October 2022

Autumn deepens. I rake leaves like I rake the archives, into neat piles. It is rich humus, essential for growth, as are the stories I have uncovered.

My favourite tree in the garden is a bifurcate oak of perhaps eighty years. The tree expert tells me that its two trunks are not the result of pollarding or early damage but arise from a self-set acorn which produced a pair of shoots growing together. Now, some four feet above the soil, they divide. From that point two trunks rise like a pair of conjoined twins and stretch fifty or sixty feet into the air.

Neither trunk is perpendicular: the more upright of the two bends towards the west and overhangs the country lane. Walkers can shelter from the rain under its canopy. The other trunk, tending eastward, is less lofty, but hangs out over my pond, and its branches seem torn between reaching for the sun and drooping towards the water. Its lower branches graze the surface, and one is a perch for kingfishers.

Since I am writing about genealogy, and family trees are the framework on which I construct a narrative, I cannot fail to point out that this tree is particularly felicitous. The roots, hidden and ultimately undiscoverable, can represent every line of descent of this or any other family. The point of bifurcation, however, is neatly indicative of that moment in time when a conjunction occurred - the union of George Root and Hannah Ellis, for example, and two became one for a brief instant before new growth and alliances led upwards, outwards, across the waters and the road.

I can see the spirit of the wood, who I will call Root, squatting silently in the crux of the tree. He grows and twists with the seasons. He is content to occupy his niche and survive. I feel him stretch his limbs and rub his back along the untender bark. He is holding an unlit pipe in the gap in his front teeth and looks slightly smug, as if he knows that he has found his place and will not easily give it up, however roughly the storms and snows or the baking sun assail him. Each autumn he can contemplate ever more abundant acorns, satisfied that he continues to spend his profligate seed. Dryads are like this: watchful, content, unambitious, perhaps, but guardians of their place and people.

I am a seeker of evidence, of verifiable facts. I should draw a line at seeing phantom dryads. Yet now old Root has something to say to me.

'You can't stop now, can you? It's your nature, to want to know everything.'

'You're right, great-great-grandfather. I need to collect every story, just as I must know the names of every tree and collect all their fallen leaves.'

He gestures across the pond, towards the sumac trees.

'You know it's impossible,' he says. 'Look at the sumacs.'

'Each year new ones pop up,' I say. 'It's the underground runners. I never know until the spring where the next will poke through.'

'Exactly. You've set yourself an impossible task.'

'With each new stem the landscape changes,' I tell him. 'With each new ancestor my landscape changes and the inheritance becomes a little richer.'

'Or more unwieldy,' he says.

I stand here, in the garden, silently conversing with a tree, but within me there is a vast company of ancestors and all their progeny, dead and living. I can't stop myself from knowing them better because they are my inheritance and this will be my bequest, though I don't yet know who I shall leave it to.

There is a breeze tugging at the remaining leaves and the old oak seems to chuckle. Root's voice inside me says,

'Look now for my Hannah's sister, Charlotte. I never knew her, but her memory troubled Hannah. In her last illness she would say, *Where's Charlotte, George. I want to see Charlotte.* I could tell her nothing, and it upset me. Tell me about Charlotte and then we might both understand our story better and you might have your inheritor.'

And from the depths of the pond, a naiad voice says,

'Yes, me, Charlotte, the bad girl. Charlotte, the neglected. Charlotte, the one they all wished they could forget. Hannah's oldest sister and your great-great-aunt, who they transported to Australia. Charlotte, whose story was never told but who has been there just the same.

'Hear my story, but I warn you, it will change you. You can never unhear it.'

I sense she is important in two ways. Her forgotten story haunted the family she left behind and, if she survived, maybe my rightful inheritors belong to her.

Tell your tale, Charlotte.

## 24: Charlotte Ellis on the *Elizabeth and Henry*

### 1848 [171]

'Restless. Her's all scrigglin' next to un! No wunder Oi'm restless. They give us no space to turn below decks after lockdown. And it's wet.'

Charlotte, in an inadequate shift, roles over on her plank, mutters to herself, and knees the woman next to her in the back. It is to teach her a lesson. Charlotte is fifteen but she will not let Lydia Childs steal her rest or her bed space. The woman is older than her, and hysterical. Earlier in the day the ship's surgeon had bled her.[172]

'Joss over, Charlotte,' squeals Lydia.

'You joss over, you maw,' says Charlotte.[173]

'I got me pains agin. I carn't help it,' says Lydia, and groans loudly, pulling her knees up to her breast. She can hardly breathe, is weak, and there is no position in which she can rest comfortably. The ship's timbers moan in sympathy and the sails flap as the vessel wallows in a long, slow sea. There has been a brief squall but now the weather has resumed its humid sullen calm, and the *Elizabeth and Henry* is making little progress on this May afternoon in the Indian Ocean.

Charlotte closes her eyes and sees the image of her family: James Ellis, her father, and Catherine, her stepmother, with the children, Isaac, Hannah, Charles, and baby Sarah asleep in the half-open bottom drawer of the dresser. Over the interminable weeks of the voyage, she has come to realise that she will never see any of them again. She steels herself against the memory. She will not recall them. She will not. She has seen other women who can do nothing but mope when they remember the world they have been torn from. She will not join them. She must make do with her new company.

It is four months since the women were driven aboard the ship at Woolwich; four months since one hundred and sixty-eight of them, from prisons across the kingdom, had been incarcerated on the prison deck. There are ranks of bunk beds behind iron bars, partitioned into groups of eight, where the women, some with babies and small children, have been forged into groups to cook and care for each other. Charlotte is with the women of East Anglia: sick Lydia, Fanny Prior, and Lizzy Hume from Essex, and Charly Church[174] from Ipswich.

A quarter of the ship is full of Scots who don't even speak a language anyone can understand, so these English women band together for mutual protection.

'Tell us your tale again, Charlotte,' says Lydia. 'It keeps me mind off things.'

'When she was the littlest slut in Ipswich,' sniggers Charly Church.

'You'd know, you trapes,'[175] says Charlotte Ellis, and pinches the girl. They have been bickering for four months; two Charlottes fighting for pecking order, fighting to climb one rung above the shit in their stifling coop.

'Tell us about the innkeeper again,' says Lydia.

'Pompous, smarmy, pot-gutted owd fool,' says Charlotte. 'Mister Castle of *The Great White Horse*. We ran him to ribbons. He never knew where us 'ud pop up next. Arter dark we could sneak all over. They say as the place had been standing three hunnerd years and there was a pale ghost round every corner. Oi never saw no ghosts but there was more rooms than you ever seed in any house, and the place was full of fine folk and skivvies so, if you was quick, no one ever noticed you. There was food to be had if you were nifty, and warmth in the stables and behind the kitchens.'[176]

'You did more than steal the chicken bones,' says Charly Church. 'You never passed a tankard without finishing the slops. And you knew the way into a pair of breeches, with the man still inside them.' Even Lydia laughs, and then hunches in pain once more.

'What if Oi did,' says Charlotte. 'I ain't proud of it but I earnt more there than I got sewing seams. You were no better, you maw.' She spits and then becomes more reflective.

'Oi 'ad friends there, too. The lads in the stables and Jimmy, the pot boy, and Sara, the chambermaid. We all enjoyed larkin' about after the quality were in bed.'

'But you weren't so clever,' says Charly, ''cos you got caught.'

For a moment Charlotte looks wistfully into a corner of the wet, wooden cell.

'There was this footman. Cheeky Albert. A right charmer. His master was staying in the 'otel and Albert was sharing a room with other servants over the stables. And we got talking. We were getting on real fine.'

'Tell them about the chaise,' says Charly Church, sniggering.

'*The White Horse* had a post chaise. Right comfortable inside. So, me and Albert gets in and Albert has a bottle of Jamaica and there was no one else about, it being the middle of the night. We closed the doors and pulled down the blinds and lit a candle. He was a clown, Albert. We bounced up and down on the springs and 'ssh, someone'll come.' So then he tickled me and I fought him off. He put his hand over my mouth to stop me giggles, but he was right up close, and he said, 'You've got lovely eyes, Charlotte,' and we kissed. We huddled in the corner of that old chaise and I was comfortable with him. His breath were warm and sweet, I remember, and he knew how to make a girl happy, what with the rum and all.

'Next I knew, there was some rough old ostler grabbing at me - I'd fallen asleep you see - and Albert was nowhere to be seen. So, this hussman[177] ranted and threatened me with his whip, and I'm trying to straighten me clothes and feeling hully ill. And I must have puked all over the poxy chaise 'cos there's the stink of rum everywhere. I got thrown out into the street.'

'What about Albert?' says Lydia.

'Albert? Oi never sees him again. But I'd found how comfortable the owd post chaise was, so I crep' in there whenever the events of an evening at the *Horse* come over me. Better sleeping there than five in a bed with me ma and pa and the brats in our room in Cold Dunghills.'[178]

'Christ, Cold Dunghills,' says Charly Church. 'That were a midden. Oi never knewed you live there.'

'What would you know about it?' says Charlotte, suddenly

defensive of her Ipswich home, 'but Oi ain't sorry to be away. I ain't.' As she denies them, the mental image of her family appears in her head once more then fades till it's no more than a pale outline, like the ghost you see when you have looked into the sun too long and then look away, and you hope it will clear.

'What's it to you, anyway?' She is angry now. 'I was free there. I did whatever I wanted and no-one stopped me. There was money to be had, and I went to *The Horse* whenever I felt like it,' says Charlotte Ellis, snarling at Charly Church but, as if to compensate for her meanness, stroking Lydia's contorted back.

As the sailors trim the sails to catch a fresh breeze, the ship heels over. The women slide and adjust their positions on the slippery planks. For a moment a breath of air rustles down the open companionway. Charlotte sighs and fills her lungs.

'So how did you get here, then?' says Charly Church, knowing that the story must end with Charlotte's downfall: she wishes to twist the knife.

'Bastard caught me again, din't he?' says Charlotte, meaning the ostler who had pulled her out the first time. He had found that she had been locked in the post chaise by whoever had been with her, with the steps put up and the blinds closed. 'Oi hadn't done nothing. Just stayed in there to sleep it off.' Charlotte goes silent.

'So, what then?' wheedles Charly, knowing exactly what.

'They takes me to the magistrate and tells him all sorts about me. How they'd had to reline the whole coach after Oi'd spewed up in there, which I knew to be a lie 'cos my friend Sara told me. The policeman says they keep finding me wandering the streets at night. Then the mayor calls my stepmother up to the stand and says, 'How is it that this child of yours, a mere thirteen years of age, is away from home at night?'

'And that's what really done for me, 'cos my blessed stepma goes to save her own skin.' Charlotte mimics her stepmother's fluting and pathetic speech:

'We're very sorry, your honour, but we cannot control the girl. Her mother died when she was small, you see, and I done my best since but she won't listen to me, and my man, her father, works hard every day to feed us all and we've got three young ones and they're all thriving, but Charlotte, well, she's just a bad lot, and she won't stay home and look after the baby, and we tried to keep her home but she keep on getting out, and whenever she do she bother all the neighbours, upsetting the washing and taking food from the stalls and running away and using the most dreadful language, and we just couldn't bear with it, your honour, so we had her put away in Nacton and that didn't do no use neither,' and she pauses for breath and looks pitiful.

'What can a girl do when her own mother turns against her?' asks Charlotte, defiantly. 'Three months Oi was in Nacton, the shithole.' [179]

'What's that?' whispers Lydia.

'The workhouse,' says Charly. 'Didn't do you no good, then, did it?'

'Oi just wanted to be free,' says Charlotte, and as if exhausted by her memories, curls up with her face to the dripping wooden walls of the ship and cries silently and secretly while Lydia moans and Charly grumbles about her own hardships, having decided the younger girl has had enough attention.

So it went on from day to day. Lydia, her pains worsening, was removed to the ship's hospital.[180] The Suffolk women had a little more room in which to bicker and to digest the misery of their situation. Charlotte examined in minute detail the knots and splinters of her prison and the iron bars and locks which separated one cage from another. She listened to the sad shanties of the weary sailors and the percussion of prison chains and the guards' keys. She was haunted by the distant melodies and, from time to time, found her voice to sing gently:

> *As I walked out one morning fair,*
> *'Twas there I met Miss Nancy Blair ...*
> *There ain't but one thing grieves me mind,*
> *To leave Miss Nancy Blair behind ...*[181]

In the profound darkness of Southern Ocean nights, she huddled next to Charly, because the soft warmth of the woman's body was a comfort, and a protection from the terrors visited upon other girls who were alone. In her turn Charlotte discovered she could become a protectress too: one of the London women had a baby and was ever happy to give it up to someone else's care. Charlotte surprised herself by spending hours entertaining little Mary and playing the games with the child that she could not remember any mother ever playing with her. She sang to her, and the other women would pause whatever they were doing and listen. Charlotte had a sweet voice.

But in the deepest night of the Southern Ocean, as the ship rolled, sails slapped and the rigging strained, while women cried out in their sleep and children grizzled, Charlotte lay awake and played back all her short life. She could find little consolation in her thoughts. She was not a bad girl. Why would no one believe it? If her mother hadn't died things would have been different. She could hardly remember who Margaret was, but one day she was there and the next she wasn't, and then Catherine Malary arrived, herself only a girl, and clueless in dealing with a stepdaughter. 'Oi didn't have to do what she said. I didn't. I didn't.'[182]

So she didn't, and there were always gangs of children loose in the muddy streets to fight and frolic with. There she found her taste for alcohol, which was a great way of seeing the world in a different way. She laughed at the way it made people seem. All these adults getting red in the face and shouting at her, and, as she swayed and hiccupped, it was impossible to take them seriously. That was the best way to deal with adults, she thought. She'd go to the Devil before she'd stay at home and look after the little brats that appeared every couple of years from her stepmother's belly. *Drown 'em, like kittens*, she thought.

She had run wild so they'd put her in the workhouse, but they couldn't keep her there and the parish said it wouldn't pay. Then some Uncle Ellis in Woodbridge had said he'd beat some discipline into her, and she was sent there to live with him and his wife and their brood. He was a whitesmith, making locks and bolts, and he rather fancied having a thirteen-year-old girl to fiddle with behind the forge. So she hopped over the wall and found herself in the yard of Master Robert Green, the shipwright who lived next door.[183] It was the work of seconds to take every garment from the pegs in the back hall - a black cloak, a worsted cape, a soft black silk cape (oh, so luxurious - she wanted to keep, it but knew she could not) and a white pinafore - and then she was away to try and hawk them round town. But, in the tight-knit Woodbridge community, questions were asked about where she had got such fine clothes, and before the evening she was locked up.

The magistrates, and then the assize, and no-one would come to speak for her.

'Previous bad character,' they said, and 'her parents don't know what to do with her,' they said.

What Charlotte wanted to say was, 'why don't you listen to my story?'

What she actually said was, 'Fack off!'

'Transported to Van Diemen's Land for seven years,' was what they said then, and she was straight into a grinding machine: iron doors, locks, chains, and rope.[184]

After the trial she was sent to Ipswich prison, which was run as a silent institution. [185]

It were so quiet. Suited me. I didn't need to speak to any of 'em, and I sure didn't want them talking to me. Three months I were there, on a small stool in my cell, picking at old rope until my nails bled and fingers were black with tar. One pound of oakum a day if you wanted your bread and broth. I lived inside my head, mainly thinking about Australia and what it would be like. One day a wardress poked me and said,

'Harder, Ellis. No time to sit and dream. They'll work you hard in Van Dieman's Land.' And then, with a sneer, 'They need girls like you out there.'

What she meant I didn't know, but I could guess, and I had dreams of running away or meeting some fine soldier or sailor. But mainly it was just trying to sleep at night and waking to the same miserable routine in the day and no windows low enough for me to look out of. No-one came to visit me, neither.

In the autumn, just as it were getting cold, they carted me off to Millbank Gaol.[186] That were much worse. Silent and damp. I were quite alone in the dark and cold in a tiny stone cell. There was water, slimy, down the walls, and it seeped into me and made me cough. Oi were frawn[187] all winter in that beastly place. You ever been in the dark so you can't see your own fingers in front of your face? That were what it were like in that cell. Day by day, whatever I 'ad in my 'ead were lost. Everything lost. I tried to see Hannah and the other children in my head, but it came so I couldn't remember what they looked like, and I wept.

We were all one to a cell. Couldn't speak to no-one else, on pain of a beating or no food. Head down and masked when we went to work or to chapel. Women in little wooden boxes coughing and scratching while parson tells us stories about Martha and Mary, Ruth and Rachel, and all of them hully unbearable women. God knowed them, but he wun't know o' me.

Winter came, and the water on the walls of the cell turned to ice. In chapel the parson said, 'On this joyful Christmas Day let us thank the Lord for his great mercies ...' and he told us how fortunate we were to be released from our sins by God who had sent his son. There was extra suet pudding that day and I wondered if Pa had bought something special for them all to eat back in Ipswich.

We froze through all of January. Now that I had been in

the prison for more than two months, I was allowed to speak to other women when we went into the yard. We talked about when we might be transported. Some said that many women died on the crossing and others said that they had heard we would all be sent to hard labour in the forests and have to live with snakes. Others said we would be made to sleep with soldiers or taken by force by the natives. No-one really knew anything, and the guards told us nothing.

Then, one day in February, we came out of our cells as if to work but were led into the yard and handcuffed. We were to be transported that very day. They led us through the gates and massive walls of Millbank and straight on to the quay side. Idle fellows stood around and called out and whistled. I remember a woman passing, an old servant in a brown drawn bonnet, who looked me in the eye and spat on the cobbles as if she were warding off evil. Another woman convict behind me screeched at her and she hurried away.

It were a fair relief to get on the steamer to take us down river to Woolwich where our ship for Australia was waiting for us. There was excitement, almost as if we were on a pleasure boat. We sat on the deck and watched the great city pass by. Some of the women had never been on the water before, and I'd never seen London and wouldn't expect to see it ever again.

'What's that?' I asked.

'You don't know Paul's Cathedral?' said one of the London women who was cradling a baby. Then she pointed out other places like the Tower of London and the great docks full of sailing ships from all over the world, bigger than anything we ever seen in Ipswich Docks.

'That's the Isle of Dogs,' she said, 'and on the other side is Deptford, where I lived.' She was suddenly silent and her eyes stared at the near bank as if trying to see inside every warehouse and factory and fix the picture in her mind for ever.

We went round great bends in the river, weaving slowly between hundreds of sailing ships moored up or at anchor, and then we came in sight of the hulks; a line of dismasted men-of-war.

'My man's in one of them,' said the London woman. She scanned each one as we passed.

'That's it,' she exclaimed. '*The Justitia!*' [188]

She stood and started waving and shouting.

'Warren! Warren!'

We were steaming so close that some men on deck looked up and shouted back, excited suddenly to see a boat full of women. One of them sprung up and climbed onto the rail. He too was waving and shouting, though I couldn't tell what he said. A guard stepped towards him, raising his cudgel, but before he could belabour the man, Warren, for it must have been him, jumped overboard and started to swim towards our steamer.

Suddenly we was all screaming and shouting for him to come across and the guards were blowing whistles and shouting. Our steamer was slowing because the ship we were to meet - the *Elizabeth and Henry* - was hard by. For a minute or two it seemed like Warren might reach us and be able to give his wife a last embrace. He was a mighty strong swimmer but the wash of our propellor and the incoming tide were against him. We began to pull away from him and he was tiring. Then he stopped swimming and was treading water, waving at the woman as she waved back and screamed at him. She held her baby aloft and flapped its arms.

Then all hope died for the pair. It was like an invisible ribbon was stretched between the two, him in the water and her in our boat, until it suddenly broke and they knew in an instant that they were apart for ever.

We saw the guards had a trustee in a rowing boat coming after Warren and when he approached the exhausted swimmer he yanked him half out of the water and pulled him back towards the hulk where the guards got him aboard. All us women groaned and thought how we didn't have a man to jump in the river for us. Then the guards on the steamer slammed us below decks before we could see more.[189] By then, it were raining fit to drown us,[190] so we were glad to get in shelter where we become quickly silent. Some wept, and we could hardly look each other in the eye.

The steamer bumped alongside the *Elizabeth and Henry* and, before that short February day ended, we had been thrust into our prison deck, taking wet and freezing steps between the lives we had and the unknown one we must face.

# 25: Peter and Charlotte

## April 2023

Months of solitary research under pandemic constraint have given me relationships I never thought to have, stories I didn't anticipate, and dialogues with a silver bowl and woodland spirits. I should like to dismiss it all as unreported symptoms of the wretched virus - oh, yes, I suffered, but I know it's more than that. As Lakshmi told me, now that I know the stories, I am changed and I can't forget. Past and present have coalesced.

Charlotte has got under my skin, and not just because we share an ancestor and some DNA. This is uncomfortable, so let me attempt to be objective.

She is a child. She has pale skin, light brown hair, and brown eyes. At the time of her incarceration she is barely four feet four inches tall, with a small round face and an upturned nose (the prison record calls it 'piggish').[191] For one hundred and forty-five days or more, she rocks in a cramped hold on the *Elizabeth and Henry* as it shuffles across the winter North Atlantic to Rio and on to Cape Town, and then the Indian and Southern Oceans to

Hobart, in suffocating summer heat; one hundred and thirty-eight female convicts and twelve children in an unkind cradle.[192]

On arrival in Van Dieman's Land, Charlotte is described as a 'nursegirl' and an Irish Catholic. She is in and out of trouble for the next four years: put out to service she runs away and is brought back to hard labour in the Hobart factory. This cycle is repeated, and again. In 1852 her record is marked, 'Not to be allowed to enter service in the District of Hobarttown.'

It seems that whenever the opportunity arises Charlotte becomes drunk and unmanageable. She takes up with a fellow convict, Thomas Outhwaite, who is at least twelve years older. They ask to marry but are refused - a token of the state's continued control over her. Outhwaite is a 'ticket of leave' man and still serving the remainder of his fifteen years for theft and burglary.[193]

I tell myself that I am back on track. No fanciful dialogue; just the available facts. I have put an appropriate distance between us. Charlotte was, after all, just a remote aunt and now about as far away on the other side of the earth as anyone could be. In this way I can't be doing an injustice to anyone, past or present, and maybe there are potential clients in Australia who would like me to take up the tale on their behalf.

Then I look at Lakshmi and realise how wrong I am.

She seems to speak to me in Charlotte's pained Suffolk voice.

'Why do you become so unadventurous?' she asks. 'I am real to you. You write in the present tense, yet you are glad to keep your distance! Coward!'

'I'm a very old man,' I protest. 'And all these ancestors are merely an intellectual challenge, nothing more.'

'You know that's not true,' says Lakshmi-Charlotte. 'Have you learnt nothing from Keziah, George, and Hannah? Why would you be so engrossed in their struggles to survive? You know they haunt you, just as they themselves were haunted by Samuel Root and Charles Mallows and the rest. Where's your courage? Are you cowed by a teenage girl, snatched from home and sent friendless round the world?'

She needles me, she won't stop, and I know she is right. I am too involved to turn back; the only thing to do is to follow. Borders, real and metaphorical, are beginning to fall as the pandemic seems to lose its potency. If I chose, if I had courage like hers, I could go out into the world again and find the paths once trodden by her and try to comprehend what has been hidden from me.

I turn from the computer archives to look for flight schedules.

In my head, Charlotte details our itinerary.

I get up from my desk, purposeful once more. Somewhere in the loft there is a suitcase I haven't used in years.

# 26: Charlotte, The Price of Gold

## 1852-1858

The first couple of years in Van Diemen's Land were hard. First, the Factory,[194] with all the other women: numbing labour by day and bundling together by night. I was young and small, and I couldn't defend myself. I learnt things … It wasn't natural, but sometimes it was a comfort.[195] We needed each other.

In the second year they let us out to work. I wasn't a good girl - kept being sent back to the House of Correction and to hard labour - but I was young. What did they expect? The rules were strict: no drinking, no tobacco, no money. They told me I couldn't go to Hobart at all, so I was stuck out in the bush, treated like a slave, cold and wet and never enough food.[196]

Then, one night, I met Possum Tommy. Thomas Outhwaite, a dark, bearded Yorkshireman with deep blue eyes. Oh, he were lovely, were Tommy. Older than me, of course, but those eyes. He were a highwayman in England, but he had his ticket of leave, and when we met he was just discharged and on a drunk to celebrate. There was singing and dancing that night. Oi could get drinks for me singing. He was sort of protective, trying to keep me out of trouble and keeping other men off. He wasn't tall but he was built like a bull. They called him 'possum' 'cos of the fur coat and hat he wore - and perhaps because he slept a lot by day but liked to be out at night.[197]

We had fun for a few months, and I thought we'd be alright together. I got my ticket of leave on 24th of February, 1852. That's not a date you forget out here. I got the piece of paper still and it's as important as my marriage lines, so the following week we went to the office to register our marriage. The bastards turned us down! I were too young, they said, and it was for my own protection, 'cos he were twelve or more years older and I could be exploited, and he didn't have a proper job, and anyway I was still not discharged and must remain under the authority of prison. But really, they turned me down because they could. Show the little maw who's boss. I cried and I swore at them.

'Perhaps we should rescind your ticket of leave,' they said, all sneery. Thomas put his arm round me and gentled me and took me out and we had a drink.

'Don't leave me,' I said to him.

'Never, my sweetness,' he said.

He did, of course! They all facking let you down, these men. If you scream and make a fuss they hit you and go; if you weep and talk kindly and sing to them they tell you they'll stand by you, and then they leave you just the same. You close your eyes, they finish, and they're off.

The last thing Possum Tommy had said to me was, 'There's gold in Victoria. I'll go, now I've got my freedom, and I'll send for you. When I'm rich they won't be able to prevent us marrying.'

It was a fairy story, and I wanted to believe it, but it didn't survive the next morning's waking and a day of drudgery. I knew I'd never see him again.

Once more, there was no-one beside me. I don't often think

of the folk in Ipswich now, but just then I thought it wasn't natural being without a father and a mother (even if she wasn't my real mother), and all those brothers and sisters and the friends we had on the streets and around *The Great White Horse*.

It wasn't long after Tommy left that I met John Henry Gilham. He were a fine young man, and no convict. He was a carpenter, and he come out to Australia with his brother and sister to be with his father who had been transported, like me, for nothing at all. He came steerage on the *Victor* 'cos he wanted to be with his daddy, and you wouldn't believe what happened. He'd got all the way to Hobart, met his dad who had just been given his ticket of leave, and the old man promptly took off to Melbourne, leaving John Henry to sort hisself out![198]

It's parents, you see. Never trust them. Here were three children who had taken themselves halfway round the world to find their father. John Henry had only been six year old when he last saw his daddy. He expected the old man to treat him like a son, but the bastard took off to the mainland with his new woman as soon as he saw him.

*Father and son fought from the moment they met.*
*'I didn't ask you to come, son.'*
*'But dad ...'*
*'I left all that behind me, son. Your mother wasn't no good for me.*
*That wretched country did me over, son, and I owe it nothing.'*
*'But family, dad ...'*
*'I owe family nothing. I got a new life here and so have you. Make*
*the most of it. You're better off not knowing me, anyhow. I'll always*

*be a Vandemonian, even with a ticket of leave. You're a free man and well set up. Forget family. It's a new start for both of us. Go your way, lad, and I'll go mine.'*

And that was all my John Henry got for his trouble, but he and I got on right fine together. We drank together and I sang to him, which he loved, and he made me behave! But he had a problem: there was no work in Van Diemen's Land at that time.

Men were leaving the place as fast as they could get passage because there was gold found in Victoria. Letters came back to Hobart and Launceston: gold, just for the picking up in the creeks; valleys where gold shone from the stream bed, just waiting to be grasped.

'Come now - before the Chinese get here, or the Americans, or the Scots ...'

'I know a fellow who got three large nuggets before breakfast. He's staked his claim. He'll be a made man ...'

'Buy a pick and a shovel when you get here. There's even more to be had just beneath the surface. I got a map ...'

It was all anyone could talk about, and when I met John Henry Gilham, carpenter and free man, in a bar in Launceston, he was no different, though he seemed to have a plan.

'Now see here,' he said. 'Not many people get rich in a gold rush, and a good many die in the attempt, so I'm not about to join the charge to dig or pan. Do you know who gets rich in a gold rush?'

'No ...'

'It's the man who sells the pick! It's the tin smith who makes the pan. It's the miller with his over-priced flour.'

'But the ...'

'Stands to reason! And I reckon as they all need carpenters! You got to have a handle for your pick and shovel, the miller needs his sheds, and all those miners got to have huts to live in and wooden cradles to sieve the gold ...'

'Tents ...' I said, 'cos I'd seen a picture in the newspaper of the camp in Ballarat.[199]

'They're building towns out in the bush and there won't be enough carpenters to go round. I reckon I can name my price!'

He talks a lot, this John Henry Gilham, without letting me get a word in, and he doesn't have blue eyes which look through you, but, rather, hazel eyes, which are more used to examining trees for felling and considering their grain than looking into your soul. But he is free! He was never a convict but came out, as he tells it, to escape the mother who betrayed his father. He is a couple of years older than me, and full of enthusiasm. I think that excites me more than the thought of gold.

'So how about it?' he asks.

'What?' I said.

'Come with me to Victoria. We'll follow the rush and we'll make money from the miners, whether they have gold or not, and then we'll be able to buy all the gold we need. You look like a girl who knows how to work hard.'

'But ...'

'Have another drink and think about it,' says Gilham.

'We've only just met.'

'You're a great girl. I knew the moment I came in. You look just like my sister. Here she is now – meet Elizabeth. Mrs Will. And this is her husband, James. Edwin, our big brother, will be along shortly. We all came out together in forty-nine to start again.'[200]

Elizabeth has a sweet smile and is very pregnant. James looks serious and is dressed like a man of business. He buys us all drinks and counts money from his purse covertly, as though he doesn't want people to see how much he has.

I look at John Henry Gilham. There is nothing much to dislike about him. His beard is untidy and wet with beer, and his hair is powdered with sawdust, but he is respectful towards me, which is unusual in a man. And I am suddenly swallowed up in a family such as I have never experienced.

John and I married within the year, at Launceston Parish Church on 22nd of January, 1853. James Will, my brother-in-law, was a witness. I lied a little about my age, claiming to be twenty-one.[201]

We were all over each other at first, every opportunity we had. Our honeymoon was the boat to Melbourne, and it were glorious. Wind and sun and freedom. I thought being married was the freest I'd ever been. Just the one master, and I was learning to halter him, so I thought. We landed at Liardet's Beach and it was sweltering, and we clung to each other 'cos the place was heaving with folk from all over the world, and the diggers with money lording it, and the many more down on their luck trying to take you for every penny. We got through town as quick as we could and out to Flemington,[202] on the goldfield road, 'cos John Henry's older brother, Edwin, was already there and had a business and rooms enough, which was just as well 'cos the prices of everything seemed ten times what they were in Van Diemen's Land and there were no rooms to be had, even if you had the money. It was all chaos but exciting and I thought, *This is it! I'm Mrs John Gilham. I got to talk properly, 'cos we'll make money, and I'm going to be a lady. No one will know where I've come from (and I'm never going back to Ipswich - though if our golden dreams come true, perhaps I could).*

John Henry got work soon enough. It wasn't exactly steady, but he could earn a guinea a day, even thirty shillings, which would have been two weeks' wages back home. They was putting up buildings everywhere and John Henry was prepared to work hard and go anywhere. We stayed with his brother, and I made a home for us, and I won't say that I was expert, but he didn't complain. There was a hotel in the village, so in the evening we could meet company, and I couldn't imagine a better life. People called me 'Mrs Gilham' and treated me with respect in the stores.

I was pregnant as soon as we'd crossed the Bass Strait. George Edward was born just before Christmas in 1853 - the hottest Christmas I ever knowed. Our room was baking under the corrugated roof and there was dust everywhere, but I thought that at least there weren't Ipswich ice and snow.

How we fussed over that baby, and I remembered the child I'd played with on the ship and thought, *I can do this.* He was a reg'lar tough lad from the off. I loved him. John Henry worked as hard as ever, but the child was mine. I made him. I was prouder of him than anything I'd ever done. John Henry could say 'That's a shack I built,' and be ever so proud - though mainly of the money he made from it. I could say to myself, 'This is a child I'm making. You'll never see a better.'

But a child does drive you apart. I could see it in John's face.

'Why ain't you paying attention to me?' he seemed to be saying, and I thought, *You owd moppet. Who's the bigger baby here?* He couldn't see that little George Edward came before everything. In those days, I'd have given my life for the child.

As the months went by, John Henry spent more time at the hotel, and I could tell he was getting impatient of me and he thought he was missing out in every way. He had less of me, but perhaps worse was that every day there were fellows coming down from the goldfields, pockets full of coin and those government papers that tell them how much gold they've lodged with the Commission and all the wealth they can collect in Melbourne. 'Look, I got two thousand pounds waiting for me. I can go home and buy an inn!' or 'I'm straight round to the office and buying me a thousand acres in New South Wales.' It was intoxication for my John Henry.

'I'm off to the diggings - find us a fortune,' he'd say.

'You're making good money here,' I'd say. 'I don't want to be traipsing through the bush with our son. Anyway, you said you'd make more money from your craft than digging a filthy hole in the ground.'

'But you should see how much they make, and how easy it is. Only last night there was an Irish fellow in the bar who said he'd been up to Ballarat, bought his concession, and the first morning, before he'd had his breakfast, he picked three large nuggets the moment he scraped the soil back.'

'And what's he doing with them?' I said.

'He's off to Melbourne. Says he'll keep sheep, now.'

'He's off to Melbourne and what he doesn't spend on whores he'll drink, and he'll be back on the road in a week.'

'What do you know, girl? You weren't there.'

'And what about all the others?' I say to him.

'What others?'

'All the men who come slinking back from the goldfields with nothing in their pockets and glad to be looking for a labouring job down at the port. The broken ones, crippled when the diggings have fallen on them. Don't suppose you asked their opinion. Don't suppose they get to drink in your bar,' I said.

I'd seen them coming back through Flemington with disappointment dragging their every step. But John Henry wasn't listening, and I could tell that I was losing him.

'We got to be off,' he grumbled. 'The gold'll be worked out before we get there. We've come all this way ...'

'We're fine here,' I'd say to him. 'Look, George Edward's thriving. We're settled. You make good money. What's wrong with us, John? Why take the road and go heaven knows where with a baby?'

We bickered back and forth, and I thought, why, when for the first time in my life I had freedom and a life I loved, did this man want to take it all away? But I was stuck with him then, you see. There's nothing a married woman with a baby can do, and I knew that in the end I'd have to go wherever he wanted to be.

John Henry bought a cart and a pair of horses from returning miners. He bought a tent and tools. He bought timber, as if to show that he still meant to do his carpentry and wouldn't throw it all over in the search for gold, and he waited until the winter floods had dried up. He wasn't completely unfeeling at that time, and I suppose he didn't want to see his wife and his baby in a bogged down wagon somewhere in the wilderness. But it came to October, George Edward was not yet a year old, and we had to set off and leave our sturdy rooms behind for a life on the road.

Once we were away, I resolved to do my best to encourage him. I needed him to look after us - me and George Edward.

It took us a week to get to Ballarat, joining with other travellers on the road to protect ourselves from bushrangers, and eventually we camped beside a stream where there was already a large group of diggers.

'We'll stay here for a day or two,' said John Henry, and I thought, 'There's no call for a carpenter here, so he'll be digging in a hole in the ground tomorrow.' I wasn't wrong. Gold was the only thing that made his eyes light up now.[203]

That was the beginning. Since then, we've been all over this state, anywhere there might be gold, at least. For five years we camped around Bendigo - up Sandhurst and Eagle Hawk - then Dunolly, and on to Ararat and back. He couldn't keep still. He'd spend his thirty shillings to licence a claim, work it, and like as not get little or nothing. At the end of the month, we were up and off again.

'Let's go back to Haverton Gully. I know there be more to be had there,' he'd say.

'You said that six month back, and there wasn't.'

'Pack up, you jade. We go tomorrow.'

That's how it got. We never settled. I did my best. When we had money, I bought rugs and china, and I polished, cleaned, and sewed. 'I can turn you out proper, and the babe,' I'd say to him, but he'd just grunt. My hands were red and blistered with trying to keep clean in the winter mud, and in the summer the dust was in everything. Sometimes there were other families and good women about. Sometimes you just had to put up with the men and their chi-iking. I could give as good as I got (and some of them were a laugh, but if John Henry were there, I daren't let him hear me).

I began to think he don't really want me or the baby around, but he don't want to let me go, either. It was the gold fever that had him. I saw he was jealous of what he had, whether it were metal or human.

Like I said, he wasn't a tall fella but he were broad and strong, and he became sort of menacing. If he felt he was being hard-done-by, or something was rightfully his, whether it was or not, he fought. I seen him square up to a man over the edge of a claim, and the other always backed down. It didn't make me feel any safer. It got so I was always on edge.

'Come here, sweet. I got something for you. That were a good pay day last month. I got you a present.' It was a gold ring.

'It's what you should have had when we married. It's three years since, but better late than never,' he said.

It was the best present I had ever had (apart from George Edward), and for a week afterwards all was good between us. Then he had another exhausted pit, and he decided we had to move on. He spent a few days on carpentry, making cradles and rockers for other diggers, but then it was pack up everything on to the cart and off to some other gully. He'd never work with others if he could avoid it. 'I do better on me own,' he would say, though I could never see much evidence of that. When it came to puddling, washing the mud off, and sifting for the gold, he had me work with him. 'Keep it in the family.' *Keep what?* I thought. We didn't seem to have much more now than when we started.

The curse of all was the sly grog shops. The grog was cheaper than beer out in the diggings. I've alus liked my rum. I suppose it's what got me into trouble in the first place, and now there weren't no stepmother nor magistrate to shake me or bang me up, and when we had the money there weren't nothing to stop us. The government said spirits weren't to be sold in the diggings, which of course was like a red rag. You couldn't always be traipsing back to a roadhouse or down to Melbourne. You needed to know which Sean or Solomon or Ted had just come up the road with his barrel of brandy or rum and was mixing grog to sell at his tent flap. Then once the sun was down and the police had gone to their beds - oh, the parties we had.

I could hold me liquor.

"Struth, she's just a midget - where does she put it all?' they said.

'Drink you off your stool,' said John Henry. 'No man here better.' And he'd be proud and put his arm round me and we laughed and sang. He'd get his pistol and he and the men would fire off into the bush at any sign of movement.

'Got to chase the ghosts away.'

There was a nightly riot of gunfire in them days and you learnt to join in or keep to your tent. You didn't want to be walking around in the dark when a dozen drunken diggers were celebrating or, more likely, moaning about the gold they didn't find. Then we'd crawl back to the tent and he'd breathe his fiery breath on me, roll on, roll off, and snore to daybreak. And I'd be so totty-headed I wouldn't care.

When we had money, I'd make him give me some so that I could sew it in my skirts for safe keeping, but then he'd not let me out of his sight. It seemed it were the money rather than me he cared about.

This one Sunday night we went up to Sandhurst,[204] to the Victoria Hotel.

'I'll feast you,' he says.

Once we were there, things became merry, and a group of well-dressed men paid attention to us. John Henry flashed his money and bought drink for the table. A fine young English man - they said he was a lawyer, named Adams - remarked on my beautiful eyes, and we took drink together. It were all harmless enough, but it does a body no harm to be admired when she's been living in the mud for months on end with a three-year-old clinging to her skirts. However, John Henry got rough and red in the face. I could see it were going to end bad. He snarled and got loud.

'Come home, John,' I said.

'Aye, take him home,' said one of the fancy men to me, 'and, when you've tucked him in, come back yourself and we'll know how to treat you properly.'

John Henry's into them with his fists and it takes five of them to throw him out the bar. I walked on behind, ashamed. He called me every name he could - stuttering angry, he was - but I didn't care. I'd done nothing 'cept smile at a well-dressed man what spoke nice. The next morning the silly drunken fool went up to the police station and summonsed Adams. He came back with his piece of paper.

'I want him to pay up,' he said. 'No man can look at you like that. I'll teach the beggar to fool around with my wife. Mine!' He threw the paper at me. 'I got to work. Take this to the police court and see they lock him up.'

I knew it were all nonsense, and the police must be laughing, but I took little George Edward and went back to town and handed the summons in, and what did the police do? They went right out to his diggings and arrested John Henry! I thought, *Serve you right, you stupid, jealous bugger.* He'd only taken out a summons against a local magistrate.

It were me that paid in the end. They let John Henry out later that night and when he came home he was in a worse rage than I ever seen. He pulled me out of bed and set to with his glass and belt and whip. I screamed blue murder and the whole camp must have heard, but folk think twice about venturing out after dark or coming between a man and his wife.

He beat me senseless and let me lie, and as soon as sun was up he went off out again. If little George hadn't gone and told some other woman in the diggings, then I'd have died on the floor of that slubby tent. They carted me off to the doc' and I pretended I'd been bushwhacked, but that magistrate put two and two together and John Henry was run off to gaol.

He was lucky I recovered: saved him swinging. And in three months he was back with us, swearing he was sorry and he trusted me, and, 'cos I had nowhere else, I stayed with him.[205]

I had another baby within the year, and I swore it were his. It may have been. We called it John Henry.[206]

I remember the piece in the newspaper about John Henry attacking me and they described me as 'a rather pretty-looking woman,' so I always had that to remind me of a young lawyer who smiled on me, as well as the scar across my forehead from a broken glass.

We went to Ararat after that, 'cos later the same year that young John Henry was born the Chinese got to Ararat and them ugly little yellow men found pretty chunks of yellow metal in the ground, and there was a general stampede after them.[207] Gilham - I'll call him Gilham now, 'cos the bastard can't have nothing to do with my sweet little John Henry - was going on the level for a bit, not wanting to be locked up again and seeing an opportunity. Many of the whites didn't want to work with the Chinese, but they had a nose for gold and they worked harder at it than anyone had ever seen. Our men, you see, had either spent their lives shirking work in the prison gangs or were too posh or flimsy to lift a pick after lunch. These Chinese worked from dawn to dusk without drawing breath, so it seemed.

'I don't mind 'em,' said Gilham. 'There's money to be made from them.'

He was right. The diggings at Ararat were rich but very wet. They was always looking for planking and shoring up as well as cradles and rockers, and Gilham could charge top dollar 'cos the Chinese was pulling gold out the ground so fast they didn't care what a carpenter charged - up to a point.

It was never enough for Gilham. Soon we were off once more, twenty mile up the road to Stawell, or Pleasant Creek, as it was then. Little John Henry had been born at the end of summer and by the time we got to Pleasant Creek and set up our camp near the store tent it was winter and wet and cold. John Henry was still at my breast - the baby, that is, not the other, 'cos I wouldn't let him near me, and he was still afraid to try his luck. But it was then that the most horrible thing happened, and it wasn't to me but some other poor woman. But it was me what was there.

I didn't like Pleasant Creek, not now, not then. It were noisy and crowded with all the nations of the earth, but Gilham stopped digging, thank God, and gave himself up to doing carpentry for the Chinese and Germans and all of them other nations.

It were difficult to find a dry camp site and we didn't have much room for our tent and fire. We had no inside oven at that time and were cooking over an open fire near the tent mouth, and that were a bugger to keep alight - and to stop young George from falling in to. All the tents were hugger mugger and you seemed to live everyone's lives for them.

Next to us we had the Shepherdsons, Lizzy and Fred. They'd come from Scotland to make their fortunes many years before and she had family down in Melbourne. Shepherdson, a thin-faced fellow, was storeman at the village shop, so he was a good man to know. His wife, Lizzy, seemed a bit lost. She was about the same age as me, but innocent. I allus thought she considered herself too good for the rest of us, but she was frit of her own shadow. I picture her curled up inside her beautiful thick tartan shawl, seeming to seek protection from the whole world.

She'd look at me with big, silent eyes. When she did speak it was to ask idiot questions like, 'Did you see where my husband went?' or 'Why doesn't he like my damper?'[208] She'd follow me around when I was close to the tents. She'd watch as I fed John Henry. 'I don't know how you manage with two little ones. What if they get sick?' I could see that she was pregnant and scared stiff about it, but at the same time I knew she thought she was better than me. I should guess her husband was little use. He probably didn't understand how the child got there. I jollied her along as best I could, but I didn't want her under my feet, and when I did need her to watch little George as he toddled about she'd say, 'Ooh, I couldn't … my husband needs me in the store,' or some such. I thought then, she ain't going to thrive here, so crawly-mawly. Her husband better take her back to Melbourne or wherever it is they come up from. She needs her ma.

She were brought to bed on a Saturday and everything seemed as it should. I took George Edward and little John Henry to see the baby and Lizzy lay there, nevvied up[209] and sad looking, though the baby looked well enough, bawling and red in the face. I gave her my finger to suck 'cos Lizzy didn't seem to know what to do.

'What you calling her?' I said, taking the child in my arms and rocking her.

'We don't know yet,' said Shepherdson, who was standing by, looking anxious, and then, 'Will you sit with them, Mrs Gilham? I must get back to the store.' He couldn't get out of the tent fast enough. Not a kiss or kind word passed between them.

The exhausted woman slumped back on her pillow and I and the children just sat peaceably on the bed beside her. The baby had quieted.

'You poor, nameless thing,' I whispered to her. I was thinking, *'tis bad luck to leave a child unnamed. What if it dies? The angels won't know how to call it home.*

It wasn't long before my two boys got restless. I propped

Lizzie up, still half asleep, and put the baby to her breast.

'Come, Lizzy,' I said. 'She needs you.'

The girl said nothing but looked at me with terrified eyes as I crept out of the room.

A couple of days passed, and I could hear Lizzy moaning from our own tent. I went to her and found her ill. I knew right away it was the milk fever.[210] She were all swelled up.

'So sore,' said Lizzy. 'The child won't feed. What do I do?'

Fred was there, looking helpless and twisting his hands together.

'Boil some water,' I said to him. 'Get a clean cloth, soak it and lay it on her breast.'

To Lizzy I said, 'Give me the child. I'll see if I can nurse her, though my little John Henry has fairly drunk me dry!' I tried to make light of it, but to look at the pair of them you'd have thought this were a death bed scene.

'You'll both be fine. You'll see. And if you're not right in a day or two, the doctor will sort you out.

The following day things were no better. Lizzy was up and walking around, wailing quietly to herself. She wouldn't go back to her bed though she was not fit to be up. 'I hurt too much,' was all she would say. Sometimes she picked up the baby and tried to feed it and then she would put it aside like an abandoned doll. I tried my best to help, nursing the nameless child, but I had my own two always beside me with George Edward toddling around and clinging to me and not liking his mother giving attention elsewhere.

At the end of the day, Fred sent for the doctor. The Doc told

Lizzy she must rest, and he gave her laudanum. He sent for a wet nurse, too, which was a relief to me.

The following day I went to Lizzy's tent to see her again. The baby was right enough but Lizzy was grey and drawn, slumped on her bed.

'Can you still not sleep?' I asked her.

'I ache. This medicine's no good. It makes me ill.'

Fred said, 'She won't take it. I put it in port and gin to take away the taste and she still won't touch it.'

'Oh, Lizzy,' I said, 'you can do this. Look at your dear baby. So beautiful.'

But she turned away from me and whispered, 'Leave me.'

Things got no better in the next two days. When I went to see her again and asked her how she fared, she said 'I'll kill meself.'

It seemed neither I nor no-one could do anything to help, and I stayed away the next day. Then that night there was a commotion after midnight. I went out into the moonlight and there was Lizzy in her nightdress, outside her tent, shrieking. The wetnurse had come out after her, pulling her back, but Lizzy was dragging the poor woman off towards the creek. Her husband came out and between us we carried Lizzy back to her bed. She was exhausted and settled down but after that night the wetnurse and Fred Shepherdson, and Mr Blyth who had the store, were in and out of the tent all the time, guarding her. She wouldn't lie still or rest or take her medicine.

Then a week after the birth Lizzy rose from her bed and left in the middle of the night, taking the baby with her.

None of us knew until the village woke that Sunday morning.

They had a crier out round the camp and soon the constables were asking about, but no-one had seen her. By the Monday, I thought, well that's her gone, off into the bush or down a pit somewhere.

Come Tuesday morning, I was washing Gilham's shirts and went down to the fence by the stockyard to hang 'em out. I was looking down the gully when I saw a splash of colour by a water-hole on the other side of the fence. The place was full of abandoned scrapes, and they might be shallow puddles or as deep as hades, you could never tell until you fell into one. Anyway, I saw this thing at the edge of the hole, and it was bright tartan, and I knew it right away as the shawl that Lizzie always wore. I climbed through the fence and found myself a long stick and went to hoick the shawl out, and it was Lizzy's, I was sure. I shouted for the men from diggings close by to come up and said, 'I reckon Mrs Shepherdson's down there. This is hers.'

The hole was deep. There was water in the bottom, four or five feet below the edge. They got some long fence bars and poked down and hit something in the water, and then I saw a sight I don't want to see again, 'cos the woman's naked heels rose to the surface, white and wrinkled. I thought of her, cold and bare and exposed to all these diggers. I supposed the baby must be down there with her and suddenly I could hardly breath.

Then they had to get ladders and clamber down and bring her and the baby up and it were the most dismal sight. That child had done nothing wrong, any more than had the woman, except she were caught up with men and their greed for gold. No-one don't deserve to end up like that. I won't forget that baby, arms out and head right back with staring eyes, and its little mouth full of mud. I ran back up the slope to our tent where John Henry was asleep in the cradle his father had made, and George Edward was playing with pieces of offcut wood to make a little house.

'Look, Ma!' he said, as I got nearer. I squatted down and hugged him. I kept him close all that day.

When Gillham came home, we went to the grog shop and drank more than was good for us. When I lay in bed that night I couldn't turn my mind off that tartan shawl, those feet floating above the water, and a nameless baby looking like it had been crucified.

In the next days, I wasn't allowed to forget anything. All the talk in the camp was of how she died and who was to blame. Some wanted to blame her husband for not caring for her, but mainly he was pitied. He wanted to blame the doctor, but the doctor said he done what he could and if the woman wouldn't take her medicine there was nothing he could do. Some said it must have been a bushranger or a Chinese what whacked her over the head and dropped her down there, though that wasn't reckoned much on. It seemed obvious to me that she done away with herself, but people said her folks back in Melbourne wouldn't like that -she wasn't no convict Vandemonian, but had family that cared about her - and she must have slipped and so it was obviously an accident. And some said she must have been mad to be wandering around in the middle of the night with her baby and climbing through the fence to get to the water hole, so she was a murdering lunatic.

It all went to the coroner and there was an inquest, and I had to give my witness 'cos I'd found her, and Gilham said 'Just say what you seen. Don't offer any opinion.'

The magistrate asked me whether I thought she was of sound mind. I said I thought she was. I told 'em I thought that mind was to do away with herself if she had half a chance.

The jury were out for a fair owd time and when they came back the head man said that they were agreed that 'the deceased was found drowned in a waterhole near her tent.'

If that's the best a coroner's jury can do, it's pretty much a waste of all those folk taking a morning off work. It seemed to satisfy everyone, but I thought, *No-one cares what the truth is. No-one cares about Lizzy. No-one cares about the baby. All that matters is what other people will think, and what gets reported in the newspaper.*

Soon after, it all came out in *The Age*. Gilham read it to me, saying 'I told you to keep your ideas to yourself.' Then, a couple of weeks after, there was a nice notice in the paper calling her the beloved wife of George Shepherdson and saying that her baby had died the same day aged nine days and the deaths were 'deeply regretted.'[211] In the end, you could just say that it was one of those things that happens to mothers and babies and let's all get on with life.

I couldn't get on with my life. Them heels coming up out of the water were in my dreams, night after night. Gilham had money, and we had the sly grog shop, so things were hazy after Lizzy died. Every day I could look across the fence and see the hole where she died. Even when they filled it in there were a patch where nothing grew. If I got up in the night and looked out of the tent, I swear I'd see her ghost wandering around the paddock, lost, looking for a hole to drown herself in. Perhaps it was just a nightmare, but it seemed real enough. It seemed like something was altered in my head.

I tried the laudanum and I spent what I could on grog, and they sure made me sleep, but they didn't help the dreams. I stayed in bed and let the boys run around and couldn't stir myself to do anything.

Gilham wanted me up before the sun to blow the fire back to life, put the tea and oats to steep, and the damper in the coals. The boys wanted their mother. I couldn't do any of that. I know I were bad, and the fight even seemed to have gone out of Gilham. Perhaps he saw what it was to lose a wife and child. He worked close to the camp, and, for a couple of weeks, he played pa and ma to the boys.

'Let's start somewhere new,' I said to Gilham. 'I hate this place. I can't live here with that - where she died - just over the fence. We still got the same old tent, and we need something better. Why can't we have a proper cottage?' I mithered on, but the more I did the more he turned his back on me.

So, I left. Three weeks after the inquest, I packed a bundle, kissed the boys, and rode a bullock cart back to Melbourne.

# 27: Charlotte in Melbourne and Bendigo

## 1858-1862

I went to Flemington, to my brother-in-law, Edwin, and his wife, Sarah. They weren't happy about me leaving Gilham and the boys. They had a house full of little children, Sarah having been married before and now with a new-born, so I helped in the cottage.[212] I had very little money, but I needed to start again. I went to the Melbourne stores and brought myself some clothes.

'On account. My husband will settle with you!'

That'll teach the bastard. I got a new green skirt and a bonnet; things I couldn't wear round the diggings. I took myself out of an evening. There was singing and dancing.

Edwin must have told Gilham where I was, 'cos after a week I got a pathetic note from him saying, 'Please come home, the boys and I miss thee.' A couple of weeks later, I got another note saying how he was pleased I was helpful to his brother, and he was surprised to receive the bill but supposed he could hardly deny his much-loved wife some new clothes, but that he would not pay for anything more and I was to make my way home 'as soon as Edwin and Sarah can spare you.'

*You humbug*, I thought, *making out as if this were all with your approval.* I bought new stockings and a fine pair of boots, the best I'd ever owned, and put them all on his account.

Monday morning, two weeks on, and Edwin brought me the day's *Argus* and said,

'What you been up to? You can't go on like this. You're dragging the family through the mud, Charlotte. We'll have to send you home.' He tapped the paper with his long, soapy finger, and I saw:

> *I will NOT be Answerable for any DEBTS my Wife, Charlotte Gilham, might contract after this date, as she has left her home and children without any cause.*
>
> *John Gilham*[213]

I thought, he can sweat a bit longer. 'Without any cause'! The bugger. But Edwin wouldn't let it drop, and Sarah said, 'I love it that you're here and helping, but we can't tear these brothers apart. Family is so important.' I looked around at all the toddling children and the newest one slurping and burping and said,

'Family ain't important for us. We ain't like you in a proper house and a business. It's wild out there. I can't go on living in a tent. I'm a town girl.' And I thought, *And women and babies die in holes in the ground.* But I knew she was right and that, besides, I was still on a ticket of leave and no pardon, and maybe I could get called back to Van Diemen's Land. I wasn't free, after all. Besides, I was missing my boys.

A few days later, I headed back up the trail, and Gilham seemed pleased enough to see me, having had enough of two small children and no woman, and we drank all evening.

'But I ain't staying in Pleasant Creek,' I said, and he said he was ready to move, too, and there was more money to be made back in Bendigo. He'd set up a carpentry business in a proper building and we'd live over the shop, he promised, and we wouldn't be traipsing through the mud of the diggings no more. We packed up, and I could leave the paddock and the wandering ghosts of Lizzy Shepherdson and her unnamed baby behind me.

In Bendigo, I went to work at *The Builder's Arms*. Gilham said we would need the money if we were to keep the new workshop, and I could get away from him of an evening while he looked after the boys. I could wear my Melbourne finery and laugh and drink behind the bar. I put on a bit of an act, too: if the pianist was in I'd get everyone singing. After a few weeks they asked me to stay over, maid of all work, and the pay was good enough and the ale was always flowing, so Gilham said 'yes,' and, for a few months, I lived at the hotel on weekends and Gilham fended for himself and the children.

My freedom didn't last long. John Bedford Lee was the landlord of *The Builder's Arms*, and he was just like all the rest and thought he could have his way in the cellar, the store, or the lean-to bedroom. I got sick of fighting him off and I left.

Gilham knew what had been going on - he'd come up the *Builder's* and drink himself silly - so, if he were short of cash, he'd ask Lee for a sub and like as not get it. *I'm like a pawn ticket*, I thought, *in and out of their pockets*.

Then I got pregnant again. It was Gillham's, and we called the baby Isaac.

About a month after the boy was born, we went out in the

trap and took Isaac and the boys with us. Just a picnic and some panning at Eaglehawk Gully[214]. We took Elizabeth from the bakery and met Mary, the teacher's wife, when we were there. It was a hot day, but the stream was cool, and we panned a few grains so were in good spirits when we got home. After an hour in the yard, we were dancing and happy and I felt like a girl again. When the sun was down, us three women climbed into bed together, giggling and laughing. The only man we had in the bed was baby Isaac. We played with him, and he sucked me well enough. Eventually we all slept. I fed the child again in the middle of the night. He was sniffly and sleepy. He woke Mary and Elizabeth, but we were warm and comfortable. 'Pity he'll grow up to be a man,' I thought. We were women and confiding together.

There was just a grey glow in the sky when I woke next. Isaac was in the crook of my arm where he'd slept all night, and I knew directly that he was dead. I know I screamed - the other two said so. He had been so likely to live. Did I roll on him? The others were afraid they'd done so.

The doctor came and they took the little limp body away. We women were in pieces.

The doctor made his report and said that the child had had inflammation and couldn't breathe, and that I was not to know, and he would as likely have died if he'd been in a cot as in my bed. But it wasn't all right, not at all. We women couldn't look at each other, and Gilham was so sad, and drank even more than usual. We both felt guilty, even though we'd done nothing wrong.[215] Isaac's death seemed like a punishment.

There's one more story that rolls around; one more picture book in my head that I can't close, and not for want of trying. It ends with me in a cell once more; black, hot and stifling.

This is how it went. I'd gone back to *The Builder's Arms* to repay money to John Bedford Lee, the landlord with the wandering hands. It was the last payment on what Gilham had from him a couple of years before, when I was working at the hotel and Gilham borrowed from him against houses he was building for some other man. It was probably not all he owed, but then again, Lee probably owed us for my various services, and Gilham thought he would call it quits.

When I got to *The Builder's Arms*, I had a stiffener or two in the bar before I went to Lee's rooms above. I had the money in a paper. 'Will this do?' I said. I had the green skirt on, I recall.

When we'd finished our transaction and he went to his office to write a receipt, I saw a mustard pot on the sideboard. It was blue cut glass with a silver cover. Very pretty. Looked like it were made to fit my silver cruet stand with its glass pepper and salt. Lee had a hotel full of mustard pots, and he wouldn't miss this one, I thought. There was whisky on the board as well, so I helped meself to both. When he came back to the room and saw his whisky glistening on my lips and me propping myself up by the door, he just wanted me out of the room as quick as possible.

'You're drunk,' he said.

'And what if I am. Who are you to fuss?' I knew I was getting noisy. 'I'm leaving now. You got what you wanted,' I said loud enough for the saloon to hear. Of course, he hustled me down the stairs quick as, and said just as loudly, 'The wretched woman's drunk again.' Before I knew it, he'd hauled me into a cab and paid the fellow to take me back to Huntly where we were living then.

'The woman's drunk,' he said again, loudly, to the cabbie, as though he wanted another witness, and then he said to me, quietly, 'and don't you voke inside the cab or it'll cost your man.' I thought, *I remember Oi done that before.* That were where my misery began, but it'd take more than the few tots I'd had to make me puke these days, and I kept firm hold on my stomach - and the mustard pot in my handbag.

A couple of days later, John Lee turns up at the house with two policemen. It was a Saturday and hot, the boys were under my feet, and Gilham was working out somewhere.

'Mrs Gilham,' said Constable Williamson, 'Mr Lee here says you have stolen a mustard pot - a valuable blue glass and silver mustard pot - when you visited his house last Thursday.'

'Of course I didn't.'

'Then what is this mustard pot, blue glass and silver, on the dresser? Is this yours, Mrs Gilham?'

'Of course it's mine,' I said. 'It's on my dresser and it's got my mustard in it.' I'd made sure to make up a little paste the moment I got it home. It had to look like it belonged.

But Lee blustered, 'My maid, Catherine Curry, will tell you it's mine, and that she missed it the moment this woman left my house,' he said.

Williamson and his mate, who no doubt knew where their next drinks were coming from, picked up the mustard pot and dragged me out of my house.

'We shall have to arrest you for robbery,' said Williamson, and cuffed me.

'What about the children?' I screamed. Little John Henry started crying and clung to me skirts; George hid in the corner and looked pale.

'Where's your man?' said Lee.

'At work. He won't be home for hours,' though I knew he was probably already in a bar somewhere.

'We'll get a neighbour,' said Williamson, and sent the other peeler to the woman next door, who was only too pleased to come in and see me in cuffs and find out what all the fuss was about. She'd have a good story when she went off to church in the morning.

I was as dignified as I could be. 'Please look after my poor children, Mrs Shaw,' I said, 'just until my dear Gilham gets back from his labours. These ruffians are taking me off on a trumped-up charge. Tell him to come to the lock-up for me.'

'Oh, you poor dear. And these children. Come with me, dar-lings,' she said to the boys, ushering them towards the door. 'Your mother will see you again soon.'

Well, she was a woman I'd never much taken to, but she surely knew how to act up to a situation. At least the men in the room looked shifty and knew better than to say anything.

Once the children were out of the way, Williamson said to Lee,

'Mr Lee, sir, are you prepared to swear that this mustard pot is your property?'

'It surely is, and I will swear it,' says Lee, thinking, I suppose, that sounding pompous must make something true.

'So,' says Williamson to me, 'you'll be taken to the lock-up and before the magistrate in the morning.' With that they bundled me outside and into the police van. A little crowd had gathered, of course, it being a hot Saturday and folk living on their porches. I held my head up and shouted, 'It's a lie!' and 'Tell my John! They've kidnapped me!'

I could tell Williamson was not quite certain what he was about. 'Come along, Mrs Gilham. Let's be peaceable and the magistrate will sort all this out in the morning.' He helped me into the back of the van where I sat behind its iron grille with as much calm as I could manage. Williamson was holding the mustard pot, and the other man drove. They told Lee to make his own way home.

I thought, It's mine, I know it's mine. They already half believe it is. Believing a story true may make it so. The moment they took the pot away, I knew it were mine. I knew where I bought it. I knew I bought it 'cos it matched the cruet and the stand. Before we reached the lock-up, I had the whole story in my head, and you would have had to doubt your own common sense to disbelieve me. For the moment it did me little good. I was in their books and there was more writing down to be done. I'd seen it all before; it's the writing what makes it true, even more than the believing.

This unsmiling policeman at the White Hills lock-up wrote my name and address and 'Charged with robbery from a dwelling,' and they threw me in the hot little cell.

'But it's mine!' I shouted.

'Tell it to the magistrate tomorrow,' said Constable Meredith, the lock-up keeper. (I know him - nasty piece of work. Beats his wife. I've seen her eye.)

That gaol brought it all back - Woodbridge, Ipswich, Millbank, *Elizabeth and Henry*, the Hobart factory; everywhere they had closed a door on me. You sit in darkness. Who's there? What comes next? And with no grog to drink, the terrors come upon me, and I see all the faces, feel all the fingers tearing at me once again. Sleep is all nightmares. Monstrous dead babies. Waking is no better.

They knew what they were doing, of course, John Bedford Lee and the Bendigo police. 'Lock her up for a day and a night. She's out of control, and we'll show her.' Just like the old fools in Ipswich. 'Out of control.' Like my bloody parents: 'Send her away and lock her up.' In the dark, where I can see, in my mind's eye, black water and a pair of white heels breaking the surface, wrinkled and pale as tripe.

Gilham came later and brought me a crust and a bottle of beer. I tried to talk to him about the mustard pot, but he said he hadn't noticed it. 'But I ain't letting that fat humbug Lee lock my missus up! I'll get you out o' here.' He didn't, but I knew his pride was hurt and he wouldn't let it lie. I was his property to do what he could get away with - he wouldn't have some other man trespassing. None of it had anything to do with blue glass mustard pots.

As the Saturday evening wore on, the lock up got more lively. I suppose this was where my past came in handy. The cell door kept opening and another and another drunken woman was thrown inside. Before morning there was five of us in there. Two of them just slept it off: drunk and disorderly. One poor young thing - a black. Almost naked. A child - crawled into a corner and trembled.

'They say they caught her stealing from a mark,' said the fourth girl. 'But it was just some man who couldn't raise his standard and needed to blame the girl. You see that all the time after they been on the drink on a Saturday night.'

This girl, Anna, had worked the goldfields for seven years. She was older than me, but she'd been through Millbank and the voyage out, sentenced as an 'habitual common prostitute.' They do like the word habitual, as though it shows that they got their judgement right.

'Yeah,' said Anna. 'Like they're habitual whoremongers and lechers, these magistrates. Imagine them with their wigs and trousers off!'

She'd been picked up for plying her trade outside and inside *The Builder's Arms*, so we had plenty to say about John Bedford Lee, 'cos it was his arms that had been round the both of us.

'Are you worried about tomorrow?' I asked.

'You watch,' she said. 'If it's who I 'spect, I'll smile at him sweetly, look demure, keep my mouth closed, and when no-one else is looking give him that special smile that he's seen a dozen times before. He'll give me the smallest fine he dares and then sometime next week he'll pay it for me, and a bit extra, if you see what I mean. It's the benefit of living in a small town and having no shame.' She laughed, and I wondered what string I could pull.

I weren't in court more than five minutes but they sent me down for another night, remanded until the magistrates met together the following day. Gilham had been there, and he said he'd see Lee and sort it all out. The next day Lee swore that the pot was his, and that I had come to his house drunk, and I swore that it were mine and I bought it in Melbourne, and that I wasn't drunk but just taken faint. I thought of Anna and I looked at the magistrates and I came over all pitiful and weak and frightened.

'I only went to Mr Lee to pay him money we owed him

and look here's the receipt and how can he be sure that it's his mustard pot, 'cos it's not uncommon, and it's got my mustard in it, and there's this mark on the glass at the bottom, and I'd know it anywhere …'

Lee didn't look as though he knew how many mustard pots he had and what they looked like, and he said that he 'couldn't completely swear to it being my pot,' so after ten minutes the magistrates had heard enough and I was let go. Discharged. 'Don't let us see you here again, Mrs Gilham.'

'No sir, certainly not sir,' and I made a great show of hurrying down from the dock and weeping on Gilham's chest and saying, 'Take me home, husband.'

When we got back, Gilham was furious. He said, 'I went to Lee, and I asked him not to go heavy on you, and he said he wouldn't so long as he could have his mustard pot back. So, what does he do, he presses the charge and has you spend time in the lock up, and what will that do to my business? It's all about reputation, Charlotte. What will my customers think if you get locked up for dishonesty? We can't stay here.'

'But I were discharged,' I said. 'It proves the pot's mine. I can hold my head up.'

'You idiot!' he said. 'We both know where that pot came from, and Lee ain't going to let it rest. Just because you fooled some dunderheaded magistrate don't mean the rest of the town won't have you down for a sneak thief and a drunk.'

He puzzled over it and got angrier and eventually said, 'There's only one way out. We'll sue him in the county court for your false imprisonment and make him pay.' And that's what we did. Two months later, the Judge heard all the evidence over again, but of course nobody agreed exactly what had happened and no-one could swear that the mustard pot was Lee's, though they all thought it was, and one policeman said he heard me say I'd bought it in Melbourne and another said I'd said I'd bought it in Dunolly, and I admitted I hadn't felt so well at the time and probably became confused, but that the pot definitely belonged to a cruet stand, though where that had come from I couldn't remember. Gilham was called and denied he'd ever said anything to Lee about not knowing the mustard pot and you could see the judge thought he'd come amongst a mob of squabbling corellas. The only indisputable evidence was that I'd been locked up for two days - me, a loved wife and mother, and the assessors agreed that Lee should pay us fifty pounds and costs. I looked faint and gave a 'Thank you, your honour,' and Gilham just tried not to look too smug.[216]

After that, we went home and were gay, and that's when, I'm sure, we made our James Isaac and put aside the Isaac that had died. Gilham went down to Melbourne and spent near enough the whole of the fifty pounds on a gold ring with a diamond, which he gave me. I think we was happy for a time then. He made money in the diggings, too. I got caught for another baby soon after James: that was my Charlotte, a darling girl at last. Charly, my love. But before she was born, Gilham got itchy feet again and we was off west, back to Stawell, in search of gold once more.

# 28: Peter, Charlotte, and Charly

## September 2023

Lakshmi is sleeping and I hear nothing from her.

From the depths of the silver bowl, glowing in the lamplight, I am sure that I can see the image of a little Suffolk woman, barely four foot six inches with a freckled, sun-baked face. She is talking to me.

'I am pleased you are seeking us,' she says.

'I am so excited to be setting out,' I whisper in return. 'What a journey you've taken me on! I had no idea about all this, but I suppose no-one in England ever knew what happened to you.'

'It happened, even if no-one knew.'

It is four in the morning. Dawn is breaking, my case is packed, and I am sitting in the porch, waiting for a car to the airport.

As I peer across the pond and the water meadow beyond, I seem to see fair, ghostly folk. Soundless, motionless, turned towards me. My endeavours to know them better mean nothing to them. They are as separate from each other as from me. No threat, no power, but nonetheless present.

'Those are all the generations,' says Charlotte. 'My children's children. My ancestors. All my kin. Your inheritors. Listen.'

They are a legion of unwritten individuals whose descendants have lived even into my own lifetime. They stand, together and alone, like the trunks of the sumac tree. There is one young woman in front, more substantial than all the rest: Charlotte's determined daughter; the daughter that she loved, named after herself, now grown to maturity. Charly. She speaks to me.

# 29: Charly Mulcahy, née Gilham

When you're a child you accept that the way you live is the only way to live. You see other children and their parents, you go into their houses, you see the food they eat, and are puzzled or surprised. You find that some of them even have a bed to themselves. You notice they have better clothes, but you learn quickly not to moan about that. I reckon it was not till I was about ten years old that I began to think that perhaps I'd got a raw deal.

Ma and Pa used to tell me how lucky I should think myself now we had a little three-room cottage with a tin roof, an iron range, and a veranda. When they first came to the goldfields they lived in a tent and camped by streams; they dug holes for a dunny and hung clothes out to dry on bushes. That was when Stawell was still called Pleasant Creek. Now it's a proper town with laid out streets and tidy brick buildings.[217]

That was no compensation for me, never knowing what state Mother would be in. She could be sweet and loving. I remember her at bedtime, singing softly as I went to sleep, or, another time, dancing me round the yard until I was nearly sick with excitement. 'My beautiful little peach,' she would say as she brushed my hair. 'Brush it forty times to make it shine.' And she would fuss with ribbons and aprons. I would suffer her kisses and her trembling hands and try not to pull away.

My three big brothers had all left by this time, working away on farms, mainly, so I was the eldest child at home. After me there was Fred and Eliza, who were three and seven years younger than me. It was up to me to look after them.

'Now, my darling, take the children for a walk and go to the store. Here's money for a quarter of tea, Charly. Get a biscuit each.'

We would be happy as we walked down Main Street. We were living near Big Hill Mine in Stawell. We might stop to play in the bit of a reserve, the children fossicking in the brush and pretending to find gold.

'Is this gold, Charly?' Fred would say, holding up a bit of dusty stone.

'Course not. T'aint shiny, is it? Look again.'

It kept them amused, and I joined in too, trying not to lose sight of either of them in case they ended up in some old diggings. Then, when we got tired of that, we'd go down to the store and I'd speak nicely to Mrs Lynch and we'd chat while she weighed out a packet of tea, and, like as not, she'd give us each a biscuit without me having to pay. I'd slip the penny Ma had given me into the pocket of my apron to add to the little box I had under our bed.

As the children got fretful, we'd walk back up the hill, and I'd end up carrying Eliza and dragging a grizzling Fred. The closer we got to home the more anxious I became. I knew Pa would still be out working, but how would Ma be? Sometimes it was all kind and protective:

'Oh, my darlings, where have you bin? You were gone such a long time. I was nearly for calling out the police,' and she'd smother us and pull us to her and gently chide us for leaving her to worry for so long. Even then I knew it to be false, like she had only realised we'd been out as we came back through the door.

Sometimes she'd shout at me:

'Where you been, you jade? I needed you. The fire's gone

out and there's damper to be made and your father will be back.'

'But you sent me out to buy tea.'

'What took you so long? You could be there and back in ten minutes.'

'But I had to take Fred and Eliza.'

'Don't you answer me back, you maw! Your father'll cane you when he gets home.'

I knew he wouldn't. I'd run off and hide my tears under a gum tree in the bush. I knew she wouldn't come after me, already being assailed by two wailing tots. On those days it was out of sight and out of mind with her.

The worst was when I'd come home and she wasn't in the parlour or the yard and I'd poke my nose into her bedroom and she'd be sprawled across her bed with a bottle, drained, on the floor. She'd snort and snuffle and nothing would rouse her, and I'd pull the children away and start to make the damper and stew for us all.

Pa would come in and see me at the stove.

'Where's your mother?'

'In bed.'

'Oh Lord,' he'd say, and look in their room and either pull the door to, quietly, or more often he'd wake her, and I'd hear a slap and shouting and he'd crash out of the house and say, 'feed the children, Charly. I'm down the 'otel.' That would be the last I'd see of him all evening. I'd do tea and put the children into the bed we shared, and often I'd join them before he came home and Ma got up. I'd snuggle up to little Eliza and keep my eyes shut tight and pretend to be asleep. When he got back from the bar there'd be an unholy row. Freddy might wake and start crying and want to go out of our room, but I'd hold the two tots and keep them with me.

'Better not,' I'd say. 'Go to sleep. All will be well in the morning.'

It usually was. Whatever had happened on those wild nights it was like the storm had passed and left no damage, all talk blown out, and a new day starting, with just mother looking paler and complaining a little about her head or her stomach or her shortness of breath. It was better, too, if Pa had gone off.

'I'm working away this week. There's a job at Bendigo.' He'd be gone, and he might be back the following day or he might be back in a week.

'I never knows where he is,' said Ma, whenever we asked her if Pa was coming home. 'Best he stays away, the beggar.' The next day she'd be complaining that she had no money and, 'Where's the fool got to? We can't live on fresh air.' She would go cleaning and work behind the bar in the hotel and then it was down to me to care for the children. Sometimes both our parents would be gone all night. When she came back in the morning she might give me a shilling.

'There, my darling girl. Treat yourself. You're a good girl.'

Then we'd eat well: fresh meat, and veggies, which were rare enough in those days.

'Where did this come from, Ma?'

'Ask no questions and you'll be told no lies.'

So I kept my mouth shut and coped as well as I could.

'Sure, you've become quite the little housewife,' said Mrs Lynch in the store. 'Where's your Pa this week?'

'Melbourne, I think. Building houses, he says.'

'And how's your Ma, dear?'

'Well enough, Mrs Lynch, thank you.'

I liked talking to her. She was Irish and told me her father had come out to escape famine back home. She guessed Ma had come out as a convict, but it's not something anyone would talk about. If I asked Mrs Lynch about the place she had come from, she'd say, 'I can't remember. I was only a babe in arms.'

And Pa would tell me never to talk about the past, though his reasons seemed a bit different:

'Never give people the bullets to fire at you, Charly. Whatever happens in the family stays here. We don't want anyone poking around. It ain't ever going to be to our benefit.'

Well, he may have been right, as events were to show. Then again, if someone had poked around a bit sooner …

I was eleven. 1875. It must have been in the middle of the summer, 'cos I know my birthday was past and the school was on holiday for Christmas. I couldn't see myself going back to the classroom since my Ma was about to have another baby. Pa hadn't been around much for nearly a year, but apparently enough to leave us with another member of the family.

'Look after your ma for me,' had been the last words he said to me. Not a word about when he'd be back.

'The work's dried up here. I'm off over the border.' Which I took to mean that he was going to New South Wales. He'd found work on the sheep stations before, and I'd heard Wagga Wagga mentioned. He had his family still in Melbourne and Tasmania, but I don't think he wanted to throw himself on any of them.

'Why are you going, Pa?' I asked.

'We don't do each other no good anymore, your ma and me. You're better off without me.' Which I know is what men say when they can't be bothered to make the effort. I've come across a few like that myself, though my husband John's a stayer and a good man.

So here we were, Ma and me, with Fred aged about nine, I think, and Eliza who was just four. Eliza stuck to me like a little koala, wide-eyed and silent. Fred was just naughty. Even I could see that Ma wasn't fit to have another baby. She couldn't look after herself. I had to tell her when to change her clothes. 'It's this heat, Ma; you stink.' She'd grumble and wash some clothes and fall into a chair on the porch and sleep. I did my best to hide the grog, and we had no money, so she was always craving it and complaining.

'Here, feel the baby, Charly,' she'd say, putting my hand on her belly. 'Is it still moving?'

'Yes, Ma.' I didn't know whether to be excited, because I really wanted to have a new baby brother or sister, or to be frightened for us all.

Ma was small - Pa would call her his 'damned midget' when he was wild with her - and the baby bump seemed especially tiny when I tried to compare with other women around the town, but most of all I didn't think she could look after a baby and I was frightened that I wouldn't know what to do.

'Ma, what we going to do with a baby?'

'Don't you worry, Charly. I've had seven before, including you.'

Yes, I thought. One died, and the two oldest haven't been near us for years. George had gone to WA by then and was a prison warder, which, knowing Ma's history, seems now to be making a bit of a point. My brother James hadn't lived with us for years, and though I did see him around the town sometimes, he wouldn't have anything to do with us. So, it was just down to me to see everything right, which was difficult because I knew there were secret things that no one ever talked about - hidden stuff that only adults were supposed to know. In our family there seemed to be more than most, though how I could tell I don't know. As children we taunted each other with the things we thought we knew.

'You're mum's a convict. What did she do? Did she kill someone? She did, didn't she? Yer mum's a murderer. Murderer!' shouted Gobby Johnson, the policeman's son, across the street.'

'No, she ain't. My Pa was a free settler.'

'Yeah, but your mum wasn't.'

'Your Ma doesn't know who your Pa is, Gobby.'

The grown-ups didn't like us shouting things like that. There were too many secrets in our little town. Nobody much wanted their history told.

'Take no notice,' said Pa. 'Your mother was a good girl. She should never have been sent here.' That's all he would say then, and, of course, I could never ask Ma. Later, after her passing, he would say to me, 'The past is best forgotten, Charly. History is no use to us. It won't put bread on your plate. We all came for a fresh start, girl, and that's what we got. The old country did us no favours and we owe it nothing. This is the beginning. Get a good man and you'll have fine children.'

This was just before he died, and perhaps he was feeling sentimental, though he seemed more at peace then than all the time I was growing up. When I had been eleven or twelve, and the oldest child left at home, that was the year it had all fallen apart.

Ma had a baby girl in January. Georgina, they called her. She died. She was two months old. Ma's feeble milk dribbled into Georgina and just dribbled out again, taking her life with her.[218] After the baby was buried, and when Ma was finally fit to do some work at the Inn:

'I'm off,' said Pa. He packed his tools and his swag and left early one morning.

'You'll be back soon, Pa?' I whispered.

'As soon as I've made me fortune,' he said, laughing.

I didn't know how to take it, and perhaps he didn't know what he intended to do, but it didn't stop him turning away towards the rising sun and disappearing into the dust along the road to New South Wales.

Everything was turning to dust. Ma was worn out, I could see. Her mouth was black; she'd lost most of her teeth before Georgina was born, and she chewed her tobacco with red gums. Her breathing was painful - you could hear the rattle in her sleep, and she coughed all the time. She was always complaining of the pains in her guts. Her face would crease, like an empty flour sack, and she'd hold back a moan.

'Get me grog, Charly,' she'd say. 'I need me medicine.' It did her no good; dulled the pain in her head but not in her stomach. So, it was just me with Fred, who did what he liked, and Eliza, who simply looked frightened.

Fred spent most of his time hanging about round the back of the store and outside the bakery, picking up scraps. We had a new railway in town, and he'd stand around the station when a train came in.

'Gi'us a penny, mate.' My little brother was turned into a beggar, and I didn't know what to do about it. I told ma.

'Did he eat to-day?'

'I think so, Ma.' So she'd laugh and go back to sleep in her chair.

We needed clothes, too.

'Can I have that old skirt, Ma? I'm nearly big enough. I can sew the hem up. Eliza can have my cast offs.'

'Please yourself.'

I took Ma's old clothes and mended the skirt and made it fit me. When she saw me in it, she said,

'That's my Melbourne skirt. Cost your father a pretty penny. It were worth it, though.' She gazed into the distance, smiling, remembering something.

'What is it, Ma?' But she wouldn't say.

I couldn't do nothing about Fred's clothes, though, and he looked more and more ragged. The red dust stuck to everything. His shirt was stained and his trousers had holes in the seat.

'Give 'em to me, Fred, and I'll darn 'em.'

'Ger off!' and he'd be gone down the street.

One time the police brought him home and spoke to Ma.

'Found your lad, Mrs Gilham. Begging by the town hall. Can't have that now, can we? He should be in school if you can't keep him at home. Where's your man?'

'Working away.'

'Well, we don't want to see the boy on the streets again.'

'I can't do nothing with him. I ain't got no control.'

When the copper had gone, she screamed at Fred, but it didn't do no good, and I knew we were marked. Next time they found him begging they didn't bring him home. She had to go to the magistrate. It was a wet winter day, and she was breathing like a steam engine as she dragged herself down the hill, hanging on to me and Eliza. I thought, what a horrible sight we are.

'Gilhams being locked up again?' shouted Gobby Johnson, loitering outside the courthouse. I could feel the burning in my cheeks.

They brought Fred from the cells. He was pale and dirty, but they'd given him a slice, and a mug of tea, and he waved at me. The magistrate looked stern, but he spoke quietly to Ma.

'Mrs Gilham, I think you are failing to care for your son. The police have found him several times begging on the street. He is not looked after. He is hungry and dirty. What do you have to say?'

'He runs away, sir. I can't control him. My husband, he's working away over the border. I haven't seen him for months. We got no money, sir.'

'Do you work?'

'When I can.' And I thought, can't they see she's sick? There was whispering between the policeman and the magistrate and some woman in a big hat who I'd never seen before.

'Mrs Gilham, we do not think you can look after Frederick. Until your husband returns, and you can care for him properly, the State of Victoria will look after him. He will be admitted to the industrial school at Sunbury. When you can show you are able to look after him then you may come here again and he can be returned to you.'[219]

We were able to say goodbye and then Fred disappeared with the woman in the hat. That was the last time I saw him for six years. He never talked much about the school, though later I heard how rough it was, and the boys were never cared for.[220]

It was the last time Ma ever saw him. How could she tell the court that she couldn't control him? How could she accept him being taken away? All she said was,

'Someone else will feed him now, and he'll get a new suit of clothes.' And then, 'If only your father were here.' And later again, when she'd had her grog and lay on her bed fussing over Eliza,

'Don't you leave me, Charly. You're a good girl. You'll look after us.'

'Of course, Ma.'

What else could I say. She was my ma, and I knew she'd had it hard and that her own mother had died and her stepmother had abandoned her - well, that's what she said. I don't know what really had happened when she was a child in England.

Father came back a few weeks later and, when he found Fred had been taken, he was angrier than I'd ever seen him. He brought money with him, so we had better food for a bit, but more whisky, too, and Ma and Pa were screaming at each other night after night.

'Serves me right for marrying a Vandemonian! Look at you. Make yourself presentable, woman.'

The house was cleaned, and I had a new blouse. I went to the store and Mrs Lynch said, 'You're a fine girl, Charlotte. I could use a young pair of hands. I can't give you much, but will you help?'

I went to the store each afternoon after school and cleaned and stocked the shelves and ran errands and I had a few coppers of my own to spend. It kept me out of Ma and Pa's way, too. The shop was a tidy place. I liked the order, and that people talked nicely to each other. Mrs Lynch would have no truck with bad manners. She spoke kindly to me and customers didn't look down on me.

Things were going from bad to worse at home, 'cos Ma was sicker and sicker. I could hardly bear to go to bed in the evening. I'd curl up with Eliza and we'd hear Ma in the next room, drawing breath like the blacksmith's bellows or crying out with the pain in her stomach. Pa spent most of his time out of the house. When he wasn't working, he was in the hotel.

One day I got home at the end of morning school and Ma was lying in bed. I stayed with her and Eliza. I could tell she was bad, but I sat and sewed until Pa come in from work. It wasn't late. I heard her call out for him,

'John, I'm bad again.' He looked at her, didn't look pleased, and went off to lie on our couch in the other room. Later she suddenly sat up and then bent double.

'Get me a basin, Charly,' she said, and when I got the old tin bowl from the kitchen, she was very sick. Eliza whimpered and ran to our bed to hide away. Ma shouted,

'John, I'm really bad. I need the doctor.'

Pa came in and must have seen how pale she looked.

'Go and get Doctor O'Donnell, Charly,' he said. 'I'll sit with her.'

I ran to the doctor. He had one of those serious offices with a stone front and a heavy, polished wooden door. It looked more permanent than any other building nearby. You could see his brass plate was polished every day. There were steps up to the door, and a bell sounded as I went inside. I suppose it was meant to say, 'Pay attention. Someone's here and needs help,' but when you're twelve and you walk into a stern, empty room it just says, 'Warning! Keep out!'

I waited for a minute, wondering whether anyone would come and whether I should stay there or run away, when the door at the back of the office opened and the doctor appeared.

'I'm from Mrs Gilham - my ma. She's been taken ill. She's been sick and she's pale and coughing. Pa sent me.'

He said, 'I'm just sitting down for my tea. I can't come now.' He looked at me closely and his silent face said, 'I know all about your family.'

'She's got no fever?' he asked.

'I don't think so,' I said. He went to the big desk, sat in the chair, opened the drawer, and took out a pad of paper. I remember he had a fat pen which seemed large in his long, clean fingers. He wrote beautifully, as if the care he offered my mother was all in that pen and piece of paper.[221]

'Here, take this to the pharmacist,' he said, handing me the prescription.

I couldn't read it properly but there weren't many words on the paper, and I thought, *She mustn't be very ill, then. How does he know?* But you can't argue with a doctor, so I took the paper and ran to the chemist. He bottled up the medicine (I suppose, looking back, it must have been laudanum) and I ran back home.

'The doctor wouldn't come, but he sent me for the medicine.' My mother sort of laughed. I think she was saying to herself, 'What else would I expect.' She took a spoonful of the tincture and threw it up straight away. She fell back on the pillow and seemed to be asleep.

'Well,' said Pa, 'there's nothing else I can do. She just needs to sleep it off. I'm going to the hotel. Got to see a man about a dog.'

'Don't go, John,' she said suddenly. 'Let me sing for you …'

But all he said was, 'You lie still now. And take no more ale. It's that what's doing you no good.' He was off out the door before she could say anything else.

Eliza and I sat on the bed with her, and her breathing became quieter. After a few minutes she arched her back and coughed cruelly and then fell back once more. I remember I relaxed and laid my head next to her and hugged Eliza and thought it were good when there was peace. I closed my eyes. *Perhaps, if I pray hard, the house will always be like this,* I thought.

We were like that for many minutes when Eliza whispered, 'Is she dead? I think she's dead.' She began to whimper.

I sat up and looked at Ma. She'd changed. I thought that when people died they went to sleep and looked calm. Ma didn't. She seemed greyer and her skin was sort of tight and angry. Her eyes were staring into space, and I knew that if I followed her gaze there would be nothing to see.

'Go and get Mr Campbell,' I said to Eliza. 'I'll look after Ma.'

Mr Campbell lived next door. He came and he said, softly, 'She's dead, child. Now take your sister and go and see Mrs Campbell and tell her, and we'll look after your mother.'

I grasped Eliza's hand, and we tiptoed out because that seemed to be what you should do, as if we might wake her, when really, I thought afterwards, we should have screamed and jumped about to try to bring her back.

We stayed all night with Mrs Campbell. Pa came home at some point and, of course, there was a fuss because he hadn't been there, and a policeman said there would be an inquest, and though I didn't really understand what that was I could tell it was serious and they needed to know if anyone could have saved Ma or had done anything to hurt her.

The next day I had to go through everything again in front of the coroner[222] and a whole lot of men who all looked solemn, though some of them looked sympathetically at me and others just looked embarrassed. They asked me questions and wrote down my answers and I had to sign, though I couldn't do my name well enough, I was so anxious, and they wrote my name and told me to put a cross. At the end, the coroner said she died of congestion of the lungs, which somehow seemed to make everyone relieved.

She was buried in the cemetery just out of town, and Pa made a small wooden cross and planted it over where her body was. Some days I would go up there and think about her. My mother had a troubled life, at least that's what my Pa said. I didn't really understand what that meant. If you have a troubled life then either someone else causes the trouble or you cause it yourself. It's what I say to my children now: don't go pretending that you're not responsible. If you did it, own up, put it right, and learn from it. My mother didn't take responsibility. She could drink and she could sing, but what use is that when your children have no shoes and can't write their names? I wouldn't stand for it and nor would my husband, John Mulcahy.

If I tell you the story now, it's not because I'm proud of her. It's a warning. Life's hard. This country is unforgiving, as John would say; it doesn't owe us anything. I'm sorry for her, of course I am. She lost her mother young, just as I lost her. You can't let it destroy you. You can't let it bring others down either, like she nearly brought my Pa down. If I'm honest, there are days when I think we were better off without her, and if that sounds hard, I'm sorry, but most of the time I wonder about all the things that she never talked about, all the suffering there must have been in her life, and I remind myself not to judge another human being unless I want all my little mistakes to be advertised to the world. And I did love her.

Pa drank less and stayed at home more from then on. He was embarrassed that Fred had been taken away, which is not to say that things went smoothly or that we lived happily ever after. Eliza was hit hard by our mother's death. I did what I could to be a mother to her, but she knew it wasn't the same.

'I'm not doing what you say! You're not my mother!' Over and over again.

'You must wash your neck, Eliza. And your feet are filthy.'

'You're not my mother. I want my mother!'

She had just had her sixth birthday when Ma died. I could understand - what a present. But then, I was feeling just as bad. Eliza took it out on all of us, especially Pa. I know she didn't understand why she didn't have her mother, but there's nothing you can do to reverse a death, so Eliza just needed to cope. Pa wouldn't talk about it with either of us.

He sorted ma's things out.

'You girls will be able to wear her clothes one day,' he said. He had no idea, of course, but put all her clothes in a bundle under the bed. Her bits of jewellery, which were mainly the two gold rings she always wore (one had a diamond), all went into a wooden box with her ticket of leave and marriage lines and a lock of her hair. Once everything was put away, that was it. Charlotte, our mother, had been packed up, and there were meals to be cooked, a house to be cleaned, and I went on learning to be a housewife. That's what you did in those days.

'I seen her again, Charly,' Eliza said.

'You're a little fool. She ain't here. She ain't coming back, so stop pretending.'

She had started to put a plate on the table for food for our mother. At first Pa got cross and shouted, but then Eliza bawled her eyes out and it sounded like we were slaughtering a sheep, so in the end we just ignored it. That went on for months.

You could see that Pa was troubled too. I'd catch him, in his room with the door half closed, going through the bundle of old clothes and rummaging in the wooden box. He'd paw at the rings and stroke her favourite dress. If he thought one of us was watching, he'd become all businesslike, pretend he was just clearing up, and put everything away again.

Then one day, about six months after Ma died, we heard a great bellowing from his room.

'Children! Come here.'

We looked into the room. The box was on the bed and all the bits and pieces spread about.

'Which of you has been in this box?'

'Not me, Pa,' I said.

'Not me,' said Eliza, who looked terrified.

'What's wrong, Pa?' I said.

'Her ring's gone.' He was almost whispering.

'The ring's there,' said Eliza, pointing to the plain gold band.

'Not that ring, child,' he said. 'The diamond ring. One of you must have taken it.'

'It wasn't me, Pa,' I said. 'I wouldn't take it. I've never opened your box,' which of course wasn't true because I'd been in it several times when he was at work.

'Not me neither,' whispered Eliza, her head dropping to her chest so that I knew straight away that it must have been her who had taken the ring. I guess Pa saw it too.

He picked up the other ring and placed it on his hand and looked sternly at us.

'I shall have to tell the police. Whoever has stolen the ring will be sent to prison if it's not found. Now come here both of you and swear.' And he did the strangest thing. He took my hand and, as he held it, he slipped the gold ring over my big finger and said,

'Swear by your dear mother's memory that you have not stolen her diamond ring.'

I nearly choked, caught my breath, then said, 'I swear. I truly swear.' It seemed like the most solemn moment of my life and even now I can't remember having to make so dreadful an oath ever again. He slipped the ring off my finger and caught Eliza's hand, put the ring on her tiny finger and made her swear too.

'I swear.' She whispered.

'Louder! I can't hear you girl.'

'I swear, I swear, I swear.' She burst into tears, pulled away from him, and ran out of the room. He put the ring back in the box and the box under the bed and as he stood up, he put his arm round me and gave me a little hug. I thought, *What happens now?*

Later he said to both of us, 'If the ring does not appear to-night, I shall go to the police station tomorrow morning.'

Which is what he did do, because no ring appeared. I asked Eliza, but she said she hadn't got it and screamed at me. I looked in her pockets and under her pillow when she was asleep, but I couldn't find it. I began to wonder whether we really had had a burglar in the cottage.

The next week he showed us a piece of printed paper, spelling it out so Eliza could understand. It was the *Victoria Police Gazette*, and it said:

> *Stolen from the dwelling of John Henry Gilham, Moonlight Hill, near Stawell, recently, a diamond ring, with 'J.H.Gilham' and 'J.F.' stamped on the inside; value £50.*[223]

'There, you see,' he said, 'the burglar will know that the police are on to him, or her. That ring cost fifty pounds, so it's a hanging offence if the criminal is brought to justice.'

He didn't say anything more, and nor did I, but the following evening, when he came back from work and went into his room to change, we heard him suddenly shout out,

'Girls! Come here!'

We rushed into the room, and he was bending over the bed with Ma's box open in front of him.

'See here! The ring's returned. I knew it would! Did either of you see anyone around the house today?'

'No, Pa,' I said. 'I was at school this morning.'

'No, Pa,' said Eliza. And then, after a long pause, 'And what will you do now?'

'I'll tell the police, of course. They can call off the search!'

He was smiling. Happier, and sort of more normal than I can remember him usually being, like he'd not only recovered from the loss of the ring. Six days later he showed us the *Police Gazette* once more:

*John Henry Gilham reports that his ring has been restored to him but refuses to say by whom.* [224]

The whole incident is one of the strongest memories I have of my Pa - one of the happiest, anyway, despite it all being because of Ma's death. I felt closer to him than at any other time, and I thought, *How clever of him to sort the difficulty with Eliza.*

It wasn't sorted, though. I did my best, but, with each year that passed, Eliza became wilder. She was like Fred had been. She wouldn't stay at home. She begged in the street and, being a girl, I knew she was asking for more than just a farthing or a clip round the ear. Pa was drinking once more, and every time Eliza ran off and was brought back by the police or some inquisitive neighbour, he belted her. It didn't work, of course, and after the police had kept her in the lock-up for a night and brought her before the magistrate, it was the lady in the hat all over again.

'She's out of control, Mr Gilham, and we really do not see any way of you giving her the care and control she needs.'

'Yes, ma'am.' Pa was exhausted, and he just seemed relieved that they weren't taking me away too. She was nine years old and taken off to the industrial school to learn good manners and housekeeping, so they said, but I guess it was just more misery. Fred was still in Sandhurst (when he hadn't run away[225]), and Eliza went to a place called St Joseph's.

She was supposed to stay there for six years but they hung on to her for eight and then licensed her out as a skivvy all over the state to any housekeeper who'd have her. I hardly saw her but once a year. She became a beautiful girl but went more and more into her shell. By the end she would hardly talk to me, and I got so I couldn't tell her about my happiness.

In 1889, I married John Mulcahy in St Arnaud, and the next year I had our Ellen, and I thought, *Perhaps Eliza will come and live with us and I can give her the home she never had,* but when I asked at St Joseph's they said she'd gone missing from her last placement and they didn't know where she was.

John and I moved south down to Mortlake and then St Joseph's said they were finding Eliza a place in the Immigrants' Home. That's a miserable workhouse by any other name, and I wasn't having that - not when we had a room to spare. I put an enquiry in *The Age* in the hope that she might see it or that someone would tell her:

*Elizabeth Gilham, left Stawell, 1880, Age about 20. Sister Charlotte Mulcahy of Mortlake wishes to hear from her.*[226]

You had to pay by the word, you see, and so I kept it brief, but just enough for her to find me if she wanted to.

There was no reply. I always hoped that Eliza would turn up again, and I did hear that she returned to the Immigrants' Home for a few days, when she was desperate for a bed I suppose, but she never contacted me. I advertised again a few years later, afraid that she might have fallen into a bad situation. I had a message put in the *Police Gazette*. When nothing came of it, I asked our MP what I should do, and he said I'd done the right thing, and he made some more enquiries and put another message in the *Gazette* with a little more information.[227] It did no good.

Pa was long since dead by this time.[228] My brothers were to the four winds across Victoria; George had got as far as Western Australia. Somehow it just seemed down to me to hold the family memory together, and I do keep looking for Eliza. One day, perhaps, she'll reappear.[229]

Our family history means little to me, except the pain Ma must have gone through all those years ago. No one here talks about their convict ancestors. It's the eve of a new century and, like everyone else, I'm looking forward to good things to come. It's all right if your ancestors were adventurers on the first fleet, but some of us have endured too many jokes about our criminal past, so I keep quiet and don't ask or answer questions about my Ma.

But I wear her pretty gold and diamond ring.

# 30: Peter

## September 2023

*A Tribute to Charlotte who struggled through life*
*A convict at thirteen, at nineteen a wife.*
*Her years were frustration, not reading or writing,*
*She mothered eight children through the travelling and fighting.*
*Her friend was the drink - a temporary release,*
*It finally gave her ... eternal peace.*[230]

It is night and the plane is somewhere over the Middle East. I
am sleepless and wondering why I am here. I have been talking,
whispering, to the retired policeman in the next seat. He is
travelling, he says, to meet his son and family in Melbourne.

'I go and visit them as often as I can. Family's got to stay in
touch, even across all this distance.'

'I'm going because I've been researching my family,' I tell him.
'I've got a distant aunt who was transported. I want to find out
what happened to her and her children ...' I start to tell him the

story, but I can see that he is soon glazing over. I'm sounding like the Ancient Mariner. I talk to myself.

I am young Charly's cousin, three times removed. Removed, because so many generations and so much time separate us that law and custom would count our blood relationship irrelevant. Yet we have a common root, a common inheritance, and I do not wish to deny it. I want to understand what it means.

We are both descended from James Ellis of Ipswich, father of the transported Charlotte. He knows nothing of Charly, or of me; could not have imagined our lives, the landscapes into which we were born, or the plane which carries me at thirty-nine thousand feet. When Charlotte, Charly's mother, was taken from the family in Ipswich, James mourned her. He died within a year of her transportation. It would be fanciful to say that he died of a broken heart: it was pneumonia that took him off in December 1849. An old soldier, Thomas Woolner, sat by him as he made his final voyage in his damp Long Lane room.[231]

Charlotte's stepmother had been dry-eyed when the girl was removed from their lives. Charlotte had been a troublesome spirit, uncontrollable and reckless. She did not care for family feelings and had rebuffed her father's attempts at peace-making. The only ally that she had was her older brother, John. Like Charlotte, he was a child of James's first wife.

John Ellis was a sawyer. When Charlotte was running wild, John was making his way in the adult world. He married within a couple of years of his father's death and named his second child Charlotte. He had not seen his sister for six years, but his family knew that he was telling them, 'She is still alive to me.' He had met

George Root, introduced him to another sister, Hannah, but John eventually moved away from Ipswich and lived out the rest of his short life in Essex.[232]

With James dead, Charlotte transported, and John married, the Ellis family of Ipswich was reduced to mother, Catherine, and four younger children: Isaac, Hannah, Charles, and Eliza.[233] And after that?

Hannah remained in Ipswich, married George, had her boy, George Lionel, my great-grandfather, and died aged twenty-six. Catherine and her other children went back to Ireland. Isaac married a girl from Limerick in 1866, and they had a daughter, Eliza, the following year. The young family returned to England, but lived in Plumstead, Kent. They were done with Ipswich.[234] Eliza met another Irishman, James Gildea Evans, a railway engineer, who took her to India - where he worked for the Imperial government. While there, she bought a small, three-footed silver bowl. All these dead. All travelling with me on a computer memory stick. In the locker above my head, Lakshmi sleeps on her silver bed. Around the darkened cabin, video screens flicker with ghostly figures. I am alone and not alone, travelling in hope.

One day, in the 1930s, the widow Eliza, in a serviced apartment in Hampshire, has a visit from her teenage cousin twice removed - my mother. The girl sees the Indian bowl sitting on the windowsill and admires it, running her fingers over the delicate engraving. Eliza talks a little of being in India, but mainly she wishes to catch up with news from Ipswich and of other family members. She is feeling her age and is thinking about her inheritance. She has been left well provided for by her late husband, but they had no children. She has lost touch with her immediate family after twenty years abroad, and so where will her wealth go next? When it is time for my mother to catch the train, back to London and onwards to Suffolk, Eliza picks up the silver bowl and wraps it in a piece of brown paper.

'Something for you to remember me by, dear,' she says wistfully.

'Oh, Aunty … but are you sure? It's lovely.'

Eliza presses the parcel firmly into her hand and sees her to the door.

They will never meet again.

James Ellis's children and grandchildren have become a diaspora. They are printers, engineers, engine drivers, labourers, and soldiers. They are to be found in Kent, Sussex, Middlesex, Hampshire, and India as well as in Suffolk and Australia. They are children of the 1870 Education Act. They can sign their names with good, cursive script and read an instruction manual or the advertisements in a newspaper. They are committed to progress and their families' security. They remind me of the dragon fish: they may be out of water, but they adapt to a new land and pass that adaptation on to their children.

There is much avoidance of the events of the past. If they are aware of their ancestors' misdemeanours, of theft and bigamy, transportation, and appalling poverty, and even if these things are too often repeated, or influence them unconsciously, there is an imperative to keep family secrets. They reckon without a small Indian silver bowl and the journey it has taken me on. They reckon without the persistent strangeness of the archives.

I can't perpetuate silence. I am not frightened of this inheritance. We are not doomed to repeat these stories, nor do I see them as shameful. I realise that, as the facts have unfolded, I have even set aside my objectivity and become proud of these ancestors. They may be 'removed,' as the table of relationships informs me, but they are uniquely related to me. They haunt me. I've lived very happily on my own for twenty years or more, but now, propelled through thin air with my fellow, sleeping, passengers, I wonder whether I shouldn't have tried harder, tried sooner, to discover the trails to my distant family.

I have understood that stories which touch me so nearly cannot be unheard. My reality is now richer, and my thin ribbon of time, which these days often seems perilously close to its frayed end, has gained substance. I need to follow it to some conclusion: not just mine, but to that of the tribe which stems from Root and Ellis. I have an inheritance to bestow on some living soul that I have yet to meet. I will sleep now, and tomorrow I will wake in Australia.

It is afternoon, the pond is still, and leaves are turning gold, or so my remote security cameras tell my mobile phone. I am using the Wi-Fi in a motel at Stawell, ten thousand miles from home. Two days ago, I landed at Melbourne and drove to McRae Street in Bendigo, where baby Isaac Gilham had died, and I saw a corrugated iron cottage which might even have existed when Charlotte was there.

I have driven through the wearying bush where Charlotte and John Henry camped, and have seen the last traces of goldrush diggings around Dunolly and Ararat. The little towns seem almost deserted in this hot season, but out of the corner of my eye I have glimpsed the ghosts of Gilhams, in the hem of a skirt disappearing through the door of a hotel, or shabby trousers flitting behind a gum tree.

Today I go to the Stawell Historical Society. They open their file on Charlotte, show me the local map, and gently point me towards Moonlight Hill, where she once lived.

I walk through the carefully tended reserve where Gilham dug for the gold-bearing quartz, where Charlotte slumped on an untidy bed, and from where young Charly walked her brother and sister down to town. Galahs shriek at me, and an ancient gum tree rustles in a gust of wind as if to say, 'and so you're here.' The afternoon has become hot. The air shimmers like dull tin foil.

What would my parents have thought about this pilgrimage? My father would have asked how much it all cost and why did I think it was worth it. I can hear the scepticism in his voice. My mother would have loved to be with me. She would have been so delighted that her silver bowl had unlocked such a journey.

'Go on, dear,' I hear her say. 'I think we're getting closer. Closer.'

A mile or so away, in the deserted cemetery, behind its old iron fence, the ground rises gently. Road trains thunder past on the interstate highway. There are some graves with dignified - if crumbling - Victorian masonry, and furthest away there are the tidy ranks of the recent dead. Most of the burials are in the oldest section, without stones or crosses. I have a hand-drawn plan from Jim at the Historical Society, and there is a grave site, number 3412, where Charlotte and her baby had been buried. I pace out the plot. John Gilham's wooden cross that once marked it is long since gone, and the grass is barren under the trees, but I know that this is the place.

I dump my rucksack on the dusty earth. A crow bounces across the ground. Australian crows, I have discovered, make a sound like a discontented toddler, and this one delivers its dying fall and then roots for grubs. All becomes silent, still, and I am left to contemplate the end of a journey.

Minutes pass. I feel that I am not alone. I try not to look behind me, but I sense that Keziah is standing there, bent almost double. Beside her are the shadowy figures of George and Hannah.

The vacant spaces of the cemetery are beginning to fill. I dare not move. There, to my right, are James Root and John Ellis. Charles Edwards stands to attention in parade uniform. Clara and PC Bragg are here together, as if to check that all is ordered and respectful. Around me, within the heat haze, a host is assembling. Some are in chains. Some I recognise but most I cannot name.

We are all looking towards the smooth, grey-blue trunk of an ancient gum tree, which marks the edge of the cemetery plot.

There stands Charlotte, holding a baby and gazing back at us.

'Thank you all for coming,' she says.

'It has taken a long time to bring us all together. It is such a long way,' I say.

There is a sigh from the grey company, like a long breath of wind.

I hear Lakshmi, in my head.

'They are all here. They each contribute, whether you know it or not.'

'Why did I waste my life looking for them when they were always with me?'

'Not wasted,' she says. 'You were made richer by the journey.'

Charlotte shimmers beside the gum tree.

Suddenly a dog barks, a small black dog on a long lead. An elderly man is approaching. He has a gentle smile and, as he approaches, sees the map in my hand and speaks.

'You looking for someone in particular?'

I am startled. I look about me and see that the old man and I are alone on a shabby piece of dried ground, and I am staring vacantly. The dog is sniffing at my rucksack.

'Charlotte Gilham,' I say. 'A distant relative. I know her grave is hereabouts, and I think this is the closest I will get.'

He stands up straight, jerks his head upwards.

'Are you a Gilham?'

'No, but Charlotte would have been a great-great-aunt.'

'Of me, too,' he says. 'I come here from time to time, just to say hello.'

I don't quite know what to say. As I stare at him, unable to speak the right words, a slight, golden young woman trots purposefully towards us.

'Hi,' she says and pauses, as though waiting for an explanation. She stoops to pet the little dog.

The man smiles again and places a hand on her shoulder.

'This is Charly, my granddaughter,' he says to me. 'I'm George Gilham.'

I feel pricking behind my eyes: I think I might burst into tears.

Is this real? I can't say a word. I hold my breath and scrutinise the pair. No, these are not ghosts but solid, glowing, flesh.

'I'm Peter Tye, from England.'

There is another pause. My name means nothing to them.

For an eternal moment I am filled with a myriad of jostling fragments of other Georges and Charlottes, and other lives, disordered, crowded, and noisy. I put my hands to my ears. I must look like a lunatic. I struggle to seem calm, to breathe and to find the right words. I say to the girl,

'I think I've been looking for you.'

'Really?' she replies. She stands and peers intently at me, shading her eyes against the declining sun.

'Yes. I have an inheritance for you.'

Over coffee, in the bakery down the hill, after Charly and her grandfather have let me gabble on about my years of research and the need to find who our family was and what has happened to them, we exchange contact details.

The Indian silver bowl sits on the table between us. It holds the memory stick with all my stories. The bowl catches the light and Lakshmi sparkles. I nudge it towards Charly.

She places it in her open palms and lifts it tenderly, as if raising a chalice, just as I have done a thousand times.

Silence again. I don't want to let Lakshmi go, yet it seems the right thing to do.

'It is important to remember,' says George. 'You see your path to the future in the folk that came before.'[235]

Charly nestles the bowl in her bag. She looks at her grandfather as if checking that this is the right thing to do. He smiles at her and nods. She stands, gathers her things, and says, gently,

'I must go. I'm sorry. I have a friend waiting. I'll message you.'

She reaches out to shake my hand. I stand.

'Thanks for the gift.' She says, 'It's beautiful.' Our fingers cling for a moment. Her grip is warm and confident.

As we break contact, I feel wrung out, abandoned. She turns away, goes through the door, and into the street. Lakshmi and the girl both gone. Yet this is what I wanted, and I will not grieve.

I turn to speak to George, but he too is going.

'I'll be in touch,' he says, grasps my hand, nods at me, and suddenly I am alone. I look down at three empty coffee cups and cake crumbs on napkins. So, this is it?

The bakery is shutting up. I close my backpack, sling it over my shoulder, and go out into the drab carpark. I watch the little town pulling down its shutters. Road trains continue to trundle past, and cars pull into the service station across the road. No one passes on the sidewalk.

Yet the spirits are all around me: Australians who dug for gold and fenced and farmed the land, those original custodians who celebrate their ancestors here within the landscape, and all our family, now documented in 'the cloud' and carried away by the next generation.

I've told my stories and passed them on. What I have bequeathed is, I hope, no burden, but something to be built on.

There are three thousand more names in the family tree. Even without Lakshmi, I can find more stories.

I climb into the hire car. Tonight, the motel, and tomorrow, home. Start again.

# The Family Trees

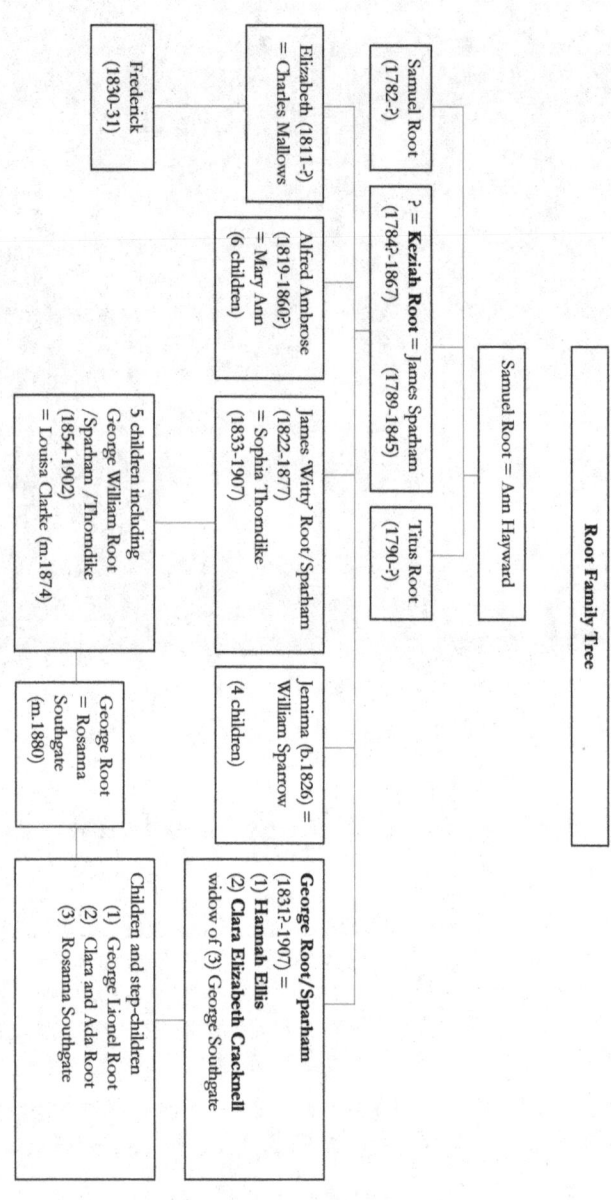

Root Family Tree

Samuel Root = Ann Hayward

Samuel Root (1782-?)

? = **Keziah Root** (1784?-1867) = James Sparham (1789-1845)

Titus Root (1790-?)

Elizabeth (1811-?) = Charles Mallows

Alfred Ambrose (1819-1860?) = Mary Ann (6 children)

James 'Witty' Root/Sparham (1822-1877) = Sophia Thorndike (1833-1907)

Jemima (b.1826) = William Sparrow (4 children)

**George Root/Sparham** (1831?-1907) = (1) **Hannah Ellis** (2) **Clara Elizabeth Cracknell** widow of (3) George Southgate

Frederick (1830-31)

5 children including George William Root /Sparham /Thorndike (1854-1902) = Louisa Clarke (m.1874)

George Root = Rosanna Southgate (m.1880)

Children and step-children
(1) George Lionel Root
(2) Clara and Ada Root
(3) Rosanna Southgate

# Ellis Family Tree

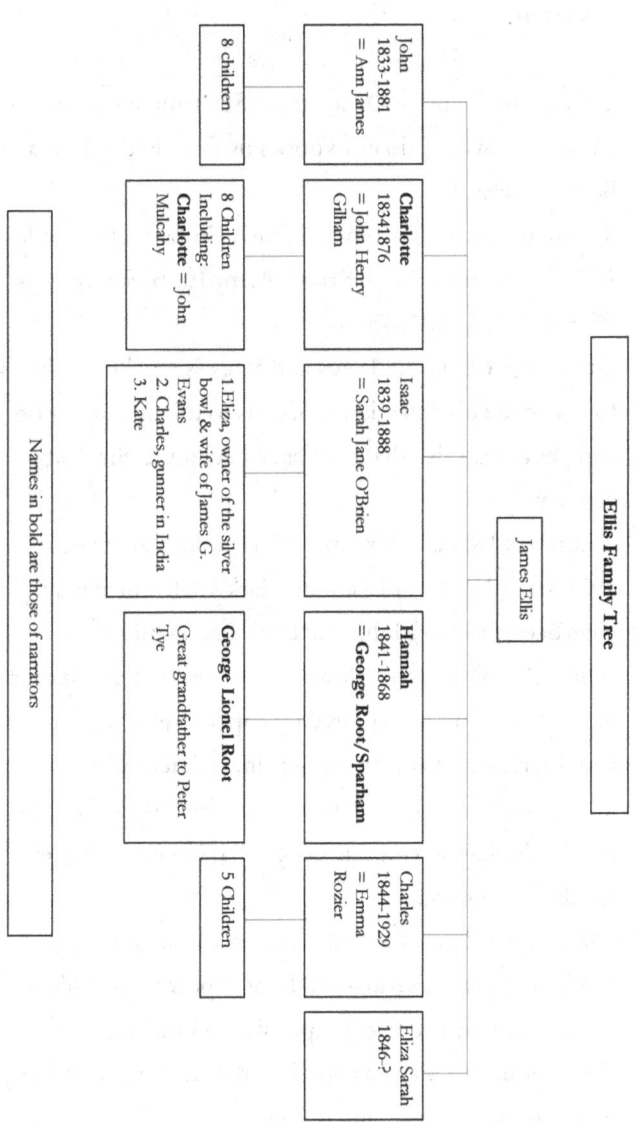

James Ellis

John
1833-1881
= Ann James
— 8 children

**Charlotte**
1834-1876
= John Henry Gilham
— 8 Children Including:
**Charlotte** = John Mulcahy

Isaac
1839-1888
= Sarah Jane O'Brien
— 1. Eliza, owner of the silver bowl & wife of James G. Evans
2. Charles, gunner in India
3. Kate

**Hannah**
1841-1868
= **George Root/Sparham**
— **George Lionel Root**
Great grandfather to Peter Tye

Charles
1844-1929
= Emma Rozier
— 5 Children

Eliza Sarah
1846-?

Names in bold are those of narrators

313

# Notes

## Part 1 - Keziah

1   He is to be found in Duke Street, St Clement's, where he
    labours - at what I do not know. His first child, Eliza, was
    born in Ireland.

2   Enlisted 22nd of November, 1887. Embarked for India
    19th of February, 1889. British Army Embarkation lists
    BL ref. IOR-L-MIL-15-46

3   Scooters were, in the 1940s and 50s, essentially children's
    toys, not the hi-tech adult solutions to urban congestion
    and pedestrian risk that they have become in the 21st
    century.

4   The Mark IX was a luxury model produced between
    1958 and 1961. It replaced the Mark VIII, which may
    have been the model that I actually had in mind.

5   The only comic I was allowed. *The Eagle* had fine, bright
    illustrations, and was printed on superior glossy paper.
    Dan Dare, an astronaut, was a principal hero who
    intoxicated me. But I still hankered after *The Beano* and all
    the World War Two comic books that circulated under
    the desk at school.

6   Platignum created the first self-filling fountain pen in
    1919. (Pre-filled cartridges did not appear until 1965, but
    these were comparatively expensive to buy, and
    generations of children soon learnt to refill the cartridges
    by syphoning from an ink bottle).

7    Is this account my petty act of revenge, perhaps? My parents are long dead: they cannot rip out these pages. I remember that, when I went to stay at my paternal grandfather's house, there was a plaque on my bedroom wall which said, 'God Sees You.' It was terrifying. I suspect I am remembering this wrongly and it really said, 'God watches over you,' and was meant to be comforting, but, when you are eight, the meaning was plain enough. God was everywhere, and every pathetic misdeed I committed left me twitchy.

8    *The Bhagavad Gita* (2.20) in the translation by Laurie L. Patton (London, Penguin Classics, 2008):
     'The self is not born, nor does it ever die.
     Once it has been, this self will never cease to be again.'

9    See premium.weatherweb.net/weather-in-history-1800-to-1849-ad

10   Head lice (Suffolk dialect).

11   Keziah was born in Framlingham and baptised at Wickham Market on 22nd of May, 1784. This would make her fifty-two at the time of these events and mean that she was forty-six when she gave birth to George. Unlikely as this is, these dates are confirmed by subsequent census records and her death certificate.

12   The mediaeval church of St Clement (the patron saint of seafarers) is in the dock quarter of Ipswich. It was at the centre of the largest and most densely populated parish. In the eighteenth and nineteenth century, the Cobbold family of brewers was associated with it.

13    Walpole, Suffolk, nearly thirty miles north-east of Ipswich. There is no firm corroborative evidence that either she or George's father did belong to Walpole. George sometimes says it was his birthplace, though he also says he was born at Bungay, eleven miles away.

14    Elizabeth, Keziah's oldest child by another relationship.

15    Scolding (Suffolk dialect).

16    Ambrose Alfred, born Ipswich, 1819, James, born Ipswich, 1822, and Jemima, born Ipswich, c.1826.

17    James Sparham appeared in court on 5th of November, 1836, and was acquitted on what seems a technicality in January, 1837 (see *The Ipswich Journal*, 7th of January, 1837)

18    Snails (dialect).

19    A court was a cul-de-sac of terraced houses and rooms, usually entered via a narrow alleyway off a residential street. They included most of the town's multi-occupancy slum housing. 'There are 106 courts in the town, containing 627 houses. The drainage from some of these is very defective.' Glyde (1850), *The Moral, Social and Religious Condition of Ipswich in the Middle of the Nineteenth Century* p.36

20    The Cobbold who Keziah met was probably Charles Cobbold (1793-1859) of Rose (or Roe's) Hill, Ipswich. In 1839 he moved to Edinburgh, where, in 1841, he became superintendent of the botanical gardens. He was involved in the Ipswich bank of Bacon, Cobbold, Rodwell, Dunningham, and Cobbold, founded in 1826.

21    The New Poor Law Act of 1834 grouped parishes together in unions which were charged with building workhouses for the poor and discouraging 'outdoor' relief. The stated aim was to reduce the cost of supporting the poor and encouraging those people who could to work. By 1836, the difficulties of administering the new system were emerging, and, while some rate payers objected to the cost, others were becoming aware of the scope for corruption and the suffering of many of the poor who faced new impediments to seeking help and to their family life.

22    Under the Poor Law regulations, the parish of Walpole would be responsible for the relief of her and her children, if this is true.

23    *Suffolk Chronicle*, Saturday, 17th of December, 1836.

24    For comparison, the average weekly wage for an agricultural labourer in Suffolk in 1851 was seven shillings. Waller, I. H. (2010), *My Ancestor was an Agricultural Labourer*, p.27.

25    The implication is that she was a prostitute, if only at times of extreme hardship. The records seem to suggest that at least two of the three children described as belonging to St Clement's, i.e. born there, were of the same father, the errant bigamist, Sparham.

26    The Blything Union had come into existence on 25th of June, 1835, and represented forty-nine Suffolk parishes, including Walpole.

27    *Suffolk Chronicle*, Saturday, 24th of December, 1836.

28    As well as George, Jemima, Alfred, James, and Elizabeth,
      Keziah had had another boy, William Henry, baptised
      in St Clement's in 1814 and who was probably the child
      whose death is recorded at Stoke Baptist church in 1823.

29    Elizabeth was born on 23rd of January, 1811, and
      baptised at St Mary, Stoke, Ipswich, on 3rd of February.

30    Charles Mallows was probably born in Framlingham
      about 1800.

31    In 1826, The magistrates' court sentenced him to one
      month's hard labour, as reported in the *Ipswich Journal*.

32    The treadmill was invented by William Cubitt, the chief
      engineer at Ransome's in Ipswich, in about 1817.

33    *Suffolk Chronicle*, January, 1828.

34    30th of March, 1828, St Margaret's, Ipswich.

35    Confused, bewildered (Suffolk dialect).

36    A square of terraced cottages built to house officers
      during the Napoleonic Wars, off Woodbridge Road,
      Ipswich.

37    Sentenced for 'having obtained several articles of
      wearing apparel under false pretences, the prisoner
      having been convicted at former sessions of similar
      offences.' *Suffolk Chronicle*, 21st of August, 1830, and
      *Ipswich Journal*, 25th of September, 1830.

38    Plural of lice (Suffolk dialect)

39    The certificate survives in TROVE, the Australian
      National Archive, and includes the physical description
      which follows.

40    The Suffolk heavy horse or 'Punch' is also known as the

Suffolk Sorrel. Sorrel is synonymous with chestnut.

41 Records for the hulks are in The National Archive (TNA) HO9/8.

42 *HMS Leviathan*, the second of four ships to bear the name, was launched in 1790. See the account on the Kent History Forum website by Stuart Waters, which also includes a detailed account of the regime on board the ship when she was a prison hulk in 1838 (www.kenthisto-ryforum.com/index.php?topic=122.0).

43 Details of the voyage of the *Georgiana*, and John Tarn's journal, are to be found in TNA HO 11/8, p.76, and on *Free Settler or Felon* at: www.jenwilletts.com/convict_ship_georgiana_1831.htm.

44 Dawes Point, known by the Aboriginal names 'Tar-ra' and 'Tullagalla,' was the site for the first major British gun emplacement in Sydney Harbour. By the time that Mallows was free to sit there, the Point was at the centre of wharves, stores, and accommodation. It is now dominated by the southern tower of the Harbour Bridge.

45 *Sydney Herald*, 7th of June, 1838, p.2.

46 Keziah Root, alias Sparham, who found herself in the Ipswich prints of 1836, was probably born in Framling-ham, Suffolk, in 1784. (She says she was, but it may be unwise to trust anything she says to a government census officer.) If so, she was probably the child of Samuel Root and Ann Hayward, who were married at Framlingham in 1782. I don't like 'probably,' but the archive gives me no other options, so experience tells me that I am 'probably' correct.

47     *Ipswich Journal,* 16th of April, 1785. According to the
       newspaper report, the brothers had ridden in a post
       chaise together to the place of execution, where John had
       made a public confession and pathetically admitted that,
       had he not been executed for this crime, he might have
       gone on to commit something worse. The local paper
       promised to publish a pamphlet itemising all his wrong-
       doings, but there is no record of this. He was executed
       alongside one John Latter, a burglar, though it is not clear
       if they were associates. The execution was at Rushmere
       Heath, east of Ipswich, where most executions in East
       Suffolk were carried out between 1735 and 1797.

48     'Journeyman' means 'one paid by the day' (from the
       French jour). Though he is skilled, and has completed his
       apprenticeship, he has no security of employment.

49     I.e. Halesworth, which is three miles north of Walpole.

50     *Ipswich Journal,* 19th of February, 1785.

51     *Ipswich Journal,* 8th of October, 1785, reprinted on 22nd
       of October.

52     The *Ipswich Journal,* 24th of February 1787.

53     At this time, there was no paid police force, and
       constables were largely volunteers - often unwilling.

54     William Ashhurst or Ashurst (1725-1807) became a
       judge in 1770, and was admired by his contemporaries
       for his 'liberal education and enlarged notions,' and for
       his clear, logical judgements. See *Dictionary of National
       Biography,* London, 1885-1900.

55    The important mediaeval town of Dunwich, together
       with its churches is now almost entirely lost to the sea. A
       local myth says that fishermen still sometimes hear the
       church bells tolling from beneath the waves. The one
       stolen by Robert Sharman in 1787 is presumably not
       among them.

56    'Judge Ashurst with his lanthorn jaws/ Throws light
       upon the English laws', DNB 1885-1900.

57    *Bury and Norwich Post*, 4th of April, 1787. Other than
       the terse newspaper report, no details of the trial have
       survived. The sentence of 'Transportation to Australia' is
       interesting because at this date the First Fleet was yet to
       sail (13th of May, 1787). Cone did not begin his journey
       until 8th of September, 1789.

58    As an illustration of the irony inherent in life's infinite
       game of chance, this further tale of Henry Cone is
       pertinent, (though not part of this narrative, because he
       never returned to England, and Elizabeth never heard a
       word from him, and there is no propinquity between him
       and me).
       Cone set sail on *Guardian*, a ship intended to supply the
       fledgling colony with much needed supplies, but, in the
       Southern Ocean, it struck an iceberg. The ship was
       dismasted and started to leak. The small group of
       convicts on board were not allowed to take to the
       lifeboats, which were reserved for paying passengers
       and manned by some of the seamen. This saved Henry
       Cone's life, since five of the six boats that were launched

were never seen again. A heroic feat of seamanship by the commander, his small remaining crew, and the convicts, led to the ship drifting back to the Cape of Good Hope after nearly two months.

The twenty-one convicts, including Cone, were now embarked on Neptune, one of the ships of the second fleet. The voyage of the *Neptune* was perhaps the most ignominious in the history of transportations: of her four hundred and ninety-nine prisoners, nearly one third died on the passage, and only seventy-two were considered to be in adequate health on arrival at Sydney. Cone again survived. What's more, in the following year, Cone was one of twelve convicts who were pardoned because of their efforts in saving *Guardian*. He seems then to have been granted land and built a house on Norfolk Island. In 1808 he moved with his de facto new wife, Mary Anne, and a child, to Hobart, where he is later listed as owning 30 acres. Some twenty years on from a conversation in a Suffolk inn, he was at last a man of property.

[For a comprehensive account of transportation and reference to *Guardian* and *Neptune* see Robert Hughes' *The Fatal Shore*, London, 1987. Wikipedia entries on both ships and on the second fleet have short bibliographies. For Henry Cone see:https://convictrecords.com.au/convicts/cone/henry/61371].

59    In *Norfolk Chronicle*, 31st of March, 1810, there is a report of a Samuel Root appearing at the Bury assizes for breaking into the shop of J. Margerom of Mutford (near

Lowestoft) and stealing several pairs of shoes.

This sounds like the kind of crime a shoemaker, down on his luck, might commit - perhaps against a man with whom he had had dealings. The severity of the sentence suggests that either the shoes were of significant value or the prisoner was well-known to the courts. There is no other evidence of this crime, but the prison records exist.

60  He was removed to the prison hulk *Captivity* at Portsmouth, where he arrived on 12th of June, 1810. From then on, the quarterly returns (TNA HO9/8) show his continued incarceration (and with what articles of clothing he was issued). He was discharged on 22nd of March, 1817, but what happened to him subsequently is unknown. He doesn't appear in the 1841 census and there is no sure record of his death. He doesn't seem to have bothered the public prints any further. There is no record of his shoemaking business. He was released from custody in time to be the witness at Keziah's wedding in 1821.

61  Following the early death of my father, and finding myself at a low ebb, I underwent a period of Jungian analysis. It was not something I was ever inclined to continue, but some bits of learning have stuck in my mind. For example, this observation from Jung in his autobiography:

'When I was working on the stone tablets I became aware of the fateful links between me and my ancestors. I feel very strongly that I am under the influence of things or questions which were left incomplete and unanswered by my parents and grandparents and more distant ancestors. It often seems as if there were an impersonal karma within a family, which is passed on from parents to children. It has always seemed to me that I had to answer questions which fate had posed to my forefathers, and which had not yet been answered, or as if to complete, or perhaps continue, things which previous ages had left unfinished. It is difficult to determine whether these questions are more of a personal or more of a general (collective) nature. It seems to me that the latter is the case. A collective problem, if not recognised as such, always appears as a personal problem, and in individual cases may give the impression that something is out of order in the realm of the personal psyche.'

Carl Jung (1963), *Memories, Dreams, Reflections*, recorded and edited by Aniela Jaffé. Translated from the German by Richard and Clara Winston, chapter VIII, 'The Tower' (kindle edition, loc. 3732).

62    The Lower Canada and Upper Canada Rebellions of 1837 and 1838 arose from frustration with a lack of governmental reform. The former was especially motivated by the grievances of French settlers against British rule.

63    Bragg was born in Bocking, Essex, in March, 1816. His military and pension record survives in the Chelsea Pensioner records, WO97, TNA, available online. He joined the Royal Artillery in 1835 and was discharged on

8th of January, 1839. I hope my account of his life and character is at least plausible.

64    See Ipswich Constabulary records in Suffolk CRO, Ipswich. All the following criminal records are either from accounts in the *Ipswich Journal*, or *Suffolk Chronicle*, or from the Ipswich Gaol books or Quarter Sessions ledgers in Ipswich CRO. Bragg must have arrived in Ipswich around the beginning of 1845.

65    Charles Dickens, who memorably located a chapter of *The Pickwick Papers* (1836/7) in Ipswich (see Part 3 of the present book), also showed a familiarity with the lives of brickmakers in his novels:

'… so your husband is a brickmaker.'

'How do you know that sir?' asks the woman, astonished. 'Why, I suppose so from the colour of the clay upon your bag and on your dress. And I know brickmakers go about working at piecework in different places. And I am sorry to say I have known them cruel to their wives too.'

Charles Dickens (1853) *Bleak House*, chapter Forty-six. Brickmaking was a major occupation in Ipswich because of the ready availability of high-quality clays. For further information see, for example, the Ipswich Historic Lettering website, specifically: ipswich-lettering. co.uk/whersteadred.html

66    Census return of 6th of June, 1841, shows James and his brother Alfred in Ipswich Gaol.

67    *Suffolk Chronicle*, 12th of July, 1845: 'A young man named James Sparham alias Root, who is a person notorious for

doing mischief, was brought before the Mayor and Magistrates on Thursday last and pleaded guilty to a charge of wilfully damaging a gate, the property of Mr Sawer of Greenwich Farm.'

Greenwich Farm is just down the River Orwell from Ipswich. The farmer had strengthened his gates and kept a strict watch, Root was caught, and the magistrate fined him nearly a guinea, including costs and damages, and threatened him with imprisonment and a public flogging if he was caught again.

68    See *Ipswich Journal*, 28th of February, and 14th of March, 1846.

69    The tattoo is recorded in the Ipswich Gaol Receiving Book (Suffolk CRO, A609/8 p.196, December 1848). The entry also describes him as a brickmaker of St Clement's, aged twenty-six. He is five foot eleven inches tall, with a dark complexion, dark hair, grey eyes, and a 'long visage.' He had in his possession a coat, waistcoat, trousers, shoes, shirt, handkerchief, and a cap, but no money or other personal effects. He is not married and is illiterate. His father is described as 'James Root [sic], sawyer, deceased'. It is also recorded that he had been in custody three times before: once for assault and twice charged with a felony, but not convicted. I can find no specific event on 7th of May, 1840 which could explain the tattoo.

70    See *Ipswich Journal* 14th of April, 1849.

71    'The brags of life are but a nine days' wonder' (George Herbert (1633), *The Temple*.

72    An inn in Myrtle Road (which runs from Fore Hamlet

down towards the docks).

73    Sixty-seven years later, John Gosling's grand-nephew would marry James Root's grand-niece. They would become my grandparents. I don't suppose they ever knew about this shared moment in their history.

74    In 1832, Sir Robert Peel's government had removed sheep stealing from the list of capital crimes.

75    Bragg may be thinking of Magwitch in *Great Expectations* (Charles Dickens, 1861).

76    Bragg may also have known that book that I love - *Bleak House* (Charles Dickens, 1853), where Esther observes: 'I was glad when we came to the brickmaker's house, though it was one of a cluster of wretched hovels in a brick-field, with pigsties close to the broken windows and miserable little gardens ... At the doors and windows some men and women lounged or prowled about, and took little notice of us except to laugh at one another or to say something as we passed about gentlefolks minding their own business and not troubling their heads and muddying their shoes with coming to look after other people's.'

77    At Kersey in 1841, and Stoke by Nayland in 1851, according to the Suffolk censuses.

78    Isaac Prentice was transported to Australia on *Rodney*, 19th of September, 1851. He served four years of his sentence before being granted a ticket of leave on 8th of June, 1854, at Launceston, Tasmania. He died 31st of August, 1895, at New Norfolk, Tasmania. He was a pauper, aged 70, having spent the previous year in the insane hospital there.

79   27th of September, 1849.

80   Whether they paid up or did the time is not recorded.
     James is clearly seen as the ringleader: George and Robert
     Friston (an iron moulder's lad living in John Street) were
     still in their teens.

81   *Ipswich Journal*, 9th of March, 1850.

82   See committal document, dated 6th of March, 1850,
     and the record of his transfer to Millbank Prison. The
     description of prisoner 5021 matches that of a few years
     earlier at Ipswich Gaol, but on his most recent conviction
     he is described, additionally, as having a long and promi-
     nent nose.

83   The Quarterly Returns of *Warrior* are held in the
     National Archive.

**Part 2 - George**

84   See 1851 Census where Harriet and George Sparham are
     at 47 Fore Hamlet. '47' is the enumerator's reference, not
     a house number.

85   Later Fisons. Coprolite is fossilised dung, high in
     phosphates, and, when treated with sulphuric acid, could
     be used as agricultural fertiliser. Deposits had been
     discovered lower down the Orwell at Trimley in the 1840s
     and extraction began on an industrial scale.

86   Ipswich was a garrison town. For commentary on
     poverty, prostitution and social conditions in this period,
     see John Glyde, *The Moral, Social and Religious Condition of
     Ipswich in the middle of the Nineteenth Century* (Ipswich, 1850,

reprinted S.R. Publishers, Wakefield and London, 1971).

87    On 20th of December, 1848, he is entered into the
      Ipswich Gaol receiving book as George Sparham,
      labourer, of Ipswich. He is five foot, five inches tall, of
      dark complexion, brown hair, and hazel eyes, with a long
      face and a scar on the little finger of his right hand. He is
      possessed of a smock, two waistcoats, trousers, shoes, a
      shirt, handkerchief, knife, cap, and a halfpenny. He says
      that he was born at Bungay and that his father was James
      Sparham, deceased. He is convicted of trespass in pursuit
      of game on the land of Sir Philip Brooke, at Nacton. He
      is given fourteen days hard labour. He is illiterate and has
      not been in gaol before.

88    For example, the case that featured in Chapter 8, or one
      which was to come to the Ipswich magistrates on 3rd of
      June 1850.

89    See Glyde, John (1850, 1970), p.25. The Wet Dock, the
      largest in the country at the time, had opened in 1842.
      Apart from coal, there was rum, cheese, corn, and brandy
      coming from the continent. Cargoes of hay and straw
      were shipped to London, the boats returning with horse
      manure.

90    Ray Island is now the site of Parkeston Quay, Harwich
      International Port.

91    At the time, and in the newspaper reports, often referred
      to as Hog Island - a piece of rising ground south of
      Ipswich, on the north bank of the Orwell, behind what is
      now Cliff Quay.

92    The report of the trial appeared in the *Essex Herald*, 28th

of May, 1850. The court reporter did his best, but the account is confused and in places contradictory. Throughout, George is referred to as 'George Sparhawk,' but in the light of subsequent events and accounts there is no doubt that it is George Sparham, alias Root. The quarter sessions' records attest to the outcome of the trial.

93    *Ipswich Journal* 1st of June, 1850.

94    'I want a hero: an uncommon want,
When every year and month sends forth a new one,
Till after cloying the gazettes with cant,
The age discovers he is not the true one.'
Byron, *Don Juan*, Canto 1.1. Ironic, of course. Will George let me down, too? Is what I write true? (I remember this poem from school.)

95    The Ninety-sixth was an infantry regiment which recruited both in Manchester and Suffolk. William R. Wittingham from Bolton had served for more than twelve years in India, New Zealand (the Maori Wars), and Australia, when he returned home in 1851 and was sent as a recruiting sergeant to Ipswich.

96    He was probably twenty-one or twenty-two. The army record shows no date of birth but 'age apparently' twenty.

97    George's attestation document, together with his service, discharge, and pension record is in The National Aarchives' British Army Service Records 1760-1915 (WO 97/3922/74), and available on findmypast.co.uk.

98　　An inch and a half taller than the last time he appeared
　　　in an official record. He has grown, but perhaps he is also
　　　standing up straighter for the army than for the police.

99　　The attestation document shows that George received
　　　two shillings and sixpence in his hand on signing up.

100　Burton had been mayor of Ipswich in 1848-9. He was a
　　　grocer and confectioner.

101　Clearly visible, George made two even strokes,
　　　intersecting precisely with the line, and exactly between
　　　the two parts of his name. It has been done painstakingly.

102　The attestation shows that it was signed at three o'clock
　　　on 25th of May 1852.

103　The dragon or dinosaur fish (proper name, polypterus
　　　senegalus, or the Senegal bichir) is an ancient species,
　　　originating, it is thought, more than four hundred
　　　million years ago. They are slow-moving, bottom-feeding
　　　carnivores. They have rudimentary lungs giving them
　　　the capacity to breath air, and may shoot suddenly to the
　　　water's surface. In the right conditions in the wild, or the
　　　laboratory, they have been known to make slow
　　　adaptations to enable them to live entirely on land, their
　　　pectoral fins operating as legs. It seems this adaptation
　　　can be passed from generation to generation.
　　　'Developmental plasticity and the origin of tetrapods',
　　　Standen et al., *Nature*, 513, 54-58 (2014).

104　Now Pakistan but then under the control of the British
　　　East India Company, supported by the British
　　　government and its armies.

105 Subsequently, Isaac Tyrrell wrote *From England to the Antipodes and India 1846-1902 with Startling Revelations or 56 years of My Life in the Indian Mutiny, Police and Jails* (ALV Press 149 Popham's Broadway, Madras 1904). It is freely available at: http://www.archive.org/details/fromenglandtoantOOtyrrrich. I have made frequent use of it in what follows, since Tyrell was in the Ninety-sixth throughout George's years in India.

106 A small Indian bronze coin, worth a quarter of an anna or sixty-four parts of a rupee

107 See Tyrell (1904

108 Tyrrell records that the regiment was heavily down in numbers. In one month of 1852 alone, some four hundred soldiers were sick and thirty-three died. Further, out of a draft of eighty-nine men (possibly including George) who marched from Calcutta in 1852, forty-two were dead of dysentery or cholera by the end of September. Tyrell also gives accounts of theatrical productions, card games, and the delights of the Shalamar Gardens, among other pleasures of Lahore, in his book (Tyrell, 1904).

109 Literally, the diamond market, which at night becomes Lahore's entertainment district, notable for music and dance. In the Mughul era, however, the highly skilled performers ('trawaif') might also trade sexual favours, and by the time of the raj the area had become synonymous with prostitution.

110 These days, a DNA test would sort things out in a few weeks. I wonder if he has, since, done one.

111    In 1947, Sir Cyril Radcliffe spent five weeks in Faletti's Hotel, where he was responsible for drawing the lines on the map which partitioned India at its independence from Britain. The result was the displacement of some fourteen million people and two million deaths. So many family lines were terminated by a line.

112    For example, *Bluegate Fields in Shadwell* (1856) - though without the people.

113    Sarinda: a bowed string instrument, played vertically by a performer sitting on the floor.

114    Sarhadi's Wikipedia entry says: 'Munir Sarhadi was passionate about sarinda musical instrument. He didn't earn much from his profession. His only source of income was his job at a broadcast network Radio Pakistan. The salary which was being offered to him, was inadequate to fulfil his medication requirements, and on May 23, 1980, he died in poverty at Peshawar, but died in a dignified manner.' His music was available on an EMI Pakistan LP LKDE 20009: *Sarinda, Sound of Khyber Valley.*

115    This anecdote is recalled by Tyrell, 1904.

116    Now Prayagraj (Uttar Pradesh).

117    Now Danapur, west of Patna.

118    Charles Edwards' pension record shows that he enlisted on 27th of October, 1842. The Ninety-sixth had arrived in Australia the previous year, and subsequently, its nine companies were stationed throughout South Australia, Norfolk Island, Tasmania, and New Zealand. Edwards is credited with five years and seven months service in

Australia followed by five years and ten months in India. He was promoted to Corporal in April 1855 and Sergeant in August 1858. He had three good conduct badges and would have had two more had he not been promoted to Sergeant. Colonel H. C. Wylly (1923, 2018), *History of the Manchester Regiment Vol I & II 1758-1922,* Lume Books, and Chelsea pensioner records, The National Archives, WO97.

119    The Forty-third Regiment of Foot was the Monmouthshire regiment. It had been stationed in England, Ireland, and South Africa, before arriving in India at the beginning of 1854. The Seventy-fourth (Highland) Regiment had recently arrived from the Cape.

120    The Crimean War began in October 1853, and British forces arrived in support of the Ottoman army in January 1854. The land war did not start until September 1854, just at the time the men of the Ninety-sixth were considering their options.

121    Tyrell, 1904.

122    The Ninety-sixth sailed in three ships: *The Wellesley, Nile,* and *Bride of the Sea,* arriving at Gravesend on 10th of April, 1855. The journey was broken for some weeks at the Cape of Good Hope.

123    They proceeded via Chatham to Liverpool and Dublin. They were stationed initially in Dublin and then at The Curragh from September 1855 to 3rd of April, 1856. That part of George's service record which survives in The National Archives lists all these movements.

124    Twenty-one years was the length of service required to

claim an army pension.

125   The Ninety-sixth marched out of Dublin on 12th of September, 1855, according to Wylly (1923:269), who also reports that the regiment was ordered to increase its establishment to twelve companies, all to be armed with the new Enfield rifle, which was standard issue to forces in the Crimean War (1853-56).

126   Deserters might be branded on the chest with a 'D'. Other punishments included prison sentences of up to six months, flogging, and transportation for seven years or longer. See, e.g., Burroughs, Peter, (July 1985), 'Crime and Punishment in the British army, 1815-1870', *English Historical Review*, vol. 100, No. 396, OUP.

127   Stew and potato cakes.

128   George's pension record shows that he deserted on 30th of January, 1856, and was 'brought back' on 28th of February. He was tried by a district court martial on 4th of March for 'Desertion and making away with clothing and necessaries', receiving fifty-six days imprisonment and stoppages. His confinement was deemed to have begun on 28th of February, but his imprisonment ran from 10th of March to 27th of April. The regiment returned from The Curragh to the Royal Barracks in Dublin in the first week of April, according to Wylly (1923).

129   The wedding on Thursday, 24th of July, is recorded at St James, Dublin. The muster roll - WO12/9630 - records George as AWOL the 24th of - 26th of July.

130   Wylly (1923:271) says that the regiment sailed in two

sections, and the *Cleopatra*, the second ship, arrived in
Gibraltar on 8th of August, the men going into the Rosia
barracks.

131   George's service record gives him ten months in
Gibraltar. The muster roll shows he was in hospital there
for the whole of January to March, 1857.

132   The census for 1861 shows Charles, Maria, James (aged
3), and George Sparham (lodger) in a house on Raymond
Street, Thetford.

133   The Crimean War had ended in February 1856. The
Indian Mutiny, or Great Rebellion, had largely been
suppressed by the summer of 1858.

134   The American Civil War broke out in April 1861. Great
Britain declared its neutrality, though this was taken by
some as a de facto acknowledgement of the right of the
Confederate South to exist as an independent state. The
union had placed a maritime blockade around southern
ports when, in November 1861, their warship, *USS San
Jacinto*, intercepted, fired on, and boarded, a British mail
packet ship - the *Trent*. On board were discovered two
would-be diplomats from the southern Confederacy on
their way to London to obtain formal public recognition.
The resulting diplomatic mess threatened to lead to war
between Britain and the union. It was in the interests of
the Confederacy to stoke the tension and there was a war
party within the union. Eventually, President Abraham
Lincoln had the prisoners released, and war was averted,
but not before Britain mobilised and financial markets

had threatened to crash. The British government
pencilled in a probable declaration of war for the third
week of January 1862. In the event of war, the defence
of Canada was to be the key strategic objective, and
during December 1861, an additional eleven thousand
troops were sent to bolster the weak, existing garrison.

135  Canada did not become a Dominion under the Crown
until 1867.

136  Cobh, from where the two ships set sail on Monday, 30th
of December.

137  See *Cork Examiner*, 30th of December, 1861.

138  This account is derived from the official regimental
history in the Manchester Regiment archive at Ashton
under Lyne, and contemporary newspaper accounts,
including that in the *Dublin Evening Packet and
Correspondent*, for 24th of January, 1862, p.3, which
concludes:
'Regardless of the sufferings of the men, who
amounted to 500, besides twenty-three officers, they are
still on board. However, one of the Citizen's Steam
Company's boats has now - one o'clock p.m. - gone
alongside the Victoria, while it blows a heavy gale from
E.S.E., with a terrific fall of rain to take 450 of them on
board and take them to Cork. The remainder, with the
baggage is to be sent up to-morrow. It is adding cruelty
to suffering to send them up the river in such a storm as
now rages. This is another result of red-tapeism.'
Nothing changes!

139    4th of January, 1862.

140    Canned corned beef, called 'bully,' was just being
       introduced to military rations at this time, though he may
       be referring to a beef soup - soup and bouilli - which had
       been a staple of naval fare for a hundred years.

141    The engineer officer, Ardagh, and all the events here, are
       as recounted in the official enquiry. Wylly (1923:272-7)
       has a similar account, but also quotes from a colourful
       personal reminiscence by Captain Reid of the Nine-
       ty-sixth, who was on the voyage. George's role is
       conjecture.

142    There are no black angels in the Bible. George is perhaps
       picking up on traditions which have their roots in Milton
       and elsewhere.

143    Details are in George's pension record, including the
       original letter: "Sir, Her Majesty having been graciously
       pleased … to restore to the soldier named in the margin
       (96 Foot 2740 G Sparham), the benefit of reckoning
       the whole of his forfeited service as a ground for other
       advantages … issued and charged from 3 February 1862
       …" The dates within the letter indicate that this
       restoration is not connected with the *Victoria* incident.
       George's military experience is full of paradox and point-
       lessness, but they kept good records. My storytelling goes
       well beyond the available archives, but it feels right.

144    Eliza's husband, James Gildea Evans (born 1868 in
       Galway), had died in 1928 and left his widow an estate of
       £7,614 and 12s 9d. He seems to have been of Irish gentry

descent and was described as a mechanical engineer to the Indian government. In 1892, shortly after he and Eliza arrived in Calcutta, he had joined the freemason's lodge.

145    HM Courts and Tribunal Service: Evans, Eliza 29/07/1934.

146    The brewer, Cobbold, had bought and refurbished this mediaeval building behind Ipswich docks in 1845. It's still in use, though not as an inn.

147    On the 1871 census, John Ellis had 'father an English-man' written above Athlone in the place of birth column.

148    'John Ellis, sawyer, was charged with neglecting to maintain his three children. The defendant went on a 'drunk' for a fortnight, and as he now promised to reimburse the parish (St. Peter) by instalment of 5s a week, judgment was suspended.' *Suffolk Chronicle*, 9th of August, 1862. In August 1864 he was in court again for assault on a neighbour, and three years' later for a drunken brawl in his own home.

149    Christchurch Park was the property of W. C. Fonnereau. Ipswich Corporation leased 13 acres from 1851 to provide a public open space, and in 1853, the Upper Arboretum was opened.

150    She had been sentenced to seven year's transportation in 1847. Her story, which Hannah never heard, will be the subject of Part 3.

151    The census from the previous year records Keziah as being aged 80 and living in a Court in Fore Hamlet.

152    8th of February, 1863.

153   Infant mortality and its probable causes were often in the local papers. For example, see *The Bury Free Press*, 31st of August, 1861, carrying an article from *The Morning Post*, which asserted that 'we know, for instance, that in 1859, out of every five deaths which took place two were those of infants under the age of five years. By far the larger proportion of these never saw their first birthday ...' The article ascribes the cause to poverty, disease, and malnutrition, but is chiefly concerned that infanticide 'is not an uncommon crime'.

154   Hannah Root died on 9th of February, 1868, with Maria Squire in attendance, and she was buried as a pauper in the public grave at Ipswich cemetery (grave reference C-21-58) on 14th of February. There is therefore no headstone.

155   And perhaps this is the origin of the family tradition, which my mother told me, that Hannah was an Irish princess, though I have assumed it may belong to her mother, and actually refers back to a much older myth.

156   'Albion Street ... the earliest nineteenth century street of working class housing in the area stretched down from Fore Hamlet towards the docks, the gas works, and the Orwell iron works. It was lined with long rows of terraced cottages on either side, many of which on its north side were two-up two-down. And behind numbers 78-82, towards the bottom, were three cramped courts, one, John's Court, with eight one-up one-down blind back dwellings.' Frank Grace (2005), *Rags and Bones*, p.84.

157   Otherwise known in official records as Rosa or Rosanna

158   'Sometimes one sees things more clearly years afterwards
      than one could possibly at the time ... It is a question of
      proportion, isn't it? And more than proportion,
      probably. Relativity and all that sort of thing.' Agatha
      Christie, 'The Dead Harlequin' from *The Mysterious Mr
      Quin* (1930). These short stories are all founded on the
      notion that events of the past can only be truly under-
      stood with the benefit of a gap in time, which I take to be
      some justification for my labours here.

159   Lakshmi hints that she may be interested in notions of
      Extended Evolutionary Synthesis, and the theories of
      epigenetics, in which psychosocial and bodily changes
      have been observed to alter the chemistry of DNA and
      cause intergenerational change. Another reason for stud-
      ying personal heritage.

160   Part of Southgate's military record survives in The Na-
      tional Archives.

161   George Southgate died 20th of December, 1864, aged
      34.

162   A pawnbroker.

163   James 'Witty' Root, alias Sparham, died 17th of January,
      1877.

164   *Bury and Norwich Post*, 14th of February, 1882, which
      carried a report of the Suffolk winter assizes

165   Clara Root, born 1870, married Thomas Betts, a gunner
      in the Royal Artillery. He later became an Ipswich iron
      worker. Ada Jemima Root, born 1873, married Alfred
      Reeves, a sailmaker from Sussex. My mother remembers

'Aunt Ada' giving her books. Both daughters had families. Perhaps I should seek them out, but time is pressing.

166    Neither of the letters survive but they are alluded to in the newspaper reports of the case.

167    The most complete account is in The *Ipswich Journal* of 3rd of January,1882, and includes Clara's testimony. *The Diss Express*, 6th of January, 1882, and T*he People's Weekly Journal*, 7th of January 1882, also report the case.

168    The assize hearing was covered in The *Norwich Mercury*, 18th of February, 1882, *Bury and Norwich Post*, 21st of February, and *Lowestoft Journal* of 18th of February, all carrying the same report - editors no doubted attracted by Thorndike's plea, below.

169    In the 1881 census, Sophia Root is living at 1 Palmers Place, Walsoken, Wisbech, in the fens, with her son, William (15), and daughter Rachael (16). She is described as a widow and 'formerly laundress'. William Cutting, Bricklayer, seven years Sophia's junior, is described as 'boarder.' In 1891 she is at 4 Palmers Place, married to William Cutting, and her son, William Root, is a bricklayer's labourer.

170    George and Rosanna are shown living together with their children in Albion Street in the 1891 census. They are known as Mr & Mrs Root.

## Part 3 - Charlotte

171    *Elizabeth and Henry* built Sunderland, 1845. Wooden

barque of five hundred and thirty-four tons. This was her third voyage, having previously carried male convicts from Dublin and female convicts from London. She carried one hundred and thirty-eight female convicts to Hobart, departing Woolwich on the 13th of February, 1848, and arrived in Hobart on the 30th of June, 1848. Master: Captain William J. Clark. Surgeon: John Smith. She seems a small ship for so many people on such a long journey. There is a picture of her at convictrecords.com. au/ships/elizabeth-and-henry

172 Lydia Childs, aged nineteen, was sentenced at the Essex quarter sessions, Chelmsford, on 18th of May, 1847, for obtaining fifteen shillings under false pretences. She had been convicted of other minor offences previously.

173 Joss over: move over - a command that might be given to a cow when it is being milked. Maw, an abbreviation of 'mawther': a girl, usually one growing to womanhood, particularly if rough and awkward. I am indebted to A.O.D. Claxton (1954), *The Suffolk Dialect of the Twentieth Century*, Boydell Press, Woodbridge.

174 Charlotte Church, aged seventeen, sentenced at Ipswich sessions on 26th of July, 1847, to transportation for seven years for theft of a calico bag containing the possessions of William Pegg.

175 A slovenly woman (Suffolk dialect).

176 'In the main street of Ipswich … stands an inn known far and wide by the appellation of the Great White Horse … famous in the neighbourhood, in the same degree as a

prize ox, or a county-paper-chronicled turnip, or
unwieldy pig - for its enormous size. Never was such a
labyrinth of uncarpeted passages, such clusters of
mouldy, ill-lighted rooms, such huge numbers of small
dens for eating or sleeping in, beneath any one roof,
as are collected together between the four walls of the
Great White Horse at Ipswich.' Charles Dickens (1836),
*Pickwick Papers*, Chapter 22. Dickens stayed several times
at the inn and has Pickwick lose himself in the corridors,
late in the evening, in search of his pocket watch.
'The more stairs Mr. Pickwick went down, the more stairs
there seemed to be to descend, and again and again, when
Mr. Pickwick got into some narrow passage, and began to
congratulate himself on having gained the ground floor,
did another flight of stairs appear before his astonished
eyes. At last he reached a stone hall, which he remembered to have seen when he entered the house. Passage
after passage did he explore; room after room did he
peep into; at length, as he was on the point of giving up
the search in despair, he opened the door of the identical
room in which he had spent the evening and beheld his
missing property on the table.'

177   Horseman - one who cares for horses.

178   Cold Dunghills was an extra-parochial area on the edge
of St Clement's parish between Eagle Street and Upper
Orwell Street, and about three minutes from The Great
White Horse. It is the address given on Charles Ellis's
birth certificate in July 1844. It was one of the poorest
slums in Ipswich.

179    Nacton Workhouse was established by Woodbridge Poor
       Law Union in 1835. That Charlotte was admitted there
       suggests that her natural mother 'belonged' to
       Woodbridge or one of the other rural parishes in the
       union. Her Ipswich place of residence would not have
       allowed her to be placed there. See also, The *Suffolk
       Chronicle*, Saturday, 3rd of April, 1847.

180    Ship's surgeon, Dr John Smith, 3rd of July,1848, reports
       of Lydia Childs that she:

'Was seized this afternoon with severe Hysteria simulating
       Hysteritis from severe pain in the region of uterus and
       left ovary ... As all are about to be discharged, I sent her
       to hospital.'

181    South Australia - a trad. sea shanty

182    The name 'Margaret Dunn' appears in various records
       as Charlotte's mother, though I can find no record of
       her marriage to James Ellis or of Charlotte's birth, which
       were probably in Ireland. It is unlikely, but not
       impossible, that (Elizabeth) Catherine Malary was her
       mother - she would have been very young - and I take her
       testimony against Charlotte as being evidence of her lack
       of relationship with the girl.

183    Robert Green is mentioned in the indictment, and a
       Robert Green, shipwright, is to be found living next to
       an Ellis in the 1851 census, but this sequence of events is
       supposition. It feels right: Lakshmi seems to approve, and
       neither Ellis nor Green are here to dispute my version.

184    'Charlotte Ellis pleaded guilty to the charge of having

stolen a black stuff cloak, one worsted cape, one black silk cape, and one cotton pinafore, the property of Robert Green of Woodbridge. The Court in passing sentence said, that in consequence of her previous bad character, her parents not knowing what to do with her, they should transport her for seven years.' The *Suffolk Chronicle*, 3rd of
July, 1847. It is typical, both of the court and the newspaper reporting, that what is described is the value of the crime and its punishment, rather than the exact circumstances of the girl, her family, and relationships, or any mitigation.

185   *Ipswich Journal*, 3rd of July, 1847, reported that the governor of the Ipswich County Gaol told the visiting justices to Beccles House of Correction of the success of adopting the 'Silent System' in his gaol. The system of unremitting labour, such as picking oakum in silence, was designed to break the spirit. Cf. Zedner, Lucia (2006), 'Women, crime and custody in Victorian England' in *Prison Readings* Jewkes, Y and Johnston H. ed.

186   *Suffolk Chronicle*, 8th of October, 1847, reported 'Removal of convicts - to the Millbank Prison - Charlotte Ellis'. At this time, Millbank, a vast prison on the north bank of the Thames in London, and built according to the Silent System, was the receiving prison for convicts from across the United Kingdom prior to their transportation.

187   Frozen (Suffolk dialect).

188   The *Justitia* had been an East Indiaman and a fourth-rate

warship before becoming a prison hulk at Woolwich in 1830, where she remained until sold for scrap in 1855. (I love finding out about the ships, whether or not it has any relevance to the story!)

189    A report of this incident is carried by many London papers, e.g., the *London Daily News*, 9th of February, 1848. The female prisoner is unnamed but her male partner is called Warren. The anonymous reporter whose story is carried across the press compares them to Hero and Leander - doubly ironic given the state of the river at this time as an open sewer. (Ten years later, at the time of 'The Great Stink,' even parliament was forced to take action.)

190    February 1848 was an exceptionally wet month with frequent squalls. (Something else you don't need to know, but it was in the records.)

191    What overbearing male bully wrote this? Charlotte's physical description is taken from court and prison records.

192    The *Elizabeth and Henry* made one of the slower crossings to Van Diemen's Land, having experienced adverse weather, but she suffered no deaths among the convicts, and the surgeon, Doctor John Smith, claimed that his rigorous cleanliness regime was responsible for this. Certainly, his very significant level of care for the women on the vessel contrasts strongly with the much more punitive approach of the surgeon on the Elizabeth and Henry's previous voyage of transportation (see The National Archives' transportation surgeon's records).

193   Search.archives.tas.gov.au/ have the record of Charlotte's
        proposed marriage marked 'refusal', 1st of March, 1852,
        and her convict record, including her banishment from
        Hobart and other instances of her going absent without
        leave.

194   The Cascades Female Factory, Hobart, now one of
        eleven Australian Convict sites on the UNESCO list of
        World Heritage Sites, operated between 1838 and 1856.

195   The relationships between women in the factories has
        been documented, as for example in the 1841 enquiry
        into a riot at the Launceston female factory, available at:
        femaleconvicts.org/index.php/convict-institutions/in-
        quiry-1841-1843

196   Abbreviated records of Charlotte's prison experience in
        Tasmania are to be found in Libraries Tasmania: https://
        libraries.tas.gov.au/family-history/Pages/Convict-life.
        aspx

197   Thomas Outhwaite born c. 1821 in Leeds, sentenced to
        fifteen years transportation in 1841 for highway robbery
        and other offences. See Libraries Tasmania (entry 196,
        above). His soubriquet, Possum Tommy, appears in a
        Victorian police record after he had been found drunk
        and disorderly.

198   Thomas Gilham of Alton Hampshire (born 1798) was
        a grain carter, sentenced to seven years transportation in
        1836 for theft. He had also assaulted his wife. John Henry
        was his fifth child, born 1830. Thomas Gilham was given
        a ticket of leave in 1841 and a pardon in 1843. He left

Tasmania on the *Shamrock* on 23rd of August, 1849, just two months after his son arrived on the *Victor*.

199    See for example 'in the Golden Point mining camp 1851' in the Granger Historical Picture Archive available online in Alamy stock images.

200    Elizabeth, John, and Edward [sic] Gilham are listed as steerage passengers on the barque *Victor* (338 tons) sailing from London on 6th of March, 1849, arriving Hobart 21st of June, 1849 (Ancestry.co.uk - Tasmania, Australia, passenger arrivals, 1829-1957). Edwin Gilham was born in Alton, Hampshire, in 1828, and died in Melbourne in 1875. Their younger sister, Elizabeth, was born in Alton in 1833 and married James Will (a former convict) of Longford, Tasmania, in September 1851.

201    Libraries Tasmania search - Tasmanian Names Index (sirsidynix.net.au). She was probably aged nineteen.

202    'Flemington is a nice little village or township, consisting of about forty houses, a blacksmith's shop, several stores, and a good inn, built of brick and stone, with very fair accommodation for travellers, and a large stable and stock yards.' Clacy, Ellen (1853), *A Lady's Visit to the Gold diggings of Australia in 1852 - 53*. First published London. Public domain on Kindle, loc 322. Flemington, now a suburb of Melbourne, is about three and a half miles from the city centre. There are birth records for Edwin's children at Flemington.

203    'money is the idol, and making it is the one mania which absorbs every other thought.' (Clacy, 1853. Loc 214).

204    Bendigo was officially known as Sandhurst in the 1850s,

though the later name was also in regular use. Bendigo.
photos/original-photographers-of-bendigo-1850/ has
a remarkable series of contemporary illustrations of the
diggings and embryonic town.

205  *Bendigo Advertiser*, Thursday, 10th of April, 1856:
'THE GREEN-EYED MONSTER AGAIN
Within the last few hours another unfortunate woman
has been the victim of the violence of a jealous husband.
Not many days since a rather pretty looking woman appeared at the Police Court with a summons issued by her
husband John Gilham, and to which he had attached the
name of the Stipendiary Magistrate. After having been
confined in the lockup for a few hours and been properly
frightened he was let go. He was, however, yesterday afternoon again arrested on a charge of assaulting his wife,
who, it appears, is lying in an extremely dangerous state
from three severe wounds inflicted upon her head by him
with a glass in a fit of jealousy. It is reported that there is
but little hope of her recovery. The unfortunate woman,
after a vain endeavour to shelter her husband has con-
fessed that he inflicted the wounds. Two other witnesses
are also able to testify the fact.'

206  John Henry Gilham, Born 18th of March, 1857, at
Dunolly. Died Heidelberg, Victoria, in 1929. I am
indebted to the many researchers who have uploaded
Gilham family trees to Ancestry.co.uk and who have
helped to verify or challenge my own assumptions about
what happened to the family in Australia.

207  See *The Star*, Ballarat, Thursday, 20th of August, 1857.

Available at: trove.nla.gov.au/newspapers/rendition/nla.news-article66043843.txt

208    Damper: unleavened bread or cake, made from flour and water, often mixed with any available seeds, nuts, and roots, and baked. Originally Australian indigenous and adopted by European settlers, especially when in the bush.

209    Exhausted (Suffolk dialect. Claxton, 1954).

210    Mastitis.

211    A full account of the inquest, including Charlotte's testimony, was published in the Melbourne *Argus*, Monday 28th of September, 1858, and the death notice appeared in *The Age* on Thursday, 15th of October, 1858.

212    Edwin Gilham married Sarah Winder, a widow with three children, and by this date they also had three of their own. Edwin had a soap and candle making business.

213    *The Argus*, Melbourne, Monday, 6th of December, 1858.

214    Eaglehawk is some four miles northwest of Bendigo.

215    Isaac Gilham, born Sandhurst, Bendigo, 22nd of January, 1860, died 24th of February, 1860. The inquest report survives:
https://prov.vic.gov.au/archive/496F8C06-F1C1-11E9-AE98-1773A08EADA4?image=1

216    The court reporter of the *Bendigo Advertiser*, Tuesday, 9th of October, 1860, presents the facts of Gilham versus Lee in the Sandhurst county court. The context and background remain a mystery and thus ripe for imaginative

interpretation. Lakshmi approves my account. Page two, available at: nla.gov.au/nla.news-article87947138.

217  See, for example, photographs in the collection of The Stawell Historical Society, a museum that is dedicated to preserving the unique heritage of Stawell from the 1850s onwards, and currently housed in the original Pleasant Creek Courthouse, which the Gilhams would have known well. The photographs are evidence of a remarkable transformation between the early 1850s and 1876.

218  Georgina Catherine Gilham, born Pleasant Creek, January 1875, died 11th of March. Cause of death given as diarrhoea. Buried Stawell Cemetery, 19th of March, 1875.

219  Fragments of Frederick Gilham's children's register record are available on PRO Victoria where he is 'child 8524.' He was committed to state care at Stawell (Pleasant Creek) on 1st of June, 1875, for six years, and admitted to Sunbury Industrial School on 4th of June. It was noted that he had been found begging, his clothes were worn out, and he had head lice. His father, John Henry Gilham, carpenter, was believed to be in New South Wales. Both parents are described as drunkards.

220  The Sunbury Industrial School was founded to educate and house destitute children. It existed from 1864 until 1879, following the implementation of the Neglected and Criminal Children's Act of 1864. Destitute or orphaned children were sent, as wards of the state, to learn a trade in the belief that this may then provide them with the

skills necessary (once they were old enough) to provide and care for themselves. The school was co-educational, although girls and boys were segregated. The school consisted of ten large, unheated, bluestone buildings arranged in two rows of five. Located on the side of Jackson's Hill, they were called the 'Hill Wards.' The open and exposed position of the buildings led to constant poor health of the children. By the time Fred was sent there, there were reports that the children were given poor food, little water, no bedding except one blanket, and many were affected by ophthalmia which went untreated, resulting in blindness. It was estimated that around 10 percent of children died within the first year of the school's operation. This fact alone led to the school gaining the nickname of the 'Sunbury Slaughterhouse.' Eventually, after public outcry, and after numerous royal commissions into the industrial school system, by 1879, the Sunbury Industrial School was closed.

221    It may be that Doctor O'Donnell's prize possession was one of the earliest mass-produced stylographic fountain pens from the USA. I love a good fountain pen.

222    The handwritten depositions from the inquest survive in the *Victoria* PRO and are the main sources of evidence for Charlotte's death.

223    *Victoria Police Gazette*, 3rd of April, 1877 (PRO Victoria).

224    *Victoria Police Gazette*, 9th of April, 1877 (PRO Victoria).

225    19th of February, 1878 Frederick and two other boys are listed in the Police Gazette as having absconded from

Sandhurst industrial school. He's described as four foot, two inches, fair complexion and hair, slight build, grey eyes.

226   *Melbourne Age,* 1st of July, 1890.

227   *Victoria Police Gazette - Missing Friends,* 21st of April, 1893, 'ELIZABETH GILHAM is inquired for by her sister, Mrs Mulcahy, Cobden. She entered the Industrial Schools in 1880, and was discharged to the Immigrants' Home on 5th June, 1890. She soon after left the Home to take a situation'.
*Victoria Police Gazette - Missing Friends,* 17th of August, 1893, 'ELIZABETH GILHAM is inquired for by Mr. R. T. Vale, M.P., Ballarat. She was once in the Reformatory Schools, where her term expired on 10th October, 1889. She was last heard of at the Immigrants' Home in June 1892, where she stayed a few days and left to go to service at Albert Park. She is 23 years of age,.

228   Died in Stawell, January 1883 and buried there 29th of January.

229   I can find no record of her marriage, children, or death. The last official record seems to be the entry for the Immigrants' Home in June 1892.

230   This handwritten verse, anonymous and undated, is in the Gilham file at the Stawell Historical Society Research Centre. It is accompanied by another verse on John Henry who, it says, has 'lain here a century under grass overgrown', so I assume that both verses were written by a Gilham descendent who was researching in the 1980s.

231   See James Ellis' death certificate.

232   He was a steam sawyer in Earls Colne and died in July 1881, aged about 48. There was a death notice in the Essex Herald of 2nd of August.

233   They are visible in the 1851 census where Catherine is a widow and a charwoman. In 1861, Isaac has left and Catherine is now supported by her three remaining children: Hannah (nineteen) is a stay maker (and yet to meet her future husband, George Root, Private Sparham), Charles (sixteen) is a labourer, and Eliza (fourteen) is a silk winder.

234   Charles may have hung around, and if he did, he made a leap up the social and educational ladder since there is a Charles Ellis, publisher's traveller, in Ipswich in the early twentieth century.

235   'You see your future in the footsteps behind you.' Margo Neale of the Australian National Museum talking of Aboriginal ideas of time in, *1922: The Birth of Now*, BBC Radio 4, first broadcast 4th of February, 2022.

# Afterword and Acknowledgements

The character of Peter Tye is fiction (though I imagine him to be my cousin on my mother's side). All the people he discovers in the archive once lived, and this novel is an attempt to give them the voices they never had or, at least, never had recorded. Despite their poverty, lack of education, or influence, they survived, they had ambitions, made decisions, and had emotional lives. They left intangible inheritances for their many ancestors across the globe.

This novel was the core of my Brighton University PhD thesis in creative writing, which was supervised at the University of Suffolk. The critical commentary, which reflects on the historical novel as a way of writing personal heritage, is available via university libraries.

I am grateful to the following, who have offered encouragement and insight at various stages (though none should be accused of responsibility for the content or direction of the book): Doctor Vivienne Aldous; the late Professor Brian McCook; Professor Barry Godfrey; Jude and Jeff Rowohlt; Denis Sheahan; Professor Harold Short; Doctor Muriel Moore-Smith; Peter Traves; Meredith Wilkie; Robert Wilson, and my sister, Professor Diana Worrall.

My initial research was conducted at the former Suffolk County Record Office at Gatacre Road, Ipswich. In the book's final stages, Jim Melbourne and friends, who gave me access and advice at the Stawell Historical Society, Victoria, Australia, helped me over the line.

My extraordinary wife, Professor Anne Worrall, has been unfailingly supportive, wherever my obsession has taken me.

I approached the historical novelist, Doctor Amanda Hodgkinson, at the University of Suffolk, with a mass of archive material, reams of unfinished writing, and half formed ideas about what I wanted to achieve. Her persistent and perceptive questioning, and willingness to read, review, and to show me the gaps in my knowledge, has been rigorous and deeply rewarding in equal measure. I am truly grateful.

This publication would not have been possible without the wonderful team at Softwood Books, Stowmarket, Suffolk.

# Peter Tye's Bibliography and Resources

Barratt, N. (2010), *Tracing Your Personal Heritage*. Barnsley: Pen and Sword Books.

Blythe, R. (1969), *Akenfield*. London: Penguin.

Cannadine, D. (2017), *Victorious Century*. London: Allen Lane.

Claxton, A. O. D. (1968), *The Suffolk Dialect of the 20th Century*. Woodbridge: The Boydell Press.

Cole, G. D. H. & Postgate, R. (1938), *The Common People 1746-1946*. London: Methuen.

Clacy, E. (1854) *A Lady's Visit to the Gold Diggings of Australia in 1852-53*. Available at: A Lady's Visit to the Gold Diggings of Australia in 1852-53: Ellen Clacy: Free Download, Borrow, and Streaming: Internet Archive

Clarke, M. (1874), *For the Term of His Natural Life*. Available at: For the Term of His Natural Life by Marcus Andrew Hislop Clarke | Project Gutenberg

Evans, G. E. (1965), *Ask the Fellows who Cut the Hay*. London: Faber and Faber.

Glyde, J. (1850), *The Moral Social and Religious Condition of Ipswich in the Middle of the Nineteenth Century*. Reprint (1971). Wakefield and London: S. R. Publishers.

Glyde, J. (1866), *The New Suffolk Garland*. Ipswich and London: Simpkin, Marshall and Co.

Grace, F. (2005), *Rags and Bones: a social history of a working-class community in nineteenth century* Ipswich. London: Unicorn Press.

Hindle, S. (2004), *On the Parish? The Micro-Politics of Poor Relief in Rural England, c.1550-1750*. Oxford: OUP.

Howitt, W. (2017), *Land, Labour and Gold; or Two Years in Victoria with visits to Sydney and Van Diemen's Land*. London: Longman. Available at: *Land, labour, and gold; or, Two years in Victoria. With visits to Sydney and Van Diemen's Land* : Howitt, William, 1792-1879 : Free Download, Borrow, and Streaming : Internet Archive

Hughes, R. (1988), *The Fatal Shore*. London: Pan Books.

Hughes, K. (2017), *Victorians Undone*. London: 4th Estate.

Kindred, D. (2002), *Ipswich in Old Photographs*. Stroud: Sutton Publishing and Lucas Books.

Kindred, D. (2003), *Ipswich: The Photographic Collection*. Stroud: Sutton Publishing.

Malster, R. (1978), *Ipswich, Town on the Orwell*. Lavenham: Terence Dalton.

Malster, R. (2000), *A History of Ipswich*. Chichester: Phillimore.

Maskill, L. (2014), *Suffolk Dialect*. Sheffield: Bradwell Books.

Mayhew, H. (2008), *London Labour and the London Poor*. (eds.) R. O'Day and D. Englander. Ware: Wordsworth Editions.

Mount, F. (2016), *The Tears of the Raja: Mutiny, Money and Marriage in India 1805 -1905*. London: Simon and Schuster.

Waller, I. H. (2014), *My Ancestor was an Agricultural Labourer*. London: Society of Genealogists.

Wilson, A. N. (2003), *The Victorians*. London: Arrow

Zedner, L. (2006), 'Women, crime and custody in Victorian England' in Y. Jewkes and H. Johnson (eds) *Prison Readings*. Cullompton: Willan Publishing.

## Newspapers: British Library, available on Findmypast.co.uk

*Bury and Norwich Post* (1786 – 1900).
*Ipswich Advertiser* (1855-1863).
*The Ipswich Journal* (1748 – 1902).
*Suffolk and Essex Free Press* (1855- 1869).
The *Suffolk Chronicle* (1810-1872).

## Internet archive resources

Findmypast.co.uk
Ancestry.co.uk
Familysearch.org
TROVE.nla.gov.au
Pro.vic.gov.au

www.ingramcontent.com/pod-product-compliance
Lightning Source LLC
Chambersburg PA
CBHW011757010726
47497CB00013B/3242